Praise for S.

'*One Way* is what would happen[ ] got together and had a baby. Deeply immersive, chilling and atmospheric enough that you will believe yourself under a cold Martian sky. An utterly fabulous book!'

Emma Kavanagh, bestselling author of *Falling* and *Hidden*

'An intense, gripping sci-fi thriller'

Adrian Tchaikovsky on *One Way*

'*One Way* is a taut and claustrophobic hard SF thriller. Morden does a fantastic job of ratcheting up the tension like oxygen escaping from a pressurised Martian habitat'   Gavin Smith

'A rip-roaring thriller that blends science-fiction with crime'

John Marrs on *One Way*

'A claustrophobic, high-tension, survival-against-the-odds thriller. It paints a convincing picture of the lethal Martian environment as well as the growing terror of being incarcerated in a deadly prison with no way out'   *Guardian* on *One Way*

'Alfonso Cuarón's *Gravity* . . . Ridley Scott's *The Martian* . . . James Gray's *Ad Astra*. Few novels measure up to these gripping cinematic visions, but Simon Morden's *Gallowglass* knocks them out of the park'   *The Times*

S. J. MORDEN

THE FLIGHT OF THE APHRODITE

This edition first published in Great Britain in 2022

First published in Great Britain in 2022 by Gollancz
an imprint of the Orion Publishing Group Ltd
Carmelite House, 50 Victoria Embankment
London EC4Y 0DZ

An Hachette UK Company

3 5 7 9 10 8 6 4

A CIP catalogue record for this book is
available from the British Library.

ISBN (Mass Market Paperback) 978 1 473 22859 7

Typeset by Deltatype Ltd, Birkenhead, Merseyside

Printed in Great Britain by Clays Ltd, Elcograf S.p.A.

www.simonmorden.com
www.gollancz.co.uk

This book is dedicated to the survivors.

Dramatis Personae

Crew of the European Space Agency
Deep Space Exploration Vessel 'Aphrodite'

Luca Mariucci – Captain

Flight crew

Hanne Aasen – Chief Engineer
Theresa Blasco – Pilot
Deirdre Colvin – Navigator
Yasmin Borner – Communications
Ove Hellsten – Life Support

Science crew

Rory Forsyth – Senior Scientific Officer, High Energy Physics
Petra Kattenbeck – Senior Medical Officer, Doctor
Benjamin Velter – Planetary Geology
Valeria Spinu – Remote Sensing
Konstantinos Tsoltos – Psychology
Laszlo Molnar – Nuclear Engineering

Part 1

Tiamat

𒀭𒆳𒁉𒉈

enū-ma eliš lā nabū šamamu
šapliš ammatum šuma lā zakrat
apsū-ma reštū zārū-šun
mummu tiāmat muallidat gimrī-šun

1

The lights of the holographic display showed the supply ship as it ought to be, not as it was: the wire frame model was whole and complete, but the object outside was far from that.

The external cameras showed it to be diseased and partial, bruised yellow and blown ragged by strange winds. The solar panels were filigree, which would explain why it was here, running on the last of its batteries, in an uncontrolled tumble, gradually falling towards the king of planets.

Mariucci looked through the hologram at the hunched shoulders of his pilot, at her leaning into Colvin's screen to check that the distances and the rate of rotation were the same on her display. 'Theresa?' was all he said, and she shrugged her name off.

'I can get this.' Blasco spoke into her screen. 'Just let me watch it a little longer. I've got the feel of it now.'

At the next console, Borner was trying yet again to access the supply ship's systems, but whatever functionality was left, she was still unable to make the critical connection to the thrusters. Something in the ship's vaulted brain had become unstuck in the two Earth years it had been orbiting Jupiter. All that way, all that time, and now, at the moment they needed the food, the water, the fuel and the spares that it contained? They couldn't dock with it.

Borner was deep in the guts of the programming, feeding in raw bytes of data in an effort to reroute what little power there was to the systems she needed. Her concentration was total, only her lips and fingers moving as she recited hexadecimal spells.

The Aphrodite had matched course with the Nimbus-class supply ship a day ago. The rest of the time had been spent crawling closer and closer. It was now just off the Aphrodite's bow, a hundred metres distant, but its motion couldn't be corrected, and for that reason it might as well have been lost to the roiling cloudscape below.

Mariucci glanced behind him, at the segment of Jupiter the external cameras could fit onto the display. Distinct and drawn white-and-ochre bands precessed across the luminous pixels, washing their colours into the subdued lighting of Command. The slow swirls were beguiling, the temptation to watch them wind and unwind was strong, especially at perijove when they made their closest approaches.

Now was not the time to become lost in the fractal detail of their patterns. He needed to call it. There was no chance the hundred-plus metres of Aphrodite could manoeuvre precisely enough to dock with the Nimbus. But if they could, then it would be a huge boon.

'Deirdre, when's the next possible encounter with a Nimbus?'

Colvin rattled her keyboard, and shook the answer out. 'We can match with Nimbus-eight on perijove seven.'

Three more orbits. Six weeks. He needed to talk to Hellsten, to see if that was going to put stress on the stores they had on the Aphrodite. Hellsten had been not quite himself recently, though, and Mariucci hadn't been having conversations with him about that, which was something he now instantly regretted and felt shame over.

A captain's duty wasn't just to the mission, or the people who'd sent him and expected – if not spectacular discoveries – sufficient new insights to justify the cost of gaining them. A captain's duty was also to his crew, all of them. A year was already a long time to spend in space. Especially with the knowledge of another two ahead of them.

Blasco gave a grunt and pushed back in her seat. Her hair drifted with the circulating air. 'We're almost out of shampoo.'

'I cannot endanger the ship for that,' said Mariucci, knowing he was right, and yet also accepting that while it wasn't a problem for him, it was a problem for her. He briefly slid his hand over his shiny scalp, then brought his arm down in case she took the gesture as unwanted levity. They were all not quite themselves, and he didn't know how to fix it. 'Will this particular Nimbus survive another orbit?'

Colvin clacked her keyboard again. 'Yes, within the margin of error. Ship systems will degrade further, and the beacon may not be functioning at that point. It'll survive, but it'll be worse than now, and we may not be able to find it again.'

Borner clicked her tongue, distracting Mariucci for a moment.

'Yasmin?'

'I thought I had it for a moment. Slipped away. Give me five minutes.'

Blasco touched the release mechanism on her chair, allowing her to swivel and face the pit. 'We can afford to wait five minutes, Luca.'

'If we wanted to make the next rendezvous, when would we need to start the burn?'

Colvin had already run those calculations, because she answered instantly. 'T plus five hours ten minutes.'

'Well, then: we can afford to wait five hours. If Yasmin can get the thrusters working, and we can get the tumble stabilised, we can attempt a docking manoeuvre. Otherwise, we initiate the burn and find another Nimbus. Agreed?'

They had one docking ring. If they damaged it – if they damaged it and couldn't repair it – then they'd be in serious trouble. Not today, not next week or next month, but later on than that. It would be about more than shampoo by then.

Blasco nodded, Colvin looked at Blasco before assenting, and Borner didn't so much as acknowledge the question. She just tightened her expression by another millimetre and let the data wash against her face.

'Call me if you make progress.' Mariucci punched his seat buckle and nudged down with his elbows against the arm rests.

He remembered briefly and vividly the violence of their orbital insertion, how they'd positioned themselves so precisely in the path of Jupiter that they had been swept up in its influence. They had almost skimmed the cloud tops to do it. So close: he'd felt he could have reached out and trailed his fingertips in them, sent eddies of smoke spinning around the planet. Strapped in his chair, listening to the tidal strains as vast forces gripped the Aphrodite and bent its orbit into new, tighter ellipses.

He'd been frightened, but he'd not shown it. It wasn't in his job description to mirror the fear of his crew, of his scientists; rather to soak it up, absorb it, hold it in, and radiate calm assurance. All would be well.

He caught hold of one of the grab rails and pulled, his feet clearing his console and straightening out behind him. Pilot, navigator and comms were busy. Mariucci knew there was no point in interrupting their work: they were the best in their professions. They knew the limits of their choices and that they needed further permission to exceed them. He had captained sufficiently, but not excessively.

He aimed for the axis, and palmed off the bulkhead frame to reorient himself. The axis tube didn't present a straight path all the way to the drive section at the far end – it kinked just over half way along, at the probe storage bay, to accommodate the four machines, two offset each side. But he could see as far as scientist country, the workshops and laboratories, where Forsyth had them crunching numbers and running models. They could have just as easily done that in the gravity section, but Forsyth wanted to keep them together, encouraging each other, competing against each other, driving each other, for as long as he could. For him, it was all about the science, and a moment spent doing anything else was an opportunity wasted.

It was a pattern that had slowly emerged after perijove one, but was now set. Mariucci thought it was too much: he knew that at some point he'd have a delegation of disgruntled scientists pleading exhaustion, and he'd be forced into a confrontation with Forsyth to try and fix the problem. He needed to pre-empt that moment without upsetting him. Forsyth, his superiors in Darmstadt had stressed, was the golden egg in his clutch.

Mariucci knew he had to line up his arguments first. Logic, not emotion, was the only way to convince Forsyth. Kattenbeck would have to help explain. Even though she was designated as science, he knew she didn't take Forsyth's, or anyone's, side on this.

And there he was, coming up the axis towards him, his spindly limbs making him look disturbingly spiderlike as he bounced off the curved walls. Pale hands and pale face and a shock of black hair set against the off-white panels and his royal blue flight suit: Mariucci couldn't envisage him ever complaining about the lack of shampoo, or anything so mundane as a physical need.

Forsyth stopped on the stern side of the gravity section's rotating hub, with Mariucci on the Command side. The openings to the four hollow spokes spun gracefully and silently around between them.

'There's a delay,' said Forsyth. 'Why?'

Mariucci calibrated his response. It wasn't personal. The scientist was like this with everyone.

'The supply ship is tumbling, preventing us from docking.' He kept to the facts. 'Yasmin's attempting to establish contact with the ship systems, but there's a severe loss of function.'

'The Europa probe is scheduled for this perijove.'

'Yes. I've instructed the crew to keep trying up until the last moment they can, before it becomes necessary to—'

'Any delay is intolerable.'

'Necessary to the safety of the ship and its whole crew to alter our course for another Nimbus,' finished Mariucci, ignoring the interruption. He'd found the constant talking-over difficult at first: Mariucci knew he'd come over as hesitant, which meant that Forsyth had doubled-down on his rhetorical trademark. But it had only taken a little while to find the tactic of simply remembering where he'd been before the interruption, and now he just carried on as if Forsyth had never spoken.

Except he was starting to struggle again, and he had to consciously make the effort to recall his last few words and his train of thought.

'This is a scientific expedition,' said Forsyth. 'We have a mission profile that we have to follow in order to maximise our data collection.'

'This is a human expedition,' countered Mariucci. 'We need the supplies in order to carry out the valuable investigations done by your team. Without them, our abilities are degraded, and the data we collect will suffer.'

'The data will be just fine.'

'I'm sure it will. However, people who are tired and hungry and worried won't function at their best. Both Stan and Petra will tell you as much.' That was also data. A human being wasn't a machine.

Forsyth, frustrated that a mind inexplicably also needed a body, turned his head while he considered this. Then he looked back. He had no fear of intimate eye contact, just a fear of actual intimacy.

'Your crew need to do better,' he said. 'Their lack is affecting my work.'

'We can't change the laws of physics, Rory,' said Mariucci mildly. 'As much as we'd like to. The space outside here is … savage.'

'Then they should have built the Nimbus ships better.'

'I'll pass that on. They've been out here for far longer than was intended. They've withstood all manner of storms and fluxes. Sometimes I think it's a miracle they've kept going this long.' But he'd used the wrong word. Nothing was a miracle in Forsyth's universe. Everything was always explicable.

'Better,' repeated Forsyth. The food he might eat or the air he might breathe was spinning uncontrollably outside the hull: it was neither his fault nor his business. He just wanted it done – completed or abandoned, he didn't care which – so that the science schedule wasn't compromised. Blaming the engineers back on Earth was simply a proxy for blaming Mariucci's crew.

The senior scientific officer had made his point. Without another word, he spidered his way back down the axis, and vanished from view, heading into one of the workshops. Not for the first time, Mariucci was left wondering how someone like Forsyth could have got through the selection procedure for a long-duration mission. The engineering team had done far better in terms of robust design than the human factors group had. But Forsyth was a brilliant, if late, entrant, on a crew of mere experts. He supposed that allowances had been made. Compromises, even.

Mariucci drifted for a moment, letting the air currents push him away from Command and into the rotating hub. An access tunnel to the wheel passed him every five seconds. The magnetic bearings were perfectly quiet, but the quality of the ambient sound changed each time the hollow pipe swung by his ears. A profound, distant silence was replaced by a close, swaddling one, and back, and forward.

Then he stopped himself, and reached out for one of the grab rails on the rotating section and waited for his body to get up to speed. He lowered himself into the tube, and placed his hands either side of the ladder.

Illuminated pictograms warned him he was entering an artificial gravity environment. The fall, top to bottom, wouldn't kill him, but it would hurt and it might injure him. Kattenbeck was a good doctor, very experienced, but that wasn't the point.

An avoidable accident was just that: avoidable. He needed to follow procedure and set an example.

The stripes on the tunnel wall tightened as he descended, to make him think he was going faster than he really was. An optical illusion, but a useful one, nudging him to stay safe. He closed his fists on the ladder, brought himself to an almost dead-stop, and consciously climbed down the rest of the way to the wheel.

One-fifth gravity at the bottom. Enough to keep water in his glass, food on his plate, and calcium in his bones. Not so much as to make him, or the rest of the crew, actively avoid the gravity section, not enough to associate it with tiredness, with exercise, with it being a chore. It was where they were supposed to sleep, socialise, eat, wash, and just be. It looked like a hotel, comfy curves and soft, noise-absorbing furnishings, carpet, fabric. There were archipelagoes of low couches, embayed coffee tables, and the kitchen area was open. Enclosed bedrooms intruded into the floor space like headlands.

It was designed to be welcoming, and easy, and normal, to draw the eye away from the arc of the floor that rose up either side of the viewer, to obfuscate that this was the inside surface of a spinning wheel on a spaceship that was itself a billion kilometres from home.

Mariucci's gaze went past Kattenbeck, who was sitting at the long kitchen table, head bowed, concentrating on the words on her tablet, to follow the curve of the floor as it rose up around the rim of the wheel. It slid down again to her back as she moved, her finger grazing the screen before her hand returned to her lap.

'Petra?'

'Luca. Come on over.' She read another few lines, then darkened the screen. She was assiduous with patient confidentiality. 'Sit with me.'

He poured himself a glass of water, learned that she didn't want one by his slight gesture and her equally minimal response, and he sat beside her, dropping gently into the chair. The water in his glass rolled as he put it down, moving as slowly as oil.

He didn't ask her what she was reading, as the question was redundant. He had to trust that she'd tell him of anything that might affect the ship. Technically, he could raid all her files. Diplomatically, he never would. Instead, he swirled the water and looked at the reflections in it before drinking it down in three gulps.

'I've seen you happier,' she said. 'You're still worried?'

'Yes.'

'Your short-term memory is, if not perfect, well within bounds. Both verbal and visual. I can continue to test you every week against your baseline, but you haven't varied more than a few points up or down. Clinically,' she stressed the word, 'you're fine.'

'You want me to talk to Stan.'

'That's my recommendation. I'm the bone and blood. Not the ...' She twirled her finger next to her head. 'He's the grey matter.'

Mariucci put the glass down and nudged it away. 'But otherwise?'

'This, this ship, this journey, is unique. Never have so few people spent so long together, so far away from land. Even in the Age of Sail. Everything that happens here is normal, Luca, even though it's happening for the first time. We're putting down the markers that everyone who follows will judge themselves against.'

'We're making history.'

'This is our Apollo moment. We're the vanguard, Luca, the pioneers. The very best of who we are travelling in the very best of what we can make. It's our duty to record everything faithfully.' She tapped the side of her tablet. 'I make notes. But those notes are only as reliable as I make them.'

'And if I don't tell Stan about my memory loss—'

'You don't have memory loss. You're concerned that you're

losing your ability to recall short-term memories, even though you're not. It's not real. It's not measurable. All you have is the fear. What am I supposed to say to that, apart from "Go and talk to the psychologist"?'

Mariucci rephrased. 'If I don't tell Stan about my concerns ...'

'Then his notes will be incomplete. Inaccurate.' She raised her eyebrows as she smiled. 'You owe it to the future, Luca.'

'Captain to Command,' said Colvin over the tannoy.

He was out of his seat before the C of Command. The chair legs – magnetic – slid back rather than flew.

'I'll wash your glass,' said Kattenbeck. 'Go. Raus.'

'I still need to talk to you about the—' He gestured to the stern of the ship.

'I know,' she said. 'It can wait until you deal with whatever.'

Mariucci climbed back up to the axis and pushed himself into Command. Aasen was there now too, the first time he'd seen her today. Perhaps it was two days? She was arm-deep in one of the floor panels, a tablet with schematics tethered to her other wrist.

'Okay, Hanne?'

'Circuit's showing an intermittent fault.'

'If you pull it now, will it affect any of the systems here?'

'There'll be a short outage, yes, before it reroutes.'

At that, Borner jerked round. 'It needs to wait.'

'I've a list of faults here, and they're not fixing themselves.'

'Hanne,' said Mariucci. 'It can wait. Yasmin – do we have control?'

'Yes. The power I can shunt to the servos is minimal, and possibly temporary. But it should be enough.'

'Port it to Theresa.' He realised the engineer was still reaching under the floor. 'Hanne. That's an order.'

Blasco folded out the twin joysticks and fixed her chair in the upright position.

'This is the delta-v,' said Colvin, and Blasco nodded curtly. She'd barely looked, but she understood she probably only had one chance at this.

Mariucci wanted to watch the external cameras, but Aasen was persisting. He pulled himself over the consoles and planted himself next to her. What had got into her? Any interruption, any delay here could mean losing the Nimbus.

'Hanne. Whatever it is, please. It must wait.'

It was the please that stopped her. She seemed to soften, then relent, pulling her arm free with her hand empty.

Mariucci took a moment to look at her properly. Her skin had a greasy sheen to it, and her hair – what he could see of it escaping from her bandana – was slick.

'When was the last time you took a break?' he asked her. 'Rested? Slept? Had something to eat?'

She shrugged rather than answer. She looked down at the open floor panel, and then at the diagram on her tablet, and he could see her jaw twitch.

'Go. I'll look after things here.' He knew Kattenbeck would still be in the kitchen area, and she'd see what he'd seen. How long had this been going on? Why hadn't he spotted it sooner? It was his job, after all. Or had he seen it, and ignored it, because repairs were still being made and nothing had gone wrong?

Aasen unclipped herself from the floor and drifted up to the handholds. She glanced at the floor once more, and Mariucci flipped the panel with his foot, clicking it shut with his toe. He needed a tool to fix it in place – Aasen had that hanging off her belt, alongside all the others – but they weren't doing any high-g vectoring anytime soon.

She almost smiled at him, just a brief flash with one corner of her mouth, then she headed for the axis. Mariucci scanned the screens for progress, but he only needed to see the look of quiet satisfaction on Blasco's face to know that whatever she'd done, she was happy with it.

'Update me,' he said. 'How did it go?'

'Permission to dock, Captain,' she said.

The Nimbus was rock steady on the display. Not a hint of

either the spin or the tumble. It hung in space, pinned against the black.

'Permission granted.'

Colvin tabbed her headset. 'Acceleration, acceleration.'

Mariucci swung himself towards his chair, and strapped himself in. Borner, to his left, pressed her fingers into her temples, blinking and gasping, like a diver coming up for air.

'Good work, Yasmin,' he said. 'Very well done.'

'You're ... welcome,' she replied.

The acceleration, when it came, was so gentle, it was barely a flutter in his inner ear.

2

They were all there in Command to watch, all twelve of them. It didn't feel cramped, which was down to the designers realising that internal space was not a luxury, but a necessity for human well-being. All the seats, banked up half the sides of the spherical chamber, could turn and face the central holographic pit without blocking anyone's view.

Mariucci sat in the front row, as was his habit, but the important people in the scenario were pilot, navigator, comms, and remote sensing. He'd give the order, but they were the ones who'd trained for this and would react if something went wrong, long before they had time to explain it to their captain.

'Are we go for launch?' he asked.

'Telemetry go,' said Spinu, the remote sensing specialist.

'Navigation go.'

'Flight go.'

'Systems go.'

He looked around Command. Those who weren't looking at their screens were staring at the pit, and he could see their eyes more than anything else, shining with colour. The hologram showed a wire model of the Aphrodite in blue, pregnant with a red hexagonal probe the size of what? A large car? A small van? That was the usual metric. They had hauled it, and three identical probes, halfway across the Solar System, and if they didn't work – if they underperformed in a way that displeased Forsyth – then there'd be a lot of soul-searching and angry accusations in the next few hours.

Mariucci caught Forsyth's gaze for a moment, and didn't know what to make of his expression. He could best describe it as furiously analytical. Certainly not emotionless, just not concerned about the softness and vagaries of humanity. 'We are go for launch.'

They'd named the probe Laelaps, after a dog. Mariucci's classical education didn't extend further than versions that might have made it into operas, so the allusion, if there was any, was lost to him. But he was content to call it that rather than the prosaic Probe One.

Blasco took control, and released the probe's retaining bolts. The hangar doors were already wide open, and at the same time the restraints were released, a pusher plate palmed the probe out into space. In the pit, the red hexagon moved through the blue lines of the Aphrodite's hull. On the screens, the heavily armoured probe slid out into the unfiltered sunlight and glittered. The camera followed its trajectory outwards, catching a slice of Jupiter as it passed.

'All systems nominal.'

'Telemetry nominal. Distance to Aphrodite sixty metres.'

'Deploying solar panels.'

Laelaps unfurled three feathers of black glassy panels that quivered as they extended outwards. They locked into position, then turned to face the distant sun.

'Power is nominal at four hundred and ten watts.'

'Beginning rotation.'

Monopropellant thrusters twisted into position and performed the slightest of burns. The probe began to spin.

'Sensor package is online. All readings nominal.'

'Preparing to pass through the Aphrodite's magnetopause.'

This was the moment of crisis: the Aphrodite had a magnetic shield to not just deflect the worst of the radiation that roared around Jupiter's orbit, but, as far as it could, shelter its occupants completely. The Aphrodite wasn't so much a spaceship as a bunker, outside of which was death in myriad and messy ways.

Inside the shield's influence, the ship and its mechanisms were safe, but it extended its protection to everything whether wanted or not. To measure the size, the strength and the sheer complexity of the radiation environment – the very reason for Forsyth's presence on board – instruments had to be placed outside where the sleeting particles and lethal frequencies were raw and unfiltered. Sensors could be spun out from the rotating wheel on cables, to be retrieved when they inevitably failed, and the probes had been hardened and designed with redundancies and error-checking simply to allow them to operate at all.

'Magnetopause in five. Three, two, one, mark.'

Someone was breathing quickly, on the verge of hyperventilating. Mariucci glanced in the direction of the sound. Velter? As the planetary geologist, he had more at stake than most on the success of the probes.

'Report,' said Mariucci. The combatants were still collecting data, but he needed to put the man at ease.

'Telemetry nominal. Distance one hundred and fifteen metres.'

'Systems nominal.'

'Sensors nominal.'

Velter held his fist to his chest as he tried to slow his breathing down. His eyes were wide and white, and his cheeks sucked in and blew out in an exaggerated bellows movement. 'I'm fine, I'm fine,' he managed as the psychologist, Tsoltos, touched him on the shoulder, giving it a reassuring squeeze.

'Manoeuvring for primary burn.' Blasco turned the spinning probe about on its axis and reoriented the rockets.

'Distance one hundred and eighty metres.'

Mariucci saw Forsyth turn away from the pit to the screen behind him. With a few dabs and swipes, he'd accessed the magnetometer data, real time, frequency and energy, drawn as a heat chart. It pulsed colours, much like an angry cuttlefish might use in a dominance display. Spikes and splashes of blue and white flickered as the probe recorded the flux around it.

The instrument held firm, despite the ferocity of the assault. A human would have already accumulated damage.

'Distance two hundred and ten metres.'

'Burn at two fifty.'

'Acknowledged. Two fifty on my mark.'

'Two fifty in five. Three, two, one, mark.'

Three spears of cold flame, almost transparent against the dark of night, drove the probe away from the Aphrodite on a trajectory of its own, heading towards Europa.

'Ten seconds.'

The pit redrew itself. At its centre was the yellow sphere of Jupiter, and around it, its inner system. The four tiny moons closest to its radius. The slight rings. The four Galilean giants. Then the cloud of outer moons, scattered and assumed. The Aphrodite's path was drawn as a white ellipse that passed over and under Jupiter like a necklace, draping as far as beyond Callisto but no further, at least on this and the next perijove.

Laelaps's proposed line was green, and it was projected to spiral around Europa in increasingly tight circles.

'Twenty seconds.'

The burn went on for a minute, and more.

'One hundred and sixty seconds. Mark.'

'Primary burn completed.' Blasco shook out her hands. 'How does that look?'

Colvin and Spinu compared notes. 'Within ten centimetres a second. If we need to correct, we can add it to the capture burn. We have a probe heading for Europa.'

There ought to have been applause, but it wasn't spontaneous and Mariucci wasn't going to force it. No doubt, when the news reached Darmstadt, there'd be cheers and claps and probably a visit to a bierkeller. There were more careers to be made or lost there than in Jupiter orbit, but the captain recognised that it felt much more real for the science team on the Aphrodite.

'Congratulations, everyone.' He wasn't going to make a speech, but good work needed recognising. 'Theresa, Deirdre,

Valeria, Yasmin, Benjamin. Textbook launch. Thank you.' He would have executed a short, formal bow to each of them in turn, but it would have looked awkward in zero gravity.

'Do you want to tell Earth?' asked Borner.

'You send the message, Yasmin. I'll write up my log and send it as scheduled. Do we have a good uplink?'

'High gain.'

'Then give them as much data as we can, archive the rest for transmission at apojove.'

There followed a moment when Forsyth looked round and stared at Mariucci as if his captain had suggested something terrible. Then he slowly turned back to his pulsating, abstract screen. No one else seemed to have noticed, or, at least, noticed anything out of the ordinary.

The crew – his crew – busied themselves with their usual tasks. Aasen unclipped herself from her seat and kicked towards the axis. She already had her tablet out, and was checking the error log as she floated by Mariucci. She seemed ... well. Better, at least. The dark circles around her eyes had faded, and it looked like she'd showered.

Hellsten also made to go towards the axis, and Mariucci reached out towards him.

'Ove,' he said. 'We need a meeting. I feel I've been neglecting you, and we should catch up. Yes?'

Hellsten was naturally pale and thin. The lighting of Command did no one any favours, least of all him. 'Yes. Yes, of course. Just. Give me some notice. Any time. Captain. Luca.'

Mariucci dropped his hand and gestured that he was free to go. Hellsten was in charge of life support. All roles were critical. That one? That one was the one that Mariucci himself had trained in, and he knew all the things that could go wrong. He watched Hellsten's feet recede and turned back to the others in Command.

Velter was talking to Tsoltos, their heads close, if not touching. The big Greek had his hand on the back of Velter's neck, and seemed to be giving him advice, a pep talk perhaps. Spinu had dabbed out instrument readings from the various sensors on Laelaps, and she was talking Borner through them, and what they might mean.

Molnar? Molnar was quiet. He was always quiet, spending most of his time not just away from the crew, but away from the rest of the science team. His job was monitoring the fusion drive, which was partly of his design. Field testing it on a round trip to Jupiter was certainly one way to make his name, but he seemed even more ill-suited to the particular rigours of a long voyage than his team leader was.

If the nuclear fire ever went out, Mariucci understood that that was it for the mission. It was both their power source and their drive. The radiators that haloed Aphrodite's stern section were there solely to dump the excess reactor heat into space.

A basket of eggs. A basket of eggs made of the finest, thinnest porcelain. That was his ship. If just one of them dropped it, everything would shatter.

Of course, no one would deliberately do that. But accidentally? He used to be a good captain, a rock, with his finger on the very heartbeat of the ship. Somewhere on the voyage he felt he'd lost that spark, that will. Was it his memory, or was it something more fundamental? Kattenbeck swore it wasn't the former.

She was looking at him now, arms folded, but she wasn't looking just at him. She was appraising everyone, watching them, seeing how they worked, how they interacted. She'd make a good captain too. She had that eye for detail that would catch things before they escalated. He should trust her more, even though she was technically science crew.

Perhaps he'd read the notes she'd made on him.

He dismissed the idea straight away. Yes, he had the right, but he wasn't going to exercise it. He wondered what she said about herself. She might not be objective, but she was someone who lived by the maxim Know Yourself.

If not his memory, what about his concentration? Was that it? It would explain why Kattenbeck's recall tests showed no hint of decline – because he was concentrating at the time. Perhaps he needed to make a list like Aasen, to keep him focused, moving from one thing to another without the opportunity to daydream. He felt that thought was progress.

But here came Forsyth, hand over hand across the top of the pit, to talk to him.

'I've decided that the mission profile needs to be changed,' he said.

Mariucci felt his mental gears grind as they meshed at speed, with no clutch to smooth the transition. 'Go on.'

'Probe One has the capability to land on Europa. It should do so. Near an emissive breach in the ice crust.'

The pet-name of Laelaps wasn't for Forsyth, apparently.

'The data would be invaluable,' he continued. 'There's no reason for the embargo.'

'The mission profile – Valeria can correct me on this if I'm wrong – already allows for multiple low-altitude passes through the plumes.' He wasn't wrong, he knew that much. 'And that has been agreed by the oversight committee to be as close to the surface as we can go.'

'The radiation environment is sufficient to sterilise the probe to beyond the required COSPAR standards. Their arguments regarding biological contamination were, and remain, flawed if not specious.'

'The oversight committee—'

'The oversight committee are not here.'

They had an audience, and Mariucci rather wished they didn't. This was, however, the arena that Forsyth had chosen, and, like any warrior, he had to fight the battle where he was.

'The oversight committee came to their conclusions almost half a decade ago when this mission was being planned. The time to challenge their findings was then, when you were among your peers, not now.' Mariucci put on his best face. 'We cannot challenge that collective decision, here, in this space.'

Forsyth had always planned this move, he realised. And it was a low blow, an argument that couldn't possibly succeed in a committee room in Paris, but possibly, potentially, might just work a year in to a mission, thirty light minutes away from a rebuke.

'I wasn't on the team then,' said Forsyth, 'which is why the profile is flawed. The issues of contamination have been grossly exaggerated, and the benefits far outweigh the minuscule risk. The probe has to land in order to collect the time-series sensitive data I require.'

'I know this discussion has already been had, Rory. They clearly didn't agree with the arguments for a landing then, and I can't agree with the arguments for a landing now. Darmstadt have the authority in this, and we must respect their final, unequivocal decision.' It was the line he was most comfortable with, so he took it. 'We'll land on Europa when we're ready. When we've collectively decided we can do so safely, for us, and for the Europans.'

'There's nothing out there. There's nothing but us. This is our future, and you're holding us back.'

Rather than involve himself in that debate – playful and engaging with most other people – Mariucci simply reiterated: 'It has been decided. The embargo holds. We can look, but we cannot touch.'

Forsyth wouldn't let go, though.

'We have the opportunity to do something remarkable. If we're not to push the boundaries of science and gain new insights into our universe, then why are we even here?'

Mariucci took a moment to answer. The way Forsyth said *our universe* made it seem like he meant *his* universe. 'I appreciate—'

'I don't think you do.'

'I appreciate that I'm just a pipes and tanks man. But I wouldn't be on the Aphrodite if I didn't want to push the boundaries of science. But we do that together. We have all,' and this was his moment to include everyone else, because there were no disinterested bystanders there, 'we have all been entrusted with the mission profile curated by our community of colleagues back on Earth. This is as much about their decisions as it is ours, and we cannot change anything without their explicit consent. For now, for this mission, the matter is settled. There will be no landing on Europa. We are forbidden to attempt it.'

He had no doubt that they'd be revisiting this conversation again, but he'd drawn a line – not that it was his line, but it was still the line – and he'd hold it against all comers. He'd have to talk independently to each of his flight crew, to let them know that they were to refuse any and all requests to change orbits or trajectories, and that they had his full, unequivocal backing to do so.

Forsyth didn't seem pleased or displeased by Mariucci's refusal. Rather, confused as to how a mere technician could possibly have the authority to deny him. He shook his head, muttered something that may have been 'some people', but his accent seemed to momentarily have more inflexion than his usual precise Edinburgh voice.

'We have work,' he announced. 'Come.'

Those who thought the summons was for them responded immediately. Spinu, Velter, Molnar, and, interestingly, Tsoltos. Kattenbeck stayed in Command, looking at the screen that Forsyth had been so intent on earlier, watching the flash and fade of fundamental particles striking Laelaps's detector array.

Mariucci unclipped and pulled himself over to her.

'Do you understand this?' he asked.

'A little. Time along the bottom, frequency up the side, intensity as colour. Any single event above this line would damage a human cell.' She raised her finger level to halfway up the display. 'The white flashes at the top of the screen – there's one – are galactic cosmic rays. Enormous energy, very bad for you.'

23

The white spark rippled down the screen and moved through the rainbow until it sank into the deep reds.

'But presumably very good for Rory.' He was about to ask her opinion on the science team's work schedules, when she pre-empted him.

'We need to talk. More specifically, I need to talk to my captain.'

'Okay.' That sounded formal. Procedural, even. 'Now?'

'Yes, why not.'

'Theresa. You have the helm. When is Laelaps's second burn due?'

'Not for another twenty-eight hours.'

'I'll be here for that.' He glanced at the ship's big clock, a dedicated display positioned where pilot, navigator and captain could all see it. Tomorrow, plus four hours from now. Time enough for this, and to talk to Hellsten, perhaps go through the inventory with him and see if they had enough supplies for the next few perijoves without having to go Nimbus-chasing again. Then some time alone to fill in his journal, and watch the view of Jupiter from one of the external cameras. And sleep and eat and do the other things too. 'If I'm not here fifteen minutes before, page me.'

'No problem.'

Mariucci pushed himself towards the axis, and could feel Kattenbeck behind him. He inserted himself into one of the access tubes and drifted down to the halfway point before descending the rest of the ladder in the proper fashion.

For someone who wanted to talk, Kattenbeck spent the next few minutes not talking. She made them both coffee, and sat opposite him at the long table, watching the roils of steam make ephemeral curves in the air.

'Petra?'

She sniffed and made her lips go thin.

'Your captain is listening.'

That dragged half a smile from her. 'You've read my biographical notes, yes?'

'Yes. Those ESA have chosen to disclose. I'm sure there's more, but there's no good reason for me to know it.'

'I'm seeing ghosts.'

'I think you're going to have to be a little more explicit than that.'

'People who've died. People I've failed to save.'

'Friends?'

'Patients. I don't even know their names. Just I recognise their faces.' She equivocated. 'That's not true either. I recognise their injuries. The faces are, I assume, theirs, but I can't be sure.'

'From ...' Somewhere in the Middle East. She had been an MSF surgeon, ten, twenty years ago. 'Jordan?'

'And Lebanon, when Jordan got too hot.' She stared into her coffee. 'There were a lot of failures.'

'I can't imagine what it was like.' He let a suitable silence follow. 'Ghosts?'

'Yes. So. A repressed memory manifesting itself as a vivid hallucination, if I was given to diagnosing myself.'

'But there's more than one.'

'Oh God, yes. A host of them. Legion.'

'Are they malevolent? Do they try and communicate?'

'No. Okay, there's often a lot of blood, shrapnel damage, crush damage, blast injuries, blunt force trauma. Sometimes whole limbs are just missing, or an eye, or a jaw, or part of the skull. Abdominal wounds are honestly the worst because you know that even if you get all the viscera back in the cavity and sew it up, they're going to die because you used your last antibiotic shot a week ago.' She looked up. 'Probably too much information. They don't try to harm me. They don't try to talk to me. They're just there. Present. Bearing witness.'

'Bearing witness to what?'

'Me.'

'Are they here now?'

'I like how you're just believing me, by the way. Or at least, pretending that you do.' She shrugged. 'They're not here now. I saw my first one – I'll need to check my notes for the exact day – three weeks ago. Young Arab man. I remember the circumstances, but like I said, not the name or the face. Civilian volunteer. White helmet? A wall had collapsed on him while he was trying to dig someone out of a ... I think it was a fruit shop. That was it. He smelled of pomegranate, and I thought the red juice was blood. The masonry had crushed his head and chest, and his friends brought him to me crying and hoping I could save him. And I couldn't. He was bleeding into his lungs and there wasn't enough time to get in there and clamp things off. I was elbow-deep in him when he died.'

She stopped and drank some coffee, apparently glad it was dark and bitter.

'I'd chosen to be there, so don't feel sorry for me. After that, different people, different times, all memorable in some way. Real. Solid. They take up space. You know what I mean by that, don't you?'

'Yes, I understand.'

'I can feel their presence. I know they're there before I see them. If I move, they follow me with their eyes. They seem to be breathing. They have their normal skin colour. But I know that each of them is, in reality, dead. And they can't possibly be here. And I must be hallucinating.'

Mariucci steepled his fingers over his own untouched drink. 'And this has never happened before, since you stopped working in conflict zones?'

'No.'

'Is it affecting your ability to work in any way?'

'No one's complained yet. My internal auditor is continually checking for mistakes, and I don't think I've made any.'

'Perhaps it's you who should talk to Stan.'

'We both ought, but I don't think either of us have much tolerance for "human factors".'

'Why now?' he asked. 'If it's been three weeks—'

'I can only apologise.'

'That's not what I meant. This is not an exercise in blame. Something significant has happened, otherwise you wouldn't be talking to me now.'

He waited, and eventually she replied.

'We're,' and she hesitated again. 'We're not a well ship, Luca. I don't know whether my condition is primarily physical, psychiatric, or psychological. I could prescribe myself anti-psychotics, but despite everything, they still carry some side effects that would … let's just say I'd rather see ghosts for now. If it was just me, then okay, but other members of the Aphrodite's crew are also exhibiting forms of mental disturbance …' She gave up. 'There's no single pathology. We're all manifesting our own unique cluster of symptoms. I've written notes, the best I can, on everything. I've not sent them to Earth.'

Mariucci let a small tut escape him.

She demurred. 'I know. Because this is an experiment too, yes?'

'You told me that yourself, and I've just had an argument with Rory about the mission profile, in front of everyone in Command.'

'That's why we're talking now. I'm coming clean. I've devi-ated from my own mission protocols, that I helped write. What are you going to do about it, O Captain my Captain?'

Mariucci drank his coffee and ran his fingers over his head and down his face, feeling the knots and ridges on his skull, his over-heavy browline, his Roman nose, his pugnacious chin.

'What would be the result of your full disclosure of the last month of medical records? In your professional opinion. If you were in Darmstadt, reading through the reports, in date order, what course of action would you recommend at this point?'

'An immediate abort of the mission, and the ship to return to cis-lunar as soon as practically possible.'

He was startled at the force of her answer. 'Is it that bad?'

'No. No, no. But it has the potential to become that bad.'

Mariucci rumbled deep in his chest. Aborting now? It wasn't completely impossible, but it would most definitely be a disaster. The Aphrodite was a poster on every single classroom wall from Nunavut to the Tierra del Fuego. They were a symbol and a sign towards an expansive future, not just a spaceship.

'Do you think your recommendation would be overruled? For practical, as well as political reasons?' Mariucci knew his way around ESA committees, and the various personalities involved. So did she.

'Yes,' said Kattenbeck. 'I imagine that it would be. But the simple act of suggesting an abort at this stage would probably end all our careers at a stroke.'

'Even Rory's?'

'Maybe not. But it would stain him, however much he protested his innocence.'

'When you say we're all affected, do you mean all of us?'

'To some degree. I'd argue I was the worst. And of course, everyone has their coping strategies so that it doesn't affect their performance. We're still absolutely on track. It's not causing any material problems.'

'That's good. But of course, you're arguing that they shouldn't have to cope alone. Can we mitigate – you, and Stan, working together with the whole crew in an atmosphere of complete trust and transparency – the effects of this,' he struggled for the right word, in any language, 'this malaise?'

'I'd hope so. I can, if you want, start hammering away at the medicals for everyone. Get them in every other day, let them know they're being looked after, cared for. And the opportunities to hide worsening symptoms diminish, when even a reluctant patient knows they're being observed.'

'My own problems?'

'You don't have problems, Luca. But, yes, you'll be expected to comply with my regime as well.'

'Rory?'

'Him too.'

That would help the science team. Mariucci weighed everything in the balance, and finally assented.

'We'll try this. For a season. No secrecy between us, Petra. No further secrecy. If anything is endangering the ship, I have to know about it. We all go home: that is my first and last law. Capisce?'

3

Those gathered in Command were a smaller, self-selected group: Mariucci, Blasco, Colvin and Borner. Pilot, navigator and comms by necessity, and captain to make sure no one tried to interfere with the manoeuvre. Even then, he asked Colvin to recalculate the burn from first principles, just to make sure her answer matched the one stored on Laelaps's computer.

It did, and Mariucci spent a moment silently apologising to Forsyth for thinking ill of him: the man's faults might run deep, but he wasn't deliberately malicious.

'How's Laelaps holding up?'

'Valeria can brief you about the instrumentation,' said Borner, 'but from our side, very well. The CPU error-checking routines are robust, the command signals are confirmed one hundred per cent of the time, and onboard telemetry matches with our observations. We have full, unimpeded control of the probe's thrusters and gyroscopes. The solar panels are delivering an average of four hundred watts to the power grid, and the battery is fully charged. I've run simulated scenarios far worse than this.'

'We can override Laelaps at any point?'

'Yes. No problem.'

'Let's get the data up in the pit, then. And can we get a feed from the camera on the screen?'

Borner ported the camera's image to the display closest to Mariucci, while Colvin brought up the Jovian system in the pit. Again, the Aphrodite was in white, Laelaps in red. Their

30

respective lines had begun to diverge yesterday, and they were now a hundred thousand kilometres apart: Aphrodite was squeezing itself between the innermost edge of the radiation belt girdling Jupiter and the cloud-tops of Jupiter itself, and the probe was lying deep in the thick, howling wind of fierce elemental energy, and diving towards Europa, the second Galilean moon.

'T minus ten minutes,' said Colvin, and popped the time to the burn under the steady tick of the ship's clock.

Mariucci contemplated Europa's form. Because the moon always kept the same face to its planet, its pale, cracked mantle of ice was subtly shaded: the side always leading the orbit was stained pale yellow with sulphur, while the trailing edge looked bluer and whiter. The fissures in the crusts were marginally darker than the ice, like scratches on ivory. Otherwise, it appeared billiard-ball smooth. No mountains, no valleys.

And beneath? Was the ice a thin veneer over a large ball of stone? Or was there an ocean beneath that crust, that ran all the way down to a small rocky core? They were here to answer those questions, and more, if they could.

That there might be a hidden ocean, forever shrouded and protected by tens of kilometres of ice, an ocean that could, just might, maybe, harbour life that had evolved independently from Earth's biota, was the reason why no part of the Aphrodite was to ever reach the surface of Europa. Water might leak up and out through the fissures, to plume and blow in the ion storm, but if something, some fragment of terrestrial DNA went the other way and escaped into the cold dark sea, the pristine environment would be forever ruined.

One day. One day, when they'd learned not to be such cazzi, they'd be back and if there was anything down there, they'd find it and greet it and see if they could learn from it. Until then, they'd have to be content with whatever Laelaps's instruments could tell them.

That right there was part of why Forsyth's attitude bothered him so much: the man didn't care about whether he might commit genocide on an entire ecosystem, just so he might collect better data than he could otherwise manage. Information over emotion. Science over souls. He'd burn down a forest just to see how much carbon it contained.

Europa was a world in its own right. It needed to be respected.

'Coming up on the mark.'

'Hmm?'

'Luca. The burn.'

'Yes, thank you, Deirdre.' He'd drifted off, drifted with the images both on the screen and in his mind. Now he had to concentrate on the pit, on what the glowing lines were telling him.

What if he ordered them to cancel the manoeuvre, to send Laelaps away from Europa and out towards the fringes of Jovian space? Save the Europans from any possibility of interference by these barely civilised ape-men?

'Five. Three, two, one, mark.'

Too late. Laelaps's rockets were firing, slowing the probe and letting the moon capture it. The green line tightened like a watch-spring, coiling around the yellow sphere of holograph-Europa. The line flicked and quivered, and as the burn continued, it abruptly switched from an open-ended trajectory that represented escape to a closed ellipse that spoke of capture.

That was it. It was done.

Mariucci sat back, dry-mouthed, heart-quickened. Forsyth wasn't going to try and land Laelaps. His request was preposterous, and so was Mariucci's reaction to it. It was them simply acting out their parts. He ought to pay it no mind from now on.

'Engines report shutdown. Laelaps is in Europa orbit, periapsis two fifty kilometres, apoapsis seven eighty kilometres. Telemetry is nominal, all systems nominal.'

'Good, good,' he managed. 'Seven eighty is low?'

'The mission profile states eight hundred kilometres, but if anyone complains –' Colvin didn't have to say who, '– we've enough propellant to nudge it up to that.'

'I have no such objections, but I'm more interested in why the orbit is measurably low. Can we find out?'

Colvin looked at Blasco, who looked at Borner. 'Yes, we can do that.'

'We are threading needles here, constantly. If something is upsetting our ability to accurately map our paths, then we need to know about it before it affects the Aphrodite. Our drive doesn't permit us to make quick corrections.'

'You're right,' said Blasco. 'We'll run some tests. It might be a navigational error, or the engines' ISP.'

'Ove tells me we've sufficient stores for more or less free access to the kitchens for the next three months based on past and current usage. If we can draw up plans for a Nimbus encounter between perijove eight and ten, or twelve at the latest, that'll give us some flexibility in our actions. You had one at seven?'

'Much easier to make on the perijove after,' said Colvin. She'd worked it out long before Mariucci asked the question. 'Why make things harder on ourselves?'

'Then we'll schedule the Nimbus on perijove eight, and I'll tell Ove to keep a close watch on what we're eating. Can we get comms on that ship so we know we can steer it?'

Borner nodded: 'Already done. Pinged it, and it pinged back. The diagnostics log reports some errors, but not enough that we can't access the engines.'

'Thank you.' He knew he had a competent team, and he didn't need to tell them how to do their jobs.

Hellsten? There was definitely something wrong, an agitation to be away and doing something else. Not like Aasen's – he knew what she was doing at any given moment just by checking the ship's repair log. He'd have to ask Kattenbeck, and he'd expect a full answer. Coping was one thing, but he wanted his crew to live well.

He needed not to think about that now: concentrate on

the crew in front of him. 'Our next scheduled probe launch is Ganymede?'

'Now at perijove eight. We can make both the launch window and the Nimbus encounter.'

Mariucci looked into the pit, at the white line that Aphrodite was describing. They were heading out of the fire of the radiation belt, into the calm beyond Callisto, at the distance where the Nimbus ships circled.

Except that one, and that other one, and the two that were confirmed lost.

If they lost too many, they'd have to cut short the mission anyway, simply because otherwise they'd be on starvation rations before they recrossed Mars orbit.

'We should work up a chart of all possible Nimbus encounters,' he said, saying out loud what he was thinking. 'Just in case. And keep it up to date.'

Colvin nodded. 'I can do that,' she said. 'And warn you of any potential problems?'

'Yes. That would be helpful.' He flexed his fingers around his arm rests, the padding yielding slightly to the pressure of his grip. 'We need to work together, yes? Our science team, the mission specialists, are less ... aware of the complexities of running a ship like the Aphrodite than the flight crew are, and that decisions we make here in Command will affect the work they can do back there. I don't know how that divide has appeared, just that it has. We have to be, all of us, flexible in our approach, to allow them to gather as much data as possible while not hiding that what they'd like and what's practical are sometimes in conflict.'

Borner looked as if she wanted to say something, but simultaneously didn't want to raise it.

'Yasmin. We speak freely here.'

'We know this is a great adventure, and how privileged we are to be ...' She gestured at the rest of Command. 'We should be having the time of our lives. But we all know that this might be the last chance anyone ever gets to do this. That we have to make the most of being here, because of the way things are going on Earth. We might never be coming back.'

'And because of that?'

'It makes us want to take risks, Luca. It makes us want to take risks, even if it means losing sensors, losing probes, more exposure to radiation. We've been entrusted with this mission, and we have so much to prove.'

'Risking our lives to cancer in five or ten years' time is one thing,' said Blasco. 'It's whether we're willing to risk something with more immediate effects, and what form that would take.'

'Food has always been there, water has always been there. The radiation alarms have so far stayed silent.' Mariucci looked at the lines in the pit. 'To date, this voyage has been, if not easy, then straightforward. We have a ship capable of reaching Jupiter, completing a years-long mission, and going home again, all with a margin of safety and a degree of comfort that would have been unimaginable ten, twenty years ago. It wouldn't have even been possible, then.'

'It'll become impossible again. Five years, and it'll be over,' said Blasco. 'They're cancelling missions. Nothing will leave cis-lunar again.'

Colvin frowned at that. She was a navigator to her very core. 'Then we make a case they can't ignore. With this ship. With this mission.'

'I wouldn't want Laszlo to think all his work on the drive might be wasted,' Mariucci rumbled into his chest. 'Thank you for your honesty, Yasmin. This is something we all need to be aware of, but we must remain steadfast in our approach to safety, while still being sympathetic to wider concerns. The ship must not be compromised, must not be put in a position where it can be compromised, because if anything is going to seal the fate of future missions, it's the failure of this one. Do I have your assent to that?'

They all said yes.

'You have your duties, and I've kept you from them for long enough. Carry on.' He dismissed himself and headed for the axis, where he was immediately intercepted by Kattenbeck.

'In the spirit of our complete openness with each other, you should go down to airlock one.'

Mariucci frowned and looked down the axis. There was no one visible, and he glanced back at the doctor, waiting for a clue, or even a hint, which never came. He gave up with a grunt of annoyance, and pulled himself hand-over-hand down towards science country.

There were twelve external modules fixed to the radius of the Aphrodite's hull in three blocks of four, behind the gravity section and ahead of the probe garage. As he drifted by the open doors to the workshops, laboratories and storage areas, he caught sight of backs bent over instruments and consoles. Two of the modules, opposite each other across the axis, served as the primary airlocks.

Airlock two was empty: he peered through the thick layers of glassy plastic in the inner door, into the lit space beyond, and there was nothing but air between him and the outer door, also sealed. The tell-tales fixed to the bulkhead told him it was at full pressure.

He turned and pressed his face to airlock one. Inside was Spinu, with her spacesuit tethered to the wall beside her. She had her eyes closed and earpieces in, listening to something that made her serene.

Mariucci saw from the tell-tale that she had just started decompressing, moving from the ship-standard mix to a more suit-friendly reduced pressure, pure oxygen atmosphere. Where was she going? What was she doing? Most importantly, why hadn't he been told of this EVA?

He overrode the decompression and, when the pressure had equalised, spun the wheel on the door. Whatever was playing in her ears was loud enough to cover both his entrance and the slight rise in air pressure, so he pushed himself from the bulkhead over to her. He waited until she realised that she wasn't decompressing, and that there was someone in with her.

It took a little while. Her eyes opened and scanned the opposite wall, then her gaze flicked towards Mariucci. She gave a little gasp, but wouldn't turn her head.

'Valeria,' said Mariucci. He took a wild guess, but it was more intuition than speculation. 'This isn't the first time you've done this, is it?'

She swallowed, thought about lying to her captain, then decided against it.

'No.'

'Despite all the protocols we have in place.'

'Yes.'

'Opening the outer airlock door triggers an event. It's logged by the computer. It's also supposed to trip a warning light in Command. Can you tell me why this is the first I've learned of your excursions?'

'I – we – downgraded the alert level.'

'Did someone tell you to do that, or was that on your own initiative?'

She didn't answer that.

'Obviously, other people know about this. Just not me. Hmm.' Mariucci reached over and pulled her suit towards him. His was still in its sterilised cover, but hers looked subtly worn. Used. He turned the gauntlets over and inspected the rubber pads. They were scuffed and striated. 'Why?'

'Things have needed fixing. Instruments on the hull. I ... volunteered.'

'If something was broken, then it should have appeared on Hanne's list.'

'They did. I said I'd deal with them.'

'So she knew, at least.'

Spinu acknowledged the gotcha with a brief tight-lipped smile, and Mariucci filed a note to talk to Aasen.

'She's the engineer, familiar with the ship's systems. You ought have been second to her first, or vice versa.'

'She didn't want to waste time in decompression. There were things that needed fixing inside, and she just looked relieved when I offered.' She stared at the opposite wall. 'I did have a second. Benjamin said he'd come with me, and I thought Hanne had reported it to you. I was following procedure then.'

'And after the first time?'

'Benjamin just refused every time I suggested an EVA. He didn't want to go outside again, couldn't go outside again, and everyone else was busy. We're all busy. I just went by myself. It was fine. It was perfectly safe.'

She hadn't been perfectly safe. She'd been lucky.

'If something needed mending, I'd never withhold permission for EVA,' he said, as mildly as he could manage. 'You'd just have to say, and we'd have found you a partner, and that would have been that.'

'You're disappointed.'

A small fire flared inside him. 'Of course I'm disappointed. How could I not be? Even now, when caught and confronted, you're not telling me the whole truth. You're not a child and I'm not a parent. Respect me enough not to make me drag everything from you, one capitulation at a time.'

She was silent again.

'I can't permit this to continue. You know that. If you don't promise me you'll stop, I'll have to do something to stop it.'

'Have you seen it?'

It took him a moment to realise they had changed subject. 'Have I seen it?'

'Jupiter. Have you seen it? With your own eyes.'

'No,' but he felt that answer was inadequate. It wasn't what she was looking for. 'Is that the why, Valeria? Is that it, so you can see Jupiter?'

Now she looked at him, intense, full-gaze, searching his face for reaction, for understanding, for agreement.

'Looking at it on a screen just isn't the same, Luca. You have to experience it. That first time, we were still on perijove one, and Jupiter was this fat, bright circle in a black sky. You could see the banding, the oblateness, even from almost outside the system. But the second time, we were closer than Metis. I climbed out on the hull and it was there. Enormous. Overwhelming. Demanding. It was glorious.'

It didn't sound like she was going to stop her trips outside the hull. It sounded like even if she gave him her most solemn vow, she would break it in a heartbeat.

'You need an EVA partner, every single time you go outside, because things happen. Stupid things. Predictable things. Accidental things. Any of those can incapacitate you, and if there is someone outside with you, they can get you back in the airlock quickly. Even the simplest of problems can overwhelm you, and if you have to wait for someone to decompress and come and get you, you could well be dead by the time they reach you. You know this. You know this already, and yet you choose to ignore it.'

How could he enforce his will? This was a spaceship. Trust was as important as air.

'Yes,' she said. Not so much an admission of guilt as a simple acknowledgement of the facts.

'I'm not forbidding you to EVA. I'm asking you, when you do it, to do it within the rules.' Mariucci would do whatever it took. Take her spacesuit from her, confine her to the wheel, chain her to him even. She absolutely could not spacewalk on her own. He had to hope, though, that she'd return to reason of her own accord.

'I hear you.' It wasn't enough. He'd sat through enough meetings with bureaucrats to realise that she was choosing words that he couldn't use against her later.

'I am your captain,' he said. 'You must not EVA without a partner. You must go by the book, or not at all.'

'Come with me,' said Spinu in a small voice, barely above a whisper. 'Please, come with me. If you see, you'll understand.'

He'd need to speak to Tsoltos, and to Kattenbeck about this. Not a well ship, the doctor had said, and this was just another manifestation of that.

'If I do this for you,' said Mariucci, 'will you do something for me?'

Again, another moment when she could go for the comfortable lie, or the inconvenient truth. 'Yes. I'll do something for you.'

He shouldn't have to bargain like this. And yet, what other option did he have? Commercial spacers travelling outside of any and all legal jurisdictions had one sanction in their collective toolbox and that was simply to throw malefactors out of the airlock, without a spacesuit. It was both brilliantly, brutally effective and open to the most horrendous abuse.

'Come and find me. If you want to go outside, come and find me first. Yes?'

'Yes. I can do that.' Then, as if she hadn't just coerced her captain, she said, 'Go and get your suit. We can decompress together.'

He'd done all of his training and completed several difficult, technical spacewalks. Being tethered to the outside of the Aphrodite while someone else did the work was no real effort aside from the time spent in decompression. Still, he felt nothing but apprehension, a fist tight around his heart, squeezing the life from him: if Velter felt the same, then no wonder the man had balked. Mariucci fought against it. He was the captain, no matter what.

It passed, and he remained.

'I'll be five minutes,' he said, and pushed himself away towards the inner door. He hadn't asked what it was they were actually replacing, or bringing in to be mended. Spinu didn't seem to have any tools with her, nor a tote bag with a plug-in unit. He should have asked, but when he turned back to her, she looked so happy, happy that she was going to be able to EVA, even happier that she had someone to share the experience with.

If there was nothing to do, no fault, no repair, then he would absolutely have to ground her. But he would do this once, because he'd promised, and to come all this way and only see Jupiter on a screen, something he could have done at home? Everybody should have the opportunity to do this once.

He didn't say anything more, just headed to the gravity section to pick up a tablet. He could read some of the science reports, because he'd given up trying to find out from Forsyth what was going on in his own ship. The daily précis the science team put together was enough to surprise them with when he quoted it back at them during mealtimes, and still he had the suspicion that Forsyth was curating the data feed back to Earth, to leave out the choicest morsels and save them for himself.

He descended to the wheel and took one of the tablets out of their dock.

'Did you see her?'

Kattenbeck was by the door of her consulting room, which would double as an operating theatre should the necessity arise. Either she hadn't been there moments before, or he'd blanked her completely.

'I saw her. I'm going out with her.'

'Are you? And you're okay with what she's been doing?'

Mariucci checked that no one was in the immediate vicinity. 'No. I'm not okay with it. This endangers the whole mission – as have all the decisions that allowed this to get to this point. I've forbidden her to EVA solo.'

'Solo EVA is already forbidden,' she said.

'So are a lot of current practices on this ship, but it doesn't stop them from happening.' He powered the tablet up and checked on its battery life. It'd last the length of the decompression and more. 'Thank you for telling me. It was important that you did.'

'And we still need to talk more about her, her physical and psychological state, and whether she's still fit for her duties.'

'And Benjamin. And Hanne. And you. And me.' He let his shoulders sag before straightening up against the weak gravity. 'We're starting to make bad decisions, Petra. This was a tight ship. A solid crew. Somewhere along the way, we – I – let it slip out of my hands like sand. Is it too late to bring it back, or are we lost already?'

'It's never too late, Luca.' Kattenbeck seemed to be looking over Mariucci's head, at something further round the wheel. He frowned and turned, but there was no one, just a cluster of low chairs.

'Is there someone there?'

'In a manner of speaking, yes.'

'Ah. One of your Arab boys?'

'A child. A girl. On the road to Al-Hadithah, if I remember correctly.'

He nodded. 'Are you going to be all right on your own? I have to get back to Valeria before she decides to go without me anyway.'

Kattenbeck snorted. 'I'm not really alone, am I?' But she still waved him away. 'I'll be fine.'

Mariucci tethered the tablet to his wrist and climbed up the ladder. He stuck his head around Command before heading back to airlock one.

'I'm doing an EVA with Valeria,' he announced. Did they already know about her? Judging by their guarded, neutral expressions, yes. How far they had fallen, so fast. 'Something on the hull needs looking at. It'll be on Hanne's list.'

Now he was just making excuses for someone else. He didn't know if either of those things were true, and most likely they weren't.

Borner looked round from her screen. 'Any problems, use channel one.'

'I will,' he said, and she had already returned to the stream of numbers coursing up her display. 'Could one of you reset the airlock alarms so they flag in Command? The appropriate event level is in the manual.'

He left it at that, to let them know that he knew, that there would be something said at a later date, and until then, they could worry about it.

Mariucci went to the suit storage bay, opened the cover of his locker and looked at his spacesuit. He held on to one of the ceiling grab straps and dug his fingers into the thin plastic wrap that cocooned it. It tore and peeled away, and as he dragged it over the life-support housing and down to the articulated waist, he had to adjust his grip to hang on to the sides of the locker, and then finally to the bottom lip. He balled the plastic film up, and tucked it tidily into a corner.

His suit, fresh out of the bag. He took a life-support pack from the rack and opened the back hatch on the suit, marrying the two with a positive click. Lights bloomed, and the system started to boot.

The last time he'd been on the hull of Aphrodite had been before they'd left cis-lunar. He'd had one of the ship's lead designers with him, and it had been very much a courtesy tour for someone who spent her life inside a virtual reality program, drawing with light. But he'd been pleased to accompany her, and had enjoyed her wonder at how the long array of coordinates she'd coded had been made real in metal and composite.

Now he was going out again, this time to gaze at the face of Jupiter, in a much more problematic situation than a leisure EVA. He could call off this excursion. He didn't even need a reason. He could tell Colvin to fire up the engines and plot them a course home, and there'd be nothing anyone could do about that.

Except disobey him.

He grimaced. That it had occurred to him would mean it had also occurred to everyone. He would have to navigate the path away from this point more surely than he had the road that had led them there.

Mariucci took his suit by the arm and towed it behind him towards the airlock.

4

Weeks could pass on board the Aphrodite without all of the crew being together in one place, and because of that, human factors had decided there needed to be a regularly scheduled event at which attendance was, barring a crisis, mandatory.

That was how the apojove meal was born, out of a conference several years earlier and a billion kilometres away. It was now in its fifth iteration. Mariucci put the work in, curating the menu, setting the table, arranging the plates and the glasses. When the time for everyone to convene arrived, rather than summoning them via the intercom, he went to find them, one by one, or however they were grouped, and invited them to share in this celebration of shipborne life.

He headed towards the back of the ship first, because that's where he knew Molnar would be, as close to his nuclear drive as he could be. Molnar was also responsible, in conjunction with Kattenbeck, for the dosimeters that they all had in their top pockets, and for the accuracy of the radiation alarm system, a duty he shared with Aasen.

So far, there hadn't been a problem with any of the three systems. The shielding, passive and active, seemed to be effective, and the drive had performed solidly throughout the long, slow burn to Jupiter.

Mariucci propelled himself past the workshops, through the bulkhead doors into the probe bay, then took the tunnel as it jinked around the garages. Beyond that, the modules became more industrial: the fifth section wore the external fuel tanks like a pearl necklace, with the necessary tubes and valves, shunts and stirrers – the whole panoply of pipework – exposed against the internal walls like a twentieth-century submarine. Then came the radiators, with cables and trunking as fat as his arm taking the excess heat away from the reactor and bleeding it safely into space, and finally the magnetic coils that both powered and shaped the invisible shield that surrounded the ship.

And beyond that? Another thirty metres of ship. The internal tank of deuterium-helium fuel, shielding, a refrigeration plant that could freeze a small moon, and the fusion torus. Stirling engines to convert heat to power and a great, flaring cone that blasted out sub-light plasma to order. No one went further back than the last bulkhead, if they could possibly avoid it. There was no door, and very few user-serviceable parts, deliberately so, past that point.

He found Molnar, back pressed against the plastic-coated ceramic housing of the shield. He was motionless, held there by air currents, or perhaps the deep bass hum of electricity that permeated every fibre of his flight suit, every pore of his skin.

'Laszlo?' said Mariucci. 'Is everything okay here?'

Molnar blinked. 'Yes. It's good. It's good here.'

'What are you doing?'

'Listening.'

'Listening to …'

'The heart of the machine. It tells me things the sensors don't.'

That was possibly the truth, so Mariucci let it slide. 'We're ready to eat. Apojove.'

Molnar pushed his hands behind him, away from the bulkhead. He drifted into the centre of the module, turning his arms at the midpoint so that he could see where he'd come from. 'I've some tests to run,' he said. 'I won't be able to stay for long.'

'Laszlo, the tests can wait for an hour, half an hour even.

46

We run our own schedules, but you have to come to apojove.'
Molnar had his back to Mariucci, so he couldn't see his expression. The lighting in the radiator module was dim, as subdued as it was in Command, but there it was deliberate, so that the screens and the pit were more immediately visible. In the stern of the ship, the white ambient lights should have been burning bright, not just the displays and the tell-tales.

'I don't like to be away for too long,' Molnar said, in a way that made Mariucci frown and start searching the shadows for shapes that shouldn't be there. He was blocking the light coming in from the axis behind him, and he pulled himself to one side.

It helped, a little. There, in the gloom, between bulkhead and wall, were drawstring bags, three of them, and what was probably a rolled-up sleeping bag, clipped to the wall. Molnar was, it appeared, living in the module.

Everyone had to sleep in the wheel, eat in the wheel, use the plumbing in the wheel, except in the obvious cases of the wheel not turning, or a high radiation event when they had to retreat to Command, with its thicker physical walls. What Molnar was doing was ... not forbidden, in that there weren't specific rules about this, but it was just not expected because that was not how the ship was supposed to run.

Someone else to talk to Kattenbeck about, to see if she already knew, to go over his medical records again and lecture him on the long-term effects of reduced gravity on muscle and bone. But now was the time for the apojove meal, and Molnar would just have to come with him.

The scientist turned again with a swing of his arms, and followed Mariucci's gaze. If he guessed that he'd been found out, any shame he might have felt didn't show.

'Come with me, Laszlo. The table's ready, and I'm getting everyone together.'

'I don't want to leave here,' said Molnar. 'It's safe here, right next to the shield.'

'It's safe anywhere in the ship. You know that. You know that from the raw data you pull from the detectors, from our dosimeters. You know it's safe in the wheel, in Command, in the workshops. If it wasn't, you'd be the first to know, and you'd tell us. You'd show us the evidence, yes?'

Molnar had a thin face, but it had become swollen with zero gravity: he squeezed at his cheeks as he worked his jaw and pursed his lips.

'You're right, you're right. I'll come.' He made no move towards the axis, even though he'd finally drifted the length of the module, and was now beside Mariucci.

'After you, Laszlo.' Mariucci gestured along the axis. He gave Molnar no choice as to when to leave, nor any opportunity to dissemble. 'I'll catch everyone else as I go. Find a place at the table.'

With one last look behind him, Molnar slowly eased himself past Mariucci, who quite deliberately positioned himself in the doorway again before following closely behind, shepherding him along, back through the fuel module and around the kink in the axis.

Mariucci watched Molnar tap and dab his way past the workshops and hesitate at the rotating section. Molnar saw his captain watching him, waiting for him to commit, and there was nothing he could do but slide feet first into the access tunnel and descend to the wheel.

Visiting each workshop in turn – and checking the airlocks – Mariucci chased the rest of the scientists out, including Forsyth who he thought he would have to at least verbally spar with, but who came as meekly as a lamb, even encouraging his entourage to cease work and do as they were bidden.

Hellsten was in the repair shop, nursing a just-made minor wound on his hand. The blood was very red against his pale skin, a puncture in the fleshy part between thumb and fore-finger, with a smear pointing towards his wrist.

'Ove, you have to be more careful.' Mariucci turned Hellsten's hand over to see the damage. Superficial, but unwelcome all the same.

'Screwdriver slipped. Sorry.'

'Hands behind the blade. You've clamps and vices for holding the work. If it takes longer, it takes longer, and avoidable mistakes are avoidable.' He folded Hellsten's other hand over the gouge, and pressed firmly down. 'Go and find Petra. She'll clean it up and dress it. Go. It's apojove.'

He shooed Hellsten out of the workshop, and tried to account for the others. Borner, Blasco and Colvin were in Command, the science team – minus the doctor and Molnar – had been in the labs. If Hellsten could be relied on to find Kattenbeck, then the only one left was his engineer.

He hadn't seen her on the way to the back of the ship, nor heading forward again. She hadn't been in the wheel, so perhaps she was back under the floor in Command. He pulled his way through the rotating section.

The three people he expected to see were all there, crowded around Borner's screen. It momentarily struck Mariucci as odd, given that she could port her information to any display in Command, but he was concentrating on where Aasen might be, and the thought bounced off him.

'Where's Hanne?' he asked, and a hand – Blasco's – emerged from the press of bodies and pointed to the very front of the ship.

They were still docked with the Nimbus – to be discharged into the Jovian atmosphere at perijove – but they'd stripped all the supplies and everything else useful from it. Mariucci pushed himself over the pit, behind the three flight crew, to the docking ring structure. The bulkhead door was closed, and he instinctively glanced at the tell-tales: full pressure at Earth-normal mix. He spun the lock and braced himself against the grabs either side to push it open with his feet.

There she was, inside the Nimbus itself, tablet in hand and using a data cable to interrogate the wiring behind a panel. She was tabbing and dabbing furiously at the tablet, scrolling and stopping, checking a line and then moving on.

He pushed the door shut behind him and glided towards her, resting his hands against the outer door of the docking ring, where the Aphrodite ended and the Nimbus began.

'Hanne? You don't have to fix this.'

'I do if you want rid of it.' She didn't look round. 'Thrusters lasted long enough for Theresa to stabilise it, and not a second longer.'

'It's apojove,' he said.

'I'd love to, but,' and she waggled the tablet.

'It can wait. It can wait for an hour.'

'Luca, I won't lie, there's a lot of things breaking down, a lot of things about to break down. I can't keep on top of them.' Her tablet pinged, and she tutted. 'Another on the list.'

'If you need help, you need to say.'

'I don't need help. I just need to get the thrusters working again and move on to the next problem.'

'I'll get Ove to work with you.'

'He is. All the broken bits go to him, to see if he can get them back, or break them down for spares.'

'Laszlo then.'

'He's busy with his engines.'

'He's not so busy that he can't help maintain the ship. That goes for everyone. I can give you an hour or two a day, until we catch up. We can get the list down to manageable size again. Tell me what's going wrong.'

'Everything. Everything is going wrong. Everything that might go wrong is threatening to go wrong. It all needs checking before it does and kills us. Do you understand that, Captain?' She stabbed down at the tablet with her finger, hard, repeatedly. 'I'm not doing this because I enjoy it, I'm doing this because I don't want us to die.'

'Hanne. We're not going to die because the Nimbus isn't powered. We can jury-rig something, an external control box, and that'll be that. Now, it's apojove, and your presence is required at the table.'

'Faen ta deg!'

'Hanne! The ship is holding up fine. You don't need to go chasing every last report. You don't.' He studied the interior of the Nimbus, for the want of anywhere else to look. 'I can relieve you of your duties for a period.'

'We'll all die,' she said, and she started to shake. 'We'll all die and it'll be my fault.'

'This ship, my ship, is in good condition. It will keep us safe and get us home.' He reached out and gripped her shoulder. 'Come with me, Hanne. All will be well, at least for as long as apojove lasts.'

She looked at her tablet and, trembling, powered it down. She threw her head back and gasped in relief. He still had hold of her, and he pulled her unresisting body after his, back through the bulkhead, then boosted her gently across Command while he sealed the door back up.

The flight crew were still squashed in around Borner's chair, and he almost didn't ask them what they were so intent on because he was afraid of the answer.

'Is that anything I need to be aware of?'

Borner pushed the data away. 'Science stuff. Valeria put us on to it. It's the first big find, and I'm sure she'll tell you about it over apojove.'

She unclipped, and the three of them drifted away at different vectors towards the ceiling, before taking hold of grab straps and bars to aim at the axis. Mariucci made sure Aasen was ahead, then let them all head down to the wheel before he did. He preferred it like this, appearing last, letting them sit where they wanted, start conversations with each other, which he would then join rather than instigate.

Command was empty. The axis was empty. It was a strange feeling, knowing that the ship represented the only place outside the orbit of Mars that might sustain human life. Aasen was right, in that if anything went significantly wrong, then death was probable. But they were all smart. They'd trained for this. They could fix – try to fix or invent a workaround for – most things that weren't going to kill them instantly.

He descended to the wheel, and took the space left for him, between Spinu and Hellsten, and opposite, he was surprised to find, Forsyth. Someone had already charged his glass with water, and he picked it up, raising it in salute.

'Cent'anni.'

An aperitif would go down well right about now, but it was a dry ship. All ships probably ought to be: he'd heard stories. He sat down, nestling his elbows between his tablemates', and started to help himself to the food nearest him. He'd gone for an Indian theme – the menu was a European's idea of Indian cuisine, a bit from the south coast, a bit from the north-east, something from the central highlands, but at least it had flavour, and the vacuum-packed naans were a favourite of his, once they'd been properly woken up with a sprinkling of water and a blast in the microwave.

He thought about the Indian diaspora, how a billion people had – not quite overnight, but still across the short span of a decade – seen their country become lethally hot for weeks at a time. The advocates for fixing Earth before venturing outwards towards other planets had a point, but he resisted agreeing with them – even if he knew two of the main agitators personally. He argued that there was the money to do both, and there always had been.

He noted that Hellsten sported a neat bandage on his left hand, and he turned to Spinu.

'Valeria. I'm told you've made a discovery.'

She glanced at Forsyth before answering. She was checking it was okay to share the details with Mariucci, which soured his mood. But he hid it, and waited for her to clear her throat.

'It's a little thing. An anomaly, but it might turn out to be significant.'

'I'm interested,' he said.

She reached out and started to move the plates into an orbital diagram. 'So that's Io, this is Europa, and then Ganymede, and they're in a four-two-one resonance. Every time Ganymede passes Europa, every seven days—'

'Seven point one five five days,' said Forsyth.

'Every seven point one five five days, at a distance of,' her glaze flicked to Forsyth again, 'approximately four hundred thousand kilometres, there's a burst of low-frequency energy between the two moons.'

Forsyth didn't correct her, and Mariucci took the opportunity to nod approvingly.

'A breakdown in the vacuum insulation?' he asked.

Perhaps the scientists had forgotten that the flight crew were also highly trained specialists with magpie minds. Spinu's eyebrows registered a flash of surprise.

'That's certainly one of the early theories. Two charged spheres immersed in a conducting plasma approaching each other like clockwork. It's a formidable distance, but if the ionospheres of the moons momentarily connect at closest approach, allowing energy to flow between them, then it's a genuinely novel finding.'

'And low frequency?'

'Yes. That's one of the more problematic parts of this. I'd have expected a burst in the megahertz range, and widely scattered. This is in the kilohertz band, which wouldn't normally make it through a radio-opaque layer, but it's also tight. There's something going on, and it's not likely to be lightning.'

'New is good,' said Mariucci. 'It justifies our presence here—'

'We don't need to justify it,' said Forsyth. 'Even if we discovered nothing of note at all, we have every right to be here. If we don't explore and record, then what are we even for?'

'It justifies our presence here to our detractors. The more we discover, the more essential we show ourselves to be, and the

53

more likely that others will follow in our footsteps.' Mariucci proffered the dish of korma. 'Rory, you're among friends.'

'They're whittling us like a stick,' said Forsyth. He took the dish, but didn't quite know what to do with it. 'And when they are done they'll break us like a match.'

Mariucci took a moment to digest the metaphors.

'The Earth was almost reduced to smoking ruin by an asteroid only four years ago, in what was a foreseeable and avoidable situation. It concentrated minds.'

'It was going to miss. And then that idiot boy Van der Veerden started his ridiculous campaign.'

'He's not alone—'

'It's monstrous. How dare he try and interfere with what I'm doing.'

'We allowed him to drive a four-kilometre asteroid into the path of the Moon.'

'"We" didn't do anything.' Forsyth gave up juggling the plate and simply held it out to one side for someone else to take. 'I don't concern myself with his business. He ought to keep out of mine.'

The rest of the table had become silent while the two older men argued. Mariucci felt nothing but resentment, more at the ruined atmosphere than the sentiments expressed, although they were bad enough.

'You do recall that the Aphrodite was the ship that disrupted KU2 and saved cis-lunar space from becoming unusable?' Mariucci looked down the table and saw Colvin. She'd been there with him. Of course she had. Somehow, he'd remembered the mission, but not her. To cover his confusion, he uncharacteristically went on the attack. 'If we'd failed, then none of us would be sitting here. We would have been shut out of space for a thousand years.'

Fractured images and scattered scenes played out in Mariucci's mind. It had been a desperate scramble: Aphrodite had been the only ship capable of stopping KU2 that could have reached it in time, and even then, it had come right down to the wire.

'But we weren't "shut out of space",' said Forsyth. 'We weren't because we could prevent it. We could prevent it happening because we were in space already. Accidents happen: we just have to be ready for them.'

'We weren't ready last time, Rory. Jack van der Veerden just wants better regulations to prevent accidents from happening in the first place. He doesn't want to shut us down.'

'That woman does. Woman? Girl.'

'If you mean Catherine Vi—'

'Yes, of course, you know her too. The gallowglass. She and Van der Veerden are two sides of the same coin. Awful people. Can't you just tell them to just shut up and go away? Let the grown-ups deal with matters?'

'Because we've made such a good job of it so far, yes?'

Forsyth snorted. 'Well, I have. I can't speak for you.'

'I'm the captain of a spaceship,' said Mariucci.

'And I'm the Lucasian Professor of Mathematics at Cambridge University. Something I'll continue to be when we get back.'

Mariucci was already on edge due to his earlier mistake. Now, he couldn't remember the last time he'd hit someone. No, that wasn't true: he had the image of one stringy child – an older child, ten, eleven, something like that – battering another in the street, next to a yellow-painted house with a blue door. He could picture that, but not recall what it had been about, nor the identity of the other child. Even whether he'd been on top or underneath.

'With such mentors as us, it's surprising that our youth are so ungrateful,' he managed sourly. He picked up his naan, tore off a strip and wadded it into his mouth. At least he would stop himself from saying anything for a while. Who would pick up the conversation now?

Tsoltos: it was, at least partly, his job to keep the peace, to mediate conflict. He began a rambling anecdote about sitting on the quayside at Thessaloniki with his uncle, eating ice cream and watching the ferries come in. Everyone was listening to him, trying, like Mariucci, to work out exactly how this story tied in with the friction between the captain and the chief scientist. Tsoltos and Uncle Spiro went to sit in the gardens underneath the statue of Alexander the Great, then they walked to a bar, and someone laughed because they thought, like Mariucci, that this was something from when Tsoltos was young, and not just before the Aphrodite had left for Jupiter. In fact, Spiro had dementia, and he was out of his care home for a day. Tsoltos had assumed the caring role, visiting the places that they'd shared before.

There was no point to what Tsoltos was saying. It was simply a story about an old man and his nephew, eating and drinking and walking their way through a sweltering day in the city, made more bearable by the sea and the shade.

When he finished his story, with a car taking them both back to the care home, and leaving again with only him, he wiped his sleeves under his eyes, left and right. He expressed his wish to cure Spiro of his affliction, and somehow the fractious words at the start of the meal were forgotten, forgiven even. Everyone seemed to be enjoying themselves at least, and whatever stresses were affecting them seemed to be put aside for the moment.

Everyone except Mariucci and Forsyth. The scientist remained unchanged, unmoved, unyielding, while the captain was full of shame and doubt as to how he could have forgotten, even momentarily, that Deirdre Colvin had been with him on that first Aphrodite mission to save the world.

5

It was up to Mariucci whether to make it known to the rest of the crew, but they were going to find out eventually: they were only forty light minutes away from Earth, not at the other end of the universe. He read the communiqué again, tried to digest its importance and its meaning, but there was nothing but the cold, hard facts, and they had experts – like Velter – who could better interpret the news for them.

In fact, it would be entirely reasonable for him to page the planetary scientist and talk to him first, then the others. Mariucci considered matters. Actually, no. He'd go and find him himself, rather than broadcast the summons through the entire ship. Commercial spaceships had a communications blackout on long voyages: spacers believed people from different cultures and different backgrounds could work together better if they weren't constantly bombarded with stories and media from home, as much domestic – who had died, who was getting divorced – as geopolitical, although ship's crew did sometimes find themselves on the opposite sides of a war that was happening millions of kilometres away.

He locked his screen in Command. Borner knew he'd had a priority message from Earth, but she didn't know what it contained. When he unclipped and pushed himself off towards the axis, he could feel her gaze follow him. She'd know soon enough.

Mariucci moved swiftly down towards the science section, and located Velter, who was using a VR headset to analyse stereoscopic images – Mariucci could see them displayed on the screens behind him – from Europa's surface. That looked like something he'd very much like to try himself: the resolution seemed pin-sharp, and it would be like hovering over the ice crust and seeing every wrinkle, every crevasse in glorious detail.

'Benjamin?' Mariucci had to try twice more, but eventually his voice broke through Velter's concentration, and the scientist peeled off the goggles.

Velter blinked, saw Mariucci, and quickly looked around to see who else was present: no one in that particular module.

'Luca. How can I help you?' A moment later, he asked a supplemental. 'Is something wrong?'

'Yes,' said Mariucci. He stroked his nose for a moment, before asking: 'What can you tell me about the Ross ice shelf?'

'I …' Velter tethered the VR goggles to the console he was next to, using a Velcro strap. 'Has it?'

'As of this morning, it's no longer attached to the continent of Antarctica.'

'I knew there was increased calving from the front edge.'

'This is the whole shelf. The crack started propagating two days ago, and it's now all the way across. I need you to tell me how bad this is, and on what timescale.' Mariucci pulled himself into the module, and used his feet to kick the bulkhead door closed. 'The report I've been sent is strong on current facts, but weak on future consequences.'

Velter had left cis-lunar with close-cropped tight coils of black hair. Now, when he ran his hand over them, they jostled like springs.

'The shelf itself isn't the problem. It's already floating on the ocean, displacing as much water as it ever will. It's the whole system of glaciers behind the shelf, and most of the West Antarctic ice sheet.' He put his fist on his sternum, deliberately taking a breath and holding it for as long as he could. Mariucci recognised Tsoltos's hand in that: a coping mechanism, self-treatment.

'How much and how long?'

'I paid some attention to what was happening. It's not my speciality.'

'Do your best.'

Velter took another deep breath, and held it, expelling it in a long, slow exhalation. 'West Antarctica – the ground the ice sits on is below mean sea level because of the weight of the ice sheet – is vulnerable to sudden melting. Sudden is fifty to a hundred years. It's happened before, in Quaternary interglacials. Not all of the ice, but enough of it. It caused at least two or three metres sea-level rise. Maybe four or five. Possibly ten. If that's true, then we could be looking at five centimetres a year, plus, for the next century, on top of what's already happening.'

'Tell me about the worst case?'

'If the whole of Antarctica melts, that's sixty metres. A civilisation-ending amount of water.'

'Five to ten metres in fifty years is perhaps enough for that. What were we before this?'

Velter shrugged. His shoulders were tight: it was more a jerk than a gesture. 'Half a centimetre a year?'

Mariucci rubbed his face, and he was surprised to find his hands were cold, properly cold, as if all the blood had rushed to his core. Stress response. He was probably pale, too. 'I need to tell the rest of the crew, but I also need to compose my thoughts first. I apologise for using you as my sounding board. Are you going to be okay? I know about the—' and he scrunched his own fist against his chest.

The man looked down at his feet, floating over the deck. 'I don't know why it happens. I shouldn't be scared all the time. But I am, and I'm sorry.'

'Sometimes we don't know what will frighten us until it happens.'

'I've been in space before. On the Moon. EVA. Hours of it. I should be used to this.'

Mariucci nudged closer. 'Benjamin, no one will make you do anything you don't want to. We can work around this.'

'Will this mean we go home early?'

'I hope not. What we're doing here – what you're doing here – is important. Perhaps more important than ever now. And it's a long haul back to Earth. If they tell us to return, we'd have to. Until then, we have our mission profile to follow. There'll be more discoveries like Valeria's. You'll make some yourself. If nothing else, it'll keep us busy, and the time will pass quickly. You'll see.'

'But what would we be returning to, Luca? We were struggling with the sea rise as it was, not as it will be.'

'We'll have to leave that to our peers, and our governments.' Even as Velter rolled his eyes in exasperation, Mariucci acknowledged that his words were very weak sauce. 'ESA have informed us of the situation. That is all they've said.'

'They will, at some point, have to justify our continued presence around Jupiter to a world that's starting to drown. That's going to become increasingly difficult, however self-contained we are.' Velter reached for his VR headset again, probably the only reasonable response in the face of such a slow-moving but overwhelming disaster, so far away: work. 'Two years ago, when they tried to blow up the Rhine-Meuse barrage? Life in prison for all them? They should have just waited. Ten years and it'll be useless.'

To Mariucci, they were terrorists. To Velter, they were that as well, but also they were people who had a point to make.

'Thank you for your time, Benjamin. I'm going to call home and ask some questions and look for some clarification. That'll delay the conversation we need to have on the Aphrodite by a couple of hours. Can I have your confidence until then?'

Velter nodded. 'Sure.'

Mariucci returned to the bulkhead door and hauled it open. Then he turned, half through the doorway. 'If there was a vote – this is not a democracy, but if it was – what would you want to do?'

'I don't know. I'd have to think about it. I ...' Velter hesitated.

'I wish I'd never come. The thought of spending every day like this, like I'm about to suffocate, it's terrifying. And yet, this is supposed to be the highlight of my career. The first manned voyage to Jupiter. I'm ashamed of what I've become.'

It was Mariucci's turn to nod. 'Something is bearing down on us. We all feel it. You're not alone, Benjamin.'

Velter pulled the VR goggles over his face, and Mariucci left him there, hanging over the face of Europa, silent and still.

He returned to his seat in Command and unlocked the screen. Borner had seen him come in, but had diplomatically pretended that neither the secure message nor his sudden departure were of any concern. She was watching something on her screen – lines, frequencies, a sine wave moving through time – and Mariucci was happy to leave her to it.

He steadied his fingers over his keyboard, but the words wouldn't come. Part of him thought of typing 'What possible good did you think telling us this would achieve?' and another part of him thought sending that wouldn't hurt at all. He was as out of reach to them as they were to him. In that, Forsyth was exactly right: they were autonomous of Earth, and it was only loyalty and integrity that kept them in line. And to be accurate, his own loyalty and integrity: if it had been down to Forsyth, those ideals would have already gone out of the airlock.

In the end, he started with something bland:

Thank you for your communication regarding the Ross ice shelf. I have consulted with Dr Velter regarding the implications of the event. He was able to give me a general forecast, but stressed that he was not a specialist in this area.

Colvin drifted in, acknowledged both the captain and Borner, and settled herself at her habitual station.

Mariucci tried to concentrate on his message. The sooner he sent it, the sooner he'd have the answers to give to the crew.

Dr Velter concluded that there are no immediate physical effects of the ice shelf collapse, and the mission profile of the Aphrodite is such that our scheduled return in 2082 will not likely be affected by any degradation in Earth-LEO capabilities that might occur.

He thought of Kourou, and Peenemünde, and how low they were, how close to the coast. There would be somewhere to land a space plane, but the number of runways might be reduced.

Of more concern is the political situation. There will be renewed and increased calls for missions such as this to be cancelled or curtailed. Such pressure is not likely to abate, but will intensify as sea level rise accelerates over the coming years. The Nimbus supply craft that are currently in orbit in Jovian space are sufficient to maintain our presence here for the duration of the mission, assuming we can successfully intercept them. Those which are en route to Jupiter will arrive in time to restock the Aphrodite, if our departure date is unchanged.

However, I can foresee a scenario where we are recalled early. At that point, the Aphrodite would have to divert from the agreed mission profile and adopt an aggressive Nimbus-intercepting course, in order to collect enough supplies to last the voyage to cis-lunar space. This would necessarily impact the science programme on board.

To reiterate: there will be a cut-off, after which the Aphrodite will not be able to return early, having used too many of the existing Nimbus craft to resupply, and will be compelled to wait for new Nimbuses to enter Jovian space. You have our up-to-date inventory and flight plan: our next Nimbus intercept is scheduled for perijove eight.

The Aphrodite's crew will make these deductions for themselves, independently and quickly, and it would be best for all concerned that I am able to either confirm or deny any variation in the mission profile immediately after making the announcement about Ross.

The ESA directors were probably already in conclave. But he had to let them know he was watching and waiting. There was nothing wrong with holding their feet to the fire: they were paid to make the big decisions, and he'd much rather not have to call it himself. Let the crew vent their anger and frustration on faceless bureaucrats a billion kilometres distant, while he remained their captain.

What else could he add? Send it now, before the temptation to change a letter here, a word there, got too great. He bounced it into the waiting transmission queue, and gave it the highest priority. The high gain dish towards the rear of the ship squirted it out in digitised form and bounced it off the relay positioned at the Jovian L4.

Colvin was looking at stars, measuring their relative positions, and checking that the Aphrodite was where it ought to be: perturbations in the gravity field would pull them away from their orbit, and corrections and calculations had to be factored in to each perijove. He stared at the back of her head. No, he remembered the KU2 mission now, and all the times he'd looked up to see Colvin's shoulders hunched over her console.

His attention slid from navigator to comms. Borner was still staring at the oscilloscope-like waveforms on her screen. She seemed concerned by what she was seeing.

'Yasmin,' said Mariucci. 'Explain.'

She leaned back, gaze still fixed on the lines. 'There's something … odd here. I can't work out if this is an artefact of the data, or a genuine result.' She ported the window to his screen, so now they were both looking at it.

Mariucci watched as the line jagged.

'This is the Europa signal that Valeria spotted. This is it cleaned up and stretched out – the x-axis is a millisecond across

– you can see it start here, frame, frame, frame, and gone. A three-millisecond burst of low-frequency electromagnetic radiation, at about four hundred and fifty kilohertz. As far as we can tell it happens within one to two seconds of the closest approach between Europa and Ganymede. That's a high level of precision I wouldn't expect for a natural phenomenon, and Laelaps has now been in the right place to record three individual events.'

'What would you expect?'

'That there would be a breakdown in the insulation as Europa and Ganymede closed, and at some threshold level conduction would begin, and then cease as they separated. The timing ought to be dictated by the local electromagnetic environment, which is going to be different every orbit. But this is, for want of a better word, astronomical. It's all down to the geometry.'

'Have you talked to Valeria? Benjamin? Rory?'

'Rory isn't that interested in this end of the frequency spectrum. If it's not in the megahertz range or above, then it's not high energy plasma. I know what this looks like, though, and I think it's worth investigating further.'

'What do you think it is?'

'It's a spark. More accurately, it's a spark-gap transmitter, like Marconi built. We were made to build one too, in the first year of my degree. The waveform looks just like that. Obviously, it can't be that, but it's got that same distribution of wavelengths, the same duration, the same attack even.'

'And Europa and Ganymede, when they draw together, are at the exact distance apart to make that spark-gap?' Mariucci watched as the process looped again, and again.

'No, that's not it. The spark-gap, the whatever-is-generating-the-signal, is wholly on Europa. And it fires at the moment Ganymede is closest. Which is still four hundred thousand kilometres away, slightly more than the Moon from Earth.' She scrubbed at her face with her fingers. 'And there's the second thing that might be happening, which is the first thing you said, that the ionospheres interact and create a tunnel at closest approach. But this signal isn't part of that. The breakdown would happen earlier and end later, like it's supposed to.'

'It's a separate phenomenon that's taking advantage of it?'

'Again, I don't see how it could. It might simply be a periodic event, but we don't see it at all outside of the closest approach. And Europa's ionosphere is weak. Ganymede has its own magnetic field, but Europa doesn't: it's just induced by the field from Jupiter, which at that point is four, five times larger than any effect it has. Even if a flux tube is being created, it wouldn't affect the propagation of the signal.' Borner stopped and turned around. She saw Colvin was still present behind her, still looking at her own screen and involved in her calculations. She unclipped from her seat and beckoned Mariucci to follow her.

They drifted along the axis as far as the rotating section, and then a little further. Mariucci hung off a rail and orientated himself in the same plane as her.

'Something is clearly bothering you, Yasmin. What is it?'

'It ...' She swallowed hard, grimaced, then blurted out: 'It looks like a transmission. There. I've said it.'

'A transmission. From Europa?'

'From under the ice. Unless there's something on the ice, and I haven't checked with Benjamin, or looked at the images myself. We should do that, because this is unprecedented. It's a ping. A beacon. Narrow frequency range, short duration. We can pinpoint exactly where the signal is coming from, but I'm certain it'll be at the antijovian.'

Mariucci took a deep breath. 'A signal? From a transmitter? And you're sure about this?'

'No, of course I'm not sure, because if I was, I would have just come out and said it, and have proof of it too. But I would swear on my grandmother's grave it's artificial. We need to find out what it is.'

Mariucci took a moment to consider matters. 'First things

first. Could it be a Nimbus? We can account for all but two of them: one might have crashed on Europa, and enough of it survived to transmit.'

'The signal is different.'

'Some sort of redundant, legacy feature? Possibly even a spark created by damage sustained in the hard landing?'

She conceded with a groan. 'Perhaps.'

'Secondly, it could be another probe. I can get Earth to send details of anything lost in Jovian space in the last fifty years. Thirdly, and most speculatively, it could be an illegal landing on Europa. Private concerns have probably had the capability to do this for the last ten years.' He frowned. 'Illegal for us. Illegal for a state organisation. I don't know how OSTO would rule on this, but I think they'd uphold the ban.'

'Can we check if Benjamin's found anything?'

'Yes. Of course we can, but this – despite everything – is not the most important matter I'm dealing with at the moment, Yasmin.' Mariucci checked his wristwatch, synced to the ship. There was still time: the message he'd sent to Earth wouldn't even have reached ESA yet. 'We can deal with some of this now. The rest may have to wait.'

Borner followed him to where Velter was still working. This time he heard them, and without prompting peeled off the goggles.

'This isn't about that,' said Mariucci quickly. 'It's something else.'

Velter could see that the comms officer was agitated, anxious even, and his hand briefly flexed against his sternum. 'There's something else?'

'Do we have high-resolution images of Europa's antijovian point?'

'Yes.' He relaxed ever so slightly. 'Do you want me to … ?'

'Please.'

Velter hooked himself to his console and brought up a globe of Europa. 'There are still unsorted images I need to tag, but I should have some from an earlier pass. Around the antijovian, or near it?'

'The exact place,' said Borner.

'Okay. Give me a minute.' He clattered the keyboard and the globe turned and expanded. The individual images were obvious now, like a pale mosaic of rectangles, each piece a subtly different shade of off-white. To the left, there was more yellow – sulphur from Io spattered across the leading face of the moon – and to the right, a more cream ice surface, cracked like a fossilised egg. Darker cracks, curved, straight, cross-cutting, every kind of fracture, separated islands of shell, and even then it was obvious that almost everything was broken. Lines were fractal. The more detailed the image, the more grooves there were.

And the ice wasn't flat any more, either. Still no mountains, but there were bumps, pits, patches of ice-crust that looked shattered and refrozen in place. The darker colouring was diffused, strongest on the lines themselves, and fading rapidly away from them, as if applied by aerosol.

It looked a genuinely terrible place, and yet, if there was an ocean underneath, then it might still be terrible, but also wonderful.

'This,' said Velter. He slid gridlines across the image. 'This is exactly on the equator, one hundred and eighty degrees from subjovian. Resolution is five metres a pixel. We'll get better images on later passes when Laelaps moves into a more eccentric orbit, down to one or two metres.'

Borner moved closer until her nose was almost pressed against the screen. She put her finger on the cross hairs of the grid. 'Can we lose the latitude-longitude markers?'

Velter turned that layer off, and they were left with just Europa, in all its sigil-written madness. Borner took her finger away.

'There's nothing there,' she said. 'Closer?'

Velter obliged and the image grew grainy, but revealed no new detail.

'How big would a Nimbus look at this scale?'

'A Nimbus? It's four, five metres across, ten metres long, plus the solar panels that extend out another fifteen metres each side. Four centimetres across. Is this about the signal?'

'We're just checking something, Benjamin. Ruling out a man-made explanation. Are there any signs of a fresh crater, anything on the surface that looks discoloured, burnt fuel, debris? Anything that might look like a lander, or something that delivered a payload under the ice – a drill, a heating element?'

Velter gestured at the screen. 'I haven't seen anything, but I've not been looking for it. You can see for yourself, the ice surface is chaotic. I can look again, though, or you can.'

Mariucci worked his jaw. There was still the possibility that Borner was seeing something that didn't exist, that this was her drawing an artefact onto the data that wasn't there. Given how everybody else was falling apart, he couldn't discount that she was too.

'Here's what we'll do. Yasmin, I want you to go over the technical aspects of this with Valeria, and make certain that this isn't instrument error, or anything else. That this signal is as you've described it to me. Benjamin, I would be very grateful if you could look at this image, and any other image you have of the antijove, and check it for anything you might deem unusual, although I appreciate that we're seeing Europa in such detail that everything might be unusual. If you send me a link to the images as well, I'll look at them too.' Mariucci's gaze skittered along the arcuate lines. 'These are pre- or post-processing?'

'Raw. You're seeing what Laelaps is seeing. I can boost the contrast, add false-colour, subtract wavelengths, sharpen, but sometimes this is just better, despite the noise.' Velter shrank the image, returning it to its original size. 'Shouldn't we tell Earth?'

'Yes, of course. And we will, as soon as we've made this preliminary search. The data is already at Darmstadt, so they can replicate anything we do here.'

'But we don't want to appear ...' He understood. 'I'll spend some time on this.'

'Thank you, Benjamin. Yasmin, can you find Valeria and get her to confirm your findings?'

She gave him, and Velter, a suspicious glare. 'Do you think I'm making this up? Luca, you saw it for yourself.'

'If I'm going to suggest to Earth there is a radio transmission coming from Europa, potentially from an unauthorised private interplanetary mission, then we need to confirm it to ourselves first. I agree with you that there is something there, it is anomalous, and that it is potentially artificial. What I don't have is the detailed technical expertise that Valeria has. I wouldn't be the captain if I didn't call on all of my crew when I needed them.' He waved his hand at the image repeated across Velter's screens. 'This has – temporary – priority. If Rory objects to my use of his scientists, then he can come and tell me himself.'

Borner turned away and went to collect Spinu, leaving Mariucci and Velter alone.

'A transmission?' said Velter.

'Something else I need you to keep in confidence for the moment,' said Mariucci. He rotated so that he could exit the module.

'Is she imagining it, or is it real?'

'It's real. Her interpretation might not be supported by the evidence.'

'And you think it's possible someone might have put a probe under the ice?'

'Are you a fan of Sherlock Holmes?'

'Tintin,' said Velter.

Mariucci took hold of the bulkhead frame and pushed his feet through. 'We certainly have a mystery on our hands, one way or another.' He let go, and drifted into the axis.

'Luca?'

He twisted his arms anticlockwise to rotate, and there was Hellsten. His face was striped with bright red blood that seemed

69

to be in his hair, and on his hands, and around his neck, and it was impossible to tell where it was coming from.

'Benjamin, page Petra on the intercom. Now.'

Mariucci launched himself towards Hellsten, caught him in a bear hug and, slowed, used his own back to cushion the impact against the section wall. Tiny droplets of blood spun and quivered in the air, expanding in a cloud until they splashed against a surface and stuck.

'Ove, Ove, what's happened to you?'

'I don't know. I don't know. I found myself like this, and I don't know how.'

Velter's voice squawked through the speakers, and Mariucci was able to say, 'Petra's coming. It's okay. She'll be here in a minute.'

And here she was, coming up behind the pair, hand over hand, taking no heed of the blood, just moving through it with a wave of her hand. Wet spots like freckles dusted her face.

'Let's get him into the wheel,' she said. 'I can't examine him here.'

She took hold of Mariucci's collar – a proper hold, gripping it inside and out in her fist so that the cloth tightened – and kicked off the wall, pulling her load like it was so much baggage. On reaching the rotating section, she thrust them down the access tube, and they immediately started falling.

But Kattenbeck was still holding on, supporting their weight with her free hand, hitting the ladder with her feet and bracing her back against the far side of the tube. The descent was rapid and inelegant, and Mariucci stumbled as his feet struck the floor.

The doctor pulled both him and Hellsten up, quickly getting one of Hellsten's arms over her shoulder and marching them in the direction of her examination room. Mariucci paused at the door.

'I need you,' she said, and kneed the door open.

With three of them inside, it was snug. Kattenbeck was

able to boost Hellsten onto the examination bench by herself: whether that was down to the reduced gravity, or she was simply that strong, Mariucci didn't know, but he could easily imagine her hefting some hulking militiaman off a gurney and onto the operating table while nurses and technicians looked on and waited for instructions on how to carefully lift their patient.

Hellsten flapped his bloody hands at her, and she pinned them against his stomach with just one of hers. She hooked a trolley-on-wheels with the toe of her ship's slipper, dragged it towards her, and bounced one of the drawers open with her hip. Her hand went in, and pulled out a gas injector.

'Get me a vial of methaqualone from the pharmacy,' she said, and Mariucci scrambled to obey.

The drugs cabinet was a whole adjacent room, and the only lockable space in the entire ship. He pressed his right thumb to the lock – it had to be either his or Kattenbeck's – and the computer logged the entry and opened the door.

There were medicines, bandages, surgical tools, the whole paraphernalia of healing in floor-to-ceiling cabinets, arranged like library stacks so that only one section could be open at a time. He was never going to be able to locate just one named bottle, but fortunately there was a map against the back of the wall.

'Where is methaqualone?' he said, not certain of his pronunciation, but the computer parsed it and lit up with a cabinet, row, and column number in less than a second.

He shifted the cabinets, ran his finger along the row until he hit the right section. There. He picked up the bottle of clear liquid, checked the label, and was back in the consulting room, handing over the drug like a prize.

Kattenbeck was shushing Hellsten, telling him it was okay, it would be okay, he'd be fine, it would go away. Briefly letting go of his hands, she slipped the bottle upside down into the empty magazine, dialled the dose and pressed the nozzle against Hellsten's crimson neck.

71

The gun went hiss, and Hellsten stopped shaking and rattling. A moment or two longer, and he visibly sagged against the wipe-clean surface of the bench. Kattenbeck patted his arm.

'You just rest. I'll see what the damage is.'

She slid the gas injector on top of the trolley and kicked it away.

'Let's get him out of his flight suit. Ove's still conscious: although he may not remember what we say, let's remember that, yes?' She was already wearing a pair of disposable gloves, and she pressed another pair at Mariucci. He more or less got them on, and by the time he had, she had already unzipped the front of Hellsten's flight suit, and dragged it as far as his waist with the ease of peeling a banana.

The man's arms were scarlet, and the sleeves dark and stiff with coagulating blood.

'How has this happened? How did he get like this?'

'Oh, Luca. He did it to himself. Consciously or unconsciously, these are self-inflicted. Get me the water bottle and the sponges. We need to clean him up. Then we have to decide what to do about it.'

6

'The signal is definitely there,' said Spinu. 'It's also more definite than that. The broadcast is directional. Straight up. Or out. Some leakage, ten degrees around the axis, but it's quite tight.'

She looked at Borner, and Mariucci guessed there was more.

'I – we – found another signal. Weaker, the same signature.'

'The same origin?'

'No.' Borner looked uncomfortable. 'It's ... it might be from Ganymede. We don't know, we can't tell. But it's two point seven seconds later. Which is twice the distance in light seconds between Europa and Ganymede at closest approach.'

'A signal from Europa, being answered by one on Ganymede,' said Mariucci. He ran his hand over his scalp. 'Every time the moons pass each other?'

'We went back through the data. It's certainly every time we're in a position to detect it. I'm willing to say it's every seven point one five five days, whether we're around to see it or not.'

'Have we better maps of Ganymede than when we left Earth?'

Spinu demurred. 'Better, yes. Comprehensive and catalogued, no. We pulled them, looking for something, anything on the subjovian point of Ganymede, and there's nothing. It's old ice, the oldest on the whole moon. Lots of craters, dark in comparison to other, younger areas. When we launch the probe meant for it, then we'll see more clearly.'

'The resolution?'

'Twenty, thirty metres, but it's oblique. We'll have to wait, or change course.'

'And you've talked to Benjamin?'

She shook her head. 'Not yet. He's still working through the Europa images.'

Mariucci hunched over in his seat and regarded his knees. 'Someone has beaten us out here.'

'Are they still here, though?' said Borner. 'This isn't radio traffic. This is timed pulses at specific events.'

'Placeholders? Homing beacons? Prefabricated structures sent ahead, waiting for crew?' He pulled a face, because he knew this one.

So did Spinu. 'Xenosystems are long dead, Luca.'

'The model's still valid. Could they be behind us, then? Using sleep tanks and a ship in a Hohmann transfer orbit? Limiting the signalling to hide what they've done. Stealth.'

Spinu shook her head. 'It's almost impossible – no, I'm going to say that it's impossible – to stealth anything in space. You can't hide excess heat. If you looked at Aphrodite in the infrared, we'd shine like a star. And if we turned everything off, we'd die. Even running minimal systems, generating enough power to run half a dozen sleep tanks will light up a ship. If we knew where to look, we'd find it.'

'Do we know where to look?' asked Borner.

'Deirdre could compute possible orbits, given likely launch dates from cis-lunar.' Spinu pursed her lips. 'What if it's not that?'

'What do you mean?'

'What if it is natural? Some phenomenon we can't explain yet, something peculiar to Jupiter, to these moons?'

Borner seemed almost insulted by the suggestion. 'We've just spent an hour going through all this! We discovered the ping-back from Ganymede. You agreed with me, it's artificial. A broadcast.'

'You can't say for certain – it could be Jupiter talking to itself, to us. We just don't know enough.'

Mariucci was getting whiplash, looking from one to the other.

'I expect good advice from both of you. There are clear areas of agreement, and areas of dissent. There is a signal from Europa. It may be being answered by Ganymede. It's unlikely to have a natural cause –' and to forestall Spinu's objections, added: 'but we cannot rule that out. The best working hypothesis we have is there is an unknown mission to the Jovian system, and we'll proceed on that basis, while understanding that we have to be flexible in our thinking.'

'It's artificial,' stated Borner. 'Obviously so.'

'Nonsense.' Forsyth levered his way into the conversation. He entered Command and strapped himself in across the pit from the others. 'There's nothing out here but us. It's an effect of the high energy environment in the radiation belts and nothing else. I will not countenance another explanation.'

'What if you're wrong?' said Borner. 'What happens then?'

'I'm not wrong.' Forsyth steepled his fingers. 'You forget that I've made a career out of being never wrong, and I'm not intending to start now.'

'Forget? How would I ever know that?'

'Well, consider this a teachable moment. We are clearly the only ship in Jovian space, apart from the Nimbus supply craft, and we've already discounted them as being the source of the anomaly. The only viable hypothesis is that it originates in the natural environment, and it's from there we have to seek our answers.' He drew breath, but he wasn't done. 'Luca, you've interrupted my team's schedule, and co-opted them in this fruitless and somewhat baffling search for objects on the surface – or under the surface – of the Europan ice-shell. I'm asking you politely to desist. How you order your own time, or the time of your flight crew, is a matter for you: all I ask is that you extend the same courtesy to me and mine. Thank you.'

He unclipped, and boosted himself towards the ceiling. Spinu was stone-faced as she went to follow suit, and Mariucci decided that now was the time.

'Rory, whatever your position is on Earth, within ESA, and

on this mission, I am captain of this ship. I have not used either Valeria's or Benjamin's time lightly, but on a matter of utmost importance—'

'To you.'

'Of utmost importance to our continuing scientific exploration of Jupiter and its moons. Persons unknown appear to have interfered with the embargo on landing on Europa: that there is one on Ganymede they've also ignored is not forgotten either. It is my duty, my first duty, and the duty of every member of the Aphrodite's crew to investigate these matters thoroughly and to the best of their ability, so that I can report back to our superiors—'

'I have no superiors—'

'Our superiors in Darmstadt, to whom we are answerable.' Mariucci thought about rising to the ceiling to confront Forsyth at the same level, but he resisted. 'Whether you like it or not, we all agreed to the chain of command. I report to those above me, and you report to me. This situation is sufficiently serious that I have temporarily inconvenienced two out of six of the designated mission specialists, for the total of just over an hour. I will not be apologising for that.'

'I did not take a sabbatical from a prestigious and ancient seat of learning, put myself through all of the training and tedium, subject myself to the indignities of the medical exams, and force myself to endure the endless media appearances, to be ordered around by a jumped-up mechanic.'

Mariucci took a moment before responding. 'Then you should have read the small print. As I understand it, being ordered around by me is exactly what you signed up for, Rory. I have no intention of abusing that privilege, but I can and will exercise it if I feel it necessary.' The whole argument was as ridiculous as the one at the apojove meal, and he was determined not to get angry this time. 'I don't know what else to say. I took you to be a man of your word. I'm disappointed that you've decided to be something else.'

Forsyth coloured up, showing an emotional reaction he was not entirely in control of. 'I don't have time for this idiocy. Don't interfere with my work again.'

'I have authority here.'

'We'll see about that.'

'Who will you see? We're a billion kilometres from anywhere.'

'Precisely,' said Forsyth, and he launched himself at the axis, far too aggressively. He had momentarily forgotten where he was and how to move, and when he put his hand out to stop himself at the bulkhead door, it was equally impulsive.

He clattered against the jamb and caromed off it, giving a gasp of pain. He disappeared out of Command, trailing thrashing feet, and Spinu was immediately after him, calling his name.

Mariucci tried to recall if anyone had warned him there'd be days like this. He unclipped, spun up to the ceiling and looked down the length of the axis. Forsyth had bounced as far as the rotating section by the time Spinu had caught up with him. He was holding his forearm rigid across his chest, warding off any help with his other hand, but it was clear that he'd hurt himself and he needed treatment.

Apparently, they were going to have to page Kattenbeck again, and she wouldn't be happy. This injury was as self-inflicted as the ones Hellsten had made.

Had Forsyth got worse though? He'd always been marginally difficult – no, not difficult, awkward – in his interpersonal relationships. Such as they were: he'd made it clear from the start that he didn't much care for any of that unnecessary and time-consuming rubbish.

Mariucci said to Borner: 'Get Petra up here, please,' then took another look at the scene in the rotating section. The pain was finally weakening Forsyth's resolve: it could do that, reduce the strongest-willed to sobbing wrecks, calling for their mothers. Spinu had been able to at least visually inspect his wrist, even

77

if she hadn't been able to touch it. Kattenbeck would brook no such arguments, and she'd still be gentle.

His presence in the same section as Forsyth wouldn't help. Their antagonism would actively hinder the situation, and he'd get a report from the doctor later. If it was a sprain, then that was one thing. If it was a simple break, then they had the casts to fix it in place while it healed. If it was more serious than that, Kattenbeck would have to improvise. He went back to his seat and clipped in. Borner was watching him for a reaction, any reaction.

'You didn't cause that, Yasmin. Any more than I did. Show your data to me again? Use the pit if you want.'

Borner turned back to her screen and laid out the Jupiter system in all its complexity. The vast mass of the planet itself – as big as a planet could theoretically get before starting to collapse in on itself – and all of its moons, swinging around it. The chief of those, the Galilean moons, three of which were permanently tied together in a dance that was potentially as old as time itself. Every orbit of Jupiter that Ganymede made, Europa made precisely two, and Io four. Only the outermost Galilean – Callisto – had escaped that clockwork movement.

But none of the moons, small or large, had avoided being tidally locked. One face always pointed at Jupiter, and one face always away, like Earth's Moon. It was nothing special, just a consequence of comparative size and distance. Each moon had a subjovian point, where Jupiter would always be exactly overhead, and, one hundred and eighty degrees away, its opposite, the antijove.

Borner shepherded the four large moons into position, and showed him the full sequence speeded up. Europa, orbiting Jupiter every three and a half days, gradually caught up with Ganymede and undertook it. The moment it did, the exact moment, a signal beamed out of its antijove. It propagated outwards, and again, the moment it met Ganymede, another signal came back, aimed at Europa.

'Is it an echo? Is it the same signal, reflected?' Mariucci was thinking out loud, but it was something that had already been considered.

'It's the same signal each time.' Borner removed the carrier wave and showed him the saw-toothed remnants of the broadcast. 'But it's not a reflection. If it was, there'd be artefacts in it, polarisation, that would be present in the Ganymede signal and which we wouldn't see in the Europa signal, but it'd be fundamentally the same. This is more call-and-response. There's an outgoing signal, and a returning one. Two sources, directed at each other. The noise around them is essentially random.'

'Call and response?'

'When you sing something, and the audience sing it back to you.'

He twitched his hand. 'I understand it. I just wondered at your use of the phrase.'

She paused while she worked out what she meant. 'In these situations, in an analogous scenario where you're polling a distant station, you send out a message which asks "Are you there?" and if it is, it responds with "I am here". Two different messages. This isn't like that. This is the same message, repeated from two different locations. Call, and response.'

'Error checking?'

She shrugged. 'Potentially. Or they're using a different protocol to what we'd expect.'

'To confuse us?'

'Maybe. I ...' She was silent for a while. 'Luca?'

'Yasmin.'

'What if it's ... not us?'

'Not us?'

'Not humanity. Not from Earth. Not us.'

'That would be very unlikely. You know the saying about extraordinary claims, yes?'

'Of course. But we're looking at the evidence. It's right here.' She sounded fervent. Invested.

Mariucci shifted awkwardly in his seat, and felt his stomach tighten. 'I don't think it says what you believe – or hope – that it does.'

'What more do you want?'

'I want conclusive evidence before saying anything like … that … to anyone else on board, or off it.'

'But what else could it be?'

'Another state, another corporation. Deliberately breaking the embargo. Trying to colonise out here because Earth is a hot mess.' He thought about the ice shelf, about what he was yet to tell the crew. 'That is what else. Do not go multiplying entities unnecessarily.'

'This could be the discovery of the century. The millennium.'

'It could still be that, without invoking –' he looked around to make certain they were alone '– aliens.'

She turned away from him and stared into the lights of the pit. 'How can you, Valeria, and Rory all be so sure? Because at least one of you is wrong.'

The noise coming from the axis had faded, and he assumed that Forsyth was now being ministered to by Kattenbeck.

'If life exists below the surface of the ice, do you think that it would have evolved sufficiently to create technology advanced enough, that works underwater, to produce a spark-gap transmitter? Do you think they could have got as far as Ganymede?'

Borner gnawed at her finger, and didn't answer. Was she succumbing to the malaise, the madness, just as Hellsten, and Molnar, and Velter, and Spinu, and Aasen – where was she? – and maybe Kattenbeck were, and what about himself? Forsyth? Almost all the crew were showing varying levels of overt psychological trauma, with very little indication of a single cause.

None of them were coping, he realised. There was something wrong, with them, potentially with the ship. They'd all been screened beforehand – those medical tests that Forsyth had been objecting to weren't just physical – and none of them ought to be falling apart, not like this. His own problems, even if he couldn't say what they were, Kattenbeck's hallucinations, Aasen's dread, Velter's anxiety, Hellsten's self-harm, and whatever it was that was affecting Spinu and Molnar. Her need to see Jupiter. His need to be near his creation.

'All I'm asking,' he said, 'is for you to consider what is probable before rejecting it. We have not lost our reason, our analytical capabilities, our good sense. A thought experiment: how would you go about proving these broadcasts were made by non-human intelligences?'

She glanced at him. She thought he was humouring her, and perhaps he was.

'Strip out all the noise, get the pure signal. See if contained any information, try and match it to known mathematical or language patterns.'

'And why couldn't those patterns be made by human technology?'

She pulled a face, the same flash of annoyance she'd shown Forsyth.

Mariucci persisted: 'If we assume the same basic technology to build a simple transmitter then the maths will also be similar. Language is different, but we have native speakers of very different languages on this ship. You speak Arabic, English, French, German, Italian. One of those is dissimilar to all the others. Would you be able to decode Finnish, or Mandarin, or !Kung?'

'The Finns or the !Kung are not out here,' she said.

'But the Chinese might be.'

She swivelled her seat back to face her screen. 'Let's just listen to it, shall we?'

Borner pulled the waveform flat again, compared it with the Ganymede signal, and slid the two over each other, adding the content and diminishing the noise. She used low- and high-pass filters to remove the background chaff caused by Jupiter's vast electromagnetic wash, and was left with a discrete series of peaks and troughs.

She shifted the signal into a range audible by the human ear, and ran the sequencer over it.

A series of individual monotones, each of roughly the same duration and amplitude, but with different spacings between them. It could be information, a series of ones and zeros. It could also be natural: just a thing that popped, randomly, creating the semblance of data.

'Have you ever read *On the Beach*?' he asked her.

'No. Is it a recent book?'

'It's over a hundred years old now. Written at a time of nuclear confrontation between America and Soviet Russia. Although, in the book, I think it was Albania that started the war. But that's not the important thing. There's an American nuclear submarine, the last of its kind, in Australia. The fallout is moving south – they know the world will become uninhabitable in a matter of months – when they receive a message over the radio. Morse code, coming from an American city they believed to be completely abandoned. The message is nonsense, but every so often there's a word. After a difficult voyage north, surfacing every so often to look at the destruction, they find out that the message is down to a sash cord from a broken window knocking into an old touch-telegraph machine.'

'Is that what you think this is?' She played it again.

'We can't discount it, nor any of the other explanations.'

'We've more than one instance of this signal. We can compare it from different orbits.'

'You're completely at liberty to do so,' said Mariucci. 'All I ask is that you keep a completely open mind, and remember that there are many options to consider, before we consider your particular one, yes?'

She struggled to agree, but she eventually gave in.

'Yes. Okay.'

He hadn't lost her after all. That was something, at least.

He needed to check on Forsyth, but perhaps not yet. There were lots of things he had to check on: he'd taken on the lion's share of Hellsten's duties while Tsoltos gave him intensive therapy, and Kattenbeck doled out the drugs. He also had his infrequent, but sometimes urgent EVAs with Spinu: he was expecting one very soon, as they rushed towards perijove and Jupiter swelled in the sky.

The person he really needed to talk to, though, was his Chief Engineer. She was – according to the fault log – working for almost twenty-four hours a day, so he supposed he could find her easily enough.

He accessed the screen. Aasen had just cleared a fault in the fuel section, and seemed to be heading forward to the probe bay, where a sensor was showing an intermittent hi-lo reading. Borner was beginning to scroll through lines of code, so he left her to it, and headed down the axis.

By the time he reached the garage, Aasen already had the panel open, and was chasing voltages down with two needle probes.

'Hanne. Can we talk?'

'Easier if you talk and I listen,' she said, moving the probes along one junction and registering a different voltage. No mechanical or electronic failure had ever impacted their safety or their ability to do science, and yet here she was.

'I want your opinion as to the origin of the signal.'

'The Europa one?'

'There's a second, from Ganymede. Yasmin called it a call-and-response.'

'A directed action. That's got a mind behind it.' Aasen glanced at the tablet strapped to her wrist, and reapplied the probes. 'Interesting.'

'Yes. Whose mind, though?'

'Sorry. I was talking about the rise in voltage. The resistance is wrong, between this box, and this one.'

'The signal?'

'Sure. Someone has set up that system, some kind of polling. Couldn't be anything else, right?'

'Valeria disagrees. She thinks it's natural, but on what basis, I'm not sure. Rory – Rory got very angry at the idea it might be artificial, and may have injured himself in the process.'

'They can disagree all they want, but if you shout "hello", and someone shouts "hello" back, then what do you think's just happened?' Aasen went back and forth with the probes. 'Maybe it's supposed to be like this, and they put it in the manual wrong.'

'Could it be an echo?'

'Sure. She discounted that?'

'Yes.'

'She's the comms officer. You should probably trust her.'

'I do.' He didn't mention her theory. Her outlandish theory. 'If it's artificial, what could it be?'

'It is what it is. All you know for certain is there's a transmitter on Europa. You can make deductions from that, but you'll never know without further evidence. You can't see it, can you?'

'No. Whatever it is, it's under the ice.'

Aasen frowned at her tablet. 'How am I supposed to fix this if I don't know how it's broken?'

'You could rewrite the manual,' offered Mariucci.

'That … no. No, that won't work. I'll swap it out, put it with the others to be checked.' She stopped for a moment, and seemed to give Mariucci brief but full attention. 'If it's under the ice, this mission will never find out who broke the embargo. That'll be something they can better do on Earth, or cis-lunar. OSTO will have to launch an inquiry. Call in the usual suspects, or whatever it is they do. But this isn't for the Aphrodite to investigate, because we can't. We don't have the equipment to do that.'

Her gaze wandered back to her multimeter, and she'd gone again. But she'd left him with her wisdom, wherever it had come from. He'd take that back to Command with him.

7

Mariucci exited the airlock, physically tired and emotionally drained. Something had inevitably come up: one of the azimuthal sensors that hung downwards – or outwards, depending on the rotational reference frame – from the wheel, through the ship's magnetopause and out into free space. They could reel it in for servicing, which they needed to do regularly because the radiation was savage on unshielded components, but this time a motor had jammed and that had only become apparent when the gigahertz receiver had stopped working and they'd tried to retrieve it.

Spinu leapt at the chance to volunteer, and again Aasen was more than happy to let her, because she couldn't afford to waste ninety minutes in decompression.

Jupiter was the size of a serving dish held at arm's length. Big, but not threateningly so. Even so, he'd had to persuade Spinu to come in. He was worried that she would have been happy to stay outside until her air had run out. Not today, though. Maybe the next time his voice, his urging, wouldn't be enough, and he'd have to leave her there.

He'd told them about the Ross ice shelf collapse. As he thought he might do, he just announced it over the intercom and let them deal with it as they saw fit. But even as he was speaking the bald words of the report, the urgency he'd felt on hearing the news faded away. There was Earth, facing an obvious manifestation of an existential threat to the whole of humanity, and here was the Aphrodite, grappling with its own crisis of confidence over the Europa transmission.

One was distant and dismissible, and the other present and all-consuming. He'd sat on the news for a couple of days as the various psychodramas on the ship continued to play out, but he had to get it out before someone from Earth just casually mentioned it. And the ship's company seemed to simply digest the information and carry on as they had done before.

Did that bother him? Yes, as much as his own disregard did.

He tugged his spacesuit after him. It didn't have that gunpowder-dust smell it might have had if he'd been on the Moon, or an asteroid. It was more Marsy: acrid, a tang that caught in the back of the throat, presumably from the tonnes of sulphur that Io belched out daily and which Jupiter turned into plasma, washing the entire system with a yellow stain. Spinu's suit was already noticeably a different colour to the others in storage, and his was starting to go the same way. Velter's was the only other suit that had been used.

They'd not run a crash depressurisation drill involving suiting up – the Aphrodite wasn't that sort of ship. It had multiple bulkheads and self-sealing liquid in the multiple shells of the hull that would expand and harden on exposure to air. It was designed to give them time to isolate the problem, repressurise the damaged section, then repair it. Not like the good old days when one fist-sized rock could kill an entire crew.

Spinu was taking her time desuiting. That was fine. He wanted to be alone for a while, to recompress mentally. Of course, all of the problems ended up on his metaphorical desk, but it used to be the case that they also came with ready-prepared solutions. These days, not so much.

He stowed his suit, plugged his life-support pack into the regenerator, and shrugged his flight suit back on. He became aware of a presence behind him.

'Luca?'

Mariucci twisted round, and there was Tsoltos in the doorway.

'Problem?'

'Laszlo's ... condition has deteriorated, while you were outside. I supposed you could only deal with one thing at a time, so we held off calling you.'

Mariucci zipped up, and made sure his dosimeter was in his top pocket. Tsoltos pushed himself into the axis, and Mariucci followed, hand over hand. Kattenbeck was in the rear section of the ship, securing an unconscious Molnar on a body board.

He glanced briefly around the walls, checking for damage, but there was mercifully none, because he was pretty certain that no one but Molnar would know first-hand how to fix any of it.

'What happened?'

'I called him for his routine medical examination,' said Kattenbeck. 'He simply refused to leave here. Stan tried to talk him down, but he had what we can professionally describe as an acute psychotic episode, or more colloquially as raving.'

'Did he say anything in particular?' Mariucci pushed himself over, and took hold of the board with a hand. A muscle in Molnar's face twitched spasmodically, but he otherwise seemed peaceful.

'How we were all going to die. That we'd never make it home again. That Earth would be gone when we got there.'

'That's not too fanciful.'

'When he says "gone", he means it. Not on fire, or under water, or just destroyed. Gone. Vanished. Literally gone, removed from its orbit and, well, I didn't spend the time discussing details with him. I just went back to the pharmacy and loaded up with psychotropics. All I have to do now is remember which ones I used.' Kattenbeck tightened the ankle straps and gave the board a slow spin. Molnar didn't fly off. 'He'll have to be relieved of his duties. Whatever benefit he gives us in fine-tuning the reactor would be lost if he managed to override the safeties and scrambled it. Or just powered it down. We'll freeze to death within a day.'

'What's the prognosis?'

'I don't have a clue. Stan might.'

Tsoltos slipped into the section and started collecting Molnar's effects: his sleeping bag, his spare food and water, and sealed containers of what looked like urine and faeces. 'I think I can cure him. Now that Laszlo has reached the point of crisis, he will accept the need to address his problems. I'll work with him, just as I'm working with Ove.'

Mariucci frowned and gestured to the softly glowing control panels. 'That's good to know, but can we ever trust him around this ever again?'

'Sure. Why not? If he's healed. What else do you suggest? The spacers' solution?'

'This is not a commercial ship. We all go home. That is that.'

Tsoltos affected a shrug. 'Then leave the damaged minds to me, Luca.'

Kattenbeck started towing Molnar towards the axis, wearing a sceptical expression that only Mariucci could see. 'I can't hide this situation any longer, Luca. I've done my best, but Laszlo is science: when his reports suddenly fall off a cliff, Darmstadt will want to know why.'

'We should never have started,' said Mariucci, but gently.

She paused at the door. 'Would you rather we'd just done one orbit of Jupiter and gone home?'

'If there's a problem with the mission that endangers the crew, then we're going to have to consider aborting. Petra, no amount of data is worth this.'

'We're here because we all thought the risks were outweighed by the reward,' said Tsoltos. 'However, I now believe there is a problem with the way this ship is designed.'

Mariucci opened his hands wide. 'You were going to tell me this when?'

'When I was more sure than not.'

'What happened to the precautionary principle?'

'If we believed in that, we wouldn't even be here, Luca.'

Mariucci let his hands drift to his sides. Kattenbeck was still with Molnar in the doorway. She knew about this already, for certain. She was just waiting to hear what his reaction was.

'The magnetic field,' said Tsoltos, 'protects us from the radiation outside the hull. It's very strong because it has to be. It's also dynamic, because it has to be. If the external detectors see the radiation environment becoming hotter, the field increases proportionately. And so far, we've not had a single alarm inside the hull.'

'Which shows it's working, yes?'

'What if it's working too well? What if the field strength is set too high, or peaks at neurologically damaging levels? That's one possibility. The other, worse, theory is this: what if the field strength required to protect us from exposure to cancer-causing radiation is sufficient to induce these neuroses, and we face a straight choice between unstitching our DNA and unravelling our minds?'

'Are either of those possible, or likely?' Mariucci looked to Kattenbeck.

She stared at the wall. 'We've never subjected human beings to such an intense, prolonged electromagnetic bombardment. Getting here, there were fluxes and spikes to deal with, but since perijove one, we regularly encounter levels of radiation that are sufficient to cause acute radiation syndrome, let alone long-term damage. The shield keeps us safe from that, and I'm glad of it, but if this is the side-effect?'

Molnar continued to tic and twitch in his sleep.

'We know – I know, at least – that targeted electromagnetic fields can induce hallucinations. And Laszlo lived and worked next to the shield,' said Tsoltos. 'Perhaps the further back in the ship you are, the worse it becomes – I've no evidence for that at all. But we might start seeing a pattern at some point.'

'What about Ove?'

'The storage facilities, the life-support systems, the suit regenerators, they're all towards the rear of the ship. Rory,

Valeria and Benjamin do most of their work and spend most of their time in the labs. At least two of them are exhibiting psychological symptoms. The other is very difficult to examine, or even covertly observe.' Tsoltos looked at his load of bedlinen and bags. 'We need to confront this situation ourselves, even if we try and disguise its extent to Earth.'

'What about the rest of us?'

'There are too many variables,' said Kattenbeck. 'We all respond differently. It might just be an acclimatisation problem, that we'll get used to it. The effect might escalate in a linear way, or according to some power law, or an S-shaped curve: I don't know. The one person on this ship who would is now incapacitated. At least now we have a tentative explanation as to why none of us are making particularly good decisions, and haven't done so for a while.'

'And if Earth orders us to return?' said Mariucci.

'Can we?' asked Tsoltos. 'Should we? As Petra says, it might be temporary. And you have me. Let me see if I can fix these things. At the moment, I feel our presence here is a sign – hope for a better future – and our return would be a defeat, not just for us, but for all of humanity.'

'We couldn't leave immediately anyway. I've already asked Deirdre to work out the intercepts on the remaining Nimbuses for each planned perijove, but we can alter our course to pick up more. We'd need another one if not two supply ships to guarantee we wouldn't be starving by the time we reached cis-lunar.' He pushed his chin to his chest. 'This is not the conversation I imagined having at this stage of the expedition.'

'Back all those years ago, you couldn't take off from Earth without medical sensors strapped to every part of you, and even inside. Mission Control were in command, and the astronauts had very little autonomy.' Tsoltos shifted what he was carrying to one hand, leaving the other free for manoeuvring. 'We have no probes in our arses now, and more agency. This is better. We were meant to be autonomous, decision-making beings.'

'I'll ask Deirdre to plot possible return trajectories. Do I tell Earth of your suspicions? At some point, if they don't decide for us, we'll have to decide for ourselves. Your medical opinions will hold significant weight when that moment comes.' Mariucci put his hand to the bulkhead that hid the shield coils, a gesture that he'd seen Molnar make. 'He knows, doesn't he?'

'I think he suspected it, consciously or subconsciously, and didn't know how to process that knowledge.'

'Take him where he'll be safe, Petra. Stan, go with her.' Mariucci bounced off the bulkhead and took Tsoltos's baggage from him. 'I'll deal with the shit.'

They took Molnar away, guiding him along the axis, past Borner's unnerved gaze. She had come up behind Kattenbeck, but had stayed silent. How much she'd overheard was unknown, and probably irrelevant anyway. They were all adults, and if anything, they needed to be more open with each other, not less.

'Now, Yasmin?'

'If you have the time.'

'Is it urgent?'

'I'd say yes. Possibly more urgent now than before I learned the mission might be aborted.'

He took that comment with a slight twitch of his lips. She was floating in the doorway, outlined by it, her hair a halo around her head. She seemed as she was when he'd first met her – first interviewed her – all those years ago, and then subsequently, training together, the delay due to KU2, and she'd stuck by the Aphrodite all that time. A few had dropped out, due to career, or family, or health, or just that they didn't want to leave Earth at that time. Borner had always been committed to the role.

What would she say to her younger self now? He wondered what he'd say to his own forty-something self, knowing that he'd be tying himself up, personally and professionally, for a decade. Would he try and talk himself out of it, and let someone else have the honour?

'Is there more?'

'Yes, there's more. Much more.'

'I need to get rid of this, and I need a drink and something to eat. If you can talk to me over that, I'll meet you in the wheel,' he said, and that encouraged her to go.

Mariucci visited various storage bins and lockers, then descended to the wheel to dispose of the bodily waste. Then dispose of the containers that had held it. None of that was particularly pleasant: they were all, more often than not, far removed from dealing with the basic functions of life. Not Kattenbeck, though. Definitely not her.

He washed his hands thoroughly, twice, and then made himself a snack of dried fruit, tube cheese and crackers. He was tempted by the sudden thought of a glass of Trebbiano, but settled for a white coffee. Borner declined anything for herself, so Mariucci sat opposite her and spread out his meal across the table.

'So,' he said.

'There's a second transmission pair,' she said. 'I should have checked for it, but why should I? One is extraordinary enough. It's between Europa and Io, every three days – Forsyth would insist I say every three point one five five days – when they're in conjunction. The same wavelengths, the same mode, different signal. From, I presume, Io's antijove point to Europa's subjove, and back. I've looked at the images, and again there's nothing on Europa's subjovian point I can say is the source, and the images we have of Io aren't detailed enough – yet.'

'Different signal?'

'The same kind of signal. But they carry different information: the peaks don't match the Europa-Ganymede pair.'

'And you're convinced it is information?'

She swallowed, even though she wasn't the one eating or drinking.

'The signal changes with each pass.'

'Randomly?'

'Incrementally.'

Mariucci put his cracker down.

'Mathematically?'

'Plus one. Each time it passes.' She got up from her seat, went to the kitchen, and fetched out the packet of crackers that Mariucci had opened, together with a sealed pot of black olives. She lined up ten of the crackers on the table, and took out an olive. She placed it on the right-most cracker.

'First pass, one. Second pass,' and she moved the olive one space to its left, 'one zero. Third pass –' She used a new olive. '– one one. And so on. A binary counter.'

'And when all these bits are full?'

'I don't know, but I'm assuming that the Europa-Ganymede signal will click over by one. With eleven bits, that works out as one thousand and twenty-four passes, once every eight years, ten months. Laelaps has only been in orbit for twelve days.'

'If Europa-Ganymede is also eleven bits?'

'Which I think it is, that will reset to zero every nine thousand and fifty-seven years. I listened to what you told me. Kept an open mind. Didn't reject any hypothesis. So this is just the data, without any explanation. Which I now invite you to provide: can you explain this?'

Mariucci picked his cracker back up and chewed slowly.

'I'll have to have someone verify this.'

'Yes, of course.'

'And I'll have to send this to Earth. Whatever this is, we have to let them look at your analysis. We are deluging them with terabytes of information, and this is down in the uninteresting end of the electromagnetic spectrum: if they ever got to this, then it might be in five, ten years' time. If at all.' He reached over and picked up one of her counting crackers, and smeared cheese on its face. 'A clock?' he finally ventured.

'At least it's not counting down,' she said. There was a flash of humour there. Yes, she was entirely serious, but while she was certain of what she'd found, she was still able to maintain her perspective.

'That *would* be bad,' said Mariucci. 'So, based on the Europa-Ganymede signal, how long has this clock been running?'

'Three thousand one hundred and fifty-seven years. Plus the Io-Europa signal of six years. Three thousand one hundred and sixty-three years. On this cycle: I don't know how to tell if it's been round before. That's the minimum age of this ... clock. If I'm right.'

'A cosmic counter, based on the motion of three tidally locked moons in resonant orbits about the largest planet in the solar system. The only place in the solar system where this happens.' He ate the cheese-spread cracker in one bite, tasting its saltiness, its smoothness. 'As old as the pyramids? I don't know, I can't remember how old they are.'

'You believe me?'

'Does that matter? If this is the evidence, we have to follow where it goes.' Mariucci recalibrated his response. 'Don't make this personal. This isn't about believing you or disbelieving you. Be dispassionate and detached about this. If it turns out to be just a coincidence, then you've not invested your whole self in it. If it's true, you should treat it that same way.'

She struggled with that. 'But this—'

'Yes, yes, I know what this might mean. Might. Remember what I said about extraordinary claims?'

'This is extraordinary evidence, Luca.'

'Which we'll have to check, here on the ship, and then pass our findings over to Earth. They may simply disagree with the data, the analysis, the method, anything, and that will negate these findings, leaving us with an interesting story and nothing more.'

'But—'

'If they have a terrestrial origin external to the ship, a probe or probes operated by another organisation, that would be incredible enough. It's much more likely that these signals are an artefact of our instrumentation or our data collection process. The data will be checked and checked again. We might be well on our way home before we get a definitive answer, one way or the other.'

He picked up his coffee. It wasn't as hot as he'd like it – he'd let it sit for too long – but he was going to drink it anyway, and then make himself another.

'We'll miss our chance,' said Borner. 'We might not get another one.'

'I understand,' he said, thinking of the Ross ice shelf, and then of Aasen. He echoed her words. 'We don't have the equipment to make these investigations. We can take as many pictures as we like, but we're not allowed to land, let alone drill through the ice. But perhaps because of us, because of this, there will be a next time, and a time after that, if they can make it safe for humans. It'll be you, and your persistence, that makes the difference.'

They needed something, anything, that wasn't going to be about high energy plasma physics. The pictures produced by Laelaps were helping, but something with drama, with human interest – how he hated that phrase, because science and space travel should be inherently interesting – might capture the imagination of enough people and keep the space agencies, especially his own, funded through the crisis to come.

She didn't appear convinced. 'Do you know about the Mayan calendar?'

'I know they had one.'

'It divides up – I'm probably going to tell this badly – into short counts of months and years, and a long count, that goes back thousands of years, from a year zero. This reminds me of that. It was in base twenty, not two, and there were five slots, not ten. It was a method of keeping track of centuries and millennia. This could be something similar.'

'For who? For what purpose?'

'I don't know. But whoever it was set it to start at zero over three thousand years ago, which means it wasn't the China National Space Administration.'

95

'Yasmin—'

'I know what I see, Luca. I know what I see. You tell me to keep some professional detachment about this, but you're calling my judgement into question. I'm not going mad. I'm not like … like them, okay? This is real.'

'If I didn't think it was real, I wouldn't be asking the opinions of the rest of the crew. I have to follow procedures. I also have to enforce them.' He drank the rest of his coffee, which was even cooler than before, and despite everything he now didn't want another, which was a petty annoyance that riled him more than Spinu's antics outside the hull, or Borner's dogged insistence that she'd found evidence of aliens. Her idea was incendiary, and clearly she wasn't going to let it go. 'Very well. Let's do it now.'

'Now?'

'Now. How long do you need to marshal your evidence, get it into a shareable format?'

'An … hour?'

'You can have as long as you like, but if you ask for just an hour, I'll give you two.' Mariucci put his mug down and stared at the food left on his plate. He needed to eat it: EVA chewed through the calories, and considering how far the supplies had come and the difficulties they'd had in securing more, he wasn't going to waste it, nor the crackers that Borner had used as counters. 'You know that Rory is going to try and tear you apart.'

'Will you let him?'

'If he's questioning your data and how you've handled it, yes.'

She stiffened, then jutted her chin. 'Then I'll have to make sure I have answers enough for Professor Rory Forsyth.'

8

'This is ridiculous.'

'Then it'll be easy to show it's false.'

'You can't prove a negative. Basic scientific practice.'

'That's not how it works.' Everyone looked at Spinu, surprised that she was the one to interrupt the to and fro between Borner and Forsyth. 'If there's a fault anywhere in the chain of logic that leads us from axiom to theory, then we can reject it. If there's anything in the data that doesn't fit the theory, we can reject it. If we can construct an alternative theory that fits the data as well as Yasmin's then, okay, we can't reject it, but we can say that there's another explanation.'

'How dare you contradict me?' Forsyth stood up and leaned over the table to speak – shout – into her face. 'There's nothing here that's worthy of my consideration, and I will not cooperate with this, this, farrago.' He rounded on Mariucci. 'And thank God I managed to stop you in time from saying anything to Earth. You – and by association, me – will be a laughing stock. I don't care about your reputation, but I care about mine. No, I won't even humour you. We're wasting valuable time, and I demand – demand – we go back to work immediately and never mention this again.'

He didn't sit down again, but stood, puffing and flushed, as if he'd just completed his mandated exercise that Mariucci knew he only honoured in the breach.

Mariucci took his cup of water and swigged from it. He'd known this would be difficult, but Forsyth had attacked everything but the data from the moment Borner finished her presentation. How had this man risen to his position? He was supposed to be brilliant and incisive, with an intellect so far above the common herd as to make many of his discoveries simply incomprehensible to all but a handful of his peers. He was also a bullying little stronzo. The two could be simultaneously true, but Mariucci currently only cared about one of them.

'Thank you for your considered opinion, Rory,' he said. 'Does anyone have that alternative theory or do we concentrate on Yasmin's for now?'

'Instrument error. Artefacts. It could be anything.' Forsyth jabbed his finger at no one in particular, and all of them in general.

'It could. We have to discount that, and fortunately we have the time to go through raw data. Anyone else?'

Spinu, who'd previously voiced scepticism at the artificial origins of the signals, shifted awkwardly in her chair. She wanted to say something, but clearly felt constrained. Mariucci caught her gaze with what he hoped was an open expression.

She shifted again. 'What if ... what if it's a biologically generated signal?'

Blasco blinked. 'Like an organism?'

'Yes?' Spinu didn't seem sure, but agreed anyway. 'A planet- or moon-wide organism. It's responding to external stimuli by generating an electrical signal.'

'The moon ... correction, the moons, are alive?'

'No, that's just—' she swatted the idea away. 'But the biosphere will be. Some kind of reflex action acting on a nervous system? There's no reason for Jovian evolution to have followed ours. Or perhaps it did, and it diverged at some point. There could be a single organism that spans the whole ocean on both Europa and Ganymede.'

'And on Io?' said Hellsten. He didn't contribute much to conversations, and his voice sounded lost. 'Is that even possible?'

'Subsurface extremophiles?' Spinu was now struggling. Io was so unspeakably hostile to anything they might consider life, it was a far greater leap of imagination than suggesting it could exist below the ice on Europa.

'I think,' said Mariucci, 'we need to agree on the nature of the signals first, before ascribing their cause. Are they external to the ship and the ship's systems? Do they present as discrete peaks? Are they representing data? Do they mark out the passage of the moons incrementally? As I've said before, the Aphrodite is not equipped to investigate the source of the signals. We have plenty to discuss, but that will have to be left to a future mission.'

'Even though you think we might have to leave early, and there may never be another mission?' said Velter. He rubbed the heel of his hand against his chest. Checking that he was still breathing.

Kattenbeck looked pointedly at the sick-bay door. 'If we can't bring Laszlo out of sedation safely, if we can't deal with some of the other manifestations of illness we're experiencing, then yes,' she said. 'My recommendation would be to leave Jovian space early.'

'That is not the mission profile,' said Forsyth. 'And if I have to follow it, everyone does.'

'This is a medical—'

'That is not my concern. He knew the risks. His body, his mind, failed him. He has my sympathy, but I owe him nothing more. I have work to do here, important work, work that will benefit the whole of humanity and change our future from the one that our captain's friends Vi and Van der Veerden have mapped out for us.' His face had gone from ruddy to pale and pinched. 'He's your patient, yours and Konstantinos's. Not mine. It's up to you two to keep him alive until this ship is ready to go back to Earth.'

'You're not the captain,' she said.

'Perhaps I should have been,' he returned.

'Enough,' said Mariucci. 'Enough. Rory, please sit down.'

He waited, but Forsyth showed no sign of complying. Instead, the man wheeled away from the table and started climbing the ladder back to the axis, with difficulty, because he could still only use one hand.

'If we're done,' said Aasen. She waggled her tablet at him down the length of the table, and started to rise. She hadn't contributed anything, and had been completely fixated on her never-conquerable fault list.

'We're almost done. Everyone here has the data. It's public on the ship. I'd like your opinion of the proposition Yasmin has put forward, sooner rather than later, and no later than the beginning of the next perijove. Privately or publicly. Remember, I'm not asking you to determine the truth or otherwise of it: I'm asking you if you think that there's something there that's worth telling Earth about, and yes, acknowledging that this may make our colleagues in Darmstadt think we have thoroughly lost our minds. I'm hoping that they don't conflate the two issues.' He put his hands flat on the table in front of him. 'You're free to go, so go,' he shooed.

They dispersed, each to their own places, except Kattenbeck.

'He shouldn't have talked to you like that,' said Mariucci.

'Rory is technically correct, while still being very wrong. It is up to me to keep Laszlo alive until we get home. Just that deliberately prolonging the time before we get home may well kill him.'

'How is Laszlo?'

'Physically, he's fine. I'm going to give him a good rest, and then wake him up gradually. I can't keep him permanently sedated for two years, any more than I could Ove. We don't have enough drugs for that, beside any other consideration. I don't know what I'm going to do, Luca. I can do the guts and sinews. Stan can do talking therapies and counselling: he's convinced he can put him back on his feet and back to work.' She pulled a face. 'I hope he can, because we don't have the psychotropics – enough of the psychotropics – to treat full-blown mania in one, let alone two patients.'

'We all go home,' said Mariucci.

'It's a good thing that you believe that.' She reached out and patted his hand. 'We all treated this as an adventure. It was only you who ever saw it as a threat.'

He shrugged off her gesture. Not that he was uncomfortable with physical affection, but he'd spent his professional life avoiding anything that might look like it. Difficult in the confines of a spaceship, especially in the early days of his career when things were inevitably more cramped and little was left to the imagination, but pretending there was privacy was a courtesy he'd always extended to everyone.

'I've not lost anyone yet,' he said.

'Try being a surgeon. Try being me, and you'll quickly realise that saving everyone is impossible. Triage taught me that. First day in the field. I walked a line of casualties with a senior colleague, and he condemned half of them to die. A month later, I was doing the same. All I'm saying is that I'm glad you're captain, Luca, and not me, and certainly not him.' She jerked her head upwards, towards the axis, in the direction Forsyth had gone.

'Thank you for the vote of confidence.' Mariucci felt he needed to be doing something, deciding something. 'The drive can maintain itself for now. Hanne can keep the fuel going in, and Earth will tell us of any adjustments that need to be made, albeit with a delay. The magnetic shield is what it is – our protection against radiation poisoning and the collapse of ship systems. We cannot turn it off, nor decrease its potency. We need to launch the remaining probes while we're in Jovian space, preferably towards their intended destinations: if we only have two or three remaining perijoves before we manoeuvre for a cis-lunar trajectory, then that might not be possible.'

'You think they're going to call us back.'

'I think I'm at the point where I'm more worried they won't.

I want to believe ESA will consider a broken ship full of dead scientists worse than the alternative humiliation of bringing us home early but alive.'

'They're not monsters, Luca.'

'No, they're just subject to pressures that we're not. If ...' He stopped and started again. 'This is my concern: if Yasmin's analysis is confirmed, then they – ESA – may put undue weight on that, against our early return.'

'If you think ESA will want to keep us out here to counter the threat to their funding, then you'll have to make the decision yourself. Rory is quite right in that respect, too. We are autonomous. We can do what we want out here, and it's only our sense of duty that keeps us close to the mission profile.' She picked up her tablet and readied herself to go. 'Do you want Yasmin to be right?'

He leaned back in his seat. 'The implications are disturbing enough if we simply invoke Valeria's moon-spanning single organism.'

'She doesn't actually think that, Luca.'

Mariucci looked up sharply. 'Oh?'

'She thinks that Jupiter is itself alive in some way. That it's using the moons as part of its neurons. The signals are nerve impulses. That what we've recorded are Jupiter's thought-patterns.'

'Oh.' He blinked. 'The giant fungus, or whatever. I liked that better.'

'I wasn't going to contradict her in front of everyone, but you need to know. Obviously, she doesn't want you to know, but if you're after an unbiased analysis of the signals, you won't get one from her. Or Rory. Who does that leave you with who's capable of doing the numbers?'

'Deirdre, Theresa, Benjamin, Hanne if she can stop fixing things for a minute, and possibly Ove. How's he doing?'

'My opinion is that it could go either way. He's capable of useful work, but if he has another episode? Stan thinks he's curing him, and to be fair, Ove's responding well to treatment. He has to call in to me twice a day for meds, but I can't watch him as I should and deal with Laszlo. Stan has to divide his time too.'

'So four, possibly five valid opinions. And I still get to make the final decision whether to tell Earth or not.'

'They'll find the data eventually anyway. In ten years' time, some junior researcher will be given the job of sifting through all our dregs, stumble across it and be awarded the Nobel Prize. Or more likely, her supervisor will. You should tell them now. Rory can go and ein schwanz lutschen.'

He raised an eyebrow, but he smiled. 'You're right. As ever. But I think I have an idea that will keep the peace better.'

She acknowledged his compliment as mere fact, and walked the short distance to the consulting room. She'd stashed Molnar in there, strapped to half a dozen monitors while still being tied to the body board: Kattenbeck was hoping for the best while being far more accepting of the possibility of the worst than Mariucci was.

He climbed the ladder to the axis, and went to sit in his seat in Command. Colvin was there, as was Blasco. He ruminated for a while over the darkened pit, imagining the light and the lines that would normally be there.

'I'm going to add to your workload,' he said abruptly. 'I need a new course.'

Colvin stopped what she was doing and turned her chair around. 'Luca?'

'I want to launch the Io probe as soon as possible.'

'That's scheduled for perijove fifteen. We're about to start perijove six.'

'I know which perijove it is, Deirdre.'

'Can I ask why?'

'There's one way to settle the origin of the signals, and that's to look for the site of the transmission. We can't see beneath the ice on Europa, we can't see beneath the ice on Ganymede.

So we look in the only place where we might see something. On Io.'

She too stared into the darkened pit. 'Possibly. We'd need to burn at perijove – before perijove – to have any chance of making the required delta-v. We may have even left it too late for this orbit.'

'On top of which, I want you to also plot in the Callisto and Ganymede launches, and at least two Nimbus intercepts. Preferably all within three perijoves. Can you do that?'

'You're joking.'

'The minimum number of perijoves, then. Deirdre, if we have to abort then I need to make sure I've saved what I can of the science, and that we've enough food, fuel and water to get us home.'

Blasco turned to face the pit too. 'You're thinking of that?'

'I'm not thinking of aborting. I'm planning for a time when we might have to abort. A lot depends on how those who are sick respond to treatment. If they deteriorate, I have to decide for all of us. I have to know what's possible and what's not.'

'Perhaps it's better to die out here doing something we think is important, than die on Earth, which is basically fucked.'

'That's a bold view,' said Mariucci.

'We were already looking at the equatorial regions being uninhabitable. Now most of the world's major cities will be underwater in a decade. I'll be honest, it's not the retirement I had planned, fighting off climate refugees with a fire-hardened stick while I scavenge the ruins of civilisation for food. Another year out here isn't going to change that.'

'Even though it might kill us?'

'We're going to die anyway.' Blasco looked straight into his face and dared him to disagree. 'With our boots on or off is about the only choice we have.'

'Theresa, I want to believe we're a long way from that. Darmstadt needs to know about our problems: there may be a technical fix they can apply to make our planning nothing more than a useful exercise.'

'If we drop the shield, the ship systems will fry before we do.'

'No one is suggesting turning it off. Just tuning its responses to allow us to function normally.' Mariucci changed the subject. 'Have either of you an opinion on the signals?'

'If there's an error, it's right at the start. Does the raw data actually contain the signal as she presented it to us? If it's not there, if it's an artefact of her processing ... if she manipulated the data to put it there?'

Colvin balked at the suggestion. 'She wouldn't have done that.'

'If the madness has got to her too, she wouldn't even know she's doing it,' countered Blasco. 'It's not deliberate. No one wants this. I'm beginning to wonder if anyone but me has thought of the implications of this.'

Mariucci raised an eyebrow.

'Seriously. If these are what Yasmin thinks they are, messages from aliens, then where the hell are they? If they were here three thousand years ago, or twelve thousand years, or however many cycles this has gone around, where are they? I'll tell you where they are: they're dead and gone, and we'll be following them to extinction soon enough.'

'We don't know that,' said Colvin.

'Then where are they?' Blasco repeated. 'They were already at space flight when we were still building stone circles: the three thousand years since should mean they're now every-where, an unmissable, a galaxy-spanning civilisation. The only answer is that they've destroyed themselves like we're doing. We missed them by this much –' She pressed her thumb and index finger together and held it up. 'And bang. They're gone.'

'Perhaps they were just passing through. We don't know. We just don't know.'

Colvin seemed close to tears, and she always appeared so un-flappable. Mariucci openly wept at opera, a painting, a flower.

He was used to it from himself, but her? This wasn't right, but he had to press on, conclude the issue and settle the crew.

'We need to know,' said Mariucci. 'Which is why I want to investigate Io. That, I think, is our priority. Physical evidence we can point to, or not, will inform what we do next. As to the other matter, it's a given that we cannot do anything about the situation on Earth, but we can do something about the one on the Aphrodite. If we cannot operate safely, then we have to go home. That is my duty to you all, to bring you back to your family and your friends, unharmed and full of stories. That is how I measure a successful mission. Yes?'

'You're the captain,' said Blasco. 'But I guarantee the scientists will measure things differently. They'll want to stick it out here for as long as they can, whether or not that puts their lives in danger. We've all seen what's happened to both Ove and Laszlo, and still no one's clamouring for us to turn around.'

It was an important point, one that Mariucci hadn't considered. 'Perhaps they don't realise how much trouble we're in.'

'Maybe. But look, we've all already factored in privation, and we've already factored in loss. No one's died yet, and even then: if you consider any one of us could have been replaced by a dozen competent people, we all have a reason to be out here that's beyond comfort, let alone safety. Even you.'

'Only one of us makes mission-critical decisions,' said Mariucci. 'Now, about Io?'

'Don't say I never warned you,' said Blasco. 'Io-intercept is doable next perijove. It comes around often enough to make some manoeuvre at perijove always possible. The delta-v we can give the probe is always the problem.'

'There's a reason why it's in the mission profile for perijove fifteen,' said Colvin.

'We won't be here for perijove fifteen.' Mariucci felt himself get testy, and he took a moment to calm himself. Orbital mechanics weren't out to thwart him: they were what they were, and he had to accept it. 'If we're not here for perijove fifteen, then we need to have dispersed our remaining payload of probes to their respective targets before then.'

'Do you want me to plot a course for that? Or for Nimbus interception?' Colvin was agitated on her own account. 'I don't think I can do both.'

'Can you at least try?' He didn't mean it to come out exasperated, but it did, and she visibly shrank from him.

'The ship,' pointed out Blasco, like she was reminding a child, 'doesn't do high-g manoeuvres. We can't just change course like that. We've used the aerobraking shield to make Jupiter orbit, and we don't have another.'

'I know, I know. All I'm asking is for you to work out if we can deliver the Io probe early. Nothing more. We know we can do Ganymede in three more orbits, Callisto in six and Io in ten. But can we get a probe to Io next perijove if we alter our course?'

'You know what Rory's going to say about that, don't you?'

'I said alter, not abandon.' Mariucci scrubbed at his face. 'This isn't a spacer ship. This is not a democracy. I want you, Deirdre, to calculate a course that allows us to launch all the probes earlier than scheduled, prioritising the one bound for Io. When you've done that, I'll look at the results and I'll make a decision.'

It shouldn't be this difficult. He was used to giving reasonable orders and having them acted on. And normally, the more constrained a trajectory, the more a navigator wanted to prove their worth. He was sure that the old Colvin, the one he remembered only in part, would have loved the challenge. But it was clear that this hesitant, timid one didn't.

He looked at his flight crew, pilot and navigator. Should he, could he, just pull the plug now, and get them back to Earth as fast as they could manage? Make a couple of quick Nimbus encounters and go for home? Or even just one, and institute rationing. Unpopular, but they'd all survive.

And now he was thinking of sleep tanks, and how they'd just skip the ten months' deceleration from Jovian space to cis-lunar like an edit. The ship would sleep with them, holding them all in its subconscious thoughts, until they woke up orbiting the bone-dry grey of the Moon. Sleep tanks worked, but there were side-effects, and there was the feeling that humans weren't made to dream months away while their bodily functions were supported with shunts and tubes. As ships had got bigger, their designers had ditched the sleep tanks.

Mariucci would have given his right arm for a dozen sleep tanks right now. Even one, so Kattenbeck could put Molnar under for the rest of the voyage. It was a mistake not having them. A big mistake.

Blasco was talking to him, and he tuned back in. Colvin had gone – stormed off, as much as anyone can do that in zero g – and now the pilot was going to have to go after her and talk her down. He shook his head, still fuzzy with thoughts of cold coffins and silent corridors.

'Yes, yes. Go. Tell me what I can do to make it better.'

He was alone, the lights of Command twinkling in the gloom.

9

'So you didn't wait for Darmstadt?'

'No.' Mariucci stared at the lines in the pit, where the white of the Aphrodite was converging on the yellow of the new orbit. 'We were running out of time.'

'Anyone looking on from the outside would see the timing of your message and the start of the radio blackout as more than convenient.' Kattenbeck sat opposite him, watching the same lines.

'If we didn't start the manoeuvre this perijove, we'd have to wait for another two. I can't drag this out any longer. It's consuming the crew.'

'It's consuming you, too,' she said. 'You're looking for reasons to stay, or go. You can't make up your mind which course to take. You could have ordered us to ignore the signals and carry on with the mission profile. You could have prioritised the Nimbus intercepts, used the probes to help capture them if there were any problems, then dumped them before bailing. Yet here we are, on a third course.'

'That's not what I'm doing. I'm looking for more evidence. This is a science ship, full of scientists, Petra. It's what we should do.'

'What happens when you find it, or not find it? Will you make a decision then?' The lights glowed in her eyes. 'Or will you kick it down the road again?'

'Petra, I—'

'I'm not blaming you,' she said. 'Just pointing out you used to be decisive. Dynamic, even. It was thrilling to see.'

'Thrilling?'

She shrugged. 'Yes. It's gone now. You have meetings, you consult, you think, you speak, but you won't commit. The options end up closing themselves out, and what's left is what we do, by default.'

'You want leading?'

'I want steering.'

'Doesn't this count?'

'Really, Luca? No, it doesn't count. Twisting around Jupiter like a pretzel so that we make an Io encounter on the next perijove – technically next but one, but we're taking two tight orbits to do it – it's just another meeting. A cosmic meeting. You want pictures of Io's antijove, but you still don't know what you're going to do when you get them.'

'Do you think it's a symptom?'

'Probably. Look, Luca, you could have just waited for Darmstadt. They tell you what to do, you do it: that's the end of the uncertainty. But you don't trust Darmstadt any more than you trust yourself. When we come out of blackout, you'll get your answer from them, but now you'll be able to say they'll have to revisit the same question once we've seen what's on Io. You've kicked their ball into the long grass along with your own.'

'You don't think I should have done this.'

'What you should or shouldn't have done is beside the point. You've done it. The problem is, you can't tell me why.'

'We need evidence,' he reiterated.

'We would have got that evidence on perijove fifteen. Why now?'

'Because it's consuming the crew.'

'So you said.' She had practical, short hair. Not spacer short, not that fine baize-flat felt they preferred; when she ran her hand over her head, the loose ends stuck outwards, held there by sweat and oil. 'By taking us further into the radiation belt, you're risking increasing the shield effects.'

'If there are such effects.'

'There has to be a cause.'

'What if we're just ...' He waved the thought away. 'We were all evaluated. Repeatedly. By the best in their field. It's just one manoeuvre, to put us within the launch window for Io. We'll be in and out of the radiation belt in five days.'

'And the next orbit?'

'Still inside, but less radiation.'

She was silent for a while, watching the pit as the moons went around. The very innermost orbited Jupiter's bloated equator three times a day at a speed of over thirty kilometres a second. Its twin, fractionally further out, the same. Between them, around them, a ring.

'No, you shouldn't have done this, Luca. We've identified a potential risk to the mission, and you're exacerbating it.'

'What if Yasmin's found something? Something worth coming back for? We're here to make discoveries, yes?'

'You said yourself that we're not equipped to investigate it. And you're right.' She was quiet again. 'Is this about Rory?'

'No, no. Why do you say that?'

'Because you want to make Professor Never-wrong eat his words. And you're willing to risk humiliating Yasmin to do it.'

'This isn't about that.' Mariucci grunted in annoyance. She was poking him, and he didn't like it. 'It's not about Rory Forsyth, and it's certainly not about making Yasmin look foolish. I'm worried, Petra. I'm worried that they're right, that this is the end, the last time we'll make it out this far, that the Catherine Vis of this world will get their way and we'll turn inwards. And it's the looking in that will kill us off in the end, not the looking up.'

'You want it to be aliens.'

Mariucci looked around, but they were still the only ones in

Command. Colvin was due back shortly to check her course, but she wasn't in earshot yet.

'The whole idea is completely ridiculous. I know it is.'

'And yet?'

'If it was, someone would have to come back. They'd have to. It'd change the entire trajectory of our future, more than whatever it is that Rory's trying to find the answers to out here. And I don't blame Vi for doing what she does—'

'But you resent it.'

'I haven't lost my island home to the sea. For her, the worst has already happened. For me, for us? Drought, disease, summer highs, falling birth rates. We face a crisis. We need a way out, something to strive for. This isn't about who's right, who's wrong. This is about hope, for all of us here, and everyone at home.'

'A post-hoc justification which conveniently aligns with what you're already doing.'

'If I wanted psychoanalysis I'd have talked to Stan.' He grunted again, but this time there was no force behind it. He'd been seen. 'Our mission here is important.'

'It's a luxury,' she said.

'Where there is no vision, the people perish,' he countered.

'You can't argue that Vi doesn't have a vision. It's just different to yours.'

'And yours?'

'I'm here to patch you up. Not to take sides. It's not going to be aliens, Luca. We're going to be the last to come here. No one will follow us. We'll get pensioned off, the Agency shrunk down, and what's left will be all Earth observation. I suppose Theresa does have something of a point: do we want to be part of that, or do we take risks up here? More risks.'

'Then what is it? One signal can be dismissed as noise. We have four, across three moons and six hundred thousand kilometres of space.'

'But do we?' Kattenbeck glanced towards the axis. There was

someone coming. 'She could have made it all up. It could be her madness.'

'We'll see.'

'No we won't. The signals – her interpretation of them – will still be there even when the images show nothing. What do you do then?' Then she shut up because the figure occluding the light of the axis wasn't Colvin, but Aasen. She seemed agitated. More agitated than usual.

'Hanne? What's wrong?'

'Spare parts,' she blurted. 'They're missing, and I need them.'

Mariucci felt his gears grind and get up to speed.

'Specifically?'

'Five-five-five timing chips.'

'What does the inventory say?'

'That we have seventy-eight of them. They're the single most versatile IC on board. We can't have run out, because I'd know.'

Mariucci unclipped himself and nudged towards the bulkhead door. 'What does Ove say?'

'I can't find him to ask him. I've literally wasted ten minutes going up and down the ship.'

'We have an intercom, Hanne.'

She waved his comment away. 'I need the chips. One chip. That's all.'

Kattenbeck came up behind Mariucci. 'You can't find Ove?'

'I don't need Ove. I need the chip. But if Ove's the only one who can tell me where he's stashed them, then … Inventories only work if the people in charge of them put stuff where the inventory says it is.'

'Show me,' said Mariucci, and received another tut of annoyance. 'Just let me take a look.'

He twisted round and saw the acknowledgement that Kattenbeck was going to hunt down Hellsten while he kept the engineer busy.

Aasen navigated the axis briskly, like someone perpetually

113

in a hurry, which she was, and headed into one of the storage modules in the science section. She checked her list, opened a locker door, pulled out a deep tray and pointed to the empty bin.

'There. Or not there.'

'Have you checked the five-five-six or the five-five-eight?'

'Luca, they're a different DIP config, and yes, of course I did, and there's a couple of each left but there should be dozens.' She opened another drawer, opened another lid. A bag drifted out with transferred momentum, and she snagged it to show him. 'Then I looked at some of the other ICs, and we're down, and raw components, and it's the diodes and transistors we're missing, and what the hell, I can't fix stuff if I've not the parts, and neither can Ove, but he can't have used all those already because the inventory says they should still be there.'

She jammed the bag back in the tray and rolled it shut. She was both furious and scared: scared that the error list on her tablet would never be finished, that something would break and they'd die and it'd be all her fault.

'I can't think of a good explanation,' said Mariucci. 'I don't know if everything from the last Nimbus was stored correctly or not. Ove was in charge of that. When he was ... ill the first time, I didn't have time to do a full, or even partial, inventory. I just logged what we used, not thinking I needed to check what was left.' He closed the door to that particular locker, and flipped over, looking through the door and out into the axis. 'The ship's not that big.'

'It is if you're actively trying to hide. Try it sometime.'

Amongst the sounds unwanted on a spaceship – the howl of decompression, the clamour of alarms, the sudden breathless silence due to the absence of turning fans – a scream was particularly unwelcome, because it didn't accurately describe what the problem was, nor how to fix it.

'Deirdre,' said Mariucci. He launched himself out of the module, and was ahead of the stream of crew heading towards

Command only by virtue of already thinking that's where he needed to be.

Aasen was on his heels, but so were Velter and Spinu and Tsoltos.

The shipwide alarm triggered. 'Emergency. Command. Emergency. Command.'

'Coming through,' he called, as Blasco and Kattenbeck appeared from two separate access tubes in the rotating section. They pulled back as he hurtled by, and he caught a handrail just inside Command, turning him and slowing him.

'Emergency. Command. Emergency. Command.'

Colvin and Borner were both there, in their seats, looking up at Hellsten, who was floating near the ceiling.

He was covered in blood. Again. He seemed stunned, like he'd been punched repeatedly. Whatever he'd done had released a massive rush of hormones, leaving him preternaturally calm.

'Ove?'

Hellsten turned to look at Mariucci, and he tried to speak. A bubble of blood expanded on his lips and burst, causing a corona of red beads to spin outwards. Then he coughed, and ... something came out of his mouth, something small and dark, flat and geometric.

'Emergency. Command. Emergency. Command.'

It spun, end over end. Mariucci lunged for it, realised that he hadn't the reach, and spent an extra second calculating its trajectory. The object travelled slowly and wetly through the air. He intercepted it before it could hit one of the displays. As he curled his fist around it, it felt unexpectedly sharp.

He immediately relaxed his grip and looked at his hand. It was an integrated circuit, black substrate and silver contacts, the latter digging into his palm as ten discrete pinpricks. His skin, space-pale, was smeared with Hellsten's blood.

What was this doing in his mouth? Mariucci was confused, even as Kattenbeck elbowed her way through and took in the scene.

'Verdammt noch mal,' said Kattenbeck. She launched at him. 'Ove. What the hell have you done?'

She pinned him against the ceiling in a single move, and waited for assistance.

'Emergency. Command. Emergency. Command.'

'Luca, when you're ready?'

'Yes. I'm coming.' For the want of anything better to do, he pocketed the chip and pushed himself towards the pair. He landed next to them and took a handhold.

'We need to get him down to the wheel,' she said, but Mariucci was checking Hellsten's face, his jaw, his cheeks.

'Emergency. Command. Emergency. Command.'

'Ove, open your mouth,' he said.

Hellsten's gaze switched from Kattenbeck to the captain. There was a minute shake of his head.

Mariucci clamped his fingers and thumb under Hellsten's chin. 'Open your mouth, Ove. That's an order.' He squeezed, and slowly, slowly, Hellsten's lips parted. 'Petra, check inside. And someone, please, cancel that alarm.'

Normally, she'd have worn gloves, but they were probably beyond clinical niceties now. Her fingers probed past his teeth, and she frowned. They went deeper, curled, and pulled, to Hellsten's momentary discomfort.

When they withdrew, they were pinching another slab of integrated circuit, glistening with spit and blood.

'Emergency. Command. Emer.'

'Fack,' she said. 'How many more, Ove? Have you swallowed any?'

He gave the slightest of nods, and Kattenbeck bit her lip to stop herself from saying anything intemperate. She looked at Mariucci with large, dark eyes, and he released his hold on Hellsten's face.

'What do we do?' he asked.

'I don't know,' she said, and she was lost. She looked at the faces staring back at her from the axis, from Colvin and Borner.

'The wheel?' Mariucci suggested.

'I … yes. I need a separate room for him – no, for Laszlo. One of them.'

Mariucci watched the slow rise and fall of Hellsten's chest. Still breathing freely, airways clear. He pressed his fingers to Hellsten's neck and felt the hard, heavy pulse. Circulation, for now, still strong. They needed to get him in a gravity section, and check him for external wounds, before trying to evaluate any internal damage. 'Petra, go ahead and get everything ready. I'll bring Ove. Out of my way, everyone else.'

Kattenbeck shook herself. 'Sorry. Yes. Bring him down. Slowly. Don't let him bend over or twist. He should be on a board.'

'But we only have one.'

'We only have one. Of course we do.' When the axis had cleared, she pushed towards it, and left a bloody handprint on the bulkhead.

'Come on, Ove. Come with me. Slowly, just as Petra said.' Mariucci didn't give Hellsten any chance to resist. He dragged him backwards towards the rotating hub, through the hatch and into the rotating section.

The others that were there, crew and scientists, were aghast and silent, and so was Mariucci. There was no reassurance he could offer, no answer as to what had happened. He lowered Hellsten the entire way down the access tube, just like he'd done before, but he was the one holding on this time, not Kattenbeck. He had the strength, but it was awkward. He was almost at the wheel when he heard her voice from below.

'Another two metres.'

Mariucci judged the distance, and before Hellsten's toes touched the carpet, another dose of methaqualone had been injected into the engineer's neck.

'Hold him,' said Kattenbeck. She dropped the gas gun with a delayed thud, and caught Hellsten from behind in a grip that went under his arms and over his shoulders. 'Let go now.'

She laid him on the floor right there at the foot of the ladder, and knelt down beside him. Her hands, before they went to his flight-suit zip, briefly pressed against her forehead.

Mariucci took the opposite side from her.

'If he's swallowed any of them, what can you do?'

'I can go in with an oesophagoscope – we do have one – and try and locate, then extract them. If they've already punctured his stomach, then I'll have to try and repair the damage. It depends on how many, how far through they've gone. If they've reached his large intestine, then it gets a lot more complicated.'

'He's only just done this.'

'Has he? Has he really? Or is this the final act in a long play that he's hidden from us?' She pulled up the T-shirt Hellsten was wearing underneath and gently palpated his stomach. 'He could be riddled with them.'

'Why didn't we notice?' Mariucci rocked back on his heels. 'Surely we should have – you and Stan should have – seen something?'

'You start by taking one or two. Wrapped in food, maybe in the plastic bags they come in. Then you get bold. You make a deliberate act of it, as many as you can.' Kattenbeck twisted around to look at the pharmacy. 'There's a box in there, with the portable fluoroscope, and all the cabling. I'll have to set it up here. It'll trigger the radiation detectors, but that can't be helped. Look, I didn't know. He didn't say anything to me, nor to Stan, and X-raying him isn't on the checklist.'

Mariucci opened up the pharmacy, located the fluoroscope, and came back to a furious row between Aasen and Kattenbeck, standing over the barely aware Hellsten.

'Hanne, it can wait.'

'He has my ICs,' she said, and while it couldn't be denied, it wasn't Mariucci's priority right now.

He reached into his pocket and fished out the tiny black slab. He ran his thumb over the top to reveal the serial number.

'There,' he said, holding it out. 'Take it and go.'

And she did. That was all she wanted.

Kattenbeck growled out 'arschloch' as she returned to Hellsten. She opened the crate one-handed, found the flat detector plate and pushed it against Hellsten's flank.

'Grab his left arm, pull it across his body to roll him up, then let him roll back.'

Mariucci complied, and Kattenbeck slid the plate under and positioned it centred under Hellsten's sternum.

'Power cable.' She launched the end at him. 'Plug it in, then walk a third of the way around the wheel. Ignore the alarms.'

There weren't sockets just lying around, but he knew where they were hidden. He ran the cable to the wall, flicked a panel open, and one was revealed. He pushed the prongs into the socket and flipped the switch. 'It's on.'

'Go,' she said, holding the handles of the X-ray generator itself and lining it up over Hellsten. 'Go. I can't press the button with you here.'

Mariucci walked around the wheel, far enough for the diptych of Kattenbeck and Hellsten to disappear.

'Radiation. Wheel. Radiation. Wheel. Radiation. Wheel. Radiation. Wheel. Radiation. Wheel.'

The alarm fell silent, and Mariucci waited a few more seconds before retracing his steps. Kattenbeck was sitting on the floor next to Hellsten, head down over the tablet in her lap. The X-ray machine was abandoned beside her, its blind muzzle pointing abstractly at some point on the wall.

She was reviewing the detector plate footage, the image moving as she'd moved the angle and direction of the X-rays. Then she put the tablet face down on the carpet.

'I have potentially three options. The first is that I do a laparotomy, get them all out, try and fix the damage while I'm in there, and probably watch him die over the next two to three weeks. The second is I sedate him while he dies over the next week to ten days. The third is I euthanise him now.' She took a deep breath. 'What do you think?'

Mariucci looked down at Hellsten. 'When you say probably, how much of a chance does he have?'

'Some of it depends on how good a doctor I am. But only a little. The rest depends on his luck. He might not be able to ingest anything for weeks, potentially for months. He'll be on antibiotics the whole time, to prevent sepsis. He's already perforated, judging from his temperature, and he's got air in his abdominal cavity. If it was shrapnel, I'd give it a go: I'd know what I was doing. But this is everywhere, Luca. Handfuls of them. Like little spiders with sharp metal legs.'

'And it's not a cure for his illness.'

'I don't have enough sedation for both him and Laszlo for the whole trip home, let alone anyone else who might need it in the future. We could be left with nothing, and he still dies having used all the medication.' She rubbed at her face. 'If this was a hospital in Berlin or Rome, with a full theatre team, bags of plasma and blood, specialist GI surgeons on call, all the imaging we needed? I'd give him a fifty per cent chance. Tearing up his gut is the single most damaging thing he could have done to himself.'

'We all go home,' said Mariucci.

'He will. Tethered to the outside of the ship in a body bag. And Hanne's going to want to have those chips back, isn't she?'

'They're vital to the running of the ship.' Mariucci dropped his hand to her shoulder, and gave it the briefest of squeezes. 'You don't have to make this decision on your own.'

'I've made worse calls in worse situations,' she said. 'The one thing about being a doctor, you get to bury your mistakes.'

'Except that for you, they're now coming back.' Mariucci pulled his hand away, and cracked his knuckles. The noise startled him enough to make him stop immediately. 'I've taken advice from the ship's doctor. My opinion is that we cannot save Ove. Given that we are not prepared to see him suffer as he dies, the only option left is that he is painlessly euthanised, according to whatever protocols we have in place. This is my decision as captain.'

'Is that what you're going to tell the rest of the crew? Earth?'

'Yes.' What choice did he have now? None. None whatsoever. He pressed his fingers to his face. He'd led them all to this place. If he'd made different decisions, earlier, he could have led them all back. Instead he'd ... what? Forgotten what he once was? He'd lost a member of his crew, and faced a situation where he could lose them all.

He looked down at Kattenbeck, squatting on her heels next to the still form of Hellsten, at the blood on her hands, his own hands. He made no effort to wash it off, because it would always be there anyway.

'We make the Io launch, and then we go home,' he said. 'I'm sorry, Petra.'

10

There was an hour to go before the insertion burn – one that would use every last gram of fuel the probe had. If Colvin had miscalculated, or the monopropellant didn't work as advertised, then the probe would end up in the wrong orbit, and their ability to get images of the Ionian antijove would depend more on luck than judgement.

Argus – the beast with a hundred eyes sent by Zeus to watch over Io after the god had turned his lover into a cow – was approaching Io through the worst of the radiation belt. Borner had already reported that there'd been damage, and that Argus would inevitably degrade further and fail. But for now, it was still sending back all the packets of data its instruments would allow, and Forsyth was more than willing to believe that this deviation from the mission profile was a concession to him, and not a unilateral decision by Mariucci.

The nature of Hellsten's affliction, more than the abrupt manner of his passing, had isolated the crew rather than bringing them together. They were looking as much inside themselves as they were at each other, wondering who was going to be next, and whether it was going to be them. Mariucci didn't know how that would translate in a vote for leaving Jovian space, not that it mattered. Neither would it matter if ESA ordered them home, or ordered them to stay. He'd made his mind up. This place, this oppressive and yet vague malevolence he'd felt for a while, had crystallised in the moment of catching the processor spat from Hellsten's mouth.

He knew that if they didn't leave soon, none of them would return.

But he'd already chanced everything on one last throw of the dice, so he was going to let that roll, then make the announcement. Argus would tell them if there was anything visible on Io that might be the cause of the signals, as interpreted by Borner, and even then, Kattenbeck was right: the absence of evidence was never going to be conclusive. If there was nothing, there was always room for more conjecture, more investigation, more prevarication and delay.

He hadn't cancelled his earlier order because he wanted to see what was down there, to save something, to make the sacrifices they'd made, were going to make, somehow justifiable. Justifiable to who? Darmstadt? The families – husbands, wives, fathers, mothers, children – of the crew? To the millions of homeless, stateless people who were washing up on northern and southern shores as their own countries disappeared under the waves or were consumed by dust? To himself?

He realised with a start that he couldn't remember the name of his own home town in the Tuscan hills, where he'd lived until the age of ten, before they'd all decamped, grandparents and everyone, to Florence. What was it? He could envisage the tight high-walled lanes and the gaps between the terracotta roofs that flashed views of the valley below. But not its name.

Maybe another cognitive test was in order, but what would that prove? Would he relieve himself of command? Or would he just worry about it, like he was worrying about it now?

The lights of the pit glittered and winked. Fifty minutes to go.

Tsoltos occluded the axis, and paused. 'Too early?'

'No. Come on in if you want, Stan.'

Tsoltos pushed himself in, and took one of the higher tier seats. 'This,' he said, 'has lost some of its excitement for you.'

'I trust it's the same for all of us. We've lost a member of the crew. We've lost a friend.'

'I've lost patients over the years. I've tried not to see it in terms of fault, nor guilt. Just a matter of fate. It was hubris to come here, and the gods were not kind to poor Ove. I, good Greek that I am, know all about hubris.'

'So you don't think we failed Ove?' said Mariucci. 'Any more than we're failing Laszlo?'

'They're human. Or were human. Mortal men. They had failings of their own that were not mine. Ove could have listened to me, but he chose to abandon reason and, like Eurydice, looked back and was lost. Laszlo hopefully won't make the same mistake.'

Mariucci had been hunched up for so long that his bones creaked when he stretched. 'I know what you're trying to say, that we're not responsible for anything more than we can do or be. That we're not saints, we don't perform miracles, and no one is expecting us to, either. But this is my ship. I've not lost anyone before.'

'The best plans, properly executed by highly trained, competent practitioners using tested machinery fit for the purpose, still carry an element of risk, and we cannot eliminate that risk entirely. That you have reached fifty ... five? and not suffered a loss on a mission or elsewhere in your professional life is simply down to luck. You've come close before.'

Mariucci nodded, and acknowledged to himself that if Catherine Vi had let go of Van der Veerden's hand, then not only would the mourners have been few, but also the political situation back on Earth far less volatile. 'You know who.'

'I've even seen the footage, recorded by the very cameras outside of this hull. A moment where it could have gone either way. As it is, we are in a universe where she was saved.' Tsoltos shrugged. 'Loss is inevitable. Do we let it teach us, or do we let it overwhelm us? I know which is the more satisfactory outcome.'

'And what of acknowledging what has happened, and allowing time to digest its consequences?'

'All good. You can be sad. You cannot fall into self-pity.'

'Is that what you think is happening here? A man, under my care, has died! It shouldn't matter that this is the first time or the tenth time or the hundredth time. This is the first Ove Hellsten either of us have lost, and we should feel that passing keenly.' Mariucci roused himself. 'Not just because of all the things that Ove did on the ship, but because of all the things he meant to us. That he loved pickled food. That he told jokes that no one could understand, and his trying to explain them was funnier than the joke. That he never remembered to reset the temperature controls on the shower unit, and if you followed him in you got freezing cold water. We've lost all that.'

'And what about the living?'

'There's enough space in my head for both the living and the dead, Stan. I can hold him in my memory there, while still caring about what happens to the rest of my crew.'

'I'm not suggesting you forget him.'

'Good.' Mariucci was irritated. Of course he wasn't going to forget. It had been barely two days since Kattenbeck had euthanised Hellsten. Both he and she had spent much of the last forty-eight hours writing and rewriting the reports on the matter. He didn't know what Tsoltos had been doing, but it didn't sound as if he'd been doing much self-reflection.

Kattenbeck had also devoted several hours to retrieving integrated circuits from Hellsten's digestive tract. That was something he'd been very grateful not to have been involved in. But he had helped her put the body in its bag which, through valves, would leak air and water to the void, and he'd taken it outside and strapped it to the hull.

Jupiter had been huge. Mighty. A full one-eighty degrees in his field of view, and so close he felt like he was falling into it. Spinu had been desperate to join him on EVA, but he'd chosen Blasco, which had resulted in a stand-up fight and a terrible atmosphere, not just between him and Spinu, but also between Spinu and Blasco.

Spinu would have let go, deliberately, pushed herself away from the Aphrodite and into Jupiter's clouds. He'd saved her, for now, and it rankled that she was angry with him. Couldn't she see what was happening to her? Apparently not. He'd been tempted – briefly – to destroy her spacesuit, slicing it open through all of its various layers and rendering it unusable. But she still might need it, and she could just take someone else's no matter how badly it fitted.

That was why he resented Tsoltos. One man was dead, another incapacitated: Molnar would be slowly revived – when Kattenbeck had the emotional energy to do so – and that still might go badly wrong. What had happened to both him and Hellsten was on Mariucci's watch, and he felt so very guilty. If anything happened to Spinu, or Velter, or any of the others, it would be cumulatively worse.

He wanted to be allowed to wallow in his grief, for just a little while. That was the reaction of a human being, yes?

Blasco came into Command. She'd showered since her EVA, and her hair was still clinging together in damp, dark curls. She looked at Mariucci, then at Tsoltos, and hesitated.

'We're in Command, Theresa,' said Mariucci. 'If we'd needed somewhere private to talk, we would have gone there.'

She nodded, and made her way across the ceiling before forward-flipping into her seat. She strapped herself in and did a few preparatory wrist exercises, in case manual control was required.

Forty minutes to go.

'Thank you,' said Mariucci.

'You're welcome,' she said. Whether she meant that or not didn't matter so much as the fact that she'd been there with him on the hull and she'd done her duty well, despite the scene with Spinu immediately before decompression.

But she really didn't want to be reminded of it. How they'd towed the inflated black sausage-shape of the body bag between them, all while it was slowly, steadily, venting ice crystals that

126

had once been part of Hellsten. How they'd anchored it to the ship down past the probe bays and between two of the external fuel tanks, using carabiners and straps. The journey back along the length of the ship to airlock one, staring straight into Jupiter's huge and ancient lined face, as the Aphrodite hung nose down over the clouds, throwing white-hot fuel behind it and forcing it ever closer.

Once they were inside, and out of their suits for the mercifully brief recompression, they'd said nothing to each other. This exchange here, in Command, had been their first acknowledgement of their joint task.

Then Borner appeared, doing what Blasco had done, scoping out who was present before going further. She'd been there when Mariucci had denied Spinu the EVA – although it was likely the entire ship had heard – so perhaps she was seeing if the scientist had already taken her place, or was yet to arrive.

It was starting to be a bad business, Mariucci thought, and they needed to clear the air properly. They couldn't carry on walking on eggshells for too long, and the journey home would take a year. After this launch, then. After he'd made his announcement.

Borner took her usual seat, checking the telemetry from Argus, polling its instruments to see if they were all still functioning. Mariucci studied her face while she did so, and he noticed the occasional – more than one, certainly – grimace.

'Damage report, Yasmin.'

She rubbed the bridge of her nose before responding. 'There's a decline in core processor speed already. The check-sums are preventing errors, but the clock is down ten per cent. The radiation is ... I had to read it twice to make sure of the numbers. We're measuring repeated spikes in the gigaelectronvolt range. The imager is still inside its housing, so it should work, for a while. Radar is returning ambiguous readings, but we should be able to clean those up post-processing. The magnetometer is fine for now, and the gas chromatograph is sampling.'

'Will the problem with the altimeter cause problems for the insertion burn?'

'No. There's a lot of cross-checking with radio pulses to and from the Aphrodite, and if all else fails, the internal clock will take over. But we can still override everything from here.'

'You can talk to Argus, and Argus responds, albeit slower than it ought, yes?'

'We have control,' she said.

'I'm content with that.'

Now, Colvin arrived. And she too did an assay of who was there and who was missing before strapping in. She opened up her software and started running through her own checklists, something she'd done every few hours since Argus's launch. So far, she'd managed to keep the probe on the wire drawn out for it, despite the battering it was receiving both electromagnetic-ally and chemically. High energy radicals of oxygen and sulphur were busy chewing their way into the outer integument with every impact, wearing it down, changing its composition into something that was much weaker and less protective.

But she gave no sign that the probe was anywhere other than where she expected it to be. The tiny spark in the pit was so close to Io, it had almost merged with it.

Kattenbeck had drifted in while Mariucci was concentrating on Colvin, and he only noticed her when the chair behind him creaked. He looked over his shoulder. Oh, but she was tired. Grey with fatigue. Doctor, heal yourself.

She rubbed her face, scratched her neck, pinched her earlobes. Fatigued, but still determined to see if there was anything to see. When the show was over, only then would she take herself to bed.

Who wasn't here yet? Velter, Spinu, Forsyth, Aasen. No, just Forsyth and Aasen, because Velter first, then Spinu behind him, were picking their seats: either side of Tsoltos, and well away from both Mariucci and Blasco. Velter looked pensive – when did he not? – and Spinu either kept her eyes down when she thought someone glanced in her direction, or stared into the pit.

After the insertion burn, it was going to be down to Velter and Spinu to retrieve, display and interpret the data. That Spinu was here was good news. That she was either mortally embarrassed by her actions earlier, or still furious at being denied her EVA, was less so. But she was present, and ready. That would have to do for now.

They'd all accepted that the camera might not last for long, but it was designed to last for long enough to take pictures of most of the moon, to a resolution no one had achieved before – if they could get the orbit right. Colvin had assured them there'd be enough propellant. They were twenty minutes away from finding out.

Mariucci noted that two of the four remaining seats were not going to be filled. It was a shame that Molnar couldn't be present, and at least aware of what was going on. But then he'd also have been aware of sitting at the opposite end of the ship from his drive. Or his shield. Whichever one of them it was that he was most attached to.

Sillico. That was the name of the town his family had moved from. It was beautiful up there. Cool, not like the heat of the plain. His mother especially complained of the heat in those first few years, and 'why can't we go back to the mountains?' but there was no work up there, and the schools were better for Luca, who was obviously and prodigiously bright.

And then there was a point when no one talked about Sillico any more, because there wasn't anyone left there, just boarded-up houses and closed shops and stray cats. The government had moved the remaining residents down the valley and just left it to decay – and that was that. Mariucci had his friends and his life in Florence and from there, the rest of the world and beyond: he'd never looked back. He wondered what Sillico was like now, and whether the cats were still there.

Forsyth came in. He didn't hesitate. He didn't care who was

129

present. He pulled himself down into a seat, front row, next to Borner, the better to crow at her when the images of the anti-jove revealed precisely nothing. She twitched with annoyance, but remained silent.

He leaned forward to catch Mariucci's attention.

'Ready for the show?'

Mariucci acknowledged him without succumbing to making the obvious jibes about the professor's wasted time.

'We're all ready,' he said. When he looked up, both Spinu and Velter had their backs to them all, peering intently, possibly deliberately, at their displays. 'It won't be long now.'

Ten minutes. Less than ten, in fact.

They'd lived on the south side of the Arno, outside the historic medieval centre, in a modernish – mid-twentieth-century – apartment. The ground floor had been a bicycle shop. Or had that been opposite, so he could see it from the window? An ice-cream parlour? No. There'd been a little bar, with a garden slotted into the shadow between two adjacent buildings, facing a square. A circle – a circus. Why were details so difficult? The colours were vivid, but the names over the doors eluded him.

It felt like he'd no sooner arrived than he'd left. First for Rome, then for Berlin, then off-planet often enough that he'd never really had a home again. Even now, the prospect of retirement, of settling in one place, seemed unnerving. He hadn't planned to retire: what forced most astronauts out was family, health, or a factor of both. He'd studiously avoided one, and as far as he knew, the other was still good. Had been good. This was probably going to be his last flight as crew.

Aasen bundled in. 'I'm not too late, am I?' A pair of pliers trailed behind her, having been incorrectly stowed on her belt at some point. They caught up with her hip as she assessed the seating arrangements, and bounced away again to the length of their tether.

'No. Just in time,' said Mariucci. And it was, more or less, time.

'And we won't have to wait too long, either? I have places to be.'

'I appreciate that,' he said. 'Some things are outside of my control.'

She flipped into her seat next to him. 'Missed anything?'

He looked at the clock. 'There's some minor problems with the electronics, especially the radar. We're not relying on that for altitude measurements, so we should get good surface data whatever.'

'T minus sixty seconds,' said Borner.

'When do we start getting the pictures?' asked Aasen.

'The camera's not deployed yet, to save it.'

'I can bring it out now,' said Spinu. 'We should pass the antijove during the deceleration.'

'We'll waste less of our engineer's time,' said Forsyth, 'and mine, if you do.'

Whatever Spinu felt about the barb, she simply sent out the commands to Argus. The travel time was less than a third of a second, short enough for Blasco to be able to steer the probe in real-time.

'T minus thirty.'

'Camera reports that it's online. We should be getting the first images shortly.'

'What's the altitude?'

'Currently, eight hundred and fifty kilometres. Final orbit will be one hundred and twenty kilometres.'

'T minus twenty.'

'Propellent systems are online. Pre-ignition checks complete. System is nominal.'

'Here we are. The trailing limb of Io, Jupiter in the background.' Velter's voice was halting, desperately trying to be the professional he was required to be. He ported the image to the displays around Command. It was a scabrous landscape, pox-ridden and pus-laden. But the technical quality of the image was sharp. Detail abounded. Dark craters, pale plains, haloed

131

volcanoes, all rendered in ochre and cream, sharp yellows and pastel reds, and pits like the black entrances to ant hills.

'Thruster ignition confirmed. Burn at t plus five.'

'Second image.'

It was closer, sharper. The colours blurred across their boundaries, in the style of an impressionist painter. The features were spaced out, so the second picture showed less of interest than the first to the untrained eye: the terminal banks of lava flows, levees and rilles, low, flat-topped rises.

'T plus twenty.'

'Altitude seven fifty. Antijovian point should be in the fourth image.' Velter pressed his fist into his sternum, and Tsoltos leaned over to whisper something to him.

The third image was needle-bright. Lobes and wrinkles, and glowing red fire in the depths of one of the pits.

'It's erupting. And it's so clear.' Colvin actually clapped her hands together, and her undiluted enthusiasm made Forsyth roll his eyes in exaggerated exasperation.

The next image. The next image.

'T plus sixty.'

The screen cleared, and another image rolled down across all their separate displays.

At first, it made little sense. It looked like curdled milk, the skin on top broken in some places, and folded together in others. It resembled salt pans, or those chemical deposits around fumaroles. Mariucci leaned towards his screen. He'd expected the landscape to be fractal, like the Moon, or Mars, or Earth, or Europa, with new features revealing themselves at every iteration. Io wasn't like that: it was becoming blander and more blank instead.

'I think we've probably seen enough,' said Forsyth. He made to unclip.

'Valeria,' said Mariucci. 'What's the resolution on this?'

'This image?' She seemed surprised to be asked, especially

by him. 'Each pixel is ten metres across. We'll get it down to two metres on subsequent passes.'

'Can you pinpoint the antijove?'

'Oh, okay,' said Aasen, looking at where Mariucci had lightly rested his finger on the display. 'That's ... quite square.'

It was at the very top left-hand corner of the screen. If the image had been taken a fraction of a second later, it would have passed entirely out of the field of view. They would probably have caught it, eventually, but not necessarily. Luck was a factor that couldn't be denied.

Spinu and Velter conferred on the coordinates, and she slid crosshairs across the image. The two lines intersected over the dark block.

'Can we ... you know?' asked Mariucci.

'Yes.' Spinu seemed shocked. 'Yes.' She cleared the grid, and zoomed in.

Everyone was staring at their screens, the count of the Argus's burn forgotten.

'What the hell is that?' asked Kattenbeck.

'I – I don't know.' Velter sucked in a breath, and held it.

It was square. It was exactly square. Even within the limits of the resolution, where the edges blurred into the surrounding plain, it was obviously and precisely a square, some nine or ten pixels top to bottom, side to side: one hundred metres across.

More than that. There seemed to be some measure of structure to it. One edge was visibly darker than its opposite, while the two were similar. A smudge of shadow on the ground appeared to suggest its height.

'Can we turn the Argus to get an oblique picture of this?'

'Not while we're burning.'

Mariucci accepted that, but he was frustrated.

'I want better pictures of it.' He chewed at his tongue. 'That is not natural.'

'Nonsense. Pareidolia, that's all. It's the face on Mars all over again.'

'Rory,' said Spinu. 'Look at the rest of the landscape. This, this object: it has hard, straight edges at ninety degrees to each other. It has volume. It's even aligned north-south, east-west.'

'It's a pyramid,' said Borner, and once she'd said it, Mariucci couldn't unsee it. The shading, the shadow, the size of the footprint. It completely fitted the description. It was there and he couldn't deny it. 'There's a pyramid on Io.'

Part 2

Imhullu

innendū-ma tiāmat apkal ilāni marūtuk
šašmeš itlupū qitrubū taḫāziš
ušparrir-ma bēlum saparra-šu ušalmē-ši
imḫulla ṣābit arkāti pānūš-ša umtaššir

11

'This is real,' said Velter. 'It's not an artefact of the camera, it's not a problem with the transmission, or the processing. We'll get more on the second pass, in less than two hours. Rory, this is actually down there.'

He had to stop talking because he'd run out of air. He panted for a few moments, then realised he was starting to flush. Tsoltos laid a hand on him, and for a moment it looked like he was going to shake the psychologist off, he was that angry with Forsyth. But then he rallied, and turned back to his screen, simply so he didn't have to look at the man.

The object was on every display except the pit. Wherever Mariucci looked, there it was, a dark square against a pale lemon background. While they were all occupied with it, the burn had continued to execute itself in the background. Argus was now in an oblique orbit around Io: not quite the polar one they'd wanted, but it was enough to capture most of the moon in exquisite detail. Two hours to wait for a better image – at a two-metre resolution, they were going to be able to pick out something car-sized, let alone the heft of a pyramid.

'The conclusion of our experts,' Mariucci said, gesturing in the direction of both Velter and Spinu, 'is that there is little room for doubt here. Either, a natural formation of high contrast and regular shape has somehow been created by Io's own internal processes – in which case, we will see several of them as Argus continues its mission – or this is a unique feature of unknown origin, and given its association with the signals and its exact position on the antijove, I have no choice but to entertain the working hypothesis that this is an artificial construct.'

His words lingered in the air, and they individually digested them. Some found them more palatable than others. One in particular choked on them.

'Benjamin, when you're ready, what else can you tell us about it?'

Velter gripped the sides of his display. He was clearly having problems, and Mariucci's gaze flicked to Kattenbeck, to see if she thought he might need medication on top of reassurance. She was squinting across Command, but she hadn't moved yet.

'Valeria,' said Mariucci, 'what about you? How does this compare with other structures we might see from orbit?'

She took a while to answer, but the impact of the image was such that any residual antipathy she might have felt to both him and Blasco was now very much a secondary issue.

'The image is raw – simply the colours and brightness that the camera collects – but the data inside the image is more than what we initially see. Because the average pixels across the whole image are bright, the target, anomaly, pyramid, structure, whatever you want to call it, being dark, will have all of the luminosity values compressed. If we alter the response of the curve to stretch those out, we lose detail at the top end in order to gain it at the other.'

Graphs, histograms, sinuous curves on an x-y plot flicked across the screen on top of the image, and she moved sliders this way and that until she was satisfied, and she brought the image back to the fore again.

Abruptly, there was more contrast, more texture, over the hundred or so pixels. In the centre of the square was another square, a mid grey that extended outwards to some half the distance to the edge. The outer half seemed banded, alternate light and dark stripes running parallel to the edges. Then there was something else, initially hidden within the shadow, but extending from the west side. A line of grey, with a wedge of darkness that abutted the structure.

'This … this piece here,' said Mariucci. 'It seems to terminate inside the object?'

'If the sides are sloped,' said Spinu, 'then it'll rest on them. It starts from the plain, and rises at a lower angle until it intersects.'

Mariucci turned his head, to try and make the crater illusion go away. 'A ramp? Is that a ramp?'

'It could be interpreted as a ramp,' she said.

'This is ridiculous,' said Forsyth. 'Listen to yourselves. Have you all lost your minds?'

Everyone else winced, if not out of sympathy, then out of self-recognition.

'This is scientific investigation,' said Mariucci. 'We have found something that requires—'

'This is a travesty of the idea, man. You're all just sitting around in this circle, right here in a spaceship, egging each other on to come up with the most preposterous conclusion. This isn't an investigation, this is a collusion.'

'—something that requires an explanation. This is not your field of expertise. Neither is it mine. It is Benjamin's and Valeria's. I intend to learn from them, probe their assumptions and their results, and then make recommendations based on those expert opinions.'

'It is axiomatically false. There are no artificial structures on Io, because nothing could have made them in situ or transported them there. Therefore we have to conclude that whatever this is, is either a flaw in the imager we have to repair, or it's natural and we must seek an explanation from that realm.'

Meanwhile, Velter had been furiously scribbling using a stylus and a scratch pad on the computer. He slid his drawing across the image, so that it sat as a layer over it. He'd drawn outlines on the structure: defining its boundary, marking out the extent of the ramp, and then inner lines to mark the contrasts.

Then – it was suddenly revealed that he had talent as a technical draughtsman – another picture in an isometric projection. What he'd drawn in top-down plan view was now in perspective.

It was a stepped pyramid. A tall first level, and five successively smaller storeys on top of that. But there was also a structure on top, another building, cubic in shape, so that the overall profile showed it was as tall as it was wide as it was deep. And then there was the ramp – a simple slope that started twice the distance away and rose up half as far.

'That's the stupidest pyramid I've seen,' said Forsyth.

'It's a ziggurat,' corrected Borner. 'It's a ziggurat, from Iraq.'

'It's clearly not from Iraq if it's on Io. It's no more than a flight of fancy. It's not real. It doesn't exist.'

'Of course it exists! It's literally right there.'

Mariucci held out his hand in front of Forsyth. 'Rory, please. No one here will lecture you about high energy physics. Show the same courtesy to the remote sensing expert and planetary geologist.'

'I would do if they weren't so clearly insane.'

'Enough.' And it was true. He'd had enough of the man. It wasn't every day a mere engineer got the opportunity to tell the Lucasian Professor of Mathematics to shut up, but he took his chance. 'If you have nothing of your own to contribute, then just listen.' He took a breath, and then: 'Yasmin. What do you know about ziggurats in Iraq?'

She looked at Forsyth, perhaps wondering if he was going to interrupt her.

'Yasmin?'

Then she shook herself. 'My grandparents on my mother's side are Iraqi. Were Iraqi. They told me stories of Babylon, how it was the first and greatest city in the whole world, how I should be proud of my heritage, my people.' She shrugged. 'They were just stories. There was never any hope of going home like they wanted, and then there wasn't even a home to go to, given it's now only a name on a map. But I also knew they weren't just stories. I had a picture book they gave me – the words were in Arabic, so I didn't understand them then, but it was about the early history of the region, the kings and the empires and the buildings. There was one picture that was not exactly like that, but it's similar. Weirdly similar.'

'A bloody children's book? You're right: it is enough. Enough to get you all certified.' Forsyth struggled to unclip himself in his fury. 'Don't you dare tell Earth anything about this. Don't you dare. This mission is hanging by a thread as it is. If you want to convince them that we ought to run back with our tail between our legs, then show them this. Children's book indeed. I outgrew them before I stopped being a child, but some of you seem to have kept hold of them long after you became adults.'

He finally managed the buckle and popped up like a cork to the ceiling. This time, he remembered not to put his hand out, instead clattering it with his back, and he still put his other hand over his wrist to make sure he hadn't done the healing ligaments any damage. He recovered his composure, and pushed his way to the axis.

How would he react when Mariucci told him the mission was aborted? He supposed he'd have to deal with that when the moment came. But already his determination, his absolute insistence that they couldn't spend any longer around Jupiter, was wavering in the face of the shared, intense curiosity of the rest of the crew. There was a pyramid – a ziggurat – on Io.

Now that Forsyth had gone, there was – not quite a sigh of relief – a lightening of the atmosphere, and a sense that Command had now become a place of serious discussion rather than acrimony and accusations.

Tsoltos turned his head from axis to pit. 'He's right in one respect: this is indeed ridiculous. No matter that we're following where the data leads, it's a very surprising finding. First the signals, and now this. Normally, when we make discoveries, we have a sense of satisfaction, that our world is more explicable than it was before. This structure? We all know that it shouldn't be there: neither have we an explanation as to how it got there. What does this leave us with? Foreboding. Unease. Awe.'

'But it is there,' said Spinu.

'Oh, it's there. Look, there is the proof. In an hour and a half,' he said, glancing at the clock, 'we'll take another picture of it, from a lower altitude and better resolution. It will most likely confirm our initial findings, and reveal detail that's currently hidden. But that doesn't address the central question: what do we do?'

'We have to tell Earth?' said Borner. 'It's unthinkable that we don't.'

'Let's think the unthinkable, then.' Tsoltos stretched his hefty legs out in front of him, and his ankles crackled. 'What would their response be to such a, a revelation?'

'They'd want to put together a mission to land, to investigate: the things that we can't do.'

Aasen tapped Mariucci on the shoulder, mouthed 'I have to go', and started to slip away. Mariucci caught her sleeve.

'You should stay. It's important.'

'So is the ship. We're deep in the radiation belt, and I've got to keep on top of my list. If something goes wrong that I could have fixed—'

Reluctantly, he let her go, and returned to the conversation.

'Yes,' Tsoltos was saying. 'But is that wise?'

'We can't decide for the whole of humanity.' Borner was frowning. 'That's ...'

'Hubris? Hubris was coming here in the first place. What if Columbus had kept the Americas a secret? What if Cook had sailed past Australia? We have already accepted hubris. Embraced it.'

'Even if we're the last people here, someone will find out about this, that we knew about this. We can't keep this from Earth, Stan.'

'My point is that we're the first, and so far only, people to

142

know about this. It's our discovery. We can do what we like with it.'

'What if it's a trap?' said Velter. In Forsyth's absence, he'd regained some composure.

'A trap?' Mariucci felt the need to stretch. He'd been sitting tense for too long. 'A technological trap?'

'Sure,' said Blasco. 'If we're thinking the unthinkable, then a scenario where aliens leave a beacon on a distant planet that's hidden well enough to be discoverable only by a spacefaring race, which then triggers a catastrophe and wipes us all out, or an invasion, or whatever? It's a standard science fiction trope. Bring it on, I say. By the time they get to us, we'll have crashed back into the Iron Age anyhow.'

'And is that your considered opinion, Theresa?'

'Go out with a bang instead of a whimper? Why not? Humanity will never recover from climate change. We've used all the easy-to-get-at resources, the coal, the oil, the iron and the copper. We've wiped out vast numbers of species, poisoned the land and the sea, and all our descendants can look forward to is war without end over what's left, while they die of diseases we could once cure with a pill. However the aliens do it to us – von Neumann machines, relativistic kinetic kill vehicle, drop a block of neutronium on us – it'll be faster and cause less suffering.'

'Humanity will come back,' said Colvin.

'Something might, in a few hundred million years, but I guarantee you they won't look like us.'

'This isn't answering Benjamin's question,' said Mariucci.

'If it's a trap,' said Blasco, 'then as well as being the first people to find it, we might be the last people who could ever trigger it.'

Colvin squeezed her hands together between her knees. 'ESA aren't the only organisation capable of putting something in Jupiter orbit.'

'At the moment. Everyone, everything is pulling back. Stan's right. This is ours. Our responsibility.' Blasco sounded like she relished the challenge. 'We should press the button.'

'We can't. We're not equipped to do that,' said Mariucci. 'Anyone else?'

'The ziggurats were temples,' said Borner. 'What if it's a temple, and the signals are a call to prayer?'

'An interesting observation. Church bells or a muezzin have not only called the faithful, they've kept time. And these signals seem to do precisely that: they record the passage of time. Who were they a temple to, Yasmin?'

'I don't know. Pre-Islamic deities. Whoever the Babylonians worshipped.' She demurred. 'I never asked, and I don't know even if my grandparents knew either.'

Spinu shifted in her seat, and Mariucci guessed what she was going to say.

'It's a temple to Jupiter. The king of the planets was always the king of the gods. We have nothing to fear from it: it's no more a trap than St Peter's or the Kaaba.'

'If it's considered holy ground, then there may be a price for violating it,' said Tsoltos.

'No, no,' said Spinu quickly. 'Not if ... we were respectful.'

She hadn't said 'if we were believers'. But it was what she meant.

'Petra, you're very quiet,' said Mariucci.

'Don't you find all this terrifying?' She sounded annoyed, angry almost, that no one shared her visceral reaction. 'We've pretty much confirmed the existence of an extraterrestrial civilisation that preceded ours, with still-working technology, and we're sitting around talking as if this were just another day in the office. It's not. It's absolutely not.'

'You think fear should be our response?' asked Tsoltos.

'Yes. God yes. Someone – something – that could put not one but four structures, assuming that there are similar ones under the ice on Europa and Ganymede, out here, three thousand years ago? If they're still around, they could crush us like ants. The only reasonable response is to hide.'

Mariucci recalled that someone had made a convincing argument earlier that any three-thousand-year-old spacefaring civilisation would be everywhere by now. 'If there was anything to hide from, they would already have found us. What if these are like the pyramids, or Stonehenge, or ...' There was another place he was going to mention. It was relevant, and he couldn't remember its name.

'Historical monuments don't broadcast timing data.' Kattenbeck huddled in on herself. 'If the people who built it are long gone, then why is it still working? We should come back in another three thousand years and see if the signals have stopped. Then, and only then, would it be safe to investigate.'

'We don't have three thousand years,' said Spinu. 'We don't even have three. You know what's coming. We need to find out as much as we can, now.'

'Something always goes wrong.' Kattenbeck dragged her fingers across her hair. 'I can't decide whether to make it Earth's problem, or just not tell them.'

'We're not equipped to investigate further,' reiterated Mariucci. 'The Aphrodite doesn't have the tools. We can look – for a limited period – but that's all.'

'This is going to be our only opportunity,' said Spinu. She was now the one getting agitated. 'This is it. We have to go further. We'll never be forgiven if we don't.'

Velter intervened. 'The surface of Io is a radioactive wasteland. None of our instruments would survive five minutes there. Argus is already degrading, and if we're still getting useful data from it in a month, it'll have exceeded all expectations. Valeria, there's no further that we can go.'

'You don't want to do it because you're scared.'

'Yes, yes I am. Petra's right. It's common sense to be frightened by this.'

Mariucci sensed they'd talked it out. They needed to come to some sort of conclusion.

'Stan, you asked the question, what do we do? What do you think we should do?'

Tsoltos ruminated for a while. 'I think we must investigate with all the tools we have. We have been presented with this unique opportunity, and we should seize it with both hands. Our humanity, our curiosity, demands it.'

'But Rory will never agree to it,' said Spinu, and Borner nodded.

'He's ideologically opposed to the whole idea, and I don't know how we'd talk him round from that. Luca, you can't let him veto this.'

They didn't know that Mariucci had already decided to leave, and he was going to disappoint his crew, one way or the other. He worried at his tongue with his teeth. They were eager, they wanted the best for humanity, and they had a good argument. Was there a way out of this? How long could he leave his announcement?

'Luca?' said Kattenbeck pointedly. She was expecting him to tell them now.

Tsoltos spoke into the gap. 'What if we ask Rory what evidence he would accept?'

'He won't agree to anything,' said Spinu.

'Then we'd know not to give any weight to his objections.' He leaned forward. 'But Rory knows that. This will force him to set out his preconditions, which we'll then hold him to. Whatever they are, we'll meet them. Personally? I don't think we should leave here without the proof of this. This is our moment. We can make history.'

That seemed to settle the matter for now, and Mariucci said nothing against it. All he could manage was a nod.

Kattenbeck was stone-faced. She shook her head and unclipped. She headed for the axis without once meeting Mariucci's gaze.

12

Pompeii. It was an iconic archaeological site, one of his country's most famous places. And he'd forgotten its name.

'It's not my short-term memory that's going,' said Mariucci. 'It's the long-term. The deep memories that I shouldn't ever lose.'

'You didn't tell them, Luca.' Kattenbeck looked down at her tablet for a moment, then brought her head back up. 'You didn't tell them you'd already decided to go home, and you let them talk, let them plan for something that'll never happen. Or did you forget that too?'

'Can you run some tests?'

'You're obsessed with tests.'

They were in the wheel, at the kitchen table, where most of their conversations occurred. Mariucci could remember that. But not the name of the family across the corridor in their Florence apartment. They'd been Muslims, second generation on from their refugee parents, and they'd kept their faith and their festivals while speaking Italian like they'd grown from the soil in their dusty back yard.

Rahimi? Rahmani? Maybe it hadn't started with an R at all.

The more he tried to recall, the less he found he could remember. It was as if someone was chipping away at his foundation, and at some point he'd end up unsupported and vulnerable to the next fierce storm. He was distressed by what he might become.

Kattenbeck turned off her screen and tossed it aside. 'I want

147

to talk about why you didn't tell them you were aborting the mission before I get into any discussion about the difference between semantic memory and autobiographic memory. Why didn't you say something? You had the perfect opportunity. Is it because you don't want to take responsibility for that decision? If they're angry with Darmstadt, they're not angry with you? Or is it something else?'

'We have to spend at least another year together. I need everyone to not hate me if we're going to get home alive.'

'The old Luca would have forced us to accept his decision by logic and example.'

'Petra, what I'm trying to tell you is I think that Luca is eroding away, like rust. It's why I want you to do the tests.'

'Honestly, I don't want to do any more tests on you, and I'm pretty certain you don't want to take any. What would it prove? That you're still capable of being captain,' and she raised her eyebrows, 'as much as I'm still capable of being doctor?'

He hadn't asked her for a while, on the assumption that if anything had changed, she would have told him.

'Do you still see them?'

'Yes. Every day now. Almost all the time. I don't know if the higher radiation environment has made it worse, but this perijove has been ... difficult. When we can get back to a polar orbit, then I'll be more comfortable. Perhaps.' She shifted in her chair. 'I see Ove.'

What was left of Mariucci's colour drained from his face.

'Ove killed himself.'

'That's a technicality my subconscious won't allow. I filled him with enough fentanyl to stop him breathing, so I still get his company. At least,' she said, and hesitated before carrying on, 'at least he doesn't complain about his treatment.'

'Oh, Petra.'

'I liked him,' said Kattenbeck. 'His reindeer impersonations.'

'Goose calls.'

'You didn't fail him, Luca, any more than I did.'

'His death made me realise it's already too late,' said Mariucci. 'We should already be on our way home, with a full crew, and that's not going to happen now. A man is dead because of me.'

'No, no: I'm the doctor. If Laszlo hadn't been so ... compromised, then I could have done something about Ove.' She shook her head. 'Because I don't know if Laszlo's ever going to be okay. I tried to bring him to the surface earlier, but he seemed to recognise where he was, and just started moaning and straining against the restraints. Look, I don't mind changing his diapers and treating his bed sores, but I can't keep him unconscious for ten, eleven months, plus however much longer it is we stay out here. The drugs I'm using, the feeding regime, the hydration: he'll die before we reach Earth unless we bite the bullet and try and treat whatever it is that's making him ill. And I don't know what that is. I don't think Stan does, either. Sure, it's a psychotic episode, but that doesn't mean shit when you're a billion kilometres away from help.'

As they were talking, the lights flickered. They grew momentarily brighter, then when they dulled again, it seemed strangely dark.

'Should they do that?' she asked. 'Because they've been doing that for a couple of days now.'

'The radiation alarms are working, we've proved that. It's ... flux from the plasma, and the shield isn't quite fast enough to compensate completely?'

'It suddenly occurs to me that one of us needs to take over the nuclear medicine side of Laszlo's work. Our dosimeters are due to be recalibrated against the standard.'

'Is it something you can do, with help?'

'I'll look into it. Honestly, Luca: a lot of my time is now taken up with nursing. That's what I need help with. We should have had sleep tanks.'

'That lack is something I've already regretted. They didn't really work, though, did they?'

'They worked well enough, and now they're better. The

side-effects of prolonged tank-sleep is, as we're discovering, less worse than the side-effects of whatever we're going through, and if nothing else, it'd keep a patient stable for long enough to get them home.' Kattenbeck put her hand over her mouth and stifled a yawn. 'We've moved a long way from your, what shall we call it, cowardice?'

It was Mariucci's turn to look uncomfortable.

'You're allowed to change your mind, Luca. But I don't think you have, have you?'

'I've asked Benjamin and Valeria to compile a report, as comprehensive as they can make it.' Mariucci pulled a face. 'As objective as they can make it. I'll send it to Earth. And we'll follow.'

'Will we?' she asked.

The lights brightened and dimmed again. They both looked up.

'Or it's shield-induced currents,' said Mariucci. 'I'll look at Hanne's list.'

'We should steer out of the belt.'

'We are. We should be out of the highest energy zone by now. I might even have to talk to Rory about this.'

And again.

Mariucci slid his chair back and stood up. 'I need to find out what this is.'

'Alarms haven't gone off, Luca. It looks scary, but it's probably not.'

'Captain to Command. Captain to Command.'

'Well, maybe it is.' Kattenbeck waved him away.

Mariucci quickly climbed the ladder and pushed his way into the axis. The ship seemed as solid and as stable as it had been throughout the entire voyage. Flickering lights were nothing, temporary and insignificant.

He entered Command and Borner pointed him into his seat.

'There's a message from Earth. For you only,' she said.

The last one like that had told him that the ice shelf that

held back half the Antarctic glaciers had collapsed. What was it now?

'I'll listen to it here,' he said. 'Can you page Hanne up here too? There's something odd going on with the lighting circuits in the wheel.'

He dropped into his chair and strapped in, fiddling behind his screen for the headset and microphone combination that he'd not used much at all. The ship was a quiet one: no roaring chemical rockets to drown out the spoken word.

He linked them to the console, and Borner ported him the message. It was openable only with his private password, like the Ross announcement. He felt his stomach tighten.

The message had been received by the Jupiter L4 relay, then sent on. Despite the error checking, the opening screen – the ESA logo, plain, two-dimensional and static – was blocky and strangely coloured, as if mosaic tilers had had a limited palette to work with.

But there was no mistaking the director general herself. Mariucci had usually dealt with the head of Robotic and Human Exploration. But this was the big boss. There was no one higher, and if she was telling him to do something, he'd already run out of appeals.

'Captain Mariucci,' she started. Her voice was very compressed – little top-range or bass, all in the squashed middle – and it made her sound like a child's impression of a computer voice. 'It is my solemn and unwelcome duty to make the following announcement. At a meeting earlier today of the ten members of the directorate, it was unanimously and reluctantly agreed that, in addition to the indefinite suspension of all future ESA missions outside of cis-lunar space, all current ESA missions outside of cis-lunar are to be immediately recalled.'

She tried to look solemn. What she looked was heart-broken. 'I'm sorry, Luca. To have waited so long, to have gone all that way, to have suffered so much loss, only to be ordered back before you're finished. This was supposed to be the start of something glorious. Instead, it looks like the end. Hopefully, this is temporary, and we'll have another opportunity in the future. But for now, we need to concentrate on us.'

She glanced down. She would have had notes, but Mariucci had rather assumed they'd be on a screen somewhere on the desk ahead of her, not written ones in her lap.

Whatever she had there, she chose to ignore. She fixed the camera with her unblinking gaze.

'The Aphrodite is to set a course for cis-lunar as soon as practically possible: ESOC will liaise with your navigator. Confirmation of the receipt of this message and the acknowledgement of its contents is required.' She leaned slightly forward. 'Come home, Luca. Come home.'

ESA logo. End of transmission.

He went to code in a receipt straight away, but he pulled his hands back from the keyboard and clasped them in his lap instead.

This was it. He was out of time and excuses. He'd known it was coming, and he'd not made the call himself because, well, Kattenbeck was right. Someone else had had to do it for him. By the time they parked at lunar L2, he'd have several lifetimes of radiation exposure recorded against him, and unless there was a miraculous repair in his memory, he'd fail the deep cognitive tests. They might find him a desk job because he was a hero for saving Earth from a killer asteroid. They might just want him out of the way because he was a reminder of when they'd dreamed larger and further.

He reached forward again to type, and withdrew again. He clenched his jaw: he knew what he should do, what his duty was to the people who'd sent him, but he also had a duty to the people he served with. His first duty lay there. He needed to talk to them before replying to ESA. He owed them that much. He thumbed the intercom.

'Flight crew to Command. Flight crew to Command.'

And he waited.

Colvin was in first, then Blasco, and the inevitable wait for Aasen while she finished up whatever it was she was doing elsewhere in the ship. It was clear he wouldn't say anything until they were all present, so navigator and pilot spent the time checking their course, and the telemetry on Argus.

Aasen eventually appeared, apologising as usual, and Mariucci turned from his screen, which was still showing the ESA logo, so maybe they knew what was coming, and maybe they didn't. He looked each one of them in the eye, much as the Director General had over all those hundreds of millions of kilometres.

'I've just had a message,' he said.

'Darmstadt?' asked Blasco.

'Paris,' he replied, and then they knew. 'We've been recalled with immediate effect.'

Blasco blinked. 'Well. Isn't that just perfect? Can we ask why?'

'You can ask,' said Mariucci. 'But they didn't give a reason. Everything beyond cis-lunar is cancelled, and that includes us.'

'It's that Vi, isn't it?'

'If the Ross ice shelf hadn't just fallen apart, I suppose whatever Catherine Vi said could have been resisted. But we're not arguing with her. We're arguing with a decade of fifty-degree summers across most of the southern and northern subtropical regions.' Mariucci shrugged slowly. 'The order came from the very top.'

'So you want me to prioritise Nimbus capture and transfer to cis-lunar,' said Colvin.

'Yes. The message explicitly said that they wanted to check the course.'

'They don't trust me?'

'It's more a question of they're aware of the impaired dynamic on the ship.' Again, he shrugged. 'They've taken the decision away from us, and told us what to do. The orders we have are clear and precise. We go home.'

'You need to tell them about the ziggurat,' said Borner. 'You need to tell them now. They'll change their minds.'

'We've been ordered home.' And still he couldn't bring himself to say it, to say he agreed with ESA, that he didn't want madame director changing her mind, that he needed to get as many of them as were left back to Earth and only that would give him any comfort.

'Luca, if they don't know about the signals, then they can't factor it in. This is the biggest thing ever to happen to the human race.'

'The destruction of our current civilisation is probably of more immediate concern to them right now. Whatever we say.'

'You've seen the pictures. The clarity. The resolution. The … everything about it. Tell them, Luca. Tell them.'

Mariucci equivocated. 'We will. When the report's ready, we'll send it. But we've still been ordered home.'

'You're the captain. You can make them review their decision.'

'I need to keep order, Yasmin. The chain of command—'

'You've seen it.' She turned back to her screen and brought up the last, best image of the enigmatic structure on the surface of Io, and ported it in front of Mariucci's ESA picture. 'You can't say that it's not real, and it's not of such world-changing importance that Earth ought to know about it.'

He looked at it. The image was raw and unprocessed, but still startling and ominous. Why did it appear so dark, when the surrounding ground was variations of acid, sulphurous yellow? Did that speak of a short relative age compared with the rest of the landscape, or was it an artefact of the camera? Even then, there should be three thousand years of sputtering with sulphur-rich compounds coating the dark stone.

And because it looked so out-of-place, it was much easier to doubt it was even there. The pyramids of Egypt were constructed of blocks of stone cut from the surrounding plateau. The temples of Mesoamerica likewise, before they were consumed by the jungle that grew up around them. This, this thing had all the appearance of something new, or worse, something still cared for.

Moreover, it looked far too much like Velter's initial drawing, the one that reminded Borner so much of her picture book. It was as if the builders had taken his sketch as a plan, rather than the scientist merely mapping what was physically there. Could the images be doctored, filtered and altered in such a way as to fool not just him, but all the experts amongst the crew?

Then there was another warning too. What if they were simply not ready for this? Too immature, too broken? As a scientific community, they'd decided not to violate the sanctity of Europa, for the Europans' sake. They should put Io out of bounds too: for their own safety, not the builders'.

'I concede all those points, Yasmin. But I can't act outside of the authority I've been given.' He pressed the tips of his fingers together. 'This is about an explicit order for us to return to Earth, regardless of our discoveries. I need to know that you're all with me on this.'

Aasen, silent until now, simply said: 'You're the captain. I'll do what you say. It's been like that since I started on the rigs, and there's no reason to stop now.'

And for all her problems, he took a moment to be profoundly grateful for her easy, uncomplicated assent.

Colvin looked specifically at Blasco, and waited for her to answer.

'It's an order,' said Blasco. 'We can call it only one of two ways. I don't have to like it. I can disagree with it as much as I want. But if you say it's come from the top, then I don't see how we have much of a choice. I'm with Yasmin, though: you should tell Earth now. We're still going to be in Jovian space for at least another couple of months, long enough for them to tell us to get back to work.'

'Valeria and Benjamin's report will be ready in a week,' said Mariucci. 'But we need to act on our orders today.'

Colvin spent a few moments looking at the screen behind

155

Mariucci before speaking. 'Yes, you should tell Earth. But yes, you're the captain. I suppose I'll start plotting those courses.'

That wasn't the ringing endorsement he'd wanted but, in the circumstances, it would have to do. He looked to his own screen, at the ziggurat, and he wondered if it would kill them in the end, no matter what they did now.

'Yes, if you could,' he said. 'Show them to me, and I'll show them to Earth, but we don't wait for their confirmation. You have my permission to alter our course whenever you need.'

Borner – he knew she was going to dissent – chose her words carefully, but they were no less cutting for that. 'It's an order based on inaccurate information. You're undermining their ability to make an informed decision, and that's just wrong. You wouldn't want us keeping things from you, so why would you do that to ESA?'

'I don't disagree with you,' he said. 'But we have an order to return to Earth, a political decision that has nothing to do with our scientific mission. I don't know what we've discovered already. I don't know what we would discover if we were allowed to continue our mission profile. All I know is that the directors have taken all that into account, and we've been ordered home. On that basis, are you with me?'

'Tell them, Luca. Show them the images, the analysis. We have to stay here ...' She visibly struggled with the idea of just leaving without investigating further. She'd cracked the signals' code, and she was invested in this discovery like no one else.

'We can't do any more than what we've already done, Yasmin,' said Aasen gently. 'We just can't. This wasn't our mission. It still isn't.'

'We won't be coming back. I won't be coming back.'

'I know it's disappointing. What else can we do? They've called us home.'

Borner let out a strangled cry, somewhere been a growl and a grunt. 'I don't want to leave this.'

Mariucci didn't take that as her final word. He stayed quiet, and waited for her to fold.

The silence stretched on, until finally she did.

'You still need to tell Earth. But yes, yes. I'll follow orders. What other choice do I have?'

13

Mariucci read over the draft report from Velter and Spinu, making notes. It hadn't taken a week. It had barely taken a day. Despite the speed of its construction, it was comprehensive in its scope, and detailed enough to satisfy certainly him. It also clearly had had input from Borner, because the signals section was almost identical to her presentation to the crew.

It laid out, in measured, unfussy prose, the discovery of the signals, their interpretation, their source, and then the unambiguous appearance of the ziggurat at Io's antijove. Everything was there: the height, the breadth, the depth of it. The most confirmed sceptic ought to be left with nothing but bluster and dudgeon.

Except, the moment the report had been completed, Forsyth had skimmed it in less than a minute and pronounced it 'unmitigated bollocks', 'fanciful nonsense' and 'our very own Brigadoon', which was a reference Mariucci didn't understand, and he wasn't going to press for an explanation either.

The weight of evidence didn't seem to trouble Forsyth. He'd made his mind up, and that was that. Mariucci found that behaviour, for a man who was the senior scientific officer on a spaceship, baffling. Unless it was a symptom, like he had symptoms, like they all had symptoms, except perhaps Tsoltos and Colvin. And even then he wasn't sure. Arrogance wasn't an illness: at least, it wasn't a new one for Forsyth. He'd always had that trait. Now it was his irresistible force against an ancient and immovable object, and neither appeared to be going away.

But it suddenly did.

One minute, Mariucci's tablet was showing closely argued technical language regarding specular and diffuse reflections affecting albedo. The next, it had gone. He did the natural, stupid thing of shaking the device first, but tutted to himself, and tried to reload the report.

The file had gone. And by gone, he discovered, he meant deleted. It was nowhere on the public drive they habitually all used for most things. Files – personal diaries, working notes, game saves – that weren't for sharing were elsewhere, behind passwords, but science tended to be done in the open, where everyone could see it and suggest changes.

That the report had vanished didn't make sense to Mariucci – until he considered who might have done it. He carefully laid his tablet down on the table, and climbed the ladder in search of Forsyth.

He found him immersed in his data. The screens around him showed the wash and gyre of plasma streaming off Io, as atoms of sulphur and oxygen were stripped of their electrons and accelerated away by Jupiter's all-powerful magnetic field. The colours and intensities danced, and Mariucci was struck by how alive they were, how organic. How voice-like.

'Rory?'

'Not now, Luca. Can't you see I'm busy?'

'I'm afraid that yes, it does have to be now. I've,' and he wondered how to frame this, 'come for your advice.'

Forsyth, floating in the middle of his displays, slowly pirouetted around. When he was facing Mariucci, he echoed, 'You want my advice?' and then let himself turn the rest of the way back to his screens.

'You're the senior scientific officer on the Aphrodite. I was hoping you might explain why the science I was reading has been removed from the public drive.'

Forsyth came around for a second rotation.

'Perhaps, being very bad science, it had no right to be there. There is such a thing as quality control.'

Mariucci gave in and cut to the chase. 'Did you delete Benjamin and Valeria's report on the Io structure?'

'Yes, of course I did. It was nonsense from start to finish. It was crap. It was,' Forsyth took time to pronounce the word carefully, 'shite.'

'I asked them to collate their findings and present them to me. Whether or not it is cacata is for all of us to decide, not just you.'

'It was my a priori assumption that their findings were not even wrong, so I saved the crew's time by removing it from their consideration. You should be thanking me.'

Mariucci had been saving it for later, but he decided on the spur of the moment to tell him.

'I've had a message from the Director General. They're recalling us. Immediately.'

That stopped Forsyth. He reached out and grabbed hold of the edge of one of the screens, which flashed angrily as high energy particles stormed Argus's detector.

'They can't do that.'

'Whatever you think of them, you know that they can.'

'You'll disobey them, of course.'

Mariucci shook his head, slowly, firmly. 'No. I won't be doing that. We're already laying in courses for Nimbus intercepts on the next perijove.'

'You're lying.'

'You can watch the transmission yourself. I've seen it, and I've communicated the contents to the flight crew. We're agreed that it's a genuine and lawful order, and we can't ignore it.'

'You put ESA up to this. You're scared, and you want to run home, so you sent a message back to Earth pleading with them. They think you're unstable, so of course we have to be recalled.' He snorted. 'You're not the only one who can captain a spaceship.'

160

Mariucci felt himself needled, because there was a grain of truth in Forsyth's volley of accusations. Scared? Yes, but not of the ziggurat. Unstable? As much as everyone else, which on its own was reason enough to abort. But he certainly hadn't done those other things. He'd sat on his fear and he'd hidden his instabilities, for the sake of the mission. They were being pulled back for external reasons, not anything that had happened on the Aphrodite – which considering they'd lost one crew member and another was incapacitated, was a bold, and potentially uncaring position.

Perhaps they'd had other things of greater importance to debate over the last few weeks. Of course they had: the entire future of the organisation and its role, if any, in a spacefaring future. But someone should have been looking out for the Aphrodite.

Probably the captain. Was he the reason why was it all falling apart?

'Either Benjamin or Valeria will have a back-up copy—'

'They will not, because I've deleted those too. Their passwords were easily crackable for someone like me. Editing the images to remove the errors so obviously embedded within them will be next, and redacting the faulty data from the electromagnetic recordings will see to the rest of it.'

'You broke their privacy?'

'I did what I had to do to save the mission, since you clearly weren't up to the job.'

'You haven't saved the mission. If anything, you've deleted the one thing that might have persuaded ESA to let us stay.'

'I have no intention of persuading anyone, Luca. We're staying, and we're finishing our mission, and that is that.'

The arrogance, the privilege, the sheer nerve of the man.

'I have my orders, Rory.'

'I don't care what they're asking you to do. I'm telling you: I'm not ready to go home yet. Just because Earth have caught a cold doesn't mean we have to start sneezing.'

'We have orders.'

'Well, I don't agree with them. We have enough Nimbi in orbit to last us for another year. There are more already launched and on their way. By the time we need them, they'll be here. We can stay out here for as long as we like.'

'This is …' Mariucci struggled for the words he needed. 'This is not our spaceship.'

'If it isn't ours, then who else's? ESA can do nothing to us. They can't take remote control of the ship, and even if they tried, we could simply cut communication with them. They won't want us to die, because that would be terrible PR for them.' Forsyth was warming to his theme. 'Where this spaceship goes and what it does is de facto in the control of the crew. You can talk about loyalty and duty all you like, but my first duty is to my research, and as for my loyalty, it extends only as far as the scientific method, as it would for any right-thinking person of my position.'

Mariucci realised with a shock that he was seriously proposing piracy. Not just piracy, but mutiny.

'That is enough!' He finally raised his voice. 'There will be no more of this. You have violated the computer systems of this ship, you have removed valuable data from it, and you have a very dangerous line of talk. I am responsible to others, and you – you are responsible to me. I am the captain of this vessel. If I say we turn for home, we turn for home. I won't let your irrational behaviour stand between it, and us.'

If there was one thing that he knew would stab at Forsyth's heart, if in fact he had one, it was the accusation that he was being illogical and not following the facts. So he used it, even if he probably shouldn't have.

'How dare you? How dare you! I am the only person on this ship trying to hold back the reputational disaster you'd inflict on us all. Aliens? Pyramids? Some vast and ancient clock? Have you listened to yourself? And you accuse me of irrationality? How … dare you!'

Two men, shouting at each other, getting in each other's faces, spittle flying in straight lines, in a spaceship orbiting Jupiter. Yes, why not, thought Mariucci. Wasn't it always going to come down to this? Except he was the one now defending their discoveries, and the eminent academic was denying them.

'Yes, Rory, I have listened to myself. I have also listened to others, which is something that you have forgotten how to do. They have hard evidence for their views. What do you have? Nothing but dogma. Blinkered, misguided faith.'

Forsyth telegraphed his first slap, because he was unused to physical contact, let alone combat. He'd spent so long inhabiting the furthest reaches of his mind that he'd almost forgotten he had a body and how to properly control it.

It meant that Mariucci was able – late, because he was as surprised as Forsyth – to block the arc of the arm with his own. It was a long time since he'd fought anyone with his fists either, but at least he'd grown out of it rather than never having done it at all. His hand instinctively clenched and he jabbed out before the transfer of momentum pushed them apart.

It was a weak blow, off target, glancing against Forsyth's cheek rather than landing squarely on his nose. They spun away from each other. All that mattered now was who was going to find a hard surface first, so they could reorient themselves and launch at the other.

Except that as Mariucci flipped over and braced his legs against the bulkhead, gaze encompassing the module, its equipment, the angles and trajectories he needed to attain, he saw that Forsyth was holding his hand over his face and spinning uncontrollably towards the back wall. He was as inept at zero gravity manoeuvres as he was when he'd sprained his wrist.

Forsyth clattered into the wall. The plastic panels warped and popped, and he bounced back out again, flailing his arms. He looked ridiculous, and all Mariucci could do was laugh.

Kattenbeck, attracted by the noise, ventured her head into

the module. She looped her arm around Mariucci's ankle and held him there.

'What are you arschlöcher doing?' She watched Forsyth slowly spin back: he realised he was close to another wall, and he snatched at a grab rail. 'Luca? Rory? Have you been fighting?'

'He hit me,' said Forsyth. 'He actually hit me.'

He showed his cheek to her, but there wasn't even a mark.

'Luca?'

'I'm not even going to dignify this with an explanation. You know what happened, Rory. And now I'm going to have to write all of that down. Do you want to explain to Benjamin and Valeria where their report went, or shall I?' He was still making a fist with his right hand, and he deliberately straightened it out. 'On second thoughts, I'll do it now. That way, I'll know it's done.'

'What?' asked Kattenbeck. 'What's all this about? Will someone tell me what this is about?'

She still had hold of Mariucci's leg, which now looked awkward. She let go, and he dipped down to her in the doorway.

'I'm more than happy to explain, but I'll wait until everybody's here.'

'You're behaving like children.'

'He started it,' said Mariucci, baring his teeth briefly in an ironic grin. But he had to acknowledge that there wouldn't be any going back on that punch. He was certain that Forsyth could hold a grudge until the heat death of the universe, and that there wouldn't be any apology for the unlanded slap either.

He pushed himself towards a screen, and, holding on to its support with one hand, he used the other to swipe Forsyth's data aside. He tapped up the intercom and bent low towards the microphone.

'All crew to module six, science section. Immediately, please.'

His own voice rang through the ship, and when he straightened up, he pushed himself away and back towards a wall.

Forsyth was eminently unsuited for this mission. He hadn't

even been first choice. There'd been another candidate slated, though for the moment Mariucci couldn't remember their name. They'd stood down after the launch delay following KU2, and Forsyth had – Mariucci supposed in his mind that he'd saved the day – stepped seamlessly into the vacancy. But perhaps he'd always wanted the position. Perhaps he'd put pressure on the other person. Perhaps he'd engineered a coup. That there was a time when Forsyth hadn't been on the crew roster was conveniently forgotten.

But this was it. He was going to announce to the whole crew that they'd been ordered to turn back, and that there was no way out. Undoubtedly, voices were going to get raised, but hopefully not fists this time.

Spinu came in, with Velter behind her. They had the least distance to come. Mariucci tried to judge Forsyth's reaction, but of course he didn't think he'd done anything wrong, so wasn't abashed in the slightest.

The two scientists looked confused as to why they were meeting precisely there, rather than in the wheel, or in Command, as did Colvin and Borner when they arrived.

'Argus is starting to fail,' said Borner, baldly, when she'd caught his eye. 'Core control functions are running at fifty per cent speed. It's going to take longer and longer to get data back, and at some point – another five, ten orbits – we're not going to get anything other than basic telemetry, which will occupy the entire bandwidth at that point. We can prioritise individual experiments, but we're going to have to shut others down soon. The onboard memory buffer has already run out of room.'

'We'll have to do what we can,' said Mariucci. He was aware of his audience. 'Do we have coverage of Io, specifically enough images of the antijove?'

'Enough for what?' asked Velter.

'Sufficient to allow for further study?'

'Yes.'

'Then if we can shut the camera down, we should do so.' He

looked back at Borner. 'Concentrate on the other instruments.'

'I'll do it when,' she gestured, 'we're done here.' She paused. 'Luca? The shouting, just now?'

'There was a disagreement,' he said. 'We need to resolve it.'

'About going back to Earth?'

Mariucci saw Velter react with surprise, but Spinu seemed frozen. 'About going back to Earth, yes,' he said.

Borner kept digging. 'And telling Earth about the signals, and the ziggurat?'

'That too. But we need to wait for the others before we say anything else.'

Mariucci felt an uncharacteristic unease. What if Forsyth, against every piece of evidence they had, was right? It was impossible, given that all the panoply of science told them the structure was real, the broadcasts were real, and yet, it was simultaneously completely believable that they were just magicking this out of nowhere, a coherent and consensual hallucination.

'What's to discuss?' asked Colvin. 'We can only give our opinion. You're the captain. It's for you to decide.'

'Please, Deirdre. We need to wait.'

'But ESA have pulled us back. What other decision is there to make?'

'We wait,' he repeated. There was an edge in his voice that said yes, he was prepared to shout again. 'Some things are up for discussion, and others are not.'

Blasco arrived, and moments later, Tsoltos. They too were curious as to both the place and the time, but Kattenbeck shook her head and they kept their questions for now.

Mariucci sighed, and swapped hands on his anchor. He was fed up with asking this: 'Has anyone seen Hanne?'

'I'll go,' said Kattenbeck. 'I think she was in fuel.'

Mariucci watched her go. Despite everything, the doctor seemed to be able to function normally, while he felt eroded, abraded. They were two crew members down, with most of the others suffering to some degree or other from a degradation of their faculties. Pointing the Aphrodite back towards Earth should have been the easiest decision of his career. But then there were these objects, alien, ancient: he had to acknowledge that it might be the last chance they had for years, even decades, and possibly for ever, to get so much as close to them. Giving that up was going to be hard for some of them, but give it up they must.

He could hear Kattenbeck arguing – cajoling – Aasen towards the module. He needed her. He needed them both. Kattenbeck guided the engineer through the door, then positioned herself in such a way that Aasen couldn't easily escape again.

14

They were all there, and Mariucci couldn't put it off any longer.

'Firstly,' he said, 'I've received a message from the Director General of ESA, cancelling this mission, and recalling us to cis-lunar as soon as we can expedite it.'

'A politically motivated order that takes no account of the scientific work we're doing,' said Forsyth into the gap before Mariucci could continue. 'I will be ignoring it. So will my scientists.'

Mariucci steadied his nerves. 'I have determined it's a legally constituted order, which we cannot ignore. However—'

'Oh, that's just so much bullshit, Luca. We can be out here until we choose to go back. What are they going to do? Send OSTO agents after us? Your friend Van der Veerden? Vi, for God's sake, and her ecofascist horde?'

What was he going to say? He'd lost his train of thought. Lost, derailed, it didn't matter. His mind was blank for a moment, and he was just staring at the faces staring back at him. The signals, that was it. The signals. He regrouped, and hoped they hadn't noticed.

'We need to decide what to do about Benjamin and Valeria's report on the Io ziggurat.'

'You said you'd send it,' said Borner.

'I cannot send what I don't have. Rory has deleted it, and all the working copies.'

Forsyth became the centre of attention, and he didn't seem

to mind at all. 'I refuse to tell Earth we think we're seeing little green men. It will reduce our credibility to zero.'

'Rory,' said Benjamin, 'we're not saying we've seen little green men.'

'No, and it needs to stay that way.'

'But the ziggurat—'

'There is no such thing. Not on Io, not on Europa, not on Ganymede.'

'But we have images of it.'

'We have images of Io, yes. But whatever surface features are there are entirely natural—'

Borner interrupted, and Forsyth looked momentarily shocked that someone would do that to him. 'The signals. The coding. The clock.'

'Again, whatever you think it is, it isn't.'

'Then how—'

'Whatever it may or may not be, it's not some alien race from beyond the dawn of history marking time using the moons of a planet as their second hand.' Forsyth had regained control. 'Honestly, we're – at least some of us are – scientists. We deal in certainties. Hard data. Not Fortean ephemera and internet conspiracies. If Earth learns about what you think you might have found, everything else is lost. Everything. All our measurements. All our models. All our images. All our interpretations. All of the science, the papers, the conferences, the positions: none of that will ever happen, because we'll be the mission that thought it saw aliens.'

'Rory—'

'I do not want to spend the rest of my professional life in committees and meetings, for God's sake! I absolutely will not countenance saying anything, sharing anything, doing anything, that might make that more likely.'

He'd finished, and his words had hit home. Mariucci looked at the faces of the science team, Spinu and Velter especially, but also Tsoltos and Kattenbeck, and they were thinking furiously.

No matter how much they had invested in the extraterrestrial theory, they all had professions that they'd like to not just continue, but advance in. There was more truth in what Forsyth said than any of them wanted to admit.

But it wasn't just the scientists. It was his own flight crew. What did they want to be remembered for? Going to Jupiter, or going mad? Because that was what it amounted to, and Forsyth had laid that out in a brutally plain manner.

What was left? Mariucci was blindsided by Forsyth's appeal to fear, to self-interest, to selfishness. All that was left was reason and logic, and he felt singularly unequipped to make an argument based on those against a man who'd seemingly guided his entire life by their stars.

Should he try, though? Why couldn't he tell them that he wanted to leave Jovian space for the sake of his sanity and the lives of his crew? Was it because he couldn't acknowledge there was an equally legitimate reason to stay, despite the difficulties they'd faced and would continue to face?

'Benjamin, Valeria, you wrote the report. Do you stand by it?'

Spinu looked at Velter, saw him twist his mouth. And she growled.

'I stand by it,' she said. 'Every word. It's there. It's there and we need to deal with that fact, no matter how inconvenient it might be to some people's careers.'

'It'll certainly end yours,' said Forsyth, and Mariucci held up his hand against him.

Spinu told Forsyth bluntly: 'Just because we don't want it to be there doesn't mean it isn't. We can't pretend that, because it's not honest. Do you remember what it was like when you were a junior researcher, and you got given the least promising work and the data that no one else could be bothered with? And suddenly, you realised that there was a pattern there, a pattern that only you had ever seen? That at that moment, you knew something that no one else had ever realised? That is what we have.' She looked directly at Velter, who couldn't look back. 'You know it, Benjamin. You know it.'

'I stand by it too,' said Borner. 'I didn't want to find the signal. I had no idea where it would lead us or what it would say. It's there. No one has come up with an alternative explanation. The theory stands.'

'No one's come up with an alternative explanation because it doesn't need one,' said Forsyth, but he was interrupted again, this time by Tsoltos.

'Rory, I think it does.'

'What do you know? You're not even a proper scientist.'

Tsoltos paused, and rolled with the blow. 'That might be to my advantage. We have two possible explanations as to how we are seeing what we are seeing, a question which is entirely separate from interpretation. The first is that we are measuring physical data related to actual phenomena. The second is that we are subconsciously imposing patterns on the environment and transmitting them as memes to each other.'

'Pareidolia. I've already said that.'

'But what you have not proposed is a way of proving your criticism.' Tsoltos eased, by degrees, into the centre of the module. 'You have, in fact, resisted all attempts to clarify what evidence you would accept to confirm or falsify the primary theory.'

'For God's sake, man, it doesn't need it. It's patently and obviously wrong.'

'Then it should be straightforward for you to provide a simple test to prove it. That you haven't is an unresolved weakness in your argument, and it's led us to this precise point. Refuting a theory is not the same as rejecting it, and all you're doing currently is rejecting it.'

Mariucci was intrigued to see what Forsyth on the back foot would look like. The psychologist had neatly skewered his position – but this is what Mariucci himself ought to have been doing. He felt dull, leaden by comparison, a bystander in his own court.

'The evidence I would accept is simply this: hard, physical evidence. Anything outside of that is unacceptable.'

'Coming from a man who's spent his life dedicated to a branch of science no one can either see or touch.' Spinu was in quick with her jab. 'I've seen your mathematical constructs. I expect there are half a dozen people on Earth who can even begin to understand them.'

'Half a dozen?' said Forsyth, and he actually seemed to be counting. 'I think that's probably an exaggeration, but never mind. This is entirely different. We're dealing here with the supposition of an actual object. If so, then asking for physical evidence isn't unreasonable.'

'What about the signals?' asked Borner. 'They're not any more or less physical than what you study. Why won't you accept the results – results which came from the same instrument that you're using to collect your data?'

'Because the instruments were designed to measure effects in the megaelectronvolt and over range, not right down the bottom where the chaff is.' Forsyth shrugged theatrically. 'I'm sorry that I have answers that satisfy me but not you. Perhaps you should ask yourselves why that is?'

Velter tried. 'Do you accept the other data from the camera – the volcanoes, the pits, the craters?'

'No, of course not. There's clearly an error with the instrument if it shows artefacts like your pyramid.'

'And the lidar?'

'What about the lidar?'

'If we get an altitude track directly across the ziggurat that gives its profile? The lidar is accurate to two centimetres.'

'If it shows it, then it's unreliable. Really, I don't know why you're having so much difficulty in understanding this.'

'So you reject any evidence that might confirm its presence?'

'Yes. Of course. Since it cannot be there, anything that tells us it is is inherently unreliable. If the camera had picked up pictures of ghosts, then we wouldn't even be having this conversation. We'd be taking the instrument apart to find out where it was malfunctioning.'

Mariucci glanced at Kattenbeck, who seemed sanguine about the analogy.

'It's not malfunctioning,' Aasen was saying. 'I should know.'

'And yet, we have pictures of ghosts.'

'Then we conclude that the ghosts are real.' Aasen glanced down at her tablet, then around at Kattenbeck, who was still guarding the door. 'I don't know what you people usually do, but I think you've got enough evidence here to make a strong case for checking out whatever it is. It's just a shame we can't do that ourselves.'

'This coming from someone who's chasing the whole length of the ship repairing things that probably aren't even broken. You've already discredited your own testimony. I won't hear another word of it.'

They were at an impasse, and Forsyth looked triumphant.

'Very well,' said Mariucci. 'We have no consensus regarding whether to tell Earth about the ziggurat, but enough to acknowledge that we need to secure the existing data against any interference, accidental or otherwise. However, that is incidental to our new orders. Deirdre, implement the plan we discussed previously. Prioritise the Nimbus encounters and confirm your course with Darmstadt. Flight crew will have to assist me on the inventory. The science team are free to continue their studies, but our mission profile is aborted, and we won't be launching any more probes. Apologies.'

'No,' said Forsyth.

'Yes,' said Mariucci. He turned towards the door.

'We have another option.'

'Not obeying orders is not an option, Rory.'

'Of course it is. How do you think anything ever gets done? We will not be running back to Earth because some bureaucrat has folded to political pressure: we're above all that. Who wants to stay? We can decide this now, on a show of hands.'

'No, we cannot.' He turned back to face Forsyth. 'This ship is not a democracy.'

Forsyth had raised his hand already, and seemed not at all disturbed that his was the only one. 'You're relying on people to do what you say because you were appointed captain. There's an expectation that they follow your orders, but if someone else was to offer sufficient inducement to do what that someone else says, then you could be the Lord High Potentate of Space and Time for all the difference it made. A leader gives orders. The led follow them. That's the only definition of a leader that's important.'

'My crew will follow me,' said Mariucci.

'Will they, Luca? You can't force us home if we won't go. I have unfinished work here, and I'm certain the rest of the people here do too. Even you, if you were honest with yourself. But whatever you say now, we'll be finishing the mission profile, and going home when we're ready. The only choice you have to make is where you spend that time.'

Mariucci blinked. 'You're relieved of your duties.'

'Oh, I don't think so.' Forsyth addressed the rest of the crew. 'Here is my proposal. You all know full well that your alien theory is incomplete. What you need is proof, proof that will satisfy me, because if it satisfies me, it'll satisfy anyone who might ever doubt you. Very well. We'll work together to get you this proof. I've calculated – trivially, but I expect Deirdre can confirm my numbers – that if the Aphrodite was in an orbit around Jupiter that matched that of Io, a probe, of which we have two left, would be able to descend to the surface of the moon, with a passenger, and soft land at the antijove. Once there, the astronaut will be able to confirm the existence or otherwise of your damn pyramid.'

'Rory, that's the most ridiculous suggestion I've ever heard,' said Kattenbeck.

'Is it, doctor? It seems to me that everyone else is taking it quite seriously.'

'Even if it was possible, whichever idiot you strapped to the probe would die. Quickly, and horribly. They would literally boil from the inside out.'

'We can ensure they'd last long enough to reach the antijove site. That would be all that mattered.'

'You'd be sending them to their death!'

'Yes, yes, I know that, and so would they. Honestly, Petra, I have actually thought this through.' Forsyth snorted. 'Curie died of radiation poisoning, Roentgen died of cancer, Daghlian, Slotin, Bugorski: people have made sacrifices for the sake of progress. Moreover, people are still prepared to make sacrifices. I'm certain there'd be someone here who would do that to get the proof, and their name would live for ever as one of the martyrs of science. Immortality, in a way.'

'Luca, you can't allow this,' said Kattenbeck.

Mariucci wasn't certain he could stop it, but he was going to try. 'Your proposal is rejected. No ethics committee, no sane human being would entertain it.'

'Well,' said Forsyth, and then he smiled. 'Quite.'

'I will not let you endanger the lives of my crew.'

'Your crew are seemingly endangered already. One is dead, one is incapacitated, and yet you have done little or nothing to protect them. You waited for someone else to give you permission to return home, and even then you prevaricated. I see you, Luca Mariucci. I see your ineffectual compassion and your "we all go home" hankie-wringing. On the other hand, I offer a hard but clear way forward. We accept the risk. We stay, and we explore, and we settle this pyramid business once and for all – that is leadership.' He twisted around so that he could look at each of them in turn. 'Who's with me now?'

No one wanted to be first, but it was clear from the unspoken communication between the members of the crew that someone was going to have to be first.

In the end, it was Blasco. His pilot. His pilot.

'Sorry, Luca. Let's pull the trigger on this thing. If it ends us, it ends us, and we go out with a bang.'

Then Borner, and Spinu, simultaneously.

'We need to know,' said Borner.

'We need to know what's in there,' Spinu elaborated. 'What it's doing there. Who put it there.'

'This is all batshit crazy,' said Aasen. 'You want to kill yourselves and trash the entire ship, drive it into the radiation belt and keep it there? I can't stop you, but neither can I stop any of the electrical and electronic systems from failing. I'm out.'

Colvin was working her jaw. 'Stay,' she said eventually. 'They're right, Luca. We have to stay to find out the truth.'

Then it was Velter's turn.

'You can't expect someone to go down to the surface of Io,' he said. 'You can't. Your plan is ... terrifying.'

'I won't be making anyone do anything they don't want to do, Benjamin. I'll be asking for volunteers. You want to study this further, yes? Are you with me?'

'No,' he gasped. 'No.' And he had to turn away because he couldn't breathe and look at Forsyth.

If they were voting – which they definitely weren't – it was already five to three, and Mariucci's pilot, navigator and comms officer had gone back on their word.

Tsoltos had pressed Forsyth for his conditions: he now had them. If there was to be solid, physical evidence, then one of them would have to go and get it.

He nodded. 'Very well. I accept. We stay, Rory, and you will be convinced.'

Only Kattenbeck was left, and she could count well enough.

'I can't take sides on this,' she said. 'I'm the doctor. I have to be impartial. Yes, absolutely, this is likely to kill us all, and I advise you not to do this because it's reckless to the point of suicidal. But I'm your doctor, and I'm not fighting in your wars.'

That was it. It was done. Mariucci had lost control of the Aphrodite.

'Luca, you're confined to the wheel,' said Forsyth. 'You will undoubtedly have passwords and executive access that I'll need. Aside from that, do what you want, but you don't interfere with the running of my ship from now on. I think we understand each other.'

15

Forsyth made a deliberate point of sitting in the chair habitually occupied by Mariucci. Where he came from, in his world, chairs were important symbols of authority. Not quite thrones, but to be given a 'chair'? You were in charge.

He fastened the lap strap and surveyed Command from there. A good view of the holographic display, and good sight lines to the rest of the seats. Whoever had designed Command had studied Greek architecture: there was more than a little of the odeon about it. He approved.

The others drifted in, and took their usual seats. They all seemed quite stunned at the turn of events, at what they'd said, and more importantly, done. That was because they were easily manipulated, even that oaf Tsoltos, who touted his understanding of the human mind as something esoteric, arcane even, when people were very simple in reality. Offer them what they really wanted, and then give them the job of getting it for themselves.

All he had to do was offer encouragement, rather than any practical help, let alone expend effort on his part. If they succeeded, he took the credit, if they failed, it was their own fault. It was a tactic that had served him well so far. He was a man who appeared to get things done. Those in authority loved him for that, and because of his reputation they swept aside any number of complaints about his behaviour.

He remained completely convinced that there was nothing on Io worth worrying about. Data was sometimes – he was wont to use an unscientific term – haunted. Patterns would emerge and appear genuine, and it was an act of bravery to discard them: he would encourage his students and juniors to strike them down, erase them, and pay them no attention because they were false. They represented a mental dead-end, so why not? So it was with these signals – of course the data was real, but it couldn't mean what Borner thought it did. The images? Yes, there was something there, but not a pyramid, because that was clearly impossible.

Using the existence of that haunted data, though, to get what he wanted? Twice over, too – he both got to stay in Jovian space, and he didn't have to suffer any association with this alien structure nonsense. That was a moment of true genius. Poor Mariucci hadn't known what had hit him. Probably still didn't, sitting in the wheel, wondering where he'd gone wrong.

Where the captain – the old captain – had gone wrong was thinking that Rory Forsyth wouldn't get to do exactly what he wanted. If only Mariucci had understood that from the start, it would have been far less painful for the man. Forsyth might now have to spend some of his valuable time organising the crew, but once they'd been given their orders, they could be left to it and he could return to his own vital work.

Once they'd all assembled – not Mariucci, not Kattenbeck, and not Molnar, and obviously not Hellsten – he looked out at their faces, and wondered what he needed to do to motivate them at this point. He'd return to Molnar later: he wanted to know whether or not the man could be brought back into service at any point, or whether he'd be an unacceptable drain on resources. They'd already euthanised Hellsten, so that threshold had already been crossed. Much easier to do it again than do it the first time.

'We appear to be under new management,' said Forsyth. 'Most unexpected, but in retrospect, it was a perfectly logical progression from where we were to where we are. First things first: we need to consolidate our position. Yasmin, I don't think we need to be bothered with communication with Earth for now – they'll only complain, and it'll be a distraction for us all. Do whatever you need to cut those lines.'

There. Let bloody Darmstadt wonder what had happened to them.

'Deirdre, a new orbit is required, one that matches our course as closely as possible to that of Io, and with as little separation as you can. If we slowly pass the antijove point at a certain radius away – I leave the calculations to you – it should be entirely feasible to use a probe as a lander. Io, being tidally locked, will have zero rotation to us as we pass: all we have to worry about is the distance and the gravity. Obviously, it means we have to transition into an entirely equatorial orbit, which places us inside the radiation belt where it is most intense. Personally, I find that prospect quite invigorating, and I fully expect the Aphrodite to perform to its advertised standard. Any problems, I'm sure Hanne can deal with them.'

Aasen looked as if she was about to say something, so he pre-empted it.

'You have my full authority to do whatever it takes to keep the ship functioning. That's what's important, and I know you'll devote your every waking hour to it. All that's left to do is to decide which of us will go down to Io, and potentially down in history as the first human to confirm the existence of extraterrestrial life.' He deliberately didn't say 'which of you', even though he had no intention whatsoever of applying for the position of sacrificial lamb himself.

He regarded each of them with his dark, serious eyes. Some of them wouldn't meet his gaze – Velter, no he wouldn't, would he? And Colvin, which Forsyth was a little more curious about – but the others certainly did. Even Aasen, but he wouldn't be choosing her. She was far too important.

'There can only be one successful candidate, of course. Anyone wishing for the honour, put your case to me, either in writing or in person, and I'll happily consider it. Deirdre will

180

confirm our ETA and our launch window, which I imagine will be in the region of a week from now, perhaps two. I will choose at an appropriate juncture beforehand, but we can discuss ways to maximise their time on Io, and how we ensure the success of the mission, between ourselves beforehand. All ideas gratefully received.'

Velter looked – continued to look – horrified. Perhaps Forsyth should try and convince him to go down to Io: he was the one who'd 'discovered' the pyramid, and if he stood by his findings, he should have the courage of his convictions. But he'd probably faint on the way down and be too scared to do anything once he'd landed. He'd die not having resolved anything, which was no good at all. They needed to get this nonsense out of the way, and then they could sail Jupiter's magnetic seas to their heart's content. Forsyth's heart, at least.

'Anything to add, Benjamin?' he asked.

'No. No.' Was he going to argue? He wasn't. He lowered his head. 'No. Nothing.'

'Good. We're all in agreement, then. We all have our work to do, so let's be about it. No more delay.'

There, he thought. That was a proper meeting. No cyclical discussions, no interminable waffle. Concise and precise. Everyone knew what they were doing and why, and a clear delegation of responsibilities so that no one would have to come back and bother him with trifling minutiae. He unclipped and headed straight back to his workspace to carry on with his studies.

Here it was, his life's work, the equations he kept on coming back to, laid out on the screens around him. Normally he worked in the abstract, building towering edifices of equations to describe exotic particles that appeared fleetingly, if at all, in the data from vast, slumbering detectors: fully half of his work was so advanced, he was still waiting for the experimentalists to catch up with papers he'd written a decade ago.

But out here, those very particles and their associated

phenomena were all around the ship. Even the notoriously difficult galactic cosmic rays, messages born a hundred million light years away, were being lensed and concentrated by Jupiter's massive magnetic field, just for him.

None of it was theoretical now. It was happening, in real time. Bright flashes of immense energy as the almost-speed-of-light particles ended their long journeys in the seething plasma fields of Jovian space, spalling off fundamental fragments of quantum matter that had never before existed outside of the most powerful machines mankind had made.

But nothing was right until everything was right. There was a relationship, an overarching way of describing the universe, and he'd been chasing it for ever. Yes, he'd already managed to propose one or two tweaks to the Standard Model, but really, they weren't very satisfactory, because he knew in his bones there was still something outside of his understanding, something missing.

That thought consumed him. His pursuit of his goal had made him who he was. It was the greatest quest of the modern age, and despite the many teams of scientists all around the world, he – Rory Forsyth – would be the one to solve it, working alone, in a spaceship, no interference, no distractions.

Immortality certainly. Peace, perhaps. So no: he wouldn't be going home without his theory of everything complete.

If there were aliens, which there weren't, obviously, then perhaps that might have been reason enough for *them* to come here, to use the unique environment around this king of planets, to discover what he was discovering. That was where the real work lay, not grubbing around in the sulphurous dirt of Io.

He was the first here, though. There'd been no one ahead of him, and certainly not thousands of years ago. There were no monument builders, no grey-skinned, large-eyed, big-headed, spindly-limbed child-monsters of popular imagination. Humanity had been first to consciousness in the universe, and he'd been the first to this level of intellect. Yes, he might be standing on the shoulders of giants, but it was he who could see further than anyone else ever had.

In his idle moments, which were few and far between, he had the time to wonder if everything that had gone before, all of history's blood, sweat, toil and tears, had gone into making the world just right so that he could arrive at the most propitious moment of history, to be on the Aphrodite, to forge the new dawn with the hammer of his intellect against the anvil of knowledge.

While it would be lovely to believe that, he knew everything was contingent. Time's arrow owed him no special favours, even if he felt that he was specially favoured.

But still, in his imagination – of course he had an imagination, and all the best scientists considered it their greatest asset – he could see how everything would change after his discovery. His theory, and the technology based on it, would liberate humanity. That luddite Vi would become irrelevant overnight. Energy, abundant and clean, available to all. The ability to repair the damage done to the Earth. Everywhere would become habitable – and more than that, people could thrive again. Quite why everyone thought him a misanthrope escaped him – his theory would be the single greatest boon mankind had ever received. An end to tyrants, to misery, to poverty, to hunger.

And not just on Earth. Where there was matter and energy, there could be people. Planets terraformed. Asteroids hollowed out. Journeys to other stars? Why not? A spacefaring civilisation, numbering not just in the billions, but the trillions, and he would be its architect, the midwife of it all.

Wasn't that worth a little suffering? A slight sacrifice? Hellsten and Molnar had thought so, enough to dedicate the last years of their lives to the Aphrodite. Only Mariucci seemed to not appreciate that, more fool him.

And wouldn't it be glorious to see that future? He never would – he would inevitably age, and sink into senescence.

Could he avoid that? Some, he knew, were actively investing in life-extension treatments – but these were the merely crassly rich, not the most worthy. If there was any justice, it would be the most intelligent who had access to the cure for death, not the most wealthy.

Perhaps a grateful population might want to reward its heroes that way.

His secret smile slipped when he realised he was no longer alone. Who dared disturb him? Hadn't he just had a meeting? Hadn't he given everyone their orders? Shouldn't they all be busy doing whatever it was they ought to have been doing?

It was Tsoltos. What could he possibly want?

'Yes, yes, what is it?'

Tsoltos took that as an invitation to enter the module, when it was nothing of the kind. He pulled himself in and positioned himself against the innermost bulkhead.

'You wanted to know who would be willing to go down to Io.'

'Yes.' There was so much work to do. Forsyth wanted Tsoltos to simply get on with his speech, now he was here.

'I would like to volunteer,' said Tsoltos.

'You would?' That was unexpected. He was thinking it would be between Borner, Spinu and Blasco. Possibly Colvin. He'd certainly be prepared to let either Spinu or Borner go down, and if he could coerce Velter, then he'd be first pick. Losing either their pilot or their navigator would be sub-optimal.

But Tsoltos? What did he actually do, but sit around all day and philosophise as to the nature of the mind, or some other level of woo? How reliable would he be as an observer?

'Go on,' said Forsyth, because the man wasn't going to give up the information without prompting, apparently.

'I've been thinking about the signals, and the structure. On the whole, I believe that they are genuine, and that the measurements we've made so far are of actual artefacts, and not noise. Proving you wrong would be, I feel, a humbling corrective to what I perceive as your unwarranted confidence in your own abilities.'

'You think I'm wrong?'

'I think you're used to being right. You've taken that to mean you are never wrong when, in fact, you take care to expose yourself to only a very limited subset of data that you already know to be correct. This? This is outside of all our experiences. I believe that you've overreached this time.'

'Fascinating,' said Forsyth. 'And this weakness of mine – you spotted that a long time ago, of course.'

'I've been watching you,' said Tsoltos. 'I watch everyone, but especially you, and how you conduct yourself. I see into your mind, Rory: it's not that difficult for someone like me.'

'Someone like you?' He considered that for a moment. 'And what do you see, Konstantinos? What do you see when you look inside my mind?'

'That you hold yourself to be great.'

'Well, I expect that to be true of most people.'

'You'd be wrong. Most people are crippled by doubt, in-securities, fear. They feel unworthy, and their triumph is that sometimes they rise to the challenge. You suffer from none of those things.'

'And why should I? By any lights, I've achieved so much, and I'll carry on in the same vein. This isn't some idle boasting, this is provable fact. Yes, I do see myself as great. Because I am. I don't have a problem with that. False modesty is not just unbecoming, it's unreasonable. It's a waste of everyone's time. But you've taken it on yourself to bring me down a peg or two, to teach me a valuable lesson in humility and remind me of my place in the world, yes?'

There was a pause in Tsoltos's side of the dialogue, long enough to irritate Forsyth.

'Out with it, man!'

'You are not the greatest, Rory. You're not even the greatest on this ship, and I will prove that to you.'

'Will you now?' Forsyth felt his hackles rise, and an un-characteristic heat flush his skin. 'That's a bold claim, given that I joined this mission late, and am now the captain of it.' But as soon as it had come, the feeling had gone, and only cold logic remained. There'd be no acting out of anger again – one sprained wrist was more than enough. 'Thank you for your petition, Konstantinos. I'll consider it along with the others when I receive them. Now, if you don't mind, I'd like to return to my work: after all, it's why we're all here.'

He turned his back on the door, and after a while, he could sense that Tsoltos had gone.

Not the greatest on this ship? Surely the psychologist hadn't meant himself? How utterly preposterous. If he wanted to die on Io attempting to make Forsyth out a liar, then why not let him?

Forsyth brought his hand up to his mouth, and his knuckle found its way into his mouth. He gnawed at it for a moment, before snatching it away. Stupid, childish affectation.

16

It was unfortunate that Molnar had had some sort of psychotic episode that had rendered him effectively catatonic, but Forsyth had challenged Tsoltos to use his much-vaunted powers to get the man on his feet quickly, and working again. It was a challenge that Tsoltos had embraced, against Kattenbeck's wishes, but she'd wisely decided that that particular battle had already been lost.

As it was, Molnar seemed to be making progress. That was good – Forsyth doubted that Kattenbeck would have attempted rehabilitating the man without his urging – and it was a visible sign of his leadership changing the way the ship was run.

Not that his motives were purely altruistic: Molnar was their radiation specialist. The plans to repurpose the probe they'd intended to use for Ganymede, hardening it further against the radiation of Io, and adding hardpoints to attach an astronaut, were coming along nicely, but the mitigation they intended for that astronaut was mired in a slurry of avoidance and blame.

Kattenbeck had pronounced the whole idea nothing short of suicidal, and swore she'd have nothing to do with it. The others on the crew were far less trained in how to survive high-radiation environments. Only Molnar had the required expertise, so it was vital that he was at least awake and talking, even if he couldn't engage in the tasks himself.

It was proving its worth. The probe only needed to last long enough to get from the Aphrodite to Io's antijove, and the astronaut from the landing point to the supposed structure:

long enough to show everyone back on the ship that there was nothing there.

Unspoken, but understood, was that the probe didn't have enough fuel to re-enter Jupiter orbit from the surface of Io. Forsyth himself was genuinely quite surprised that anyone was prepared to actually strap themselves on and endure a one-way trip to such a toxic environment – but it wouldn't be the strangest thing about the mission. If one of them wanted to sacrifice themselves in a hopeless endeavour then it would, at least, shut the rest up.

Tsoltos might have been the first applicant, but he certainly hadn't been the last. Forsyth's predictions that both Spinu and Borner would volunteer were confirmed, but Blasco had stayed out of it. Colvin seemed undecided. He kept wanting Velter to step up, to own his convictions, but the geologist seemed to have worked out a way of avoiding Forsyth altogether.

No matter. Just one candidate would be enough to put an end to the nonsense.

He was going to have to choose who, at some point. It should have been straightforward, but he knew if he picked either Spinu or Tsoltos, there'd be trouble from the other, and if he picked Borner, he'd have trouble from both. Spinu seemed utterly reckless in her approach: hers was a determination to simply be there at the antijove site, almost as if it was a religious duty she had to perform. Very odd indeed. He'd never understood that kind of compulsion.

Oh, he wanted to get back to work, his actual work, the great work that he was going to be remembered for. A few more days and all talk of aliens would be over. The flight crew could steer the ship, and leave him alone. Being captain was all well and good, but he hadn't realised that it took time to do. How was it that normally competent people who ought to be used to just getting on with things without being told, would suddenly appear with an utterly mundane piece of information, as if he needed to be told of it at that instant?

He wanted to ask Mariucci how he'd coped, how he dealt with the constant interruptions, the constant juggling of half a dozen different issues, the balance between this action and that, the sheer strain of always being on duty. How the crew could be so needy.

He didn't though. He realised that it came with the job, no matter how much he wished it didn't. What he needed was some sort of factotum to stand between him and the crew. He was available in Command for at least an hour a day: what more of him could they possibly want?

He was there now, listening to Borner explain that they'd lost contact with Argus: the probe had effectively become both blind and mute, and fallen into a recursive loop of shutting down and rebooting. It would sail on until its solar panels turned into lace, and then the power systems that kept its wholly damaged central core alive would fail. Another month, another week, it didn't really matter. There was no telemetry coming from the probe.

Forsyth clicked his tongue in annoyance, without listening to much of the detail. The data he'd received from the detectors as Argus had spun around Io were invaluable for plotting out the radiation map of Jupiter. The Io torus was alive with energy, and he'd only just started scratching the surface of that region.

No matter. When the Aphrodite was parallel to Io's orbit, the shipborne instruments would be able to take over the task, and that would be soon: Colvin had assured him that they would be alongside Io in another few days. They were between Io and Europa, and breaking obliquely, so that they both orbited in the plane of the inner moons, and faster than Io travelled. They were moving inwards: by the time they and Io coincided, their relative velocity would be almost zero.

He glanced up at the ship's clock. He'd been in Command quite long enough for now, thank you. If anyone had anything else to say to him, he'd be there, same time tomorrow.

Borner was still talking when he unclipped himself and nudged up towards the ceiling.

'Just shut it down if you can,' he said. 'There's nothing more to do with it.'

'We were supposed to send it into Jupiter,' she said. 'COSPAR regulations?'

'According to you, someone's already breached them. And in any event, there's nothing we can do about it now. There's no life down there, nothing to contaminate. When it crashes in a few decades, it'll get recycled into ions like everything else.' Command was empty but for him, her, and Colvin, whose rounded back was now more familiar to him than her face. She was disappearing into the background, and that suited him perfectly well. 'If anything else happens, try and deal with it first before bothering me, please.'

He left them there and pushed through to the axis, where he encountered Aasen, who was just floating motionless in the rotating section. That she was still was unusual, but of no concern to him. He went to move by her when she reached out and unerringly caught the arm of his flight suit, despite having her eyes closed.

'Can you hear that, Rory?' she asked.

'Hear what?' He tried to pull away.

'That sound. That ... sound.' She shushed him when he tried to speak again. 'Listen.'

Realising that he wouldn't get any peace until he'd at least humoured her, he stopped and listened. There were the usual hums and whirrs, the slight opening and closing of the reflections caused by the rotating tunnels. Nothing else. He frowned.

Wait. There was something. A slight hissing noise, rhythmic, swelling and receding.

'What is that?'

'I don't know,' said Aasen. She opened her eyes and let go of Forsyth's arm. 'I just know it shouldn't be there. These couplings are magnetic. There's no friction. No bearings. No contact. It should be completely silent. And yet there's noise.'

'Does it need fixing?' To lose the wheel for a time would be inconvenient, but not impossible to live with.

'That's the other problem.' She shook the tablet attached to her forearm off its cradle and into her hand. 'It's not on the list. If there's a fault, it needs to be on the list. And it's not. So as far as the computer's concerned, there's nothing to fix.'

'But you can hear it.'

'Not on the list.'

'But you can hear it,' he repeated. 'There's something wrong there.'

'It's not on the list of errors I need to fix. If and when it comes up, it'll tell me, and then I'll fix it.'

'The wheel is important to the functioning of the ship.'

'So is everything on the error list, otherwise it wouldn't be there.' She flipped over and braced her feet against the bulkhead, ready to push off down the axis towards the rear. 'I just thought you'd want to know.'

'Hanne, this is preposterous. Why would you do this?'

And she was gone, dabbing her hands against the walls as she moved swiftly away. She left him with the soft susurrus of sound, like breathing. He couldn't now unhear it, and he clenched his jaw in frustration.

Perhaps Aasen should go down to Io. He still had no firm evidence that she was actually doing anything useful. He knew that Mariucci had been going to do an inventory of everything, including the allegedly faulty components stacking up in the workshop, but he hadn't had the opportunity to do so.

Forsyth could tell him to do that. After all, Mariucci was still a member of the crew, and he'd be acting under Forsyth's authority. It was information a captain needed in order to make the correct decisions for the ship, so he wouldn't begrudge him that, surely?

He was already in the rotating section. He dropped down one of the ladders, and stalked the wheel until he found the ex-captain jogging slowly the other way. How many laps had he made? How many more did he have to go?

He looked at Mariucci, and Mariucci slowed to a stop some distance away. He was wearing only a pair of white shorts, no shoes. For a fifty-something man who'd spent a year in space, he seemed lean and fit, used to his body in a way that he didn't see it as either an extravagance or an encumbrance.

'Luca,' said Forsyth.

'Rory.'

'I need to ask you about Hanne. Her work—'

'No,' said Mariucci, and he even waggled his index finger like a gun. 'No.'

'I had hoped—'

'No,' he repeated. 'Just no.'

'You don't even know what I'm—'

'No.' His muscles tightened, as if he was ready to start running again. 'It's your responsibility now. All of this.'

'I require my crew—'

'I required mine, and this is where we are now. They have either actively mutinied, or they have acquiesced to it. I have no obligation to you any more, nor to them.'

'What about to—'

'If you're not going to relinquish command back to me, I see no reason to say anything further.'

'Will you stop in—'

'Do you find it annoying, Rory?' Mariucci spread his arms out wide. 'Everything here is your problem now. You wanted this. You convinced the crew they wanted this too. Everything that happens from now on is down to you. These are your consequences.'

How disappointed did he appear? The hero who saved cis-lunar space, reduced to this, either amusing himself to death on a neutered tablet that would only access the Aphrodite's entertainment library, or running himself ragged around an endless track.

'I should make you regret those words,' said Forsyth.

'You've already done your worst. There's nothing more you can do that will hurt me.'

They stared at each other across the distance, each having to look up slightly because of the curve.

'I don't need to speak to you,' said Forsyth. 'It was more out of courtesy.'

He didn't even feel contempt for the man, just, well: there he was, making the place look untidy, eating the food and breathing the air. At least he hadn't tried to break his quarantine, nor attempted to talk the crew into accepting his orders once more. That would have meant Forsyth having to do something more drastic.

But if Mariucci was afraid of being ushered into an airlock without a spacesuit, then he didn't show it. Forsyth wasn't sure whether the same crew that had voted to depose their captain would also vote to kill him, let alone carry out the sentence themselves. Better, possibly, to leave that unspoken than put it to the test. People were fickle. Squeamish, even.

He tried one last time: 'Hanne has found—'

'No,' said Mariucci firmly. 'I will not discuss this with you. You are in charge now, and I am nothing. Moreover, you'd be a fool to listen to anything I have to say, because you cannot trust me to tell you the truth.'

'Really?' Forsyth thought about that for a moment. 'I had you down as an idiot, but an honest idiot. If it was a question of saving the ship, and its crew, then you'd do what needed to be done. So having already agreed that, I don't understand why you won't work with me now to pre-empt that moment. Peevishness? Revenge? You might see me as that sort of person, but I know you're not.'

'We learn new things about ourselves all the time, Rory. Isn't that what these long voyages are for? Not just discovering what lies beyond the horizon, but discovering what type of people we really are. How's your voyage of discovery going?'

'Mine?' He was in charge of a spaceship, and on the verge of a scientific revolution. 'Very well, thank you. Yours?'

'Enlightening,' said Mariucci. 'And at least now I've plenty of time for introspection. So if you'll excuse me, you have your duties, and I have ... this.' He indicated his spartan athletic form.

'I can make you cooperate with me,' said Forsyth suddenly. 'I can make you do what I want.'

'You can try.'

'You care too much, Luca. It leaves you vulnerable.'

'I have my run to finish.'

'What if I was to offer you the chance to save one of your crew from certain death? To save them from themselves?'

Mariucci rested his hands on his hips and he shook his legs out. The slight sheen to his skin was fading as it cooled. He seemed impatient.

'Yes, I was wondering when this was coming. I take their place on the Io descent, and disprove the presence of the ziggurat, meaning I boil my guts inside my spacesuit and suffer overwhelming neurological damage before dying in agony for nothing, rather than someone else suffering the exact same fate.' He snorted. 'That's what you're suggesting, isn't it?'

'Greater love has no man, and all that,' said Forsyth.

'I would lie to you with my last breath. I'd tell you it's there, and it's real, and it's huge, and it's magnificent, and it's covered in carvings and writing, whether it was there or not.'

'Your camera suit would record everything.'

'I'd turn it off. All you'd have would be my voice, cursing you and praising them.'

'Then we would—'

'Rory, there is nothing you could do to me, my suit, or the probe after it's left here. You could tie me to the probe's hull, like some ... some ...' He waved the lost thought away. 'I would still find a way to subvert you. I would fight you every step of the way, every moment. I know what you want – certainty. But I'll never give it to you.'

Mariucci chopped one hand into the palm of the other, three times in quick succession, then marched past. Forsyth had to dodge to one side to avoid being barged. As soon as the path was clear again, Mariucci restarted his slow, long-strides journey around the wheel.

'Someone will go. Someone will die,' Forsyth called out after him.

'They're not my crew any more,' came the wounded reply. 'They're yours. You deal with it.'

17

The Ganymede probe – the crew named it Aquila, after the eagles who had carried the boy Ganymede to Olympus to wait on Zeus, while Forsyth called it simply Probe Three – was almost ready. Aasen had done her best in interpreting Molnar's instructions, and Borner had helped in reconfiguring the probe's computer to replicate some of the error-checking tasks that Argus had by design. The radiation environment on Ganymede, the only moon of Jupiter that possessed its own magnetic field, was considered tame in comparison with that surrounding Io, but it had local hotspots. And while Forsyth thought it a shame that they would lose that close-quarter data, at least they could try and replicate some of it with the Aphrodite itself.

Or they could use the Callisto probe to go to Ganymede instead. That was always an alternative. He'd decide later.

The roughly hexagonal brick-shape of Aquila had been modified with extra shielding, but most of the changes had been internal. The most visible alteration was the hardpoints, where they would anchor the water bubble.

It was a surprising solution to the problem, but actually followed sound reasoning – Molnar hadn't been raving when he suggested it. Water was an excellent barrier against high energy radiation. The Aphrodite itself stored its own water in spaces between the inner and outer hulls, and specifically in the walls of the wheel. What Molnar proposed was a sealed container of water, inside which the astronaut would float safely until touchdown.

A spacesuit could keep out water, in exactly the same way it kept in air. In the old days, before easy access to space, almost all zero-g training had been done in swimming pools.

Aasen was in the probe bay now: the outer doors were sealed, and Forsyth stood in the axis and watched her work through the open inner door. She had cables draped and flexed over the jambs as she tightened the seals and glued the ports.

He still needed to choose who was going down to Io, but his decision hadn't got any easier to make. His ad hoc attempt to coerce Mariucci had failed. Velter was in hiding, somewhere on the ship: probably because he was afraid of what might happen if he emerged, but Forsyth didn't have the time or the energy to track him down.

It was realistically between Tsoltos and Spinu, and if he could have sent both, he would have done. Such were the constraints on fuel that there was only space for one.

He allowed himself a small grunt of displeasure. Was it worth going back to Mariucci, now that the time had come? Present him with his choice, and ask him if he really wanted them to die, and wouldn't it be the chivalrous action to step in and save them? A far, far better thing that he did now?

The old goat was stubborn, though. He wouldn't budge, even to spite himself. What if Forsyth could find someone on the crew he could use as leverage? Colvin was the obvious answer: she'd served with him on the KU2 mission. If he threatened him with sending her in his stead, how would that work?

It was useless, though. No matter what he threatened, Mariucci had been exactly right: once the probe had been launched, with just him on board, he could do anything he liked, and it wasn't as if they had probes to burn. This one, and one other, and that was it.

Kattenbeck? No. Even if everyone hated her, which they didn't, she was the doctor. They might need her sooner or later. He himself might need her. And her Hippocratic oath seemed solid. She wasn't a threat to him.

Molnar? Too unstable, and he had his uses. Definitely not Aasen, despite everything, despite that damnable hissing in the wheel's hub, despite her increasingly filthy, unwashed form suddenly appearing where she hadn't been asked to be and diving behind a panel to do something inexplicable because the computer told her to do it.

Borner? She was flight crew too, but if they weren't talking to Darmstadt, then her role was reduced to talking to the probes, Laelaps mainly, which was still circling Europa and feeding back reams of data. At some point, he'd need to reactivate the downlink to cis-lunar, to communicate his theory of everything to a grateful planet, and he didn't know how hard that would be. Keep her for now.

Tsoltos or Spinu, Tsoltos or Spinu? Who would be best? Honestly, he didn't know if Tsoltos added anything to the crew. In Forsyth's opinion, Tsoltos wasn't a scientist, and Spinu did at least know her way around the remote sensing packages that collected his data. So, on balance, Tsoltos, but Spinu would then be furious with him. She might refuse to work with him again, which would be difficult and unnecessary.

He watched Aasen move purposefully from task to task, momentarily envying her directed existence. Everything she did, she did because the list on her tablet told her to do it. Whether the computer had generated it, or she'd written it herself, she was enslaved to it. What was more, the list broke down her problems into manageable chunks. It wasn't as if 'solve the theory of everything' could ever be considered one item.

And yet it was. The whole structure needed to be imagined at once, the scaffolding mirroring the void inside.

Aasen glanced at her list again, tablet strapped to her forearm. She holstered one set of tools, and retrieved a different set for the next task.

Well, that's hackable, thought Forsyth suddenly. He could exploit that. If he interviewed the candidates together in front of a panel of their peers, and made them fight it out between them as to who wanted it most, then everyone would get a vote, and he'd not only make sure that everyone's hands were equally unclean and complicit in the action no matter how they voted, he could also be certain that his preferred candidate was chosen.

That seemed by far the most practical solution. If he hadn't been so preoccupied by the other demands of captaincy, then he would have thought of it sooner.

'How long are you going to be?' he asked Aasen.

She glanced down, and used a finger to scroll the list. 'On Aquila? Another fifteen minutes or so. But there's a stack of other problems that have come up while I've been doing this. They need fixing. Urgently.'

'Of course they do,' said Forsyth. 'But they can wait. Aquila first.'

She said nothing in response, just grimacing as if in physical pain at the thought of her to-do list.

He withdrew, and went back into his module, his workspace, with all the data flowing around him on screens. Even that he was floating in zero g made it feel a more complete experience.

First things first, though. He used the captain's log-in to access Aasen's list. He checked where the work on Aquila finished, and the work on the Aphrodite restarted, and inserted some lines of text.

Hanne, take a shower.

Hanne, change your flight suit.

Hanne, come to Command for a meeting.

That should do it. It would obviously confuse her, because she'd think it was the computer talking to her, but she was so wedded to her list that she'd most likely just follow the instructions without even realising that was what she was doing.

One last line.

Hanne, vote for Konstantinos.

Now to gather the rest of the crew together – not Mariucci, because he would use the occasion to grandstand and not for its intended purpose. But everyone else should be there, even Molnar. Kattenbeck should be able to bring him, and he wanted her there too. Make them all just a little bit grubby, because that was how he could keep them in line in the future, by reminding them of the time they participated in sending one of their colleagues to their death.

He needed to flush Velter out, too. Spinu usually knew where he was, and Forsyth would tell her to drag the geologist along. He might mention something about her commitment. That would ensure they were quorate.

He closed the log-in screen and went along the axis, through the rotating section and its damnable noise – why had no one else commented on it? – and into the subdued lighting of Command. Borner was on duty.

'Yasmin. Can you page the crew?' He looked up at the clock. 'Everybody – and I mean everybody except our former captain – needs to assemble here in ten minutes. We won't start until and unless we have complete attendance.'

It was like he was back giving tutorials. Students were rightly terrified of him. The undergraduates still had that invulnerability of youth, but the post-graduates knew that if they didn't perform, their careers would be over before they started. If they could survive, they would flourish. If they couldn't, it was no matter to him. And since he never started until everyone was present, no one, but no one, ever wanted to be late.

And he sat there, and waited. He could feel himself becoming more righteous by the moment. His ship. His crew. His mission. Nothing was going to go wrong, because he was in charge of everything now. Not like when Mariucci was captain. He didn't know why he hadn't done this sooner. He could have seized control after they'd left cis-lunar: all of the Nimbus supply ships had been launched by then, and perhaps poor Hellsten would still be alive under his command. Any talk of what was to happen to Molnar had ceased completely now he was up and awake, and in some sort of proper state.

It was a microcosm of how he expected Earth to be, when

he'd finished his theory, when everyone realised what a benefit it would be. The sick would become healthy. Peace would reign. People would know their jobs, and their places. There would be no need for dissent, because there'd be nothing to complain about. All would be well.

The rest of the crew came in one by one, two by two.

Eager Spinu – she knew why they were meeting, and she thought she knew how it would go. She was a ball of energy, excited, almost dizzy. When she strapped herself into her seat, it could barely contain her.

Then the other contender, Tsoltos: he was not just calm, but over-confident. He believed he'd got the place sewn up, that it had already been decided. It sort-of had, but Forsyth wasn't going to either let on, or subvert the process. It was still open, and Tsoltos's swagger – how did he effect that in zero-g? – was unbecoming and not a little previous.

Borner was already present, and it was difficult to tell what she was thinking. Was she intimidated by Spinu or Tsoltos? She didn't show it.

But if Spinu was here, where was Velter?

'Valeria? Is Benjamin on his way? We can't do anything without him.'

She was momentarily startled by his question, as if it was an unexpected test that she'd forgotten to take.

'I'll get him,' she said. She was going to drag him into Command, even if it was the last place he wanted to be. She unclipped and headed out again, almost colliding with Kattenbeck leading Molnar.

'Laszlo, delighted you could join us,' said Forsyth. 'You're looking in fine form.'

Honestly, he didn't look that well, but Kattenbeck had done enough for the man to be present. He was more physically there than mentally, like an aged faculty member who'd long finished their useful work and was now just wheeled out for functions and to introduce keynote speakers. But even while they pottered around in their office, they had their occasional flashes of insight. Worth keeping around.

Kattenbeck even strapped Molnar in to his seat, not just with the lap strap but the full five-point harness, before clipping in next to him.

Then Blasco and Colvin. Blasco seemed flushed. Colvin appeared pale. Was there ... was there something going on between the two of them? Forsyth genuinely didn't care, as long as it didn't affect their work, but they were pilot and navigator. Any disagreement between those two roles signalled a problem larger than the merely personal. Why couldn't people be professional, like him?

Now, Aasen. She was, as the computer had ordered, on time, clean and neat, and rather than feel any shame at manipulating her at one remove, Forsyth realised that he could now count on her voting as he intended. She seemed bemused. She kept checking her tablet to see if there wasn't anything else she ought to be doing, whether the list had made a mistake, but each time she looked, there was a period of time blocked out when she needed to be in Command and so that's where she was.

They were all waiting now, in studied silence, not looking at each other, not looking at the pit where the display was empty and too uncomfortably like a void. No banter. They were waiting to solemnly decide who was going to die, willingly, by their own hand.

Finally, finally. Velter, almost shoved into the module by Spinu. Once he was properly in Command, and there was no possibility of retreat, he looked around for safe harbour, and thought he'd find it next to Tsoltos.

Spinu, however, went to the other side of the space and strapped in there, almost but not quite facing her rival.

That was everyone, except Mariucci: let the games begin.

Forsyth started with an apology.

'We're here because I'm finding it impossible to choose between the three – very excellent – candidates for our first contact mission. I thought it fair that they should be given one last opportunity to state their cases in the court of their peers, in the hope that it becomes clear who should have the honour.'

'They're going to die,' said Kattenbeck.

'Petra, that's accepted by everyone, and we've moved past it. We're not here to rehash old, tired arguments, but to announce who will become our intrepid explorer.'

'Briefly,' said Kattenbeck. But she subsided, and Molnar, next to her, turned his head this way and that, trying to make sense of the proceedings.

Without waiting for an invitation to speak, Tsoltos leaned forward.

'It's obvious that only someone with complete control of not just their body, but their mind also, will be able to complete the mission. Someone who possesses both clarity of purpose, and strength of will. We know that Rory doubts the existence of the phenomena that we so clearly see – all of the evidence points to a single explanation – and I believe that doubt is not rooted in reason or rationality, but fear. Fear that his whole mental edifice, that he is something special, unique, in the history of mankind, the man who is never wrong, will come crashing down.

'This is why someone who is his exact opposite – someone who wholeheartedly embraces their humanity and counts himself as a representative of us all – should be the one who will undoubtedly and unambiguously prove the existence of the structure on Io. As Adam was our progenitor, so I will be the one who brings in a new era. I am the archetype, born and raised in the cradle of civilisation. If there are aliens there, then who better to make first contact than someone who has lived in the shadow of Mount Olympus?'

'Cradle of civilisation?' said Borner. 'I don't think you've any idea—'

'We're not at the stage yet where we interrogate the other candidates, Yasmin.'

'But what we've just heard is—'

'Konstantinos has made his representation. You are free to make yours.'

'I discovered the count. I made the connections between the moons. I worked out the code. I identified the structure as a ziggurat. I've made all of the running here. It's my discovery: we wouldn't even be here, now, if it wasn't for me. This is mine. The builders—' and she stopped as she regrouped. 'The builders gave this message to me. To no one else. They meant it for me, and if anyone else goes down to Io, they're not going to be welcomed.'

'Bullshit,' said Spinu. 'They'll welcome me. They didn't need electronic signals to give me messages. They've been talking to me ever since we arrived in Jovian space. You need your antennae and your processing software, and all you're doing is intercepting the messages meant for me. It's me they're calling. Me. Not you.'

'No one is calling you, either of you,' said Tsoltos. 'How could they? If the gods were speaking, then they would speak to me first. But until someone opens the door between this world and the divine, we won't hear them. I will open the door.'

Forsyth listened with mounting astonishment, and not a little disappointment. All his candidates were acting out some kind of religious mania – Borner's technological explanation was by far the most sane of them all, while Spinu seemed to believe that aliens were beaming messages into her brain, and Tsoltos? What had happened to him? He seemed to think he was a supernatural being, either in whole or in part.

None of them appeared suitable for the mission: all of them would prove unreliable narrators of their journey. They would see what they wanted to see, and report accordingly. Unless someone more rational volunteered, he'd have to call the whole thing off.

He half-listened to the to-and-fro across Command, each of the three candidates trying to prove that they had been specially invited to make the journey to Io's antijove. All they were doing was trying to convince each other and their audience who was the most fervent. If he didn't intervene soon, they'd end up whipping themselves to show their loyalty.

But, and he realised this all too well, he'd brought them to this point. They'd only given his coup support because he'd offered them the option forbidden by Mariucci: to find out once and for all what was down there. They'd cut ties with Earth, deposed their lawful superior, thrown their mission profile out of the airlock, and some of them were willing to die for this cause.

It wasn't such a great step between being willing to die for something, and being willing to kill for it. And these three were fanatics. Absolute fanatics. Someone had to go, clearly, but would those left behind accept the testimony of that one? Or would they automatically see their statements as tainted, those of an unbeliever?

This whole thing was preposterous. First the idea of aliens, and now the response of the crew to that idea. He should just send Aquila down on its own, and trust Blasco and Colvin to get it as close as possible.

That was going to be unsatisfactory to the three zealots, though.

They were still going at it, arguing about who was worthy, and who was not. Tsoltos the demigod, Spinu the prophet, Borner the acolyte. How patently ridiculous to abandon all sense of rational thought.

He had to end this. But how?

Molnar looked completely bewildered, as if he'd woken up in a surreal nightmare where people he recognised were utterly changed. Next to him, Kattenbeck had her palms pressed against her face, blocking out all sight. Colvin was shrinking even further into herself, if that was possible. Velter was horrified, his head snapping around at each further deranged declaration of divinity. Only Blasco looked like she was enjoying the show.

Aasen blurted out, 'I choose Stan,' and the whole of Command fell silent.

The engineer blinked, looked down at her list to check, and yes, it told her that she should be doing exactly that: vote for Konstantinos. She could tick that off now, and get back to repairing a failing ship.

'I think Hanne's right,' said Forsyth. 'We should move to a vote.' He thought Blasco would be most likely to take part, so he picked on her. 'Theresa?'

'Sure. Stan. Why not?' She shrugged apologetically at Borner, who sat closest to her. 'If he wants to go, let him. You'll thank me later.'

'This is not about "letting him". It should be me. At least, it should be someone who doesn't believe they're a god.'

'Presentation time is over,' said Forsyth quickly. 'Benjamin?'

'No. I, just no. I refuse to take part in this.'

'We're all taking part, Benjamin.'

'Vote for me, Benjamin,' said Tsoltos, closing his hand over Velter's. 'I want you to vote for me.'

'If it'll stop this madness, then yes. I vote for Stan. May God have mercy on us all.'

'How about you, Petra, or you, Laszlo? Have you decided yet?'

'Oh, I've decided all right,' said Kattenbeck. 'Not taking sides. You do what you do. And Laszlo doesn't have the capacity. Anything he says will be void.'

'Deirdre?'

She was silent, and then mumbled, 'I don't want to lose anyone else. But if I had to, I'd want Yasmin to be our representative.'

'Well,' said Forsyth. 'The maths is quite clear. Assuming that Yasmin and Valeria both vote for themselves, then there's nothing I can do to change the majority verdict. Konstantinos will go down to Io on probe three, and investigate the antijove.'

Decision made, hands washed, and about time he got back to work. He unclipped, and left.

18

He didn't care that they hated him. He was used to that. Ruling by fear, malice, division and suspicion was perfectly valid, just as long as they didn't dissent. Tsoltos was their explorer, and that was that.

Why then were there recriminations, arguments, black looks and shunning? All signs that even though the decision had been clear-cut and democratic, it wasn't actually accepted.

Forsyth comforted himself with the fact that after Tsoltos had landed, reported that there was nothing – much like Gagarin who, once he'd achieved the first ever orbit, had declared that he couldn't see God – Spinu and Borner would have to acknowledge that they were wrong. How that would manifest itself, he didn't know, and neither did he care, just as long as they shut up, did their work, and left him alone.

The Aphrodite had drawn up behind Io in its orbit, close enough now that it was temporarily falling towards it, the rate of descent ameliorated by the Aphrodite's nuclear exhaust. That was the number that Colvin had to watch most carefully. For all its power, the motor couldn't hover the spaceship. The moment after the probe launched, the Aphrodite needed to turn and swing obliquely past the moon, leaving the probe to its braking manoeuvres. Once away, they would spiral out towards and beyond Europa, to explore the space between Europa and Ganymede, and then Ganymede and Callisto. Months of research lay ahead, all to be collected and analysed, made concordant with his new physics and then—

Return home triumphant, the message going ahead of them from Jupiter that humanity had not only been saved, but that it had a new purpose.

The data flowed around him, above and below him. Huge energies washed around Aphrodite's shield, which responded with electronic reflexes fast enough to hold them at bay. Just. He could almost feel the magnetic field lines tighten around him, as if they were real threads drawing a net together and not just fluctuating values in four-potential space.

Is that what Molnar felt too? Even saw? He'd rather ignored him as a mere technician, but what if there was something more the man could offer? He might even be the only other person on the ship who could recognise his theory for the breakthrough that it was. He'd have to press Kattenbeck to bring him on further.

Aasen came by to tell him that Aquila was ready for launch, and Tsoltos was in position. Now that Forsyth had realised that he could simply insert his own thoughts into the engineer's head via the faults list, he'd used her to organise both the probe and the crew. He'd said he needed a factotum: now he had one, even if she neither realised nor agreed to it.

He left his data, and drifted down the axis to Command. Who was there? Who was doing their jobs? That was all he asked of them, but clearly for some it was too much.

Borner was at her station, radiating resentment, but she was present, and that was enough for now. Blasco and Colvin, pilot and navigator, good. Not Spinu. He frowned at that. And not Velter either. Expected, but disloyal all the same. Kattenbeck and Molnar were both in attendance, though. The doctor looked as if she'd come to witness an execution, and in a way she had, but this was qualitatively different: Tsoltos was a willing – more than willing – participant. Molnar still seemed both bemused and interested in everything that he saw, as if finding himself on a spaceship in orbit around Jupiter was a constant source of surprise.

Aasen looked at her list and saw she had to sit down and strap in, so she did.

Forsyth waited a moment, then asked, 'Are we ...' He tried to remember the jargon. 'Go for launch?'

'Flight go.'

'Systems go.'

'Navigation go.' Borner paused. 'Also, telemetry go.'

That had been Spinu's job previously. He should really drag her up here – get Aasen to drag her up here – and make her do her duty.

What had Mariucci said? That was it: 'We are go for launch.' Then he waved his hand and expected everything to happen. Which it would, of course. Tsoltos, imprisoned in his plastic bubble filled with water, might want to indicate his readiness too, but honestly, that was the least important factor in the whole operation. The sums just about balanced, and if they didn't launch now, they'd have to abort for another attempt in another orbit, in another one and a half days' time.

'Probe bay doors open,' said Blasco. 'Stan, launching in five. Three, two, one, mark.'

The Aphrodite gave the smallest of shudders – more of a shrug – and Aquila was away.

'Separation confirmed, sensors online, video feed commencing.'

New windows opened on screens all around Command, and in the pit, a small spark of light split from the larger one. The images showed the Aphrodite half in shadow, half lit by the distant sun. The silver radiators and white hull, where visible, were yellow with sulphur stains. From Tsoltos's suit camera, the toxic glare from Io, so bright it was almost a luminous green. This close to the moon, even Jupiter was eclipsed, hidden by Io's discoloured limbs.

'Probe at sixty metres. Ship rotation. Acceleration acceleration.'

On the screens, the Aphrodite started to heel over.

'Probe rotation. Copy that, Stan.'

'Copy.' His voice sounded wire-tight. If there was any doubt in his mind, such thoughts were useless now.

'Panels deploying. Initial thrust manoeuvre.'

The spin-stabilised probe sent back its last image of the Aphrodite. It slid out of view, and turned instead to the surface of Io. Tsoltos's suit camera looked up at the slowly diminishing shape: the bulbous node of Command, the wheel, the workshop blocks and the open pod bay doors, the burr-like fuel tanks, the great thistledown radiators and the solid bulk of the nuclear pile. The bright, ghostly jet of the exhaust.

'Aquila passing through magnetopause.'

And suddenly, it wasn't an adventure any more. The probe, and Tsoltos, were moving outside the ship's shielding, into the teeth of an electromagnetic storm.

The first blue streak came as a surprise, a flashbulb, but almost lightning-like. It speared through the water and faded almost instantaneously.

'Look,' said Molnar. 'Cherenkov radiation.' It was the first words he'd spoken in public in weeks.

Forsyth leaned forward to his console. Sub-atomic particles were striking the bubble and decelerating in the water, spending their energy in the dense liquid which then gave it out again as light. As the probe fell further, and left the shield behind for good, it lit up like a neon bulb.

'Try to stay in the centre of the water, Konstantinos,' he said.

Tsoltos let out a low moan. The suit camera had shown a crystal clear, if lensed, version of the outside. Now it seethed in blue. Kattenbeck twisted her seat around and tapped at the screen.

'External temperature is rising. He's being boiled like a frog.'

'The suit will keep him cool,' insisted Forsyth. 'That's what it's for.'

'He's already taken a lethal dose of radiation.'

'He knew the risks.'

'There were no risks, Rory. Just consequences.'

Tsoltos's moan started to rise in pitch. Now it was more a strangled cry.

'Altitude forty kilometres.'

'He's not going to make it to the surface alive.'

'Nonsense. This will pass.'

'How?'

Inside his bright blue bubble, Tsoltos was screaming.

'Can we … can we turn that off?'

'I think we should leave it on,' said Kattenbeck. 'Touchdown isn't for another twenty minutes.'

'Turn it off!'

Before Borner could do so, the screaming became choking, as Tsoltos vomited, not once, but repeatedly, coughing and retching.

'He's in a spacesuit. That's not going anywhere.'

Forsyth seethed. It was almost as if Kattenbeck was enjoying her narration. 'Turn it off. Yasmin. Now.' He rounded on Molnar. 'You said. You said this would protect him.'

Molnar looked to Kattenbeck for help. All she did was shrug, and all he did was copy her gesture.

'Will he live long enough to do what he needs to do?' asked Forsyth.

'If he doesn't drown in his own emesis,' said Kattenbeck, 'he might have a period of lucidity before he has a fatal seizure or can't function through ataxia.'

Barely any of those words meant anything to him. 'Can we get him down quicker?'

'No?' said Colvin. She was as white as a ghost. 'If we alter the descent burn, he'll just fall. The thrusters aren't rated high enough to brake him in time.'

'It'd be a mercy,' said Kattenbeck.

'No. We have to settle this.' Forsyth clenched his fists.

'I told you,' said the doctor. 'You wouldn't listen.'

If he could have cut her transmissions too, he would have.

This was all Molnar's fault. The water didn't provide anywhere near enough shielding. How could he have trusted him – even thought about trusting him? The whole scheme was doomed to failure because someone who he'd thought was an expert in his field had got his sums wrong.

'We wait,' he said. 'We wait and see.'

Tsoltos's suit camera was still broadcasting nothing but blue glare. At any other time, watching the unearthly glow from decelerating charged particles would have been dramatic, and nothing more. But Tsoltos was immersed in it. Energy was sleeting through him: slowed, but not by enough.

The camera underneath Aquila was working well, though. The field of view was such that they didn't have sight of the antijove yet, and wouldn't until the last minute or so. There was some lateral drift that the thrusters had to negate first.

But the Aphrodite had cameras on the hull. Not spectacular ones like the probes, but more than good enough, a mix of wide-angle and narrow-field lenses. And from their altitude of sixty kilometres, the resolution was sufficient that they could pick out individual creases on the surface of lava flows.

If Spinu had been in Command, she would by now have turned the cameras away from tracking Aquila, but because Borner had her hands full already, watching the numbers and checking the probe's systems, she only thought of it as the probe dropped below ten kilometres, and the landing zone was starting to resolve on the edge of the screen.

She scrambled across the keyboard, and the scintillating blue jewel moved away.

'Hey,' objected Blasco, whose job it was to guide the probe to its landing point. 'That's ...'

Her voice trailed away as the ziggurat slid into view. Resolution was twenty, thirty centimetres. Enough to pick up a sheet of paper resting on the surface. Borner adjusted the camera in real time, zooming in, nudging its centre as the Aphrodite powered on, across the face of Io.

The detail was startling. Light and shadow. Walls. Steps. Perfect right angles. Some kind of structure at the very top. A cube. With openings.

They were passing it now, and rather than looking straight down on it, their angle to it grew increasingly oblique. They could see its shape, its size, its bulk. All rendered in black, sulphur-sputtered stone.

Everyone in Command looked at Forsyth and waited for him to say something.

His expression was blank, while his mind raced furiously. He wasn't wrong. He was never wrong. His denial of these images was exactly why he'd gone to the lengths he had. There was nothing there, no stone, no structure, no shadow, no shape. A trick of the light against an unfamiliar surface.

'Concentrate on getting Tsoltos down. That, and that only.' He looked to Kattenbeck. 'Is he still alive?'

'He has a heartbeat, if that's what you're worried about. It is at two twenty a minute, which is not sustainable, and his breathing is panicked, so he's almost certainly inhaling his vomit. Aspiration won't be a problem, because he's already absorbed somewhere in the region of fifty grays. He has minutes of life left.'

'Talk to him, Petra. Tell him he has to hold on.'

'Since his entire nervous system is on fire, I'd prefer it if he just died. If you want someone to talk to him, do it yourself.'

Damn her. Damn her but he had no choice. He could go around the rest of the crew and hope someone would take on the task, but the precedent had been set. He clicked on his microphone.

'Konstantinos? I know you can hear me. You're almost there. You're almost at the ... at the antijove. Theresa is guiding you in. You just have to stay conscious. That's all you have to do.'

He glanced around, and apparently more was expected of him. He wasn't going to sink into meaningless platitudes or pop psychology – although saying 'I believe in you' might enrage Tsoltos enough that he'd take on a new lease of life. Or at least latch on to the dregs of the old one.

'You wanted this. You argued that this was your destiny. That no one else could do this – only you. You're now doing it. You're minutes away. If this is your destiny then it would be risible to fail now when it's in your reach. Minutes, man. Sixty seconds at a time. That's all.'

'Five minutes from the antijove. We have five minutes of fuel left,' reported Blasco.

'Then it'll be enough.'

'If we're even one second short, we'll be coming in hot.'

'What does that even mean?'

'It means Aquila will crash,' said Colvin. 'It'll crash into the ground.'

'It'll be a mercy if it kills Stan,' said Kattenbeck.

'There will be no crashes, no "coming in hot", and he will not die. Do you hear me, Konstantinos? You will get there.' Forsyth rounded on Colvin. 'You checked the numbers. You agreed with me that we had enough fuel for this.'

'These things aren't perfect,' said Blasco. 'The numbers might add up on the computer, but in the real world, sometimes they don't. There's no margin of error, no reserves.'

'Just concentrate on getting him down. I don't care how it's done.'

Kattenbeck brought Tsoltos's audio back on line. Scream. Breathe. Scream. Breathe. Scream. She snapped it off again. 'If we turn the engines off now, we plough the Aquila into Io, and that'll be the end of it.'

'No. He did this of his own free will. We're just following his wishes.'

'That's bullshit, Rory, and you know it. He thought he was an actual demigod.'

'Four minutes.'

Forsyth straightened his back. 'It's four minutes. We give him that long.'

Borner drove the Aphrodite's cameras back to lock on to Aquila. The bubble of water was burning blue, bright against the salt-flat surface below. Blasco took hold of two fold-out joysticks and pushed VR goggles over her eyes. The probe and the dark angles of the structure were in the same frame now, even at a larger scale.

Molnar kept looking at Kattenbeck, then to Forsyth, and back to Kattenbeck. He was trying to make some kind of connection between what he thought was happening, and what was actually going on, and, clearly, couldn't make sense of it, and finally Forsyth had had enough.

'Pity's sake, Laszlo, stop that. This is your fault. You said the water would protect him, and it's done nothing of the kind. He'll be lucky if he's aware enough of his surroundings to even set foot on the moon, let alone do anything useful.'

Molnar didn't react to his scolding, just kept on doing the thing that Forsyth hated.

He turned his back on him, and the rest of Command. He concentrated on the screen, and the images displayed. The blue jewel. The surface of Io, pale and cracked like dead skin. He tried to ignore the black shape. It seemed remarkably persistent. He could see it every time he blinked.

An alarm sounded. 'Fuel low. Fuel low.' Blasco, blinded by her goggles, still managed to reach out to a screen and kill the alert.

The slowly spinning shape of the probe started to merge with the landscape. Its shadow crossed the ground. Haze – sulphur dust stirred up by the thrusters – obscured the landing site as seen through Aquila's downward-facing camera.

'Hundred metres,' said Borner. 'Eighty. Sixty. Fifty. Forty.'

'Fuel low. Fuel low.'

This time Blasco didn't let go of the joysticks.

'Thirty. Twenty. Ten. Five.'

'Thrust zero. Thrust zero.'

Blasco sprang her hands from the joysticks, unable to do any more, and Aquila fell the rest of the way to the ground.

Aquila's camera went black, either obscured or broken by the impact. Borner rattled her way through the diagnostics.

'Offline. Offline. Offline. Central processing is at sixty per cent. Power generation failed. Battery at ninety-five per cent.' She snorted. 'Magnetometer is online.'

At least something had gone right from this debacle. Forsyth checked Tsoltos's suit camera – clearly the relay was still working, but the image was indecipherable. The view from Aphrodite's hull cameras was now so oblique as to be on the very edge of the limb of the moon, but the blue glow had gone. He concluded that the bubble had ruptured in the crash.

'Is he still alive?'

'Yes,' said Kattenbeck. She sounded surprised. 'Yes, but not for long. Either his suit or he goes first.'

Forsyth opened his microphone again. 'Konstantinos. Listen to me. Listen to my voice. You're on Io. You have one chance to prove yourself.' In another minute, the Aphrodite would be over the horizon, and whether any signal would reach them after that was impossible to tell, but most likely it would cut off.

The view from Tsoltos's camera didn't move.

'Konstantinos. Stan. Get up. Get up this second. You have work to do.'

And it shifted. The image – smeared and partial – moved, although it still showed nothing of anything.

'Put him on speaker,' said Forsyth, and he tried again. 'Stan. Get up. Look up. It should be right there. You're right there. Look around. Tell us what you see.'

The sound coming from Tsoltos's throat wasn't even human any more. He was an animal in excruciating pain. But something that could be identified as a gloved hand moved past and ahead of the camera. The ground seemed to lurch.

'Get up, Stan. Get up. It's barely one-sixth Earth gravity. You can get up and stand up.' Forsyth glanced at the Aphrodite's position. Almost at the horizon. Seconds more. 'Get up now, you idiot, or it'll have all been for nothing.'

Tsoltos's hand came back into view. Then the other one. They braced in the powdery dirt, presumably as he tried to get his knees underneath him.

'Up! Up!'

And with a roar, Tsoltos rose to his feet. For one brief second, the camera held still on a dusty, hazy tower, yellow-grey against the black of space. Then it was gone. The camera showed the sky, and nothing else.

'He's down,' said Kattenbeck. 'Life-support failure.'

'Get up!'

'Rory, he's dead. He's dead.' The camera cut out. They were over the horizon. 'There's no point in shouting at him any more.'

Forsyth put his hand to his mouth, the knuckle of his forefinger between his teeth, and gnawed at it. They were waiting for him to say something. The screens showed three blank panels and one of Io receding behind them.

Finally, he pulled his hand away and unclipped his waist strap. 'The experiment was inconclusive,' he said as he headed for the axis. 'We'll have to go again. We use the last probe, and find another volunteer. Just … sort it out.'

Part 3

Etemenanki

ibnū-ma ziqqurrat apsī elīte
ana anim enlil ea u šāšu ukinnū šubtu
ina tarbāti maḫar-šunu ušib-am-ma
šuršiš ešarra inaṭṭalū qarnā-šu

19

Kattenbeck thumped her hand against the bulkhead, loudly and long enough to attract Forsyth's attention away from the dance of elemental particles.

Forsyth eventually and reluctantly turned himself around, flailing his arms in a way that didn't really fit a captain of a spaceship. 'What is it, Petra? I'm very busy.'

But behind her, he could also see Aasen, and realising that she wasn't hurrying off to deal with the next alleged fault was more worrying.

'It's Laszlo,' said Kattenbeck.

Forsyth hadn't forgiven him for misleading him about the radiation protection measures – the use of water was sound, but Molnar had grossly underestimated the volume required. Somewhere in the region of an Olympic-sized swimming pool might have worked, while a couple of bathtubs obviously hadn't.

'What about him?'

'He's dead. Hanne found him.'

'How can he be dead?'

'Well, apparently hanging still works in one-fifth gravity. It might take a lot longer, but it's still effective, eventually.'

Damn him. Damn him. He'd failed, and yet he still might have been useful. 'Who did this?'

'For fuck's sake, Rory, he did. He saw what happened to Stan, and he killed himself. He knotted some cabling, tied it to a ladder and just hung there in the access tunnel until he strangled.'

'Well, where were you? You were supposed to be looking after him!'

'I was asleep. I can't stay awake permanently. It gets worse, the more tired I get.' She didn't elaborate. 'And I'm not going to restrain him or drug him every time I need a rest.'

'What about everyone else?'

'You mean the ones who are left alive?' She pushed the heel of her hand into her face and scrubbed at her eye. 'Benjamin spends his time hiding from all of us, in case he meets you. Valeria is furious with you, and us, for not siding with her. Yasmin sits in front of her screen, counting. Deirdre and Theresa? Maybe they've patched things up between themselves, but one or the other is usually on duty in Command. Hanne found him on her way to another job, and then there's you and me.'

'What about Luca?'

'What about him?'

'He could have watched Laszlo. He could have stopped him.'

Kattenbeck sighed. 'He could have stopped him this time. But since he's forbidden from leaving the wheel, and accessing the ladder means leaving the wheel, I don't quite know how he was supposed to follow Laszlo while he set everything up. They were your orders, Rory. So, no, Luca didn't know, and couldn't have stopped him.'

'Does he know now?'

'Yes. I told him.'

'What did he say?'

'He said he'd help me stow the body against the hull, if he was allowed. Then he started crying.' She glanced towards the fore of the ship. 'He probably still is.'

Forsyth tutted. It was all very inconvenient, but Molnar had been so damaged that it was probably for the best that he was out of the way. He'd taken up far too much of Kattenbeck's time, when she should be concentrating on keeping the remaining crew fit and healthy.

'Luca has my permission to assist you,' he said, and after

he'd said it, wondered why Kattenbeck was still there, and why Aasen wasn't following her list. 'What is it now?'

'Hanne can't keep up with her repairs – it's either that, or make the changes to the probe. Not both.'

He looked around the doctor at Aasen. 'How much progress have you made?'

'Some,' she said, then blurted, 'The mass. We can't add any more.'

'Then take something else off,' he said. 'It's really very simple.'

'It's not that simple.' She was on the verge of pleading. 'It's a single unit. Unless you want me to disassemble it completely—'

'You have your orders. We need a bigger water bubble, or more radiation protection, or a combination of both. Just sort it, Hanne. You don't need to keep bothering me over the details.'

'Rory,' tried Kattenbeck. 'Whoever goes down is going to die, no matter what Hanne does.'

'I know that! And so do they.'

'And what about the repairs?'

'Unless and until everyone agrees with me that there's nothing more than a mirage on Io, then the probe conversion takes priority over ship maintenance. Now, go.' When neither of them did, he started to get angry. 'Go!'

Aasen disappeared from view, but Kattenbeck remained. Forsyth tried to stare her down, but she stayed as stone-faced as a statue.

'You know full well it's too late for any act of defiance. You're just as culpable as everyone else, because you acquiesced to my rule.'

'Your rule?'

'Yes. My rule. My command. My captaincy. It turns out I'm rather good at running things. Good enough that I'm considering doing more of that when we get back to Earth.'

'I have no idea what you're talking about.'

'Someone has to take the fight to Vi and her lapdog, Van der Veerden. It strikes me they've had far too easy a time of it, and that our current crop of technocrats and politicians seem utterly incapable of resisting their particular unpleasant brand of anti-technological populism: so why not me?'

'You?' She jerked away, as if he was something revolting and she was disgusted by him.

'Don't let me keep you, Petra. We've lost three of the crew already, and their refusal to accept my position is going to cost us another. Perhaps you could talk to them about that.'

If she could convince Spinu and Borner not to pursue their stupid beliefs in an alien presence in the Jovian system, then that would be something. Redacting all the data relating to the episode would be even better. It was either that, or someone else was going to have to die to extinguish that belief.

Just as long as it wasn't him, because it hadn't sounded a very pleasant way to go.

Shame about Molnar, though. He might have been persuaded to take the next trip to Io, and that would save him the trouble of Valeria Spinu. Obviously, she was eager to go and meet her alien gods, or whatever she thought they were.

And for that reason he thought he might just deny her the opportunity. He knew how it was when someone was so clearly desperate for a particular role: he just knew they'd fall flat on their faces – in this case, literally so. Someone calmer, more level-headed. Less fanatical.

That would probably rule out Borner as well, because although she was less demonstrative than Spinu, she was also one of those true believers. Some rational scepticism would be needed to prove – or disprove – the existence of the structure.

Had he made a mistake allowing Tsoltos to go? A mistake? No. A miscalculation, perhaps? No. Rather, he'd tried it their way, and it hadn't worked. Of course it hadn't. Why on earth should he expect anything else?

Next time – and there was going to be a next time, Kattenbeck aside – it would be different. There'd be no self-selecting candidates. He would choose.

Given that, who?

Obviously, not Spinu and not Borner. That left Blasco, Colvin, Kattenbeck, Aasen and Velter. And Mariucci. He'd still like to get Mariucci on board, on the probe, and down to the surface, for no other reason than that he'd be rid of his malign presence on the Aphrodite. It could be worth giving it another go: Mariucci actually liked these people, and now that Tsoltos had died, he might be more persuadable. But he'd also made it perfectly clear that he'd sabotage the mission, just to spite Forsyth. In many respects, he was as much a fanatic as Spinu was, only it was hate, not adoration, that drove him.

Would Colvin let Blasco go, or vice versa? Personal relationships unduly complicated matters that should be, in and of themselves, straightforward. Their utility shouldn't be to each other, but to him. Could Blasco handle the navigation software? Could Colvin pilot the ship? He might only need one of them after all.

Velter would be the ideal candidate. He was science, a planetary scientist no less, so the prospect of being the first to set foot on a moon of Jupiter ought to sway him. Then Forsyth remembered that Tsoltos had been the first, even though his stay hadn't lasted very long. Would Velter settle for being second? Potentially, yes.

But Velter was terrified of Forsyth. And actually, that was good. If he was more scared of him than he was of dying, then he'd climb into his spacesuit and get into ... whatever jury-rigged contraption Aasen would strap on top of the probe.

He'd have to find him first, but really, it wasn't a big spaceship. There were only so many places to hide in.

Kattenbeck, definitely not. No point in even considering her.

Aasen? Yes, she was the engineer, but in the absence of anyone else, he could slip a command into her list: Hanne, volunteer to go to Io. That would work, and honestly, everyone would believe her witness. She was trusted. Even if she kept on trying to fix things that weren't broken.

Velter then. Give him a way of escaping Forsyth for ever. There would be pain, yes, and he'd be alone, yes, and he'd die, yes, but he would be free. And if he could prove he saw something there, then he'd die a happy man.

Forsyth looked back to his work, and supposed that he could leave it for a little while. The data streaming across his screens was telling him it was really very stormy outside. Some of the spikes were so severe that whatever programming was being used to visualise the intensity of the radiation was topping out. What should have been brightest white was being rendered in jagged black, opening and closing like tiny mouths as they sparked.

They looked like tiny mouths. He blinked. It was data. It was just data.

He left the module and headed towards the back of the ship, past the dogleg of the probe bays, through the industrial pipework of the fuel tanks, and into the radiator section. At the rear of it was the blank-faced slab of the shield that protected them from both the nuclear reactor on the far side of it, and the boiling plasma wrapping around them outside. The field lines would be tight, constricting inwards as the radiation intensity increased, closing like a noose. Like it had around Molnar's neck.

He shook his head quickly, violently. Such thoughts weren't worthy of him. Weren't worthy of a leader. He drifted free for a moment, pressing his fingertips into his temples. He had a headache all of a sudden. There was a crushing pressure building up, like a vice around his skull. Painful, nauseating, almost blinding.

Forsyth swallowed hard, and kicked off against the shield. For a moment, he'd forgotten what he'd come down there for, but it was Velter. Flush him out. He obviously wasn't in the rear section, and not in the next either, unless – unless he was hiding amongst the pipework, behind one of the screens that covered the next layer of unsightly tubes and valves and switchwork. He paused, catching hold of one of the rails.

'Benjamin?' he called. 'Benjamin?'

He listened carefully, trying to catch the sound of breathing, of movement. But the ringing of tinnitus in his own ears obscured any noise that Velter might have made. He pushed himself towards one of the panels and peered through the mesh, but there was hardly enough room behind them for the machinery, let alone a stowaway.

He nudged himself away, back to a handhold, and onwards towards the bow.

The probe bays were next. They were almost empty – just one probe left out of four. Aasen was in one of the bays, the probe seemingly undressed with its carapace in pieces, floating in orbit around her.

Shouldn't they be tethered? It looked like the moment after an explosion, when everything was in motion and nothing had been resolved. He concluded that she knew what she was doing, and his cursory glance through the open door told him that Velter wasn't in there with her.

The other bay should be empty. Both probes had been launched. There was no reason for anyone to be in there. The door, solid and sealed, might not be opened for the rest of the flight.

The controls were there, just to the left of the frame. Forsyth swung down to examine them. The bay was pressurised: he didn't know if that was routine, or not. The probes didn't need an atmosphere, and were most likely stored better without one. The bays were designed to open out into space, and already the external doors to this one had done so, twice.

He put his hands to the wheel, bracing his feet in the doorway, and spun it around until the closures undogged. He adjusted his grip and pushed, and the door swung inwards. The bay was in darkness, and he looked back down to the control panel for the lights. They bloomed bright, but only for a moment: no sooner had they come on, than they switched off again.

A fault. An actual fault inside the ship. Yes, they were losing sensors that were lowered from the spinning wheel, through the magnetopause and into the space outside them, but nothing appeared to have gone wrong with the workings of the Aphrodite until now.

His eyes narrowed momentarily. How likely was it that was the case?

He swung himself inside the bay, listening to the way the acoustics changed from close to echoing. The light coming from the door splashed the surfaces and, more faintly, the far wall. The near wall, just the other side of the bulkhead, remained in darkness. Except Forsyth could feel that someone was there, their hand hovering over the light switch on the interior control panel.

'Hello, Benjamin,' he said.

Whatever breathing there had been, ceased.

As Forsyth's eyes adapted to the dark, he could make out the slight outline of Velter against the pale panelling. His dark skin was flat black. Either his eyes were screwed tight shut, or he had turned his head away.

'I can see you, Benjamin. This is no way to behave.'

'Leave me alone.'

'Come now, I'm not going to hurt you.'

'Stan's dead because of you.'

'Konstantinos is dead because he gave his life to science. Unfortunately, a little too soon for anything to be concluded.'

'No.'

'No what? I haven't asked you anything yet.' Forsyth tutted. 'It would be easier if you just came back out into the axis.'

'Easier for you.'

'Yes, easier for me. But easier for you, too.'

Forsyth saw that Velter had moved slightly away from the control panel, and the status indicators were illuminated. The border of the light switch was now visible, and he took the opportunity to swing around, dab at it, and keep his hand in the way.

The lights brightened swiftly, and Velter saw there was no point in dimming them again. He turned to face his tormentor.

'I won't do it.'

'You don't know what I want.'

'I do. I do know what you want. You want to get rid of me, like you got rid of Stan. I know that's what you're thinking.'

'I want you to be happy, Benjamin. Don't you want to be happy too?'

'I'm not a child!' Velter clenched his fists, one of which was holding on to a grab rail down the side of the door. 'I know you want me to go down to Io. I know, and I will not.'

'It's the only way you'll be free of me, Benjamin. Because I'm not going anywhere.'

Velter tensed. His face was rigid. A muscle along his jaw line stood proud under his skin, casting a deeper shadow across his cheek. 'There's more than one way to be free of you,' he said between clenched teeth.

Forsyth frowned. He had no idea what Velter meant. 'You're quite wrong. Of course you are, because you're disagreeing with me, but still: you're wrong. I'm staying right here. Now, I know you believe there's something down on Io—'

'Shut up, shut up, shut up! You arrogant little snotneus, in love with the sound of your own voice. Listen, for once in your life. Listen. You know there is something on Io. You know it. You know what it is, where it is, what shape it is, you've probably even estimated its mass and volume and age. But because you don't and you can't admit defeat, you want to intimidate us into agreeing with you that we cannot trust our own eyes, our own instincts, our own instruments.'

'You can't—'

'I said shut up! We helped design these instruments. We are experts too. I know it's there. I don't have to go and die in order to prove it to you. It's there. It's there. And you are afraid of it.'

'Don't talk nonsense, Benjamin. I'm afraid of nothing

because the whole universe is explicable by equations that only I understand.'

'You're scared. Of the ziggurat. Of what it represents. Of the unknown, of the things you're not able to fit in to your neat little equations. You're terrified. You're, you're mad with fear.' He finished and he was panting, gasping for breath.

'I think you should be relieved of your duties. You're clearly unfit to continue with access to the whole of the ship, so you're confined to the wheel.'

Velter laughed. Loudly. At him.

'Confined to the wheel? With Luca? Soon there'll be more of us down there than up here.'

He pushed past Forsyth, deliberately – so Forsyth thought – barging into him and knocking him against the door frame. But there was no apology in the offing. Velter continued up the axis, and for a moment, Forsyth thought he should follow, to make sure that the scientist took one of the access tunnels to the wheel.

But who would dare disobey him? No one.

And yet, he still hadn't managed to persuade Velter to take the last probe down. Ah, but that was it, wasn't it? He hadn't ordered him to go. The next time they had this discussion, that was what he'd do. No argument. Just instruction.

20

Forsyth's screens were dancing. They were singing. They were a fully costumed Wagnerian opera, reaching the climax as lightning flashed overhead and thunder rolled. It was glorious, and Forsyth was rapt.

The mouths that flew open and snapped shut were nothing to be feared: they were the chorus, praising the cosmos in this moment of crescendo. His new physics was there, right there, just beyond the hull, and the formulae to describe it was here, right here, within his grasp. He felt the numbers shift, the vectors spin and the variables winnow themselves towards a fixed result.

A moment longer and he'd have it. A perfect way of describing everything that would ever exist. So, so close.

Then suddenly, the sound became discordant. The high notes were still as sublime, but the left hand was clanging.

'Radiation warning. All crew to take shelter. Radiation warning. All crew to take shelter.'

He turned around, his concentration broken. The lights seemed to be throbbing, both in his module and outside in the axis.

'Radiation warning. All crew to take shelter.'

'Turn it off,' he called. He waited.

'Radiation warning. All crew to take shelter.'

The lights made him screw his face up. The doorway blurred, and he had to blink to bring it back into focus.

'I said, turn it off. How am I supposed to concent—'

'Radiation warning. All crew to take shelter.'

Fuming, he pushed himself away from his work, and towards the door. He leaned out into the axis, to see what else was going on, who might be passing. The corridor was empty, but he could see it now, the strobing effect of the lights as a pulse that seemed to ripple down from Command towards the stern.

'Rory,' said the intercom. It had Kattenbeck's voice. 'Where are you?'

'I'm trying to work,' he shouted, only realising that no one was going to hear him after his words had faded away.

'Radiation warning. All crew to take shelter.'

There was a thing – a protocol, they called it – that he ought to be doing. Going to Command, closing the doors fore and aft, pumping the hull voids with water. The shield should be sufficient though, at all times, so he'd not heeded that part of the training, or he'd pretended to heed it and knew he'd never comply.

'Rory? Don't make me come back there.'

Forsyth tutted. He'd not get any peace until he cancelled the alarm and told Kattenbeck she was overbearing, and he could look after himself quite well enough, thank you very much. He pushed out into the axis and went hand-over-hand towards the rotating section. He could see Spinu in the doorway, glaring at him, and he glared right back.

'Out of my way,' he said, when he was still ten metres from her.

He passed through the rotating hub, caught momentarily the soft hiss of friction in the supposedly frictionless bearings, and was through. Spinu dropped out of sight, moving behind the door, and when he was through, she pushed the bulkhead door closed behind him. The forward bulkhead was already tight.

'Didn't you hear the alarm?' said Kattenbeck.

Forsyth moved to his habitual chair – the captain's chair – to find it already occupied. By Mariucci. He looked over the

232

rest of the seats, and there was Velter too. So he ignored the doctor's question.

'What are they doing here?'

'It's an emergency, Rory. The ship is hot, or hadn't you noticed?'

'My orders, the captain's orders, were that they were to be confined to the wheel.'

'The emergency?'

'The orders, Petra. The orders.' He moved towards Mariucci, who was studiously looking anywhere but at him. 'Out of my seat.'

Kattenbeck argued back. 'The protocols clearly state—'

'My orders also clearly stated, but that seems to have meant little to you. Luca, you're in my seat and I demand you move right now.'

Mariucci did look up now, right into Forsyth's eyes. 'There are other seats, Rory. You can be captain in any of them.'

'I asked, Petra, why he and Benjamin are here. I haven't received an adequate answer yet.'

'Because if they'd stayed where they were, they ran the risk of being exposed to harmful rates of radiation. Bremsstrahlung is rattling through the hull and it's that that set off the alarms. Surely you must have noticed?'

Forsyth dragged his attention away from Mariucci, sitting in his seat, and to Kattenbeck.

'What concern is that of mine? They were confined to the wheel. The wheel is where they should be. Those were my explicit orders.'

Kattenbeck, holding loosely on to a monitor that was pulsing red and black with the alert, stared across the pit at him.

'If you want to be explicit, a radiation warning is an immediate danger to life, and as such, it classifies as a medical emergency. In those circumstances, as the senior medical personnel on the Aphrodite – as the only medical personnel left on the Aphrodite – my orders override yours.' She turned back to the screen and contemplated its words. 'I can call you sir, if that makes you feel better about it.'

'Cancel the alarm,' he said. 'Get everybody back to work.'

Kattenbeck looked at Colvin, then Blasco, then back to Colvin. There was something unsaid that needed saying.

'Out with it,' he said, and he didn't even need to try to sound bored. He was bored, already.

'We need to change course,' said Colvin, almost inaudibly. 'We need to leave the radiation belt.'

'We have the shield,' said Forsyth.

'It's not enough,' she said, then more strongly. 'It's not enough.'

'It's not,' said Aasen. She lifted up her tablet and tabbed a function on its grease-smeared surface. The chimes of new items being added to the list of faults sounded like a Great Peal. 'The ship is being destroyed.'

'That's just ridiculous hyperbole,' he countered. 'The ship is doing perfectly well. All the systems are functioning. We don't have a problem.'

'The ship is built on multiple redundancies and error-checking, like the probes. Things are breaking down faster than I can replace them. That's what's happening. When systems actually fail, it'll be because it's the last possible circuit breaking, not the only circuit.'

Blasco shrugged. 'When it goes, it goes. If we can't fix that critical part, we risk never being able to move again. Your decision, Rory.'

'We haven't settled your Io problem yet,' said Forsyth. 'A day or two, or three, isn't going to make any difference at all. Unless everyone wants to concede there was nothing there, no signal, no structure, and no need to change course for the radiation belt in the first place ...' He glanced at Mariucci, who was mercifully silent, 'then we proceed as planned. Hanne needs to get back to work on the probe, and Luca and Benjamin need to return to the wheel.'

'The signal is real,' said Borner. 'The signal is real. The ziggurat is real.'

'Well, then.' Forsyth turned back to the bulkhead door, where Spinu was. 'Valeria, if you could open this up. And somebody, please cancel that infernal alarm.'

'You can't go out there,' said Kattenbeck. 'It's too hot.'

'I'm not used to taking orders from a mere medical doctor, Petra. Perhaps you should be confined to the wheel as well.' He hung off a rail in front of the bulkhead. 'Valeria, please?'

Spinu went to open the door, but hesitated with her hand on the mechanism.

'Only if you let me go down to Io.'

'If you're trying to blackmail me, I can probably find the wit to open the door myself,' said Forsyth.

'I want to go down. Stan wasn't worthy. He died because of that. I am. I am worthy, and they'll protect me.'

'Valeria, not this again,' said Kattenbeck.

Spinu glared at her. 'He owes me this.'

'You'll die as surely as Stan died. In agony, drowning in your own vomit, boiled from the inside, skin sloughing off from the out. Blind, mad, spasming.'

'They won't let it happen!'

'They're not there now, Valeria. If they ever were, they're long gone. All that's left is these ... buildings, and they may as well be mausoleums for all the good they do us.' Kattenbeck pinched the bridge of her nose. 'I'm coming to the conclusion that Benjamin's right: they're traps. Nothing more than bait. And look: it's working.'

Spinu turned back to Forsyth. 'I'm going. I'm taking that place.'

'What if it's not yours to take. I might have offered it to someone else.'

'Who? Yasmin?'

'It was my discovery,' said Borner.

'It was mine!'

'We are not doing this,' said Kattenbeck, raising her voice over the top of everyone. 'We are not sending anyone else to their deaths. We're three crew members down already. Three colleagues. Three friends.'

She looked at Mariucci, and Forsyth followed her gaze. Rather than being a threat, it seemed to him that the former captain was lost. Lost and bitter in a way that indicated he neither knew what he'd lost, nor why he was bitter about it.

'People have their own agency,' said Forsyth. 'They can choose to sacrifice themselves if they want. For science. For knowledge. For humanity. That's why we all came here in the first place, wasn't it? Wasn't it, Benjamin?'

He glared at Velter, who resolutely stared into the pit. As much as it would be best for him to go down, the only volunteer he was going to get was Spinu: hardly an objective observer.

'Deirdre? How about you? Why did you come here? Break new ground? Achieve something that had never been achieved before? Or are you here because you thought this would be good for your career? Or that you might meet that special someone?'

Before Blasco could react, he turned his spotlight on her.

'And our pilot. Theresa. Is this just a job to you? Is it the same as hauling metals from L4 to low Earth orbit, day in, day out? Is the Aphrodite nothing more than some space tug? I'd rather hope it was something more meaningful than that.'

He moved on. 'Hanne? Tell me this isn't the greatest privilege you've ever experienced. To be here, to be in this company, at this time? Yes, there are problems, but they're problems you can fix. Your whole life has led up to this point. Why wouldn't you want to take that one last step?'

Spinu caught on to what he was doing. 'I've already said I'd go,' she said.

Forsyth waved her away. 'When you get there, Valeria, and there's nothing to see, you might be tempted to make something up. I'm sorry, but it needs to be said. Someone who's kept their objectivity would be ideal. Someone like Deirdre.'

'You have to let me go!'

'This is exactly why you shouldn't. You've lost all scientific reason. If you were more rational—'

'Like you?'

'Yes, like me.' He let his irritation show. 'Really, who else did you expect as a benchmark?'

'Rory,' said Velter, 'let's just tell Earth.'

'Then there'd be no point in ever going home, would there?' Forsyth said. 'No point in us being here, no point in the sacrifices we've already made. And absolutely no point in us pretending to be a serious scientific mission at all, if you're determined to undermine our credibility like that. We're only in this position because you collectively insist there's an alien artefact, and with the best will in the world – this one or any other – insisting is not proof. There's two ways out of this impasse, and no one appears to want to take either of them.'

'Enough. Enough.' Mariucci finally stirred himself. 'If it will save lives, I'll go.'

Forsyth sniffed. 'You ruled yourself out by saying you'd sabotage the probe and lie about what you might see. I have no confidence that your offer now is made in good faith, nor that your position has changed.' He addressed the rest of the crew. 'Your former captain has shown himself to a be a vindictive and spiteful crewmember, who will not keep his word.'

'I will still do it.' Mariucci looked up with hooded eyes. 'If they trust me.'

'But I don't trust you, and it's my opinion that's important here.'

'Perhaps they should ask themselves why that's the case.'

'I'm not just captain and the senior scientific officer. I'm the senior scientist here and anywhere I'm present. My word is authoritative. It has weight, if you prefer. I speak, and other people listen. They accept what I say. And if I say there is no ... thing ... on Io, then that is the truth.'

Mariucci laughed. Not just laughed, but laughed at him. 'It

was a mistake bringing you here. Oh, it was a mistake bringing this ship here: the shield doesn't work, or at least doesn't work as Laszlo intended, or it does and there are unintended consequences. Yes, we have our various neuroses, our visions, our dreams: they're are all part of it. But you? You have become a monster.'

'And you should be in the wheel, Luca. You can remember the way?' Forsyth cast his gaze around Command. 'Benjamin might have to show you.'

'I know the way. I also know that the alarm is still ongoing. You'll have to suffer me until it passes.'

'We have difficult decisions to make. They are best made without your presence.' Forsyth affected a sigh. 'We can leave the radiation belt just as soon as someone reliable takes the last probe to Io.'

'Why does it have to be someone else?' wondered Mariucci. 'If you're the standard against which we're all measured, why not you?'

'Don't be preposterous, Luca. I'm the captain.'

'A captain brings his crew home.'

'Well, you've clearly failed. As the good doctor has already noted, we have two bodies strapped to the hull, and we've left another on Io which, unfortunately, we're not going to be able to retrieve.'

'I'm aware enough of my failure to realise that I need to protect what's left of them from you.' Mariucci looked down into his lap. 'I know that much.'

'They don't need protecting from me. They needed liberating from you. Now, Deirdre: I require some quid pro quo from you. If you want to lay a course that takes us out of the radiation belt, you can do that. But you only enact it after we make a second pass of Io to launch the probe. Since our planetary geologist refuses to lend himself to the endeavour, we need another investigator. I've decided it has to be you.'

Spinu growled in the back of her throat. 'I'm taking that place. I'm going to meet them.'

'Anyone would be a better candidate than you. But Deirdre is my choice.'

'You can't do this to me.'

'It's in your own best interests. I thought you wanted to prove the existence of your alien gods, or however you think of them? Deirdre is far more suitable. Calm, objective, a neutral observer. Her testimony would be valid evidence, one way or the other. You'd make yourself a laughing stock, and put the whole theory firmly within the category of crank. That's what would happen if I chose you.'

Colvin looked increasingly bewildered. 'But I don't want to go.'

'Nonsense. You want to solve this mystery,' and he gave the word air-quotes before reattaching himself to his handhold. 'And you want to do so in an unambiguous and unequivocal way, so that your fellow crew can get on with the rest of the mission.'

'But I'll be dead.'

'And everyone else you might care about will be alive. Which is surely what you want. The alternative is that we stay in the radiation zone for longer. That probe doesn't get launched until we have a reliable astronaut to go with it.'

'No one is going to Io,' said Kattenbeck.

'The crew disagree. When can we next manoeuvre past Io, Deirdre?'

'Twelve hours?' she said.

'Then plot the course, and the one after to move us out of the equatorial plane. By the time we make the pass, either you'll agree to go, or we're stuck here, going around in circles about Io.'

'The ship will fall apart,' said Aasen. 'It won't last.'

'All the more reason for Deirdre to – I believe the expression is – take one for the team. Now,' he turned back to a seething Spinu, 'open this door. I have work to do.'

21

Forsyth watched Colvin through the small glass panel in the airlock door. She was in her spacesuit. She was decompressing. She'd climb outside the hull when she was done, and join Aasen in the probe bay, to be fitted for the Arcas's journey to Io's antijove.

He'd won, in the end. It was inevitable, and quite why she'd fought him so hard for so long was a matter of regret. For him, not her: all that time wasted.

Aasen had made further modifications to the probe. Now, the water bubble was enhanced with hard shielding about its circumference, and that might be enough. Jupiter was particularly stormy at the moment, and nothing was guaranteed. But it was time to go, and the mission was as well equipped as Aasen could make it.

Of course, Aasen had needed guidance through the computer list. He'd told her that fitting out Arcas had priority over any other repairs, and that any objections that the other crew might raise were to be ignored. The computer knew what was best for her, and if she followed the list, all would be well.

She didn't know why the computer was telling her to do things that went against her every instinct, both as an engineer and a human being, but she was too lost in her mania to start questioning it now.

Forsyth quite liked the idea, that he could order her about without appearing to be doing so, that he could torment her. He liked it so much he allowed himself to smile. Only for a moment, though. The muscles in his face resented being contorted so.

Soon, they would be free of this curse – that was how he saw it now – and they could sail on to make more credible discoveries, and he could incubate his theory. It was right there, like it was on the tip of his tongue. When he closed his eyes, he could see the symbols sliding into place, like tumblers in a lock. The shape of the key was within his grasp, and with it, greatness.

He resented the energy he'd had to spend managing the crew. They ought to know their jobs by now.

At least Colvin had seen sense. She was doing what was required of her. They could manage without a navigator, surely? It was just maths. Not even particularly complicated maths. She'd already laid in the next course that would untangle them from the radiation belt. All Blasco had to do was follow it.

He turned himself around using the handholds, and pushed himself obliquely back towards his module. Half an hour before departure. Enough time to immerse himself in his data, to see his glory reflected back at him, to hear the chorus sing his praises.

He paused at the door. Kattenbeck was coming down the axis from Command. Blasco was close behind her. He frowned, and wondered what it could be this time. It was always something.

Borner was behind Blasco. And Velter! How dare he break his curfew.

And Mariucci.

'What is the meaning of this? Get back to work, all of you. And you – you two – shouldn't even be here.'

Kattenbeck took a handrail a few metres from Forsyth. 'Do you know where Valeria is?'

'Valeria? No. Why should I know where she is?'

Borner squirrelled past Kattenbeck and headed down the axis. Velter and Mariucci headed to the foremost modules. Blasco stayed at Kattenbeck's shoulder.

'She said something to Theresa. About not being denied. Then she disappeared.'

Borner emerged from the spacesuit storage module. 'Her suit's missing.'

'Check airlock two, and the empty probe bay. She can't have come past Command.'

Velter and Mariucci moved to the next module clockwise.

'Why can't you keep these people under some sort of control?' Forsyth looked inside his own workspace, scanning the corners and up along the bulkhead to see if Spinu had secreted herself there. If she was angry with one specific person, it could well be him for telling her the truth about her reliability.

Borner looked into the darkened airlock, and then dialled up the lights. 'She's not in here.'

'Go in. Check.' Kattenbeck stared at Forsyth. 'Rory, this has gone far enough. We're getting Deirdre out of there, and we're going home.'

'You'll do neither such thing. You forget, I'm captain now.'

'As the Senior Medical Officer,' she said, 'I'm relieving you of your position. You're unfit to command.'

'And you are?' He barked a laugh into her face. 'I've seen you, talking to yourself, muttering and murmuring.'

'If I was talking to myself, it wouldn't be so bad, Rory. None of us are fit to command. So we'll just have to make the best decisions we can together. We shouldn't have let things get so far, but this is what happens when a bunch of mad people are let loose on a spaceship.'

'I absolutely forbid this.'

'How are you going to stop us?' said Blasco. She pushed off in the direction of the primary airlock, and landed unerringly across the doorway. 'That ... that's not Deirdre.'

'Repressurise the airlock,' ordered Kattenbeck.

Borner bounced across to Blasco, and looked to the airlock controls. Blasco slammed the heel of her hand against the door. It only served to alert Spinu, who looked at the face behind the porthole, then pushed herself over to the outer door. She started to pump the chamber down towards vacuum.

'Do something. Where is she?' Blasco pressed her face to the glass. 'Valeria! Where is she? What have you done with her?'

Velter and Mariucci redoubled their efforts to search the modules, while Forsyth suddenly found himself without authority, or purpose.

'I can't do anything from here,' said Borner. 'I'll have to go to Command.'

'Then go,' said Kattenbeck.

'I'm in charge here,' he said. 'I'll say who goes where.'

'Rory? Shut up. Yasmin, tell Hanne she needs to get out of the probe bay. Now.'

'I'm in charge!' Forsyth shouted, and Kattenbeck was close enough to land a stinging smack against his ear. She spun away, and Forsyth rebounded against the bulkhead.

'I said shut up, you labertasche.'

'She's opening the outer door.' Blasco pushed off backwards towards the spacesuits.

'Theresa, you don't have the ninety minutes to decompress.'

'Then I'll go out without it.'

'You know how it works: you can't.'

Forsyth, half his face red, partially deaf with his head still ringing from the blow, put his hand up to gingerly cup his ear. 'How dare you.'

But she wasn't listening. Neither were Mariucci, heading towards the probe section, or Velter finishing his inspection of the last of the modules.

'Outer door open. She's going out.'

Blasco jerked backwards suddenly. She moaned, low and deep. Kattenbeck used a wall to reach the now-vacated airlock door, and looked inside for a moment. Then she thumbed the mechanism to close the outer door, and again to repressurise the module.

'Benjamin! Get me my resus kit from the wheel. Now! The paddles. Everything.'

Velter flew past, dangerously fast, dangerously close to Forsyth.

He'd had enough of this. Time to reassert himself.

He ducked through into his module, and heaved the door shut. He took a moment to spin the wheel, before going to his screens and his keyboard. He held the arms of his seat for a moment, pulling himself into contact with the back, before clipping the lap strap across him.

He started typing.

'Hanne. Ignore what Command are telling you.'

'Hanne. Listen only to me.'

'Hanne. Deirdre isn't coming. Valeria is.'

'Hanne. She can't be allowed to take her place.'

'Hanne. You'll have to go instead.'

'Hanne. Get into the bubble. Fill it with water.'

'Hanne. Tell me when you're ready to launch.'

He ignored the sounds of wailing from outside. He surmised that Spinu had killed Colvin, stashed her body up against the bulkhead wall, and assumed her place in the airlock. A casual observer would see what they wanted to see. He conceded it was actually very cunning. Spinu probably thought she was on the verge of getting exactly what she wanted.

But she hadn't reckoned with his backdoor into Aasen's mind.

He didn't know if he could override the commands that Borner was going to give from her workstation. Presumably, using his captain's credentials, he could. The automatic systems would guide Arcas to the antijove, not as accurately as Blasco might, but it would be close enough.

It was a shame about Colvin, but Aasen was an acceptable alternative. He tutted once, and then entered his passwords on the ship's system.

The file tree was confusing. There were a lot of dead ends and false starts before he could find the probe functions, which were coming online as Aasen activated them. The physical docking mechanism was elsewhere, and he had to assume that Borner could access all those same controls from Command. He needed to shut her out, at least until it was too late and Aasen was on her way.

He found Borner's permissions, and simply revoked them. It would take her a while to realise what had happened, and longer to work out who was responsible. She'd put it down to damage, and keep trying the same things over and over again, in the hope that next time they'd work.

The commotion outside had died down. Good. It made it easier to concentrate.

'Hanne. What stage are you at?'

Could Spinu interfere with the launch? What if she attacked Aasen beforehand? Or damaged the water bubble in her attempt to oust the engineer from what she'd see as her rightful place?

Aasen wasn't responding to him. Of course she wasn't. The tablet was for giving instructions, not asking for information. He'd have to talk to her instead.

There was a headset and microphone combination some-where nearby. He distinctly remembered having one at the start of the voyage and thinking that he was never going to use it, because why would he? It was only this peculiar set of cir-cumstances that dictated his rapid retrieval of it from wherever he'd put it.

His search, like everything else, was methodical. And he found it, taped to the rear of one of his screens. He tore the plastic open – it was still in its bag – and put it on. The ear which Kattenbeck had struck was still very sore, throbbing and swollen, so he eased that part away and behind, so that it rested on his scalp. He had to plug the headset in, because it wasn't charged up and wouldn't make an automatic connection.

'Hanne? Hanne, this is Rory. Can you hear me?'

'Rory? What's going on? I can't fix the ship if I go to Io.'

'I know. It can't be helped. The computer's telling you to go, so what choice do you have? Are you in the bubble yet? Are you filling it with water?'

'It's not possible, Rory. It's not possible.'

'What do you mean?'

'I can't do this on my own. I can't be both inside the bubble, and filling the bubble up.'

'That's ridiculous. Who designed it that way?'

'I did. I designed it that way. This was always the way it was supposed to work.'

Spinu was somewhere on the hull, working her way around to the probe bay.

'Are the outer doors open or closed?'

'Closed, still.'

'Are you under pressure or in vacuum?'

'In vacuum.'

'Good. Make sure you keep both inner and outer doors shut until I tell you otherwise. This is what I want you to do – I'm sure the computer will agree with me in just a minute. I want you to work out a way of inflating the bubble with you inside it.'

The ship vibrated. He could feel it through his tailbone and up his spine. He'd never felt anything like it before, and he wondered what it was. It couldn't be the engines, because he knew that slight sound and had grown used to it. Thrusters? Possibly? What were the crew doing out there?

'Hanne? Do it as quickly as you can. It doesn't matter how, it just needs to be done.'

'But I don't have the parts, Rory. I can't physically do it.'

'I'm absolutely certain that someone as resourceful as you can work this out.' He reached for the keyboard and started typing. 'Hanne. Listen to Rory. Get in the bubble. Fill it with water. It's important. I need you to do this.'

Again, he could feel the vibration in his seat. The monitors all quivered. And this time, it didn't stop. Something was happening. Despite the pain in his ear, it told him he was in motion.

Which was nonsense. He was completely stationary, and in zero gravity.

The screens were shaking now, fast and hard, chattering on the ends of their booms and pivots. There was a down direction forming towards the far wall, the one that pointed out into space. He looked behind him at the bulkhead door that led out into the axis, which was slowly, inexorably, becoming up.

He hastily pulled the plug on his headset, unclipped himself from his seat, and found himself moving, unbidden, towards the array of screens. He twisted around and grabbed the back of his chair, using it as a ladder and standing on top of it to boost himself further, jumping – having to jump – for the door.

The gravity was very slight, but very disconcerting. It made judging movement almost impossible. He could feel himself slowing as he approached the door, and he had to cling to the wheel to stop himself dropping back. He wedged a foot into a grab rail, and twisted the closing wheel back open again.

When the door came loose, it swung open all on its own, ponderously and possessing all of its inertia. It nearly knocked him from his perch. He scrambled through the doorway and into the axis, where a degree of normality returned.

At the very centre of the axis, there was still zero gravity. But everything was spinning about that axis, gaining speed. He slid through the zone of no gravity to the other side of the corridor, and bounced off the far wall.

And when he tried to stand up, every sense he had told him what he was experiencing was bad and wrong. His head was light, but his feet were not. He felt immediately sick, and ducked right back down, getting his head as close to the axis wall as he could.

It was like being in a washing machine. The whole of the Aphrodite was turning, when it should only have been the wheel.

Except: if the bearings had failed, the wheel was going to transfer its entire momentum to the rest of the ship.

He started to crawl towards Command, on his hands and knees. The low gravity made him bounce, and he lost contact with the wall as if he were a toy balloon in a breeze, the lead from his headset snaking along behind him as an ersatz string. He tumbled head-over-heels, and grabbed at a rail as it went past.

He clung on as his body settled against the wall again. He needed to get to Command before any of the others did, and lock himself inside. No one was going to usurp his authority. He started moving again, going hand-over-hand. No one.

22

Forsyth hesitated at the edge of the now non-rotating hub, and tried to imagine what was happening in the wheel. It would be spinning slower now, much slower as it transferred all its rotational energy to the main mass of the ship: the water, the fuel, the nuclear reactor and the radiators. The wheel was further away from the axis, so more gravity there, but a lot less than before. Loose objects would fly at unpredictable angles, and there'd be accidents where someone might stand up too quickly and bang their head off the ceiling.

Certainly more than enough confusion to occupy everyone there, and allow him to get across to Command without grabby hands reaching for him out of the access tunnels.

He clambered carefully around the mouth of a tunnel and continued on. He could use any part of the wall as down, just as long as he was connected to it. He swarmed over the door frame to Command and went around behind it to push it shut. Borner was there, but she was preoccupied with … counting? She was counting in binary, out loud, facing her screen, strapped in to a chair which had automatically tried to adjust to the local direction of down. It had failed to compensate enough, and it had left her head dangling at an awkward angle.

'… zero one one zero one zero zero one …'

She wasn't paying any attention to anything else but the stream of numbers that slid up her display. More importantly, she hadn't even noticed Forsyth.

He levered the bulkhead closed, and spun the hand-wheel.

He didn't need to do anything about Borner – something he was relieved about because he didn't want to touch her any more than he wanted to be touched – so he climbed over the backs of the chairs to his captain's seat and strapped in.

It felt almost, but not quite, normal: the angles were slightly wrong. He supposed Blasco could counteract the spin with a burst of the cold gas thrusters, so this configuration wasn't permanent, and it certainly served a purpose for now. He gathered up the trailing end of his headset cable and plugged it in in front of him.

He logged in, and again had to shuffle his way through the file tree.

There was no instruction for sealing off Command.

Because why would there be? What sort of possible disaster might befall a spaceship in a solar system with precisely one spacefaring species that would mean they'd need to lock an internal door?

There was still Aasen, though. He had to launch her.

'Hanne? Hanne, are you there?'

'I'm going to the temple. I'm going to the temple.'

It wasn't the voice he was expecting. 'Valeria?'

'I didn't wait. I couldn't wait. I'm going by myself.'

Forsyth frowned. 'Valeria, where are you?'

'I'm going to the temple.'

He found the external cameras and cycled his way through them. Then back. A white blob moved through the field of vision. If it was a spacesuit, then it was beyond the radius of the radiators and moving away from the Aphrodite.

'Valeria, did you let go of the ship?'

'I'm going to the temple. You can't stop me now.'

He cycled the cameras again. Jupiter, huge. Io, massive, bright, sulphurous. Spinu, drifting away. There was no snaking safety line visible. She'd either loosed it, or never had one in the first place.

'I'm going to the temple.'

Then she crossed the magnetopause, and he had to pull the headphone plug out.

'Valeria, you stupid, stupid woman.'

She'd arrive on Io for certain, because they were very close and the attraction of the moon was sufficient to sweep her up in its path. But she'd hit the ground at over a kilometre a second, not that she'd live that long to experience the impact.

'You little idiot.'

He switched his attention to Aasen. With Spinu gone, she could now safely open the outer probe bay doors and launch. He navigated his way to the fault list and started typing in some new instructions.

'You have to stop, Rory.'

'Not now, Luca.'

'Yes. Now.'

Forsyth straightened up in his seat and saw that the door to Command was half open. Mariucci was holding on to the grab rail on the door itself.

'What do I have to stop? I expect you can't remember.'

Mariucci moved closer, climbing across the chair backs just as Forsyth had done. He got halfway, and looked at the palm of his left hand.

'It says here, you have to be stopped. It's in my handwriting, so at some point in the past I thought it was necessary.'

'It's not necessary now, Luca.'

Mariucci looked at his hand again. 'No. It says it's still necessary.'

Forsyth pushed the headset off and unclipped his seat strap. He should be able to evade Mariucci by slowly moving around Command, and then end up back at the door. From there, he could go anywhere on the ship.

But as a long-term strategy it wasn't particularly effective. He needed to lure him into a place he couldn't escape from. One of the modules, in fact: all their entrances were now at the top, in their ceilings, like medieval oubliettes. Push him into one of those, and seal the door, and it was unlikely that Mariucci would be able to escape.

For now, he dropped to the wall of Command, near the new equator of the sphere, and waited for Mariucci's somewhat laboured approach. He watched as he climbed over the captain's chair, and then the one next to Borner – he paused to rest his hand on her shoulder and squeeze it – and then judged the distance between them.

Forsyth jumped across the sphere. The sensation was of up, then suddenly down. He couldn't rotate fast enough, couldn't get his legs under him, and hit the opposite side hard, shoulder first.

It hurt. It made his eyes swim with pain. When he looked up, though, he could see Mariucci looking up at him from the antipodes, ready to jump himself. Forsyth started to scramble uphill towards the door.

Mariucci managed to land on his feet, because even though the memories of years of zero g manoeuvres might have fled, the muscles still retained the images of them. He looked at his hand, at the black pen-marks he'd made there.

Trust me, it said. *Stop Rory. Do whatever you have to.*

That was why he was here. He climbed towards the door, surely and carefully as the gravity fell away. Forsyth was almost within reach. Then his quarry was through, and he'd lost sight of him. He pushed himself upwards and forwards with a thrust of his arms, and then he too was looking along the axis.

The soles of Forsyth's ship-slippers were a few metres ahead, and receding. Mariucci looked at his hand, and efficiently headed after him, never letting go of one handhold until he'd made the next. He'd been somewhere like this before, a microgravity environment, but it had been open to space, and a single false move could have killed him. It wasn't like that here, but he knew what it was to have some, and also not enough, gravity.

They passed the hub, and into the next section, where there

were twelve openings around the circumference in four lines of three. Forsyth scuttled around the perimeter until he was above Mariucci, then he launched himself across the distance, fists out in front of him like a superhero.

They hit Mariucci in his flank. He spun sideways, out of reach of Forsyth's follow-up grapple, but he rattled around the axis until he could reorientate himself. As he did so, he was struck again, this time in the back, and he clattered against the plastic panels. He bounced, and determined to be ready next time when he finally stopped moving.

He took hold of a grab rail, and almost instantly received a two-footed kick in the chest. Now he did go flying, backwards in a tumble, and he banged against the aft bulkhead.

He looked at his hand, reread the writing there, and saw Forsyth lining up another leap. They were too far apart for that – the gap between jumping and striking was suddenly enough for Mariucci to swing himself aside and even wait for Forsyth to flail at him before crashing himself into the bulkhead. Then he swung himself back, and he used his strength to get his hands behind Forsyth and find a grab rail in order to pin the scientist against the wall.

They were almost face to face. Forsyth had one arm trapped, but with his free hand he pushed into Mariucci's nose, straining his neck, widening the gap between them. Mariucci pulled tighter, and Forsyth's breath squeezed out of him with an audible *oof*.

Forsyth's hand came up again, and this time clawed at Mariucci, at his forehead, his cheek, and eventually at his eyes. Mariucci shook his head violently to deflect the nails, and increased the pressure on Forsyth by jerking his grip, crushing Forsyth between him and the wall in a series of hammer blows.

Then they were spinning and twisting, bouncing and jarring across the axis, moving from one side to another, across the up and down to the walls, locked together, pulling and gouging and pushing and writhing. Forsyth redoubled his efforts against

Mariucci's face. There was blood now, red against the white plastic, red against the pale skin.

Mariucci could either hold on and have his skin torn off, strip by strip, or let go and regroup. There was something written on his hand that would help him, but he couldn't see it right now. So he let go, and simultaneously pushed hard, throwing Forsyth almost the entire length of the section.

He twisted onto his front, took hold of a grab rail and consulted his palm.

Trust me. Stop Rory. Do whatever you have to.

That seemed unequivocal.

He raised his head. Forsyth was at the fore bulkhead, holding on one-handed like he was, his other hand clutching his bruised ribs, breathing hard and fast. Mariucci's face felt wet, and he used his sleeve to wipe some of it away. It stained the material in dark streaks, and it didn't really help him either.

What did 'Do whatever you have to' mean? He had a moment of doubt, but it was cleared away with a glance at 'Trust me'. If he'd meant anything more explicit, he would have written it down. 'Whatever' gave him freedom. 'Whatever' was not prescriptive.

He started forward, closing the distance, and for the first time in this strange, almost silent battle, Forsyth looked worried. He came towards Mariucci, but obliquely, trying to cross more wall and end up on the opposite side of the axis.

Mariucci angled his attack to narrow the difference, and Forsyth suddenly jumped across – awkwardly, so that his attempt to jump straight back and on top of Mariucci was telegraphed. Mariucci twisted aside, and Forsyth thought better of it. He pulled himself back, and Mariucci took the opportunity to move forward.

That felt good. He kept on moving, forward and sideways, keeping Forsyth off-balance and retreating, until they were up against the fore bulkhead, and Forsyth was looking over his shoulder through the door and back to the hub.

As he did so, Mariucci pushed himself forward and got his head below Forsyth's chin. His arms went around Forsyth's back, and he locked his hands together. He jerked, once, twice, three times, each time making Forsyth give a gratifying gasp of pain.

Hands made fists and beat at his back, his neck, his head, but with his face hidden, there wasn't much that Forsyth could do. They rolled. They turned. Forsyth managed to get both hands on two separate grab rails and slammed Mariucci's back hard against the panelling, but it was the plastic that flexed and dented, not Mariucci's spine. It hurt him, but he was shaking Forsyth like a wet dog.

'Get. Off. Me.'

'Stop Rory. That's what it says. Stop Rory.' Mariucci broke one of Forsyth's handholds by dint of twisting side to side.

Ninety degrees from them was an open door. He recognised it – rather, recognised the symbols around it. He twisted again, Forsyth let go with his other hand to try and prise Mariucci off him. They rolled. They rolled again. And again. The open doorway grew closer. And with a last effort, they were next to it.

Mariucci rolled a final time so that Forsyth was underneath, and then he let go with one hand. He reached for the door frame, got a purchase on his second attempt, and pulled. They both dropped through, falling slowly towards the far wall.

He let go of Forsyth, brought his knees up into the gap between them, then stood up on Forsyth's outstretched body. Forsyth grabbed for Mariucci's ankles, but he was too slow, too surprised by what was happening. Mariucci jumped upwards for the door, driving Forsyth down.

It was enough. Mariucci got his hands and then his elbows through the doorway, swinging his body up and out and snatching at a grab rail before he went too far across the axis.

Below him, Forsyth smacked hard against the airlock's outer door. He bounced, and landed, bounced and landed. He groggily lifted his head, looked around him. The realisation of where he was crossed his face, just as Mariucci started to close the door on him.

Forsyth coiled his legs under him for a jump, bracing himself using the handrails on the outer wall like a swimmer holding on to the poolside. He kicked, and met Mariucci's swinging fist coming down. Mariucci was still knocked aside by the momentum, but Forsyth was stunned by the blow. Using the door to lever his actions, Mariucci grabbed hold of Forsyth's flight suit and stuffed him back in to the airlock like a parcel.

He pushed the door against the jambs, and closed the locking mechanism. He spun the wheel, and leaned over the little window in what was now the floor. He could see Forsyth, reeling and rotating, trying to get himself vertical in an attempt to assault the door again.

Mariucci consulted his hand. *Trust me. Stop Rory. Do whatever you have to.*

Whatever you have to.

He shuffled to the controls. Which one? That one. He hit it with his thumb, and a pump started up.

'Luca? Luca! Let me out. Let me out of here.'

Mariucci rested his forehead on the glass, and there was a thump the other side of it. A hand was briefly smeared across the viewport, but it soon dropped away.

'Luca! You don't know what you're doing. I can save everyone. I can save the planet. I can save the future.'

Thump.

'Luca! Let me out. I demand you let me out. I am vital for the survival of humanity. Only I can save us. You're killing everyone. The whole species. The whole planet. If I die, we all die. Luca! Luca?'

Thump.

'Luca?'

He waited for the thump. It didn't come. Forsyth tried to stand, tried to reach the door. Even though the emergency override was right next to him, right next to the outer door, he seemed to have forgotten its existence. Or perhaps he'd never bothered to learn about it.

It was one thing, at least, that Mariucci could remember. But he didn't pass that information on.

Even though he was looking up, Forsyth wasn't looking at Mariucci. He was focused on something else. 'I can see it. Oh god, finally I can see it. It's glorious. It's glorious.'

Forsyth sank down to his knees, bowed his head. He raised it again for a moment, but his eyelids fluttered, and he slowly subsided to the floor. The pump kept puttering away.

Forsyth curled into a ball. As the pressure dropped, the moisture on his skin, the moisture in his mouth, in his nose, behind his eyes, began to turn to vapour. A thin white mist twisted up and around him, and the pump carried it away just the same as it did the air.

The pump stopped. The airlock was in vacuum.

Mariucci looked at his hand. *Trust me*, it said. *Stop Rory. Do whatever you have to.*

He patted his pockets for a pen, so that he could put a line through the instruction.

23

Mariucci climbed down the ladder to the wheel. Kattenbeck was in the treatment room, with Colvin strapped to the table, Blasco hovering close by outside the open door. Velter emerged from the pharmacy with a bag of vials: he was struggling to keep his feet in contact with the floor, and ended up holding the bag in his teeth to keep his hands free to hold on to things.

The wheel didn't have the rails and straps that the rest of the ship had. They could fix some up. If they wanted to.

'Luca?'

He looked at his hand, then showed it to Blasco. 'I stopped him,' he said.

'Your face is a mess.'

'Yes.'

'I'll get some antiseptic wipes,' said Velter. He delivered the drugs he was carrying through the door to Kattenbeck, then inched his way back to the stores.

Colvin had been in the airlock with Spinu during decompression. The damage to her lungs and soft tissue due to vacuum exposure was nothing compared to the steady erosion of oxygen deprivation. She could well die, and even if she lived, find herself very much like the ship – all those multiple redundancies that should have kept things going reaching the end of their utility. Still just about functioning, but not as intended.

'Where's Hanne?' asked Blasco.

Mariucci looked at his hand, but that was of no use now. 'I don't know. Where was she before?'

'In the probe bay.'

'Is she still there?' Kattenbeck was struggling with being in just one place, able to do just one thing. 'Someone needs to get her. Now.'

'And Yasmin?' asked Blasco.

Mariucci frowned. 'Command?' He had an image of her, counting. She was surrounded by screens, and yes, there was the pit behind her. 'Command.'

'Valeria?' It was clear she didn't want her to be safe, that she was a problem better swept away for what she'd done to Deirdre. Sitting opposite her while she slowly suffocated.

'I ...' Mariucci recalled Forsyth talking to someone, and he didn't think it had been Borner. 'Still outside? I don't know.' He seemed to be saying that a lot. 'I'm sorry.' And that.

Blasco hurried up the ladder. Kattenbeck lunged at Mariucci with her gas injector loaded and ready to fire.

'What happened with Rory?'

'He's in the airlock,' said Mariucci.

Thump.

'Will that hold him? For now?'

Thump.

'Luca?'

Silence.

'Yes.'

'Did you kill him?'

'I think so? He's in vacuum now. So, I think yes.' He looked at his hand. '*Stop Rory*. So that's what I did.'

'Give me the side of your neck,' she said.

'These are the ...'

'Antibiotics.' She pressed the nozzle against his skin and pulled the trigger. The pain was sharp, but it quickly faded. She twisted the vial out, put it in her pocket before it could drift to the floor, and loaded up another. 'Other side.'

Mariucci tilted his head the other way, and there was another burst of bright pain.

'And that was methylphenidate. I'm hoping it might work something on you.' She pushed the gas injector aside, and retrieved a blister pack from her top pocket. 'Take one of these as well. We'll see soon enough if there's any effect.'

He turned the pack over in his hand while Kattenbeck went to fetch some water: her attempts to fill a glass were disastrous, with it ending up everywhere except in the container, and in the end, she went up to Command to get a water bottle.

Velter had found a packet of wipes as he'd promised. 'Can you sit? It'd be easier if you sat, and held on to the arms of the chair.'

All the furniture had magnets deliberately installed in their bases, so that they would stay in contact with the floor whatever the gravity regime. Of course, it was now difficult to get enough friction to move anything to a new location: Mariucci's initial attempts at pushing a chair closer to Velter just resulted in him sliding his own feet away from it. He solved the problem by lifting one side, then the other, and when it was loose, dropping it – very slowly – where he wanted it to go.

Velter did the same with another, and sat opposite him, hooking his feet around the tubular legs, while Mariucci gripped the low arms.

The wipes contained enough alcohol to be considered at least a finger of spirits. It stung his wounds, and left his skin more raw than before. Kattenbeck would probably want to give him a shot or two of something. Fingernails, even on a spaceship, were dirty.

No, she'd already done that. Then she appeared. Where had she gone? Water. She'd gone to get some water.

'I saw Yasmin,' said Kattenbeck. 'Was she counting when you were there?'

'Yes. Ones and zeros.'

'I'll have to see to her in a minute. Was Rory in Command too?'

'Yes.'

'And what was he doing?'

'He was in my seat.' That was right. It had been his seat, and then it hadn't. 'He was typing something out.'

'You interrupted him trying to get Hanne to take the probe down to Io. She – look, Luca, this is all a little complicated, and I'm going to wait until the drugs kick in. But well done. It looks like you got there just in time. You saved her.'

'And Valeria?'

Kattenbeck shook her head. 'She's gone. Her suit's offline. I can only assume she's overboard, lost at sea. We can play back the ship's event log, potentially, if it's still working, and find out what happened. Just sit here, let Benjamin clean you up, and see if you feel better in a while.'

She pressed a pill from the pack into his hand and left him with the water bottle, before going back to look at Colvin's vital signs.

Mariucci tossed the pill to the back of his throat, swigged the water, and swallowed. He could feel it slide slowly down inside, and he made a face.

'All right, Luca?'

There was something happening to him, just as Kattenbeck had said it might, but Mariucci wasn't sure he liked it. Everything was starting to become just that bit sharper, faster, harder, than it was before. Like he was accelerating into the future.

'I feel … odd,' he said. 'Like I'm not quite there. Here. Like I'm getting ahead of myself.'

'All that's happening is that you're sitting down and I'm trying to repair the damage Rory did to you.'

'I fought him,' said Mariucci. 'I didn't think he had it in him, but he was fierce, and persistent. He could have won. He could so easily have won.'

'But he didn't.' Velter took hold of Mariucci's chin and guided it first to the left, then to the right. 'You're not going to win any awards for that face, and neither will I. I think I've done what I can. Petra can have the last word.'

'She usually does,' said Mariucci. He smiled and squinted. 'Is that right? Is that what usually happens?'

'Yes, Luca.' Velter smiled back, and he gathered up the bloody wipes and wadded them together.

Mariucci looked around him and saw the scene for what it was. His smile turned to a grimace. 'This is not good. What happened to us? How did we let get like this?'

'*We* happened. What we were, what we are, our sum and our remainder. This is how we got like this.'

'Ove's dead, isn't he? And Laszlo. Stan. Valeria. Rory.'

Velter put the wipes into a bag, and knotted the handles. As he did so, the intercom buzzed.

'Acceleration, acceleration.'

What scant gravity they had faded away. Things already at rest maintained the habit, while those in motion no longer fell, but moved in predictable, straight lines.

Then the engine started, and its low but constant thrust started everything crawling towards the back of the ship.

'We're on our way,' said Velter.

'But where are we going?'

'I don't know. Away. Away from here.'

'Back to Earth?'

'I don't know if we can.' Velter unhooked himself from his chair and, carefully choosing his angles, pushed off towards the consulting room where Kattenbeck was struggling with treating her patient in only slightly less than zero gravity.

'I should go and do something,' said Mariucci. 'Go to Command, perhaps.'

He looked behind him at the ladder, which was redundant now, and perhaps for ever. He flipped over the back of his chair and he glided towards the base of the access tunnel. He was right about everything being sharper and faster, but it was also clearer. Much clearer. His thoughts felt less jumbled, and more explicit.

Whole sections of his life had been edited out. He couldn't

remember leaving cis-lunar on the Aphrodite for Jupiter, even. But he could just about remember arriving, the hard braking manoeuvre they'd done in the outer fringes of the Jovian atmosphere, the aeroshield they'd used and discarded. That had been something, hadn't it? A spectacle for the people back home.

The ladder rungs scrolled by him, and then he was at the axis, meeting Aasen coming from the aft, Blasco shepherding her from behind.

'Hanne, how are you?'

Aasen screwed her face up. 'The ship's broken, Luca. There's nothing more I can do.'

'I know. I think we're all a bit broken too, and that's okay.'

She unstrapped her tablet, and gave it to him. 'I tried. I tried very hard. And I don't know why I did some of the things I did. But I suppose it made sense at the time.'

'Get something to eat, something to drink, although it might be difficult in zero g. Then come back to Command. We need to talk to each other.'

Aasen nodded. 'Are you our captain again, Luca?'

'I don't know if that would be a good idea. But perhaps we can work something out together.'

She nodded again, and Blasco eased her down the access tunnel. Mariucci continued on into Command.

He looked at Aasen's list, scrolled back up through it. He could see why she'd finally given up. The faults were legion, and there was no way she could solve them all. Now, it was simply a question of finding out what still worked, and what might be able to be made to work again. For the want of anything better to do, he strapped the tablet to his own forearm, and pushed himself towards his seat.

Borner was still at her screen, calling the numbers – chanting them, in fact, as if speaking them out loud might cast a spell and summon the authors.

'Hello, Yasmin,' he said. 'They're not coming. I don't think they've been here for a very long time, so it won't matter that we leave their monuments alone for a little longer. I've got a more important job for you. Can you find Earth, or the relay, with our transmitter? We should re-establish contact with them.'

Her voice faltered for a second, then redoubled its efforts.

'Yasmin. We're moving away from Io. Look.' He turned to his screen. Could he do this? Could he remember how? His blunt fingers hovered over the display, then tentatively started dabbing at instructions.

The pit bloomed into life. There was the Jovian system, tracking in real time, and the blue point of the Aphrodite following a white track that spiralled outwards, leaving Io behind, passing the orbits of Europa and Ganymede, beyond Callisto, and then just a little further than that. Quite where that would put them, he didn't know, and their navigator had potentially laid her last course.

'Do you see, Yasmin? We're leaving. We need to plan what happens next.'

The pit lights broke up. An error message hung in the air for a moment before disappearing too.

It had been enough, though. Borner's recitation tailed off, and she folded her hands in her lap. Her head was bowed.

'I'm not angry with you, Yasmin. We're beyond that now. But it's important that you find a way of getting a message back to Earth, to tell them that we're not lost after all.'

She looked at the numbers on her screen. Then she reached forward and slid them to one side, and started tapping out instructions.

Eventually, they were joined by the remnants of the crew. Velter, Kattenbeck, Aasen, Blasco. They sat close together. There was no pit display to watch, and perhaps they needed the comfort of proximity. They were united again.

Mariucci sighed. 'Well,' he said, 'perhaps a damage report is required.'

Kattenbeck cleared her throat. 'We are all probably – I'll

need to have everyone's dosimeters and work out how to read them – chronically overexposed to radiation. Our chances of developing cancers are enormous, if not a certainty, within a few years. On top of which, we are all severely psychologically damaged for whatever reason. We've lost crew members who are vital for the functioning of the ship's systems, and if any one of those goes down, we're left with trying to read the manuals, which may themselves be corrupted and useless. If the life support fails, or the radiators feed back, or the shield malfunctions, then we'll probably die very quickly. If they don't, we'll probably die very slowly.' She shrugged. 'That's as much as I can say. Deirdre is in a coma. I can keep her stable. But as it was with Laszlo, it's not a long-term strategy.'

She reached out and patted Blasco's arm. The pilot rested her own hand over hers, and stared into the middle distance.

'Yasmin?'

'I ... I can't turn the primary dish. I can't turn the secondary dish either. The motors are entirely unresponsive. The circuitry to them is still working, meaning we can broadcast, but not where we want to. The error reporting across the ship is damaged beyond its capacity to be accurate. Too many false positives and negatives have made it decide it can't function properly, and it's just shut down. We simply don't know what's broken and what's not any more. Electricity generation is down by thirty per cent, but that might simply be a response to our decreased usage. The radiators are working, which is why we're still here to talk about all this.'

'Thank you, Yasmin.'

'Can I ask,' she said, 'what's going to happen to us? What Earth might do with us?'

'You are still my crew. That's all we need to worry about for now. The other things can wait until later, when they become important.' Mariucci raised his gaze to Velter. 'Benjamin?'

'Most of the external sensors have gone. Most of the mechanisms for bringing them back to be serviced are also gone. We still have the cameras. With the receivers down, we can't get anything from Laelaps, which I assume is still orbiting Europa. We have the Arcas probe left. The ship's systems contain all of the data we've collected so far, including all of the data we've not sent. Some of that will probably be irretrievable or corrupted, but I won't know until I do a scan of the memory. I haven't because it uses up a lot of computer time, and I don't know if it won't just forget to pump air or keep the lights on if I start the process. Luca, we should probably make telling Earth about the ziggurat a priority, because we might not be able to if we leave it until later.'

'Hanne?'

'The Aphrodite won't make it back to cis-lunar space. Or rather it might, but we won't. The voyage is too long, and our damage too great. Something will fail, like Petra says, and it will kill us quickly or slowly.' She laced her fingers and squeezed her palms together. 'I can give you chapter and verse, but we'd be here for a very long time. I'm sorry. We're not going home, and we should make our peace with that.'

Mariucci pursed his lips and clenched his jaw. He'd failed them utterly. None of them would get to see their families, their parents, their children, their siblings, their friends, their neighbours, again. It had been his duty, and he had failed in it.

He knew his parents were both dead, but the realisation of it struck him with fresh force, and he began to weep. He might not know their names any more, or their faces, nor anything about them, where they lived, grew up, worked, died. It was just the raw fact that they were gone which brought him low.

He rallied, dried his eyes with his blood-stiffened sleeve, and swallowed. One last person to ask. 'Theresa. Can we still fly?'

'Yes. I don't know what Laszlo built the engine from, but it's survived intact. We can burn as long as we have pumps for the fuel, and fuel for the pumps. The internal gyroscopes are still spinning, but the readings from them are untrustworthy. We can't use them to steer, but we still have cold propellant enough for limited manoeuvres. We should use it sparingly until we make a final decision about what we do with the ship. If Hanne doesn't think we can make it back, then we have the fallback protocol we're supposed to execute.'

'Can we use the thrusters to align the transmitter?' asked Mariucci.

'Yes. That would work. The beam's tight. We'd drop out after a time – three, four minutes – so we'd need to continually readjust. Potentially fuel-heavy.'

'Then we should probably send a short message now, warn them of our predicament, and also let them know what kind of news we have for them. Everybody should write a report. A truthful one, as best they can. Then send them all out together. After that, we can decide what we do with the rest of our lives.'

24

'We've lost the Jupiter relay,' said Borner. 'It's almost certainly there, but it's not coming up in any of our sensors.'

Mariucci stared for a moment into the empty pit. 'Can we work out where it should be?'

'Yes. The Jovian Lagrange points are entirely predictable, and the calculations aren't difficult, but I've already tried, and we've wasted fuel doing so. I'll try again if you want me to.'

'If we can't do it, we can't.' Something was troubling him, a thought, a memory, the absence of which was causing him physical pain, right down in his guts. 'We can predict where Earth is, though? They will be listening, no matter what.'

'The Deep Space Network will pick us up. Our broadcast amplitude will mean they'll spot us immediately.'

'Then we point the ship towards Earth.' That was it. Early space history. Getting pictures back from Apollo, and one of the receiving dishes had gone out of alignment, and they didn't know which way to point it, until they realised that if they just aimed it at the Moon, that would be enough. Why could he remember that, and not the name of his doctoral thesis, nor the university he'd got it from? 'No, we turn the ship to the Sun. We can align it through the cameras. The beam spread will cover the inner solar system from out here.'

He sat back, pleased with his work.

Borner called Blasco to Command. She needed to cut the engines, turn the ship, let Borner make the broadcast, and then reverse the process. Their store of propellant would be slightly, but irrevocably, depleted. There'd be no more supply ships, no more … what were they called? They had a name, and it was gone.

He was aware that, like the Aphrodite's systems, there were now gaps he couldn't bridge. That whole swathes of his past were gone, and he could never bring them back. Kattenbeck's drug regime clawed back what it could. The rest simply had to be abandoned.

There was a certain purity to giving in to that position. Everything that had happened before, all the choices he'd made, all the decisions, both good and bad, that had led to this point: it was forgotten. And if it had been forgotten, it had also been forgiven.

It was in forgiving himself that he found most solace. He was aware of the part the actions of others had played – their betrayal of his authority, Rory's usurping his position, Spinu's deliberate maiming of Colvin – but it was in a past that had been largely erased, along with his own mistakes. There were three bodies strapped to the hull: Hellsten, Molnar, Forsyth. Tsoltos had died on Io. Spinu was lost to space. Colvin was in a coma.

Those were his mistakes. They were on him, and he just couldn't remember them well enough to mourn.

Aasen slept most of the time now, trying to make up for weeks and months of constant activity. Blasco spent her time at Colvin's side, and that gave Kattenbeck some relief. Her ghosts were ever-present, and if Mariucci was suffering a deficit of memory, her problem was a surfeit of it. He preferred it his way. She was haunted, drawn and distracted.

Velter – Velter's anxiety had been inextricably interwoven with his efforts to perform, to belong, to succeed. None of that mattered now. There was no one left to impress, nor to let down. He was probably the sanest of them all. He rewrote the report he and Spinu had previously written, which Forsyth had deleted. He included the most salient and convincing images.

He confirmed Borner's analysis of the signals. His conclusion was simple and decisive: that an intelligence had visited the Jovian system long before humanity, and had left structures and devices that had lasted centuries, if not millennia. That they resembled the ziggurats of ancient Mesopotamia was an enigma he was unwilling to engage with formally, but one he covered with the catch-all phrase, 'further study is required'.

Off the record, he supposed that if they'd built a ziggurat on Io, and potentially others in the seas of Europa and Ganymede, then perhaps they'd built one on Earth too, and that legends about warring gods were humans attempting to interpret what they'd seen, and what they'd experienced.

Blasco suggested that it made a future war in the Near East far more likely. Borner pointed out that it had always been that way: a scramble for prehistoric alien technology buried under the scorched soil of Iraq made as much sense as fighting over oil, or trade routes, or fertile land.

Nevertheless, they would send the report. They had hesitated long enough, and now it was almost too late.

Here was Blasco now, her usual confidence undermined by her vigil. She listened to the plan, agreed with its execution, and assumed her position at the flight controls.

'Acceleration, acceleration.'

The faint buzzing that made its way from the engine to Command ceased. The slight pressure in the inner ear relaxed. Then with the cameras showing the bright star of the Sun, she nudged the length of the ship about so the frozen primary transmitter dish pointed into the inner system.

'We … are receiving,' said Borner. She leaned forward to look at the data streaming into the buffer. 'I can pick up signals. So this has worked, so far.'

'Press send, Yasmin. Tell them what we know.'

She dabbed at her screen, and a progress bar appeared. She saw that Mariucci was watching.

'Yes, that's a bit old school. I think one of the programmers was having a little joke at our expense.'

'Can we keep at this angle, Theresa?'

'This will take a minute or two, at these baud rates. There's no error checking, either at our end or theirs, so probably best if we repeat it a few times in case some of the message drops out or gets distorted. They can simply swap the pieces in and out of the raw data.'

'It's not encrypted. A simple binary signal, with a start and end code,' said Borner, and recognised the irony of her words. 'Timeless, really.'

'Do we know where we are?' asked Mariucci. 'Our trajectory is constant thrust away from Jupiter, but at some point we cross the orbits of the other Galilean moons.'

'This was all Deirdre's world,' said Blasco. She clammed up for a moment. 'I'm a pilot, they teach you this stuff, knowing that you'll almost certainly never have to use it. I'll see what the cameras on the hull can pick up. We can, at least, get a raw distance between ourselves and Jupiter simply by measuring the solid angle.'

'Will we know if we're going to hit something?'

'I can try and get a lock on some stars, compare it to the ephemeris. If it's still accurate, we'll get some advanced warning, and we might be able to take some kind of evasive action. I can only trust that Deirdre didn't plot a course that would make it necessary.'

'A course we're now interfering with.' Mariucci sighed. 'It can't be helped. Our priorities have changed, and our actions must also change.'

He waited out the first cycle of the progress bar in silence.

'Again,' he said. 'As often as we can do it within this period, and then we wait to see if we get confirmation that they've received it. If we don't, we repeat it until we do.'

'What if they never reply?' asked Borner. 'What if something's happened down there that means they can't? Or won't?'

'We were recalled. Not abandoned. Not exiled.'

'There could have been a disaster. Another one like KU2. Or a war. With nuclear weapons. There might be no one listening to the Deep Space Network.'

'You picked up signals, Yasmin. Earth is still there. They'll hear us if we keep broadcasting.'

She settled, and repeated the operation.

'What if the Earth is behind the Sun?'

'Then we'll find out in a hundred minutes.' Mariucci glanced up at the clock which, despite everything, still ticked over the time, second by second. When you have one clock, you know what the time is, even if it's wrong.

Also, that hundred minute figure – was that right, or had he just plucked the number out of thin air? Neither Borner nor Blasco had objected. The travel time for light between Jupiter and Earth and back had to have a maximum. If that was it, he must have remembered it.

That, yes. Of leaving Earth, joining the Aphrodite, nothing at all. Had there been a boost phase, accelerating them out of the inner solar system using solid fuel rockets, or was he thinking of something else?

He had always been on the Aphrodite. He had always been in orbit about Jupiter. He knew there'd been twelve crew members, and there were now seven. The other five had stepped away into the shadows.

He wondered if the drugs Kattenbeck had given him were starting to fade, or whether it was that they were working and it gave him the clarity to know what he knew, and know what he didn't.

'We should take the time to give our personal testimonies,' he said. 'Our wills too.'

'We did that, Luca,' said Blasco. 'We did that back on Earth.'

'Did we?' He frowned. He didn't know who was going to get his possessions, nor what they amounted to. Was he rich, or poor, or somewhere in between? Not that it mattered any more. 'In that case, just our testimonies.'

'You've already asked us to do that too,' said Borner. 'We're doing it, just as you suggested. In video, in audio, and text, in case our bandwidth is compromised. How is yours going?'

Had he started it? Had he finished it? Definitely time to find Kattenbeck again.

'Well enough,' he said, and changed the subject. 'How many times have we sent the report now?'

'Four times.'

'That will probably do. Theresa, can you reorient the ship and resume the course Deirdre laid for us? And possibly, find out where we are.'

'I'll try,' she said. 'Acceleration, acceleration.'

He waited for her to put the drive back on, and to feel that familiar tug in his inner ear, before unclipping and going down to the wheel.

The whole point of the wheel was its artificial gravity, and with its rotation stilled, its purpose had gone. Water still came out of the taps, but it splashed in the sink below before dispersing into chaotic, wobbling clouds of liquid that went everywhere except where it was wanted. The heaters still warmed the food, but ripping the lid open now risked some or all of a meal escaping its container. Coffee – how were they supposed to make coffee now? The gravity toilets were there. The showers were there.

They had a vacuum toilet. They had emergency berths in the axis. It wasn't the same. It would never be the same.

He pushed himself to the treatment room, where Colvin lay like an effigy in marble, and Kattenbeck hovered like an angel over her.

'How is she?'

'I'm keeping her alive for Theresa. That's all. She's not brain-dead per se. But I'm certain her higher functions have been eroded to a significant extent. She's not there any more,

Luca. We couldn't have done anything different, and yet, we can't do enough.'

'I knew her, didn't I? I knew her from before,' and he whirled his finger around, 'before all this.'

'She was your navigator on the Aphrodite on the KU2 mission.' Kattenbeck saw his confusion. 'You saved the world, Luca. You both saved the world.'

He stared at Colvin for the longest time, but nothing would come back. No memory. No grief, even.

'I think I need more of your magic drugs,' he said eventually.

She sighed, and pulled out the blister pack from her pocket. What was there was already half gone. 'At least we don't have to worry about addiction.'

'We don't?'

'No,' she said pointedly. 'There won't be time for that to be an issue.'

She popped a pill into her hand and closed her palm over it before it could go anywhere else. A bottle of water with a sticky bottom was on the counter, and Mariucci squirted some into his mouth before taking the pill between thumb and forefinger, and pressing it between his lips.

He sloshed and swallowed.

'Thank you.'

'Are we any further forward?'

'We've sent Benjamin's report. We'll know they've got it if they respond.'

'If?'

'Yasmin was worried some disaster had happened, and we were all that was left of humanity.'

'The disaster is happening, but I don't believe it would have wiped us out just yet. Can you imagine us being the only ones left? That would be ironic, considering.'

'Yes, yes it would.' Was the pill working already? 'Theresa talked about a fallback protocol. I can't remember what that is.'

'We ram Jupiter in order to prevent our contaminating any-thing else.'

'Ah,' he said. 'That makes sense. We're currently moving away from Jupiter, out of the radiation belt, but we don't know exactly where we are. Theresa's trying to find out. Once we're in a stable orbit, and out of immediate danger, and we've sent as much of the data we hold as we can, we should probably think about that protocol.'

'I agree.'

'Good. I should probably write that on my hand somewhere. Do you still have that pen?'

She did. He bit the top off and wrote carefully on his left hand, *The fallback protocol is crashing into Jupiter. Do this when necessary.* He put the lid back on, and waved his hand around so that the ink would dry faster.

'How's Hanne?'

'Asleep. I make sure she wakes up for meals, to go to the toilet. Otherwise, I let her be. She spent so long doing what the computer told her to do – thinking that that was what she had to do – she no longer has any motivation. Did you know that Rory used her list to control her?'

'No. I didn't know that.'

'Benjamin was going through the ship's event log. It's all there. He's going to try and compress it, get it small enough to send.'

'The more information they have the better. The next time, if there is ever a next time, they'll have to do things differently.'

'This ship was the best we could build at the time, Luca. We always send the best ship we can build, even while better ships are being planned.'

'They may have to put a line through those, and start again. At least the drive worked. Spectacularly well.'

'Almost everything did, except us. We were the weak link in the whole mission.'

'No, no,' he said. 'I'd change the ship. But not its crew. We were the best thing about it. We came all this way, we did all these things, and of course it's a shame we won't get to go back and talk about them, but we can still let them know what it was like, what we saw, what we experienced. Whatever it was that went wrong, we were here. That's what they'll say. They'll say we were the best crew, and we still are. You're the best doctor we could have asked for.'

'And you, Luca, out of the two captains we had, I can say honestly that you were the best one.'

'I should go, and do some things, while the drugs are still strong.' He could feel his face twitch, his jaw clench. 'Have you recorded your statement, or whatever we're calling it?'

'Some of it. It's hard to tell the truth about yourself. I keep going back and being more brutal.'

'Don't. Be more kind.' Mariucci turned himself around and took hold of the door frame. The wheel looked as it always had, but it felt very different. 'I'm going to review mine, and see what else there is to say.'

He pushed himself towards the rack of tablets, and took one as he passed overhead. The next opportunity he had to change direction was when the floor curved around to meet his trajectory. He bounced to the next ladder up, and hauled himself up to the axis.

His bed, a padded cloth sleeping bag tethered to a wall in one of the modules, was where he retreated to read, comfortable and cocooned. He hadn't set a password on his files – he'd had Velter remove them all, because at some point he was bound to forget, and this far into the mission, why did he even need passwords? – so a simple tap opened them up. There was his face, his biography, his service record, and it was like a work of fiction based on the person of Luca Mariucci.

He recognised none of it but his name.

Pushing it to one side, he accessed what promised to be his personal report, but when it opened, it was just a blank page. The cursor blinking invitingly, asking him to type something, anything. He didn't know how often he'd done this: written a few words, deleted them again, closed the tablet down and slept.

Many, many times, he was certain, but he couldn't prove it.

So, to start.

'My name is Luca Mariucci. I was the captain of the spaceship Aphrodite. We are in orbit about Jupiter. I can tell you very little else, but I will try.'

25

'Yes, Yasmin, what is it?' Mariucci was grateful for the interruption, as it meant he didn't have to keep revising his statement.

'I wondered about telling you at all. I feel responsible for
everything that's happened, even though I don't think any of it
was my fault, but,' and she hesitated. 'There's a signal between
Ganymede and Callisto.'

Mariucci looked up at the ship's clock as it blindly took its
toll of the seconds and minutes. Why wouldn't the ziggurat
builders do the same? It didn't have to mean anything except
marking the passage of time.

'Show me,' he said, and she ported the data to his screen.

As far as Blasco could determine, Colvin's course had them
spiral out in the equatorial plane to sit just beyond the orbit of
Callisto. It was far enough away from the inner radiation belt
to be safe, and it had been easily accessible from where they
were. They hadn't completed the burn yet, and they were now
in the gap between the third and fourth Galilean moons.

'Ganymede orbits Jupiter once a week – every seven point
one five five days. Callisto isn't in orbital resonance with any
of the others, too far away, and Benjamin will be able to tell it
more and better, but it orbits at sixteen point seven days, at a
... I'm sorry, none of that is important right now. We know
that when Io passes Europa, there's a signal that passes between
them, up and down. When Europa passes Ganymede, there's
another signal, up and down. It appears there's a signal passing

between Ganymede and Callisto when they pass. But it's just one way. There's no acknowledgement.'

Mariucci grumbled into his chest. 'Why would that be the case?'

'Either something has broken, or it's deliberate.'

'You mean, it's a message.'

'All the information that was generated on Io is passed through Europa, and on through Ganymede, and it's finally sent to Callisto.' She shrugged. 'Why would the mechanism break just there? When the one on Io is in an environment so radioactive that we can't function. Well, we can't, can we? Or in the seas under the ice crust on Europa and Ganymede?'

'It is a surprising finding.' He ruminated on it. 'What do we know about Callisto?'

'Some things. Again, Benjamin will know.'

'Is it rocky, is it icy? Is there an ocean?'

'The answer to all those is yes. We were supposed to use Arcas to study it further, and settle some of those questions.'

He twirled his finger in the air. 'The transmitter on Ganymede, it's beneath the ice, yes? No sign of anything at the antijove?'

'Nothing.'

'And Callisto? Have we images of the subjove there?'

'Not ones that are high enough resolution.'

'We should let Benjamin amend his report. Does he know about this yet?'

'I haven't had a chance to tell him. He's busy curating the images, writing notes for them, queuing them up in the buffer and waiting for a transmission slot.'

'You should tell him. Perhaps I should tell him.' Mariucci looked at his screen, where his own words lay hidden beneath the layer of binary code. 'I'll tell him. I'm not doing anything important any more. I should have stuck at ... whatever it was I did before they made me do this.'

'You were an engineer. Life-support engineer.'

'Was I? That appears to have more utility than messenger boy, but if that's what I am now, then so be it.' He unclipped from his seat. He reached above him for a grab strap, and caught a glimpse of the writing on his palm. There was a line through one of the messages, but the other was clear. The fallback protocol. He wondered who Rory was, and why he'd had to be stopped, but only for a moment.

'How did you find the signal, Yasmin? So many of our detectors are dead, or malfunctioning.'

She looked away, then back.

'I looked for it. I thought it might be there, so I looked. I'm sorry, Luca.'

'Don't be. It was a good guess.' He needed to go, before he forgot why he needed to go. A message for Velter.

He pushed off for the door, and then drifted down the axis to the science modules. Velter was in one – the only one that was lit – and he knocked on the bulkhead before entering. Velter was surrounded by screens that showed many of the images they'd captured. Most were of the surfaces of the moons they'd explored in detail, Europa and Io, but on one screen of thumbnails there were pictures of Jupiter's clouds, showing the intimate detail of bands and vortexes.

'Yasmin's found another signal,' said Mariucci. 'And I said I'd tell you. And ask you about Callisto.'

'Is there a ziggurat on Callisto?'

'The signal from Ganymede is one-way. So we don't know.'

'Callisto is strange,' said Velter. 'Its surface is ice, but we don't know how far down it goes, whether there's an ocean, or whether it's just undifferentiated rock and ice all the way down. As large bodies go, it's potentially very primitive. It hasn't undergone the same melting as even the larger asteroids have, so its surface is potentially almost as old as the solar system itself. We don't see that anywhere else.'

'You wanted to learn more.'

'Of all the moons, Callisto is the one I wanted to see. Io and

280

Europa get all the attention, and Ganymede is the largest moon anywhere and it's bigger than Mercury. But Callisto is what the solar system was like at the start. We could have found out so much, and now we never will.'

'We have a probe. We have Arcas.'

'We don't have the bandwidth, Luca. We can't receive the data from Laelaps as it is, let alone another probe. Our chance has gone. I'm resigned to that.'

'We'll pass Callisto, quite close, if Theresa's right. We still have cameras on the hull. The astrogation camera gives quite detailed images. You can still do some useful science with it.'

Velter managed to look sad and unimpressed at the same time. 'Luca, we don't need to be here any more.'

'A little longer. Benjamin, we owe it to Earth, to the people who designed and planned this extravagance, to do what we can with what we have left. We might even be able to solve this last mystery before we head back towards Jupiter.' Mariucci looked at his hand, at the nature of the fallback.

'It's not a terrible suggestion,' said Velter. 'But what do we do if there is something there? We can only do what we've always been able to do, which is take pictures. That didn't convince Rory, did it? And I suppose he was right in his way. That we need better evidence than that.'

It took Mariucci a second to work out that he was referring to the same Rory that was written on his hand.

'We have a probe,' he said. 'What if there was some way of riding on it, down to the surface? I don't even know if that's possible, whether it has enough fuel for that.'

Velter closed his eyes and pinched the bridge of his nose. He looked as if he was in pain. 'Luca ... oh, never mind. Yes, yes, it's possible. We did try it before. Do you remember Stan? Konstantinos Tsoltos? Big man, told lots of stories.'

'Stan? No. Who was he?'

'He was a member of this crew. He went down to Io, but

281

he died of acute radiation sickness before he could get to the ziggurat.'

Mariucci frowned. If this man Stan had been a member of the crew, then he should have known that. 'I'm sorry,' he said. 'I'm having some problems today.'

'You should go and see Petra. Get some more Ritalin. But let's suppose there is another ziggurat there. The radiation environment is very different to that on Io. Obviously more than on Earth, but it won't kill you. It won't damage your suit. It won't destroy the probe either. And the surface gravity is less, so there's a fuel saving there. There is the question of preserving the environment, but it looks like the damage has already been done.'

'If landing on Io was so dangerous, why did this Stan even try it?'

'It's complicated, Luca. We were all in the grip of a kind of madness. We went to some very questionable lengths to get the evidence we needed. All the while, it may have been right here, where we could have got at it more easily. Not without cost, though. Whoever goes down can't come back. The probe doesn't have enough fuel to make orbit again.'

'But we're not going home, so if I wanted to, I could choose to do this.' Mariucci checked his hand. He was right: they weren't going home. 'If there's a ziggurat – Benjamin, can you show me a picture of a ziggurat. I've forgotten what one looks like.'

'Yes, yes. Of course.' He tapped some menus on his screen, and the large monitor above his head showed a short animated sequence, taken by one of the probes – it had a name, which was gone – as it orbited Io. The images had been stitched together so that they transitioned seamlessly, showing the black shape as the camera had seen it, travelling overhead.

It was obviously solid, with a height equal to its base, tapering upwards in stepped tiers. A wedge-shaped ramp led up from the ground to the third tier. The tiers continued to almost the top, where they ended at the base of a cubic structure on the pinnacle. There may, or may not, have been archways that allowed entrance to it.

The animation gave the ziggurat a reality a single image couldn't. Every time it reached the end of the sequence, with the probe's distance to the target increasingly oblique, it began again as the probe closed in on the structure from the other side.

'What is a ziggurat?'

'It's a temple,' said Velter. 'It's an ancient form of temple that was built by one of the first significant cultures on Earth, in what's now Iraq. Yasmin said it looked like a ziggurat, and the name just stuck. But the similarities are more than just superficial. It really does look like one of the Babylonian ziggurats.'

'Maybe they built one on Earth too.'

Velter gave a grimace, and then a smile. 'That's possible. There's an ancient legend that goes with the ziggurat. Do you want to hear it?'

'Yes. I think I'd like that very much. Even though you've probably told it to me before, and you'll have to tell it to me again.'

Velter demurred as to whether that was true.

'In the beginning there were the gods, separate and the same, their essences flowing in and out of each other. There was Tiamat, who was the salt water, and Apsu, who was the fresh, and there was Mummu, who acted as their mind. Tiamat and Apsu gave birth to other gods – who in turn made more. Tiamat wanted to destroy them, but the lesser gods found out about her plan, and managed to subdue both Mummu and Apsu. But Tiamat could not be so easily defeated.

'Tiamat created an army of monsters to fight the new gods, and many of them went over to her side, seeing that defeat was inevitable. Nothing could stand in her way. There was no hiding place safe from her, and she was relentless in her search. Desperate for a way to fight her, the gods killed Apsu, and used his heart to create a champion, Marduk. Marduk was the brightest and the best of them, the strongest and the wisest, but he told them that in return for killing Tiamat, he was to be crowned the head of all the gods, and he would rule them for ever.

'The gods built Marduk a throne and raised it off the ground at the top of a ziggurat. There, they gave him gifts, as well as weapons to defeat Tiamat, and when he had been worshipped, Marduk set off in his chariot. He confronted Tiamat and her monstrous army, and they fought each other. He wrapped her in a net so that she could not escape, and she tried to swallow him whole. But he filled her mouth with a divine wind, meaning she couldn't bite him. He then killed her with an arrow to her heart, and single-handedly routed her army.

'All that was left to do was to create the world from her body. Marduk tore Tiamat in two, with one half becoming the sky, and the other half the land. With her blood he made men, and he also made the moon and the stars. At the end, the gods sat down to a feast that goes on to this day.'

Mariucci nodded. He thought he might have heard it before, but it was still a good story, and Velter was a good storyteller.

'Does it mean anything, though? That was a myth, and these ziggurats are real. They're out here, where they shouldn't be, and they seem to be working in some way.'

'The myth isn't true, because it's not meant to be true. It's meant to explain the world to a people who can't understand it any other way. The land, the sky, the sea, their own existence, the calendar, natural events.'

'But what if it is true?'

'What if we were made from the blood of a dead goddess instead of billions of years of evolution? It's not true, Luca. We have to look for another explanation for these kinds of creation myths.'

'Yes, but what if they contained the seed of the truth? That a race of gods once visited Earth, and fought each other there, and afterwards they left their monuments when they went away again, and people didn't know what to say to each other about it. They gave us these stories which tried to explain the inexplicable.'

Velter looked up at the Io ziggurat as the probe's images continued to repeat. 'It's possible,' he said eventually. 'Before I came here, I would have called such theories both mad and stupid. Now, I can't, even though I know I should. I don't know what any of this means. I don't know if it means anything at all. What I do know, is that these objects are here, and we have to accept that, no matter how inconvenient it is.'

'Our – who sent us again?'

'ESA. The European Space Agency. This is their symbol, on our chest.'

'Yes, ESA. What do you think they'll say when we tell them?'

'We have told them, Luca. They know what we know, apart from this part about the Ganymede-Callisto connection. They haven't really said anything yet. I expect it'll take a while for them to check all our results, all our images, everything. When we broadcast the report to Earth, we didn't broadcast it to just them. We had to blanket the whole planet, the whole inner system with the message. Other people will have picked it up, decoded it, read it, and they'll be discussing it. I don't know what they'll say, either.' Velter swiped the ziggurat away. 'It's ironic. We came looking for answers, and all we ended up with are questions.'

'Will we need to do anything to the probe, if I am going to go to Callisto?'

Velter left his screen and ushered Mariucci out of the module and down the axis. When they got to the probe bay, he checked that the inside was pressurised, then undogged the door. He pushed it aside, and turned on the lights.

At the far end of the bay, Arcas sat locked to its clamps. Its hexagonal body was obscured by sheets of insulation and plastic struts, all tied together with clips and straps.

'It's already done,' said Mariucci, surprised.

'Hanne was working on it, before. Rory wanted someone else to go to Io after Stan had died, but even though Valeria begged him, he got Deirdre to go instead. So Valeria tried to take her place, and she ended up outside the hull, floating away. It's still ready, though. We'd need to wake Hanne up to check it over.'

Mariucci inspected the works.

'So everything's ready?'

'I think so. There's no guarantee this will succeed. You know that?'

'But someone should still try, shouldn't they?'

'The others will try and talk you out of it.'

'Not you, though. Why not?'

'Because if you don't go, I'll have to. And I remember what happened to Stan.'

'But I don't. That seems fair. I used to be captain. I can just say that it's my job. My duty. They'll have to do what I say then.'

'That didn't work before,' said Velter. 'I think it might this time.'

26

The six of them who could still make it to Command met there, for what was probably the last time. Velter had brought up on everybody's screens what the astrogation camera had picked out on Callisto's surface: a smudge, nothing more, about three pixels wide, at the subjove.

Callisto was already incredibly dark and startlingly bright. The contrast between the surface coating of sputtered carbon and the eroding ice peaks was stark, and strangely beautiful. It would have been easy to miss the slightly deeper black mark, or discount it as a camera artefact or as a natural variation in albedo.

They knew, though. At least, they had convinced themselves that they knew, that it was probably worth one last throw of the dice to confirm not just to themselves, but to everyone, what it was they'd been chasing and dreaming for months.

'I'm against this,' said Kattenbeck, because she always would say that she was. It was in her nature to herd her patients away from harm and shield them.

'We're planning to ram Jupiter,' said Blasco. 'The point is already lost.'

She waved away the objection. 'This just seems unnecessarily cruel. To all of us, but to Luca in particular. What if he gets there and can't remember why?'

'We'll be with him to the very end. We can spend fuel, knowing how much we need to keep in reserve. I'll keep the Aphrodite on station for as long as we need to, and we can talk

287

to him on the suit radio. It'll carry fifty, a hundred kilometres, line of sight. We can write instructions down for him, too, in case that breaks.' She looked to Borner for confirmation, and received a nod from her.

The lights flickered, on cue.

Kattenbeck rubbed her face. She was exhausted. 'I don't want to see more ghosts. I don't want to see his ghost in particular. Ove's was bad enough, but I get all of them now. All of them. Rory Forsyth. Stan. Laszlo.'

'Valeria?' asked Blasco.

'Her too.'

'We're going to end this in a pillar of fire and smoke,' said the pilot. 'I wondered what those dreams meant for a long time. I thought it was about what was happening back on Earth, that everything was burning, burning, and there'd be nothing left when we got home, and that we'd somehow triggered the apocalypse down there by doing something up here – and it felt good. It scratched an itch. Turns out it's how *we* die, not how they die. And that's okay too.'

'But what about Luca?'

'Luca gets to choose.'

'He's not got the mental capacity to choose.'

'Neither have we. And he's also sitting right there. Luca?'

He looked up. He was feeling reasonably alert, but he was also aware they were talking about things that he now only knew because he'd been told, not because he'd been there, seen them, experienced them.

They were in Command. They were discussing whether he should take the last probe to Callisto to find the ziggurat. Everything else was uncertain.

'I choose to go,' he said. 'You don't need me any more. I'm more of a danger to you than a help. You'll defer to me, because you still think of me as captain, and I'm not that person now. You can't expect me to make the decisions I once did. But this? This I can do.'

'You can't come back.'

'By the time I get there, I won't remember there's a back to come to.' He laughed. 'This condition, this disease I have, it's not getting better. No matter how many pills you give me. I've lost almost every memory, and when the process is complete, I'll be in an ever-present now. I have an idea of what that might be like – quite pleasant, probably – but when I start forgetting I'm on a spaceship is when I become a liability.'

Kattenbeck snorted, but she didn't say anything more.

'The probe is ready to go,' said Aasen. 'I don't have to do anything to it. But I'll take off the shielding that was meant for Io, because we'll get a fuel saving, and we won't have to use the water bubble either. The only question is really, can we get you there?'

'Yes,' said Blasco.

'Without crashing the Aphrodite into Callisto?'

'Yes?' she answered, less certainly. 'This was always Deirdre's thing. She could balance it on a knife edge, and still know which way it was going to fall. I'm not that good, and I know it. I'll be leaving a larger margin of error, but whatever I do, the ship can only ever pull point one g. Our approach path needs to be on rails, and I'm not saying we've lost our navigation software, just that it's less reliable than it was before because it now has very few inputs. If we don't know where we are, I can't tell when to make the turn.'

'I don't want to put you or the ship in danger. More danger,' said Mariucci.

'It's dangerous anyway. We were never meant to do these kinds of manoeuvres.' She shook her head. 'We don't have to go so far down the gravity well this time. We can skim it and use the probe motors to kill the extra delta-v. It'll be fine.'

'How hard will we hit the ground if you get it wrong?' asked Velter.

'Hard enough that you won't have to worry about surviving,' she said.

'That's not a comfort. We have the nuclear power plant to think about, and the potential contamination of the surface, the largest pristine ancient planet-sized surface in the solar system.'

'Quarantine's already been broken,' said Borner. 'By them.'

'I realise that, although, as far as we can tell, they haven't spread radioactive decay products over half the moon.' Velter looked back to Blasco. 'Just, be careful?'

'I'll do my best. I will, of course, be trying to fly the probe as well as the ship. It's a good job I can multitask.'

'The longer you broadcast,' said Borner, 'the more we'll be able to send back to Earth. You'll need to look at everything that you pass. Properly look. Hold the camera still for a second, or all that'll come out is a blur, and people will be arguing over a particular shape of a carving for the next hundred years.'

'You'll think there'll be carvings?' asked Blasco.

Borner gave a tight smile. 'I hope there'll be carvings. Inscriptions. Something to tell us who they were, and why they came. It's what we'd do. It is what we did do. The Voyager discs. Plaques and flags. We left memorials and sent messages.'

'What if they're not like us?'

'They have to be a little bit like us, otherwise they wouldn't have left things for us to find.'

'And if they did it just for themselves?'

'Yes, that's possible. I don't know whether the similarities will be enough. I just hope that there'll be something to read, even if we don't understand it for a long time.' Borner tensed up. 'Call it professional curiosity if you want. It's not a demand.'

'I didn't mean it that way. I'm sorry.' Blasco turned away for a moment and composed herself. 'Shall we get this over with? All those in favour of Luca going to Callisto?'

Everyone but Kattenbeck raised their hand.

'You know why,' she said. 'Let the record show there were five votes for, with one abstention.'

Blasco cracked her knuckles and looked up at the clock.

'Right. I need to call this. Three, two, one. Mark. Acceleration, acceleration.'

The ship started to turn.

'We should get into decompression,' said Aasen to Mariucci.

'I'm coming too,' said Kattenbeck. 'I'll need to administer more drugs before he sets off. Yasmin, you're on Comms,' she added, redundantly. 'Benjamin, can you go and sit with Deirdre for a while? You know what to do.'

'Yes, I know what to do.'

Velter left first, heading down towards the wheel, and Aasen, Mariucci and Kattenbeck carried on down the axis to the spacesuit storage. Aasen took her suit to decompress in the probe bay. Mariucci and Kattenbeck headed into the secondary airlock, so that the journey across the hull wouldn't be so far.

He clipped his suit to the wall, and marvelled at its ingenuity, while she sealed the door and set the conditions and the timer. Over the next ninety minutes, the pressure would fall to a third Earth standard. About an hour in, she'd inject him with something fast-acting, and give him another pill, then they'd both climb into their suits.

'Is there anything you want me to do for you, Luca? I probably draw the line at singing, but most other things are okay.'

'I don't know,' he said. 'I don't really know you any more, do I? I know that I trust you. That's probably the most important thing, isn't it? Anything you tell me now, I'm going to forget it soon. I just don't know.'

'I don't want you to be alone, Luca. We've had our disagreements. And I've let you down: I didn't back you when Rory took over, and I should have done, and I feel incredibly guilty about that because I could prevented a lot of pain and a lot of death.'

'I can't remember that. I know it happened, but it happened to someone else. There's no need to feel guilty. I forgive you.'

'You don't know what it is you're forgiving me for.'

'No. There is, though, continuity between who I was and

291

who I am, so I can still forgive. This is quite liberating for me. People who are about to die, I expect they think of all the things in their past which they regret, or wish they could still change and now can't. I won't. I'll go, not blaming anyone for anything. Not you, not me, not—' He looked at the crossed-out name on his hand. 'Not Rory. What was he like?'

'He was an arrogant son-of-a-bitch. He always had to be right. Annoyingly, he usually was, but it didn't make him a better person. It made him a worse one. His own personal madness was one he brought with him: he just perfected it here.'

'He doesn't sound very nice.'

'He wasn't the first choice for the mission. He demanded to be on it, and ESA thought having the famous professor on the Aphrodite would be good publicity. Or something. So they bumped the old senior scientific officer, and gave him the place instead.' Her face went sour. 'Not such a good idea after all.'

They lapsed into silence for a while, as the whispering from the pumps made sleepy background music.

'You saved the world once,' said Kattenbeck. 'Do you remember any of that?'

'No. Perhaps. I sometimes see things. Get a sense I've been here before, but I've been on this ship for months, haven't I? So that's to be expected.'

'You've been on this ship for almost two years, Luca. Before that, there was an asteroid that was going to just miss Earth, break up, and hit the Moon. The secondary impacts would have killed millions, and we'd have ended up with a cloud of debris around the planet that would have meant we'd be trapped on Earth for thousands of years. You stopped it. You had help, obviously, but you were the captain. They named schools after you. Luca was the most popular boys' name for both 2076 and 2077. You did it all from the Aphrodite.'

'I'm glad he – I – did.'

They fell into silence again. She clipped her spacesuit next to his, and tethered herself to the wall. She did the same for him, and slid her hand into his. She gave it a squeeze, and let the contact reassure him, and comfort her.

When the hour was up, she jabbed him with her gas gun, and took out a single pill from her pocket.

'The suit has a water dispenser inside it. I forgot to bring any with me, so just put it in your cheek for now, and swallow it in a minute.'

He looked at his suit, this second skin he had to wear. It looked odd and compelling, and as his thoughts began to speed up and crystallise, he reached out for it, touching the transparent faceplate and leaving it marked with his fingertips.

'I know this,' he said. 'I've done this before.'

He turned the suit around and he studied it, taking in the hump of the back, the hard torso, the control panel on the left sleeve. He manipulated the gauntlets.

He opened the control panel, touched a button, and the display there lit up. Kattenbeck reached over his arm, but he said, 'No', and tentatively guided himself through the menu until he found the option for opening up the back shell. It hissed aside, and he inspected the warm, dark folds of fabric that would wrap around his chest and arms.

He unzipped his flight suit, shucked his ship slippers, and climbed inside: leg, leg, arm, arm, head. He pushed the crown of his head through the seal and into the helmet. She did intervene now, tabbing the suit closed behind him.

The fans started. Almost instantly, he was neither cold nor warm, neither too dry nor too humid. His breath misted the plastic in front of him, and it grew clear again in an instant. The pill was still stuck to the inside of his cheek, and if he turned his head this way, to his right, there'd be a tube, and if he sucked on it, water would come out.

There was, and it did. He eased the pill off with his tongue, and swallowed.

He watched her collect his clothes, stow them in a drawstring bag, and then get rid of her own. She disappeared around the back of her spacesuit, and then she reappeared again behind her helmet's faceplate.

'Luca, can you hear me?'

'Yes. I can hear you.'

'I can hear you too,' said Borner. 'All systems are nominal. Time for launch is sixty minutes away. Descent time is calculated to be thirty-five minutes. I'll let you know when you need to egress and proceed to probe bay two.'

'Thank you, Yasmin,' said Kattenbeck. She took hold of Mariucci's helmet in both hands. 'We can call this off at any time before launch. Don't feel that you have to carry on, just because you've come this far.'

His head hurt slightly. Everything was just a little jagged, a little too sharp. It was the drugs, the high of combining the fast-acting and slow-acting doses, and he would calm down shortly as they plateaued.

'I want to do this, Petra. I want to see what's there.'

Her gaze directed him to his right sleeve, on the inside of his forearm. There were just four words written there, in black ink.

Go up.

Travel well.

That was it. It seemed simple enough: it was what he was supposed to do when he got to Callisto. Go up. Travel well. He nodded, and realised that she might not see that. 'Acknowledged,' he said.

She made him check his lights – it might be dark where he was going – and his camera, which was to the right of his faceplate, in its own nacelle. She made him do it twice, in fact, although it was unlikely he was going to remember it better through repetition.

Then they settled back, no longer holding hands, only alone with their thoughts. Borner conjured up some music, and something in Mariucci leapt at the opening chords. He recognised it. He had no idea what it was, but it was clearly a favourite. He might even have brought it aboard with him, to play at times when he needed it.

He listened, rapt. He imagined the musicians, the singers, the costumes, the lights.

Then it was time. Kattenbeck had already unhitched herself from the wall, and she did the same for him. She headed to the outer door, and used the controls there to pump the remaining air away. The sound from the airlock dwindled and vanished, while the sounds in his ears soared and built.

She opened the door onto space, and led him out.

27

Aasen had jerry-built a five-point harness to keep him securely attached to the probe. In lieu of the water bubble, there were woven straps and a buckle. She invited him to present himself to the upper surface of the probe, facing it, so that she could strap him in, and also make certain that he could free himself again when he needed to.

It felt like being chained to a rock. He had no clue as to where that allusion had come from, but it was there, and he struggled for a moment with a cold knot of fear deep in the pit of his stomach.

But he acquiesced, and she and Kattenbeck manoeuvred him into position, fitting each strap in turn into the buckle until he was held fast.

'The landing could be bumpy,' said Aasen.

'The landing will not be bumpy,' corrected Blasco. 'The landing will be perfect.'

'If the fuel runs out, or the connection goes down, you could come down hard. Just hold on. It's better that the probe takes the impact than you. I also made these for you.' Aasen held out two sticks where he could see them. Each was a metre and a half long: they had loops at the top he could put his fat, gauntleted hands through, and at the bottom, they ended in sharp spikes. 'Don't stick them through your feet.'

'What are they for?'

'Ice walking. Callisto has an ice crust. I just thought that these might help you keep your balance.' She used tape to fasten them next to Mariucci. Three pieces: top, middle and bottom.

Mariucci couldn't turn any more. His suit was held fast, and although he could look around his helmet, his field of view was limited to the probe and the parts of the other astronauts that crossed it.

Even that was going to be taken away. Aasen had fashioned a cradle for his faceplate, realising that one good knock would crack it open. More tape and insulation had gone into it, and when she slid it between him and the probe's casing, it blotted out everything. He was left in the dark.

'Sorry, Luca. There's no other way. It's either this, or you go down on your back, lying on your life support, and that's even worse.'

'We could have got him a chair,' said a voice. Kattenbeck? Borner?

'It'd change the whole moment of inertia of the probe. I vetoed it.' Blasco. The pilot. 'Our window is opening. We should call this, if we're ready.'

'Comms and telemetry, go.'

'Flight, go.'

'Engineering, go.'

Velter: 'I don't have a role as such, but go.'

'I ...' Kattenbeck. 'What the hell. Go. Go with my blessing, Luca.'

'We are go for launch. Petra, Hanne, move to the far end of the bay, please.'

Mariucci, immobile and blind, was now having things done to him. He had this one last opportunity to speak out, to call it off, to stay. When he was climbing across the hull of the Aphrodite to get to the probe bay, he'd had the opportunity to look at both Jupiter – the size of a double fist, pale and bright, its ribboned clouds clear and sharp even at this distance – and Callisto. Callisto was huge and dark, rimed with white ice in splashes and broken circles.

It had made him feel like a fly, crawling up a wall. Insignificant. Tiny. Brief.

A jolt in his chest told him that he was on his way.

'Arcas has cleared the probe bay.'

'Ten metres.'

'Twenty metres.'

'Can you still hear me, Luca?'

'I can still hear you,' he said. He was weightless for now.

'Report, please.'

'I'm … good. Buono.'

'Closing the probe bay.'

'Wait.'

'Petra, it needs to happen. You'll have a better view in Command.'

'I just. Okay. Do it. Close the doors.'

'Luca, you're passing through the magnetopause now. You shouldn't experience any adverse effects at all, but you might see the odd flash of light. It's just stuff hitting your retina.'

'Yes. I understand.'

'Ready for acceleration?'

'Yes.'

'Okay, Arcas. Acceleration, acceleration.'

Mariucci felt the straps around him slacken as he was pressed into the probe. The vibrations translated into sound: a low grumble to start with, then a medium-pitched, continuous hiss that was constantly threatening to turn into a roar.

'I need to move the Aphrodite. Hanne, tell me when the probe bay is clear.'

'Acknowledged.'

'Two hundred metres.'

'Four hundred metres.'

'Clear.'

'Let me dig us out of this gravity well. Aphrodite, acceleration, acceleration.'

'Still okay, Luca?'

298

'Yes.'

'Sorry that this isn't more exciting for you.'

'Six hundred metres. Recalibrating to altitude over Callisto. Fifty-five kilometres.'

'We need to clear you from the Aphrodite's exhaust, Luca. Acceleration, acceleration.'

The sound stopped, and he had the distinct sensation of falling.

'Fifty-four kilometres.'

'Acceleration, acceleration.'

Then it was back, the pressure against his chest, the weight of his life support held up by the rigid torso, though it creaked slightly. Nothing profound, nothing worrying. Just a subtle adjustment in the geometry of his suit.

'Progress report, Luca?'

'I'm still here.'

'Your suit looks fine. Heart rate, breathing, all nominal. We've got a good signal to Arcas. Control is nominal. Engines nominal. Fuel at ninety-five per cent.'

'Who is this?'

'Yasmin, Luca. It's Yasmin.'

'Thank you, Yasmin.'

'Aphrodite is increasing its distance from Callisto. We'll drop behind, then move up again to keep you in sight. Easier on the subjove than the antijove. Let's concentrate on getting you down in one piece, Luca. Altitude check?'

'Fifty-two kilometres.'

'Let me do some off-book calculations.' There was some dead air. 'It's going to be tight, but that's what reserves are for. Armstrong did worse. Davison did a lot worse. You'll make it, Luca.'

There was some popping in his ears. Not from a change of pressure, but some other person plugging in.

'Luca, it's Petra. How are you feeling?'

'I don't know. Like I've been in this suit for ever?'

'Is there anything you'd like me to go over for you? Anything you're not sure about?'

'All of it?'

He heard a deep breath.

'Okay. From the beginning. You are Luca Mariucci, the captain of the ESA deep space exploration ship Aphrodite. We are two years out from Earth on a mission to survey the Galilean moons of Jupiter, and Jupiter itself, primarily its magnetosphere. There were a crew of twelve of us when we left cis-lunar: you, me – Petra Kattenbeck, Hanne Aasen, Theresa Blasco, Yasmin Borner, Benjamin Velter, Deirdre Colvin, Ove Hellsten, Konstantinos Tsoltos, Laszlo Molnar, Valeria Spinu and Rory Forsyth.

'In order to protect us against the radiation environment in space, we used a generated magnetic field to deflect the charged particles around and away from us. Our health as we entered Jovian space was generally good, but it rapidly declined. As we encountered more radiation, the shield automatically strengthened its response, but that may have accelerated our problems. We don't know yet, but it's our best guess.

'We fell apart as a crew, starting to manifest different symptoms of psychological and psychiatric disease. You did your best to hold everything together, but we, your crew, were unfaithful. After Yasmin discovered a code within a broadcast from under the ice of Europa, and that there was a response from Ganymede, and that it seemed to be counting, we ended up dividing completely.

'Rory manipulated us, but really, we allowed ourselves to be manipulated. Ove killed himself. Stan thought he was a demigod. Valeria a priestess. My head was full of ghosts. Laszlo died too, after what we did to poor Stan. We lost Valeria to space, but not before she did irreparable damage to Deirdre. Hanne tried to fix everything, but couldn't. Benjamin did the only sane thing and went and hid. Yasmin – Yasmin's stopped counting along with the broadcasts now. Rory ... is dead. And then there was you: your memory began to go, earliest first, and now you struggle to lay down new memories, let alone recall old ones.

'Which brings us to now. You're strapped to our last probe, Arcas. We're trying to land you on Callisto, the fourth Galilean moon of Jupiter, because you asked to go. We think that there's a structure on the surface, built by an extraterrestrial race – aliens – and left there thousands of years ago. There was one visible on Io, but the conditions there were lethal. On Callisto, they ought to be survivable, at least until your air runs out.

'This is a one-way trip, Luca. There's not enough fuel in Arcas to get you back. Whatever you find there, you have to document, for as long as you can, the best that you can. We'll stay with you to the end, and then when we know you can't talk to us any more, we're going to take the Aphrodite and we're going to crash it into Jupiter. It'll take us a couple of weeks to do that, if all the ship's systems hold out for that long. But we'll program it in, so that even if we're dead, the ship goes down anyway. It's good to keep things tidy.

'When you get to Callisto, Theresa will try and get you really close to the structure, but if not, you'll have to listen very carefully to our instructions as to which way to walk. When you see it, you'll have to walk around it until you find the ramp that'll let you climb up it, and inside it. Once you've started going up, keep going up. There's a message written on your hand. *Go up*, it says. That's all you have to do. Go up. If you remember nothing else, it's that.'

'Thank you ...'

'Petra. Petra Kattenbeck. We were – are – friends. I had hoped the drugs I'd given you would have worked better, for longer, but you'll have to try and keep listening to us instead. We'll be right there, in your ears and in your head, to the end.'

She stopped abruptly, and Mariucci thought he might have lost contact with them, with the Aphrodite, completely.

'Still looking good, Luca.' A different voice. 'We're going to

301

check the landing site, and take you towards it. You're at thirty k, so plenty of time. Stand by for acceleration, Arcas.'

Mariucci felt the bumps and nudges as the probe adjusted its trajectory.

'We're getting there. A little while longer.'

More sudden shifts of direction, and in between, free fall.

'You're in the tube. When we're a few kilometres up, we'll do a final adjustment. The view from the camera on the probe is very clear. We've caught sight of the ziggurat at the subjove point. It's definitely there, Luca. We'll guide you in.'

'It's Benjamin here, Luca. I'm looking at the ground conditions. There are literally craters everywhere, from the largest, all the way down. The surface has been saturated with impacts: a lot of the older crater rims are worn down, ablated, but there's going to be a considerable variation in elevation locally. Once you land, you'll have a distance to horizon of three kilometres, so we're going to do everything to get you within that radius from the target.'

'I can do that. I can do better than that,' said someone.

'It's just in case. Luca, Hanne says remember to take your poles with you, in case you need to walk any distance. The ice is going to be hard, and you don't want to fall. A lot of the surface will also be covered in carbon black. It's a very fine carbon powder that forms due to the plasma interaction with the sublimating carbon dioxide ice and atmosphere. I call it an atmosphere, it's barely there. It might be greasy, and on top of the ice, difficult to walk on. Did you hear all that, Luca?'

'I heard it. Greasy. Difficult to walk on.'

'Gravity is low, about an eighth Earth standard. You're going to need to skip, not walk. You've been in low g environments before, so your legs will remember how to do it, even if you don't.'

'Skip. Got it.'

'Ten k.'

'Fuel thirty-eight per cent.'

'All systems nominal.'

'Aphrodite altitude ninety-seven kilometres.'

'Check.'

Mariucci carried on breathing evenly, the feeling of being face down now as constant as the background noise of three rockets burning. He was doing something important. He was doing it for other people, not himself.

What it was, was elusive. Every time he snatched at it, it danced away. A fleeting image of a tower, built from black stone, tiered like, like what? Tiered. One block on top of another, with stairs so that he could Go Up.

That was it. That was what he had to do. Go up. Go up.

Currently, though, he was going down.

'Five kilometres.'

'Final course corrections. Ready, Luca? Arcas, acceleration, acceleration.'

Free fall, accompanied by bumps and knocks.

Then a moment of silence, followed by constant rocket thrust, starting to get louder and higher.

'Call the landing site, Benjamin.'

'Here. Due south of the ziggurat. That's a kilometre away. We won't damage it, if—'

'I'm not going to crash the probe.'

'Fuel twenty-nine per cent. Four kilometres.'

'We can't risk damaging it.'

'Now is not the time to ramp up the anxiety, Benjamin. I'll land where you say, just let me do it.'

'Three kilometres. Fuel twenty-two per cent.'

'Luca? We're go for landing.'

'We're going to come in hot.'

'Benjamin. We are not coming in hot. Now shut up.'

'Luca, it's Petra. It'll be a few minutes now. Don't do anything until we tell you it's safe to do so. And when you do, no sudden movements. You'll bounce off the probe, and the engine casings will be red hot. Just sit tight.'

'Two thousand metres. Fuel fifteen per cent.'

The rocket noise rattled his bones.

'Fifteen hundred. Twelve per cent.'

'...'

'I've got it. I've got it.'

'One thousand.'

The sound. It owned him, took over every part of him.

'Eight hundred.'

He pressed with his hands to lever himself up, to see where he was, to see what was making all that noise, but he couldn't. He was held fast.

'Six hundred.'

What was it? A strap, a series of straps. He pushed again against them, but they weren't going to give.

'Four hundred. Low fuel lights.'

There was a buckle. He remembered that. Under him? If he could move his hand under him, he could release it. He'd be free.

'Two hundred. Low fuel lights.'

He got his left hand, and slid it across the black plate of the probe towards his chest. He grunted with the effort.

'Hold on, Luca. Don't do anything but hold on.'

'I can't move.'

'Don't move! Don't move, Luca. Lie down, flat as you can. Press your helmet into the padding. Brace.'

'One hundred. Low fuel lights.'

'Throttle back.'

'I told you I've got it!'

'Fifty. Forty. Thirty. Twenty. Cut-out lights.'

'Me cago en dios!'

'Ten. Five. All engines cut out. Impact.'

He felt it. He felt the engines cough their last, the indescribable bliss of the sudden stillness, then the smack as the probe dropped the last two metres to the ground. His head came forward with a mighty jerk, and he hauled back against it.

'Luca? Luca, are you there? Please respond.'

Now his breathing quickened. He was head down, tied down, silent and immobile.

'Luca?'

But this was what was supposed to happen, yes? The voices would talk him through what happened next.

'I'm here,' he said. 'I'm still here.'

28

The straps that held him in place fell away. He lay there for a few seconds longer, then put his hands either side of him and pushed slowly. The rigid torso made it difficult: he couldn't bend his spine, but he could just about get one knee under him.

'Slowly, slowly,' said the voice in his ear. 'Just make certain of each movement before you make the next one.'

He slid his other knee up to join the first one, then flexed his fingers to ease himself into a kneeling position.

The world glittered at him. Stubby protrusions of white ice broke through the dark crusted layer.

'We can see what you see, Luca.'

'How? Where are you?'

'We're on the Aphrodite. It's a spaceship. We all lived there together, and now you're on Callisto.'

He tentatively stood up, and looked out over the white-and-black landscape. 'Where?'

'Callisto. It's one of the moons of Jupiter. Luca, can you turn around, slowly? We need to see where you are, and where you need to go next.'

He complied. He stepped in little steps, pausing at each moment, so that they could look too.

Then he saw it. A blot that was darker than the ground, darker than the sky. It was rising from the plain. Tall, wide, stepped.

'What's that?' He was certain it shouldn't be there, but it was also the only thing, apart from ice and soot, that was visible.

'That's the ziggurat, Luca. That's where you're heading. It's directly under Jupiter: if you can look up without falling over, you'll be able to see it. But don't do that just yet. You need to get off the probe first. Do you see the sticks that Hanne made for you, taped to the deck? They should be right there by your feet.'

He looked down, and there they were.

'Peel them off. Don't worry about the tape, just get the sticks and pull slowly.'

That was easier said than done. His fingers were fat, but he could get hold of the loops at the end of each piece and lever them up.

'I've done that,' he said. He noticed that he had something written on the inside of his arm. *Go up. Travel well.* He wasn't sure how that had got there, but there was something familiar about it, the way the letters were formed.

'Now, sit down on the edge of the probe, and slide off to the ground. It's not far—'

'One point five metres,' said another voice.

'It's not far at all, and gravity is low. You'll just sink down. Put the loops over your hands, hold the top of the poles, and keep the points pointing down to stop you from pitching forward. Go to a side that doesn't have an engine on.'

He lowered himself to a sitting position, and eased himself away from the side of the probe. He fell, not too quickly, nor too slowly, to the ground. The ridged soles of his boots squeaked down as if they ...

As if they were being pressed into newly fallen snow.

An image of a white vastness. Everything white.

He put the spikes down into the surface, and leaned against them as his body over-rotated. They stayed put, and so did he.

'Done that,' he said.

'Straighten up a little, Luca. Turn your helmet – that's where the camera is – so we can see the ziggurat.'

'The what?'

'The structure. The building. You saw it in the distance just now.'

He had? He had. He shuffled around, and there it was, less obvious now that he'd climbed off the top of the probe.

'What is it doing here?'

'We don't know, Luca. That's something you might find out when you get there. Point yourself towards it, and remember that you need to skip, carefully. Use your sticks but don't poke your feet with them. Keep them away from your legs. If you get a puncture, the suit will compensate for that, but it'll make you ill, and you could lose the use of that leg at some point.'

He checked his position, pushed his left foot down, then his right. Just little taps, but he soared off the ground. He cushioned the landing with his sticks and his knees. Little black puffs squirted out from under his boots when he planted them down again.

'Keep going. You've about eight hundred metres to cover, but there's no need to hurry. Slow and steady.'

He skipped and skipped, and fell into a rhythm. He concentrated on where he was putting his feet and his stick-points, studying each landing site before he reached it. A field of ice mounds was coming up, each one taller than he was, and as broad as they were high.

Every time he stopped, and looked up, the black structure was closer. It began to loom upwards, getting progressively larger and closer, until he couldn't not look at it.

The first tier was the tallest, reaching halfway up the total height, and there were six smaller tiers on top of that, each set inside the perimeter of the one below, but all of the same straight-sided, block-like construction, until the very top, where the subtle changes in ratio made that tier look taller than it was wide.

Then he was there, at the base of a ramp that started by his feet and rose all the way up to the base of the third tier, where it passed through an archway. The ramp was smooth, sputtered with the same carbon as the ground, and the slope not so steep that he couldn't walk up it. It was broad, too. Even though there was no balustrade, or any kind of guard rail, if he stuck to the middle he'd be perfectly safe.

'Take a moment to look around, Luca. At the ramp, at the sides of it, then up at the structure itself.'

He did that. He skipped to one side: the ramp was solid underneath the whole length of its rise. He skipped back, and stood again before it.

'We don't know what's going to happen from now on, Luca. So if we drop out, it doesn't mean we can't see you, or hear you. Keep looking purposefully at everything you see, go slowly, and if you're in any doubt, look at your arm. That's what you need to do.'

He turned his wrist. *Go up. Travel well.* He could do that.

He dug first one stick, then the other, into the ramp, and gave a cautious lean on them. He shuffled forward. He appeared to have plenty of grip, so he repeated the process, stick, stick, foot, foot.

He climbed up the ramp, rising over the plain. When he judged he was halfway, he turned around, took in the view, the strange bicoloured lumpy landscape, the eroded rims of craters, the white rays of excavated ice, and even leaned back to catch a glimpse of Jupiter directly above him. He carefully turned around again, and resumed his ascent.

'How are you feeling, Luca? Your suit stats are looking good.'

'I'm good too,' he said. He glanced up the slope ahead of him, to where the ramp met the main structure.

His feet stepped on a sandstone step so aged and worn it was looped. The sun was hot on his back and inside was cool, dark, still air.

He stopped for a moment. Where had that come from?

'Luca?'

'It's okay. I—'

'Tell me.'

309

'Something's happening to me. I'm seeing things. Dreams. Visions. I don't know.'

'What of?'

'Me. They're of me.'

'It's a memory, Luca. Of things you've done. Don't be afraid of them.'

'But I don't remember them happening.'

'Then perhaps they will.'

He pressed on, towards the arch at the end of the ramp, leaning forward on his sticks. There was nothing behind him except the cold airless vista of Callisto, asteroidal patterns of ice, and the ever-more-obvious curve of the moon. He looked behind him once, but felt a sharp tug of vertigo. His balance wavered, and he decided that Go Up was good advice. He wasn't going to turn again.

He'd reached the arch. Its face was blank, covered in carbon.

'Turn on your lights. The control panel is on your right arm. Hold it where we can see the menu, and we'll guide you through it.'

Lights bloomed. The black sucked most of the extra illumination away, but inside the arch, in the lee of the crown, the stone was merely dark and crystalline.

'Stop, stop. Luca, look at the columns.'

He shone the light there. It was covered in carved lines, grouped together in symbols, then in lines, then in blocks. He leaned closer and ran his finger over the indentations, then looked at his forearm.

'It's writing,' came a breathy voice, 'it's writing. Look on the other side too, Luca. Look at it.'

He did so. The text, the carvings, seemed to run from the top of the arch and fall down each side, a chiselled rain that carried no meaning for him but that clearly meant something. The writing was too strange, too busy, to be able to spot any repeating patterns. He touched them and let his fingers catch on the hollows, so that he knew they were real – another time, another place, he traced the letters in a piece of marble, just one of hundreds, set out in a grid of grass, while birds rose and fell twittering above.

He lingered long enough for at least some of the carvings to be captured on camera. The archway revealed its inscriptions but kept its secrets. The ramp had ended. He stepped onto the level ground.

'Can you turn around and look out?'

He shook his head, but the voices couldn't see or hear that. 'I ... no.'

The wind was strong, buffeting his small thin body, whipping at his clothes, and the cliffs were precipitous. Far below, a patchwork of fields showed through the haze, and the silver line of a river.

'Luca, are you sure you're all right?'

'I'm still seeing things. Things about me.'

'Are they frightening you?'

'Yes.'

'We're here, Luca. We're here. You're not alone. What's ahead of you?'

His road had seemingly ended in a wall. He pressed it, and it didn't give. It didn't feel gritty, just solid.

'Benjamin thinks there's another arch on this level, on the next side. Turn right. Keep close to the wall. Put one hand on it so you don't drift from it.'

He did as the voice said. Having put his back to the empty space, the vast view, he now had to confront it. It pitched in from the side, the sheer drop next to him making him squeak with fright. He looked to the wall, to his hand still wrapped with the loop from his pole, his fingers against the black stone.

It was worse when he reached the corner. He froze as the sky yawned wide.

'Luca, you need to get past this. You can't stop here.'

'I can't go on.'

'There's no back to come to. Look at your arm, Luca. What does it say?'

He squinted. '"Go up. Travel well."'

'No harm will come to you. Go up. But in order to go up, you have to go round. It's a test, and you've never failed one yet. Keep to the wall, keep your hand on it. When you reach the corner, you turn, and you'll see the arch. Then you'll be inside, and hopefully you'll be able to go up again. Can you do that, Luca? Can you pass the test?'

He looked at the angle of the corner, and he crept forward. His hand trembled around the sharp edge, and he went crab-like around it, even though it was wide enough for two. No rail. No balustrade. What monsters had made this?

The voice was right, though. He could see there was another arch piercing the middle of the side he was now on, and he screwed up his courage in order to reach it.

He almost fell through into the darkness, and he had to wait for a second for his eyes to adjust before he could go any further. The lights resolved a wall of script ahead of him, dense and cryptic, while the arch proclaimed something similar. Now the writing was everywhere. A libraryful of it. Logorrhoea. Someone, something, had wanted to leave not just a message but a manifesto.

He took in as much of it as he could, but through the arch, to the left and right, there was a short ramp that led up to the fourth tier, and he knew that he had to face the emptiness again, because there was a pattern here, a meaning to this: to go up was a trial. If he wanted to keep going up, he needed to be brave.

And being brave wasn't about ignoring his fear. It was embracing it, holding it tight, and carrying it with him. He was afraid, and he would never not be.

He turned right. He climbed the ramp quickly, when his flanks were enclosed, and slowly when they weren't. The ledge he was on now, the fourth tier, seemed narrower than the third.

312

Of course. If this was a test, then it would become harder, not easier. That was the nature of tests.

'Luca, keep going. You're doing so well.'

A trodden path. The smell of meadow grass. The feel of its feathery heads brushing against his open palm held down by his side.

The writing petered out. There would be more, inevitably. Whatever story was being told was episodic. The first arch. The second arch. The hoped-for third. Each part separated by effort, by time, by emotion. It could not, would not, be hurried.

He approached the corner, and steeled himself. His fingers once again clicked over the sharp edge and dug in as he made the transition. Less room than before. He was earning this.

The transition between the fourth and fifth tiers was another riot of symbols, just as between the third and fourth. They were crammed in, smaller possibly, simply to make room for them all. Lines and grids and stars and angles, running in chiselled-out containers that might give an order to it all, or just represent a paragraph or a page, pressed into the stone at random and set there for ever.

Go up. Travel well.

The ledge on the fifth tier was wide enough for him, but it felt inadequate, given the drop, given the star-speckled void, given Jupiter hanging over his head. He navigated it all the same. He wanted to close his eyes and simultaneously was terrified of closing his eyes.

A single bell echoing across a valley. Motes of insects hugging the river bank, as he jumped into the pool beneath the broad oak tree. The water had been snow not so long before. The cold was shocking.

'Luca, we're struggling to maintain position. Hanne's trying to fix the problem, either the cold thrusters, or the gyroscopes, one of the two. We have at least another ten to fifteen minutes with you. Can you make it to the top by then? It's not long, but can you try for us?'

'I can try,' he said. He didn't know if he could.

If there'd been more gravity, it would have been easier. Something to anchor him to the stonework, to hold him down, to maintain his grip. As it was, he felt like he might fly away at any moment.

He made the fourth arch. He wanted to linger, to point his camera here and there and everywhere, but now he had to hurry. He could have hurried at the start, but he – and they – had thought that they had more time. Screeds of writing. The story was accelerating, growing dense, telling all, but it would have to wait. The sixth tier. But the ramp. Instead of going left and right with a wall ahead, he was being channelled inwards, but still upwards. Into the centre of the structure.

He hesitated. *Go up.* It said go up. *Travel well.*

Every surface now inscribed: not just the walls, but the floor he walked on, the ceiling he passed under. Everything. There was a lifetime's worth of reading just here.

Then he arrived, and he understood. The seventh tier was simply the roof. He was at the top. He had emerged into a central chamber, taller than it was wide, but the walls were pierced with more archways: rooms that led off from the landing. He circumnavigated the top of the rampway, standing in front of each doorway in turn, shining his suit lights inside, but making no move to enter.

'Can you see this?' he asked.

There was no reply.

White-headed waves on a grey lake. A small boat bobs and strains against its tether, tied to the end of a wooden pier that juts out over the water.

'Hello?'

Nothing.

He turned to his left and then to his right. Then back to the centre again.

Was there a light through there? If he was right, it might

314

take him back outside, to the ledge around the sixth tier. The voices might speak to him again if he could see the stars.

He started forward, heading for the arch.

𒀭𒁺𒌋𒌍𒀀𒁹𒉡𒈨𒀭𒌋𒈨𒐊𒁉𒐊𒀭𒀀𒌋𒌋𒁉𒈨

𒈨𒐊𒌋𒍦𒁹𒈨𒐊𒁺𒌍𒐋𒐊𒈨𒁉𒌋𒈨𒐊

𒀭𒁺𒌋𒌍𒈤𒌋𒁹𒈨𒀭𒈨𒈨𒌋𒌋𒐊

𒁉𒈨𒐊𒌋𒐋𒌋𒁉𒈨𒌋𒁺𒐊𒈨𒁉𒈨𒌋𒐊

nēberu nēberet šamē u erṣetim lū tameḫ-ma
eliš u šapliš lā ibbirū liqeʾʾū-šu šāšu
nēberu kakkabšu ša ina šamē ušapū
lū ṣabit kunsaggī šunu šāšu lū palsū-šu

Coda

It has been twelve hours since we lost contact with
Captain Luca Mariucci. His life support will be exhausted:
his batteries flat, his air tanks empty. His passing will be
mourned in all the places he was known and loved.

His legacy is what we will attempt to pass to you now.
The following video footage was captured by his spacesuit
camera as he climbed the Callisto ziggurat. The files
are unaltered, and only divided by us to enable easier
transmission. We assure you that there has been no
processing, enhancement or tampering. The accompanying
audio file is the total of the radio traffic between the
Aphrodite and Captain Mariucci. An additional file,
recording conversations in Command, is contemporaneous
with this, and can be synchronised by the time stamps.

We trust you will make use of these. We do not know
what they mean, what effect this may have on the human
race, even whether or not you will believe them. We only
recognise that they are important. We would like to think
you will use them to unite, not to divide. But we will not
be there to see the results of our research, nor of our
sacrifices.

The Aphrodite cannot return to cis-lunar space. It is too
damaged, the crew too few, and further critical systems
failures are not just expected, but predicted. Rather than
risk a collision with, and contamination of, any of the bodies
in the Jovian system, our protocols state that in the event

of our mission being compromised, we are to scuttle the Aphrodite in the Jovian atmosphere. This is what we plan to do.

We have set a course that will bring us into contact with Jupiter in fourteen days. Our life-support systems may not last that long, but we hope that the automatics will keep the ship on course after we are gone.

We will continue to transmit data gained during the mission for as long as we can. Loss of signal may be abrupt, permanent, and for any number of reasons.

It has been an honour to serve on the Aphrodite. Our love and best wishes to you all, now and for the future.

Dr Petra Kattenbeck, for the crew of the Aphrodite.

She pressed send, and watched as Borner queued up the messages, waiting for the moment Blasco slewed the ship round and presented its primary dish to the Sun. Velter was in his workspace, still prioritising images. Aasen was with Colvin, and had been for a while. She should probably be relieved from her watch.

But Kattenbeck stayed there for a moment longer, studying the purposeful actions of those who still had such a role. In two weeks, they would plunge into Jupiter's towering cloudscape, burn up and break up, and add their atoms to the king of planets. Which meant that any doctoring she might do was more or less redundant.

Still, it might be good that they all went together. One last act of solidarity. It might also be awful, and what they'd choose to do would be to sit alone and apart as the ship turned to plasma around them. It was something they hadn't discussed properly, and of course there was always what was in the pharmacy. She needed to bring all of that up, at some point, but not now.

The effort of writing that message had exhausted her, and when she got tired – more tired – was when she was most likely to be distracted.

'I'll be in the wheel if anyone needs me,' she said. Blasco, wrestling with unreliable controls and uncertain software, didn't acknowledge her, but Borner glanced from her screen for long enough to nod, before turning back to her regulation of the flow of bits and bytes towards the inner planets.

Kattenbeck unclipped from her seat, and nudged herself towards the axis. The lights there brightened and dimmed, but they never went out, which was one thing to be grateful for. Mariucci had said he'd change the ship but not the crew. She wasn't so sure: the ship was a good one. The Aphrodite had taken so much damage, and yet it was still afloat, still sailing, and it would take them all, their breath or their bones, to its final fiery end.

She pushed herself feet first into one of the access tunnels – her orientation no more than force of habit now the whole ship was in zero g – and let herself glide down towards the wheel. Once there, she was again struck by the strangeness of it, how it was so clearly designed with an up and down in mind, and yet now had all the artificiality of a stage set. She boosted herself across to the sick bay, where Aasen sat tethered into a chair, and beside her, Colvin, strapped onto the examination table.

'Any change?' she asked the engineer.

'None. For better or worse.'

'Thanks for taking over for a bit. Go and rest, Hanne.'

She deserved her peace. They all did, but Kattenbeck wasn't going to get hers for a little while yet. Aasen left the door open as she exited, and yes, here they came, the faces and forms of the lost and the let-down, those that Kattenbeck felt she ought to have saved but hadn't, or couldn't, or wouldn't.

Her hands weren't clean. She'd worked in some really dirty places, where it hadn't been so easy to wash the blood away.

This time, though, she was going to sit among them. She checked Colvin over, read her stats off the machines and made a note of them on the whiteboard on the wall, dampened her lips and mouth with a sponge, opened her eyes and carefully squeezed liquid from a dropper onto the eyeballs. She administered the injections she was required to do, and she tidied everything away into its proper place.

Then she pushed herself out into the main part of the wheel, snagging a chair and pulling herself down into it. She hooked her feet behind the metal legs, and held herself against the cushioned seat and back.

She looked up, along the curve of the floor to where it went out of sight around the circumference of the wheel. There were two dozen people there – not there, but still present nevertheless – watching her, silently, not even accusingly, just bearing witness. People with shattered bones and crushed chests, with ragged, missing limbs and gaping, open wounds, and people who were just dead with no visible cause.

She fixed each of them with a forensic stare, remembering each and every one of them, where they'd crossed paths and how long for. But none of them were who she wanted to see, who she was waiting for. She held on to the arms of the chair, untangled her legs and stretched them out in front of her.

Time passed. Others came and went. And she waited.

Acknowledgements

Making a science fiction book's plot fit into the (known) actual science of the time often means the author is a hostage to both fortune and the future. I've done the very best I can with these books (which start with *One Way*), but throughout there has been considerable numerical and design input from Sam Morden, who is my chief spaceship designer and gravity wrangler. Without him, there'd be a lot more hand-waving and a lot less veracity. Cheers, lad.

Credits

S.J. Morden and Gollancz would like to thank everyone at Orion who worked on the publication of *The Flight of the Aphrodite*.

Agent
Antony Harwood

Jake Alderson
Georgina Cutler

Editorial
Rachel Winterbottom
Brendan Durkin
Aine Feeney

Contracts
Anne Goddard
Ellie Bowker
Humayra Ahmed

Copy-editor
Elizabeth Dobson

Design
Nick Shah
Tomás Almeida
Joanna Ridley
Helen Ewing

Proofreader
Bruno Vincent

Editorial Management
Jane Hughes
Charlie Panayiotou
Tamara Morriss
Claire Boyle

Finance
Nick Gibson
Jasdip Nandra
Elizabeth Beaumont
Ibukun Ademefun
Afeera Ahmed
Sue Baker
Tom Costello

Audio
Paul Stark

Inventory
Jo Jacobs
Dan Stevens

Marketing
Brittany Sankey

Production
Paul Hussey
Fiona McIntosh

Publicity
Will O'Mullane

Sales
Jen Wilson
Victoria Laws
Esther Waters
Frances Doyle
Ben Goddard
Jack Hallam
Anna Egelstaff
Inês Figueira
Barbara Ronan
Andrew Hally
Dominic Smith

Deborah Deyong
Lauren Buck
Maggy Park
Linda McGregor
Sinead White
Jemimah James
Rachael Jones
Jack Dennison
Nigel Andrews
Ian Williamson
Julia Benson
Declan Kyle
Robert Mackenzie
Megan Smith
Charlotte Clay
Rebecca Cobbold

Operations
Sharon Willis

Rights
Susan Howe
Krystyna Kujawinska
Jessica Purdue
Ayesha Kinley
Louise Henderson